HUNTED

BY
CYNTHIA EDEN

MILLS &
BOON®

First Published in Great Britain 2017
By Mills & Boon, an imprint of HarperCollins*Publishers*
1 London Bridge Street, London, SE1 9GF

© 2017 Cindy Roussos

ISBN: 978-0-263-92899-0

46-0717

Our policy is to use papers that are natural, renewable and recyclable products and made from wood grown in sustainable forests. The logging and manufacturing processes conform to the legal environmental regulations of the country of origin.

Printed and bound in Spain
by CPI, Barcelona

Cynthia Eden is a *New York Times* and *USA TODAY* bestselling author. She writes dark tales of romantic suspense and paranormal romance. Her books have received starred reviews from *Publishers Weekly*, and one was named a 2013 RITA® Award finalist for best romantic suspense. Cynthia lives in the Deep South, loves horror movies and has an addiction to chocolate. More information about Cynthia may be found at www.cynthiaeden.com.

I want to thank the wonderful staff at Harlequin—
Denise, Kayla, EVERYONE at Harlequin Intrigue.
It is truly a pleasure working with you.

Chapter One

Josh Duvane broke from the surface of the water, pulling the regulator out of his mouth and then shoving back his mask. "We found her," he called to the team up on the boat.

He heard someone swear. Probably the local sheriff. Josh knew the guy had been hoping to find the victim alive. No such luck. Josh swam to the boat. The ocean water lapped against him, dark and rough because a storm was coming. If they were lucky, they'd be able to get the victim up before the storm hit.

A big *if*.

He grabbed for the ladder on the back of the boat and pulled himself up.

"Are you sure it's Tonya?" Sheriff Hayden Black asked as he reached out a hand to Josh.

Tonya. Tonya Myers. The twenty-two-year-old college coed who'd vanished a week ago. And, yes, unfortunately, he was sure. "It's her."

He glanced back at the water. The waves rocked against the boat. As one of the FBI's elite USERT members—Underwater Search and Evidence Response Team—his job routinely took him to the deepest depths. He searched for clues, he searched for evidence and, on damn unfortunate days—days like today—he searched for the dead.

"That makes three bodies," Hayden gritted out. The waning light glinted off his blond hair. "Three bodies in the last three weeks."

And that was why Josh was there. The FBI knew they had a serial hunting in the quiet coastal town, and Josh had been sent to provide backup to the local Bureau team—and to the sheriff.

Josh and Hayden had crossed paths in the past. Once upon a time, they'd trained together as SEALs. They'd worked together on a few missions years ago, then had gone their separate ways. Josh had joined the FBI and Hayden—hell, Josh never would have figured the guy for a small-town sheriff.

I would have figured wrong.

"This town has already had enough heartache," Hayden muttered. "The people need peace, not more fear."

More divers went into the water. Josh had done his job and located the body. His team would work to bring the victim to the surface.

"We just put one killer behind bars." Hayden raked a hand over his face. The sheriff's star on his uniform gleamed. "Theodore Anderson's trial is barely over. Now some other jerk is terrorizing *my* Hope."

Not just terrorizing the town of Hope, but killing mercilessly. The victims taken were all women in their twenties, attractive, fit. And they weren't locals. Hope was a beach town along the Florida Gulf Coast—popular in the early summer for its pristine white beaches. The victims had been tourists.

The killer had a twisted MO. He took the women,

then he immediately called the sheriff's station, taunting the authorities. Telling them to hurry and find the victim before it was too late.

But so far, they'd always been too late. Each victim had been stabbed to death. The first two victims had each been stabbed five times, and then their throats had been slit. Josh was betting that when the ME had a chance to check the body of Tonya Myers, he'd find the same wounds on her.

After he'd dumped his victims in the water, the perp made a second call to the authorities. A brief call that just gave longitude and latitude coordinates. The dump site location for the body.

In Josh's experience, most killers didn't offer up their victims that way. For someone to do that—to deliberately call the authorities and just spill the location of the dead—it meant one thing.

The perp wants attention. He wants the world to know what he's doing.

And the guy was getting that attention. News crews were camped out in Hope, desperately trying to get a scoop on the new case that was transfixing the nation. Murder was always big business.

"He'll be going after a new victim soon," Josh said quietly. His wet suit stretched as he strode to the bow of the boat. "You need your deputies to be on high alert. You need to warn the people in this area to stay extra vigilant. Because if we aren't careful…" His words trailed away. The killer was very careful. He didn't leave evidence behind, none of his taunting calls to the sheriff had been traced back to him…he was always one step ahead of the authorities. "If we aren't careful, soon I'll be searching for another body."

THEY'D FOUND THE VICTIM. Cassandra "Casey" Quinn tensed when she saw the black body bag being unloaded from the boat. "Another one," she whispered as sadness tightened her heart. Another woman who'd been struck down in the small, coastal town.

"Should I start filming?" her camerawoman asked.

She should say yes. The other camera crews were already rolling, capturing the moment when that body bag was transferred out of the boat and onto the stretcher. The ME was there. He'd be taking the body back to his lab.

"Casey?"

How long had the woman been in the water? One day? Two? Tonya Myers had finished up her bachelor's degree at Florida State University just two weeks before. She'd gone to Hope to relax. To have a little fun in the sun.

Not to die.

"We're missing the shot, Casey," Katrina Welch snapped.

Right. The shot. The story. That was why she was down there, after all. Why she'd left New York and flown down to face the already blistering Florida heat. "Keep the camera on me and the sheriff," she directed. *Not the body bag. I just... I can't.* "Maybe I can get him to share an exclusive with me." Doubtful. So far, Hayden Black had been like a vault.

Good thing she was pretty good at safecracking.

There were about half a dozen reporters gathered on the dock. Most of them were filming the body bag. Some were rushing toward the ME, and yes, two others had tried to go after the sheriff. He waved them back. She heard the growl of "No comment" that came from

Hayden. Typical. She'd discovered that even though he was a native Florida boy, Hayden wasn't exactly big on the southern charm.

Her gaze darted over him. Tall, blond, strong…the sheriff walked with a furious intensity, his body practically vibrating with tension. He didn't like what was happening in his town. Not one damn bit.

But there was another man with him. Also blond, but his hair was a darker shade, shaggier than the sheriff's. This man moved with a predatory power, and his gaze swept the scene, as if looking for threats. *Dangerous. This guy is seriously dangerous.*

"That's the USERT guy in charge, right?" Katrina asked as she pressed closer. "I think I saw him go out on the boat that retrieved the body."

Victim, not body.

"He looks mad." Katrina lifted her camera and aimed it toward the sheriff. "They both do."

"Probably because they don't like finding dead women." She swallowed. "And, yes, he's USERT. His name's Josh Duvane." As soon as the USERT group had arrived, she'd begun digging up information on them. Digging up information was sort of her thing… almost a compulsion. She didn't even date a guy without doing a full background check, and Casey knew that was weird. But with her past, it paid to be careful. "Ex-SEAL, tough as nails, swims like a fish." And he'd been the guy to find all three of the victims.

She swallowed. "Maybe he's the one who'll talk." Maybe. She smoothed back her dark hair, straightened her already straight blouse and lifted her chin. "Let's just see what happens." Briskly, she walked toward the two men, with Katrina at her heels. "Sheriff Black!"

Casey called out brightly. "Can you confirm that the body of Tonya Myers has been recovered?"

Hayden turned toward her, and his golden eyes were sharp with barely leashed fury. "No comment, Ms. Quinn. None."

Figured. The guy was far too tight-lipped.

She lowered her microphone. Voice softer, she said, "Don't you think the public has a right to know what's happening here? People are dying, Sheriff. And if you found Tonya's body, then that means another victim will be taken soon."

He stared at her. Then he gave a grim nod. "Film me."

He'd just said—her eyes widened and she gestured to Katrina. *Film the man. Film the man!* Before he changed his mind.

Hayden stared into the camera lens. "There is a predator hunting in our city. I would like to ask every citizen to be extra vigilant. If you see anything suspicious, please do not hesitate to call the sheriff's office. I am working in conjunction with the FBI to track down and apprehend this criminal, and I ask that all individuals—particularly women in their twenties who may be visiting our area—take every precaution—"

"Is that because the Sandy Shore Killer has a special victim type?" Casey cut in. "He only kills women in their twenties? Women who are vacationing in Hope, not locals?"

His eyes glittered. "Turn off the camera."

Well, at least they'd gotten something. Casey waved toward Katrina and made a quick, slashing motion across her throat.

Katrina's sigh was very, very loud.

"The Sandy Shore Killer?" It wasn't Hayden who'd spoken. It was the FBI agent—the USERT supervisor, Josh Duvane. His voice was deep, dark and sexy. Not that Casey found the guy sexy. She was at a crime scene for goodness sake. She had a job to do. She wasn't there to lust after some agent.

Her gaze swept over Josh Duvane, studying him, assessing him. Tall, over six feet, with broad shoulders. His thick blond hair was still a little wet. His skin was tanned—probably because of all the time he spent in the water—and his hard jaw appeared freshly shaven. He had a faint scar on his right cheek, a slash of white that told her the scar was old. His eyes were hazel. Not a warm and cozy hazel, though. They were stone-cold.

Chilling, she would say.

Or maybe that was just the look he was giving her. *Like an ice glare. He's freezing me out.* Because if Casey had to guess, she'd say that FBI Agent Josh Duvane did *not* like her very much. A pity. When sources didn't like her, they had a tendency not to share information. She really needed him to share.

"Who the hell gave the guy the moniker of the Sandy Shore Killer?" Josh wanted to know.

She nodded briskly. "That would be me."

He rolled his eyes and cursed. "Lady, giving the guy attention—"

"Cassandra. Or Casey. Either one works."

His lips—rather sensual lips, nicely sculpted—pressed into a thin line. "Giving the guy attention… giving him a freaking *name*…does nothing but feed into his fantasy. You're building him up when we want to be tearing him down."

She didn't let her expression alter. Casey hadn't

wanted to give the guy a nickname, but her producer had insisted. "You can only call a guy the *unknown perpetrator* for so long, you realize that, right?" She gestured to the beach behind them. "And he *does* place his victims in the water off the sandy shores here. It seemed fitting at the time." The name had certainly stuck.

"Vultures like you just do more damage." Josh turned away from her. "You don't help anyone."

She didn't flinch, but his words shot straight to her heart.

Josh and the sheriff headed toward the parking lot.

"I'm not trying to do damage." Maybe she should have kept her mouth shut but...no, he'd just insulted her. Casey figured that she deserved a chance to defend herself. "I'm trying to help this investigation. I'm trying to *help* the victims. They deserve justice."

Josh put his hand on the sheriff's shoulder. He leaned in close and said something quietly to Hayden. The sheriff nodded and then strode to his patrol car.

Josh turned to glance back at her.

"If looks could kill," Katrina muttered, "I think you'd be dead on the ground right about now."

Casey swallowed. She thought Katrina might be right. If possible, Josh's gaze had grown even colder. "Why don't you go back to the hotel? I'll meet you in a little while."

Katrina nodded and hurried away. She took the camera—and Casey's microphone—with her. Katrina's red hair was cut short, a pixie cut that accentuated her delicate features. But there was nothing delicate about Katrina's personality. The woman was a fireball, and Casey normally loved working with her.

Right then, though, she wanted some space. If she

had a chance to speak alone with Josh, she might be able to convince him that she wasn't the bad guy.

Possibly.

Josh crossed his arms over his chest and studied Casey in silence. She wondered what he was thinking. What did he see when—

"Are high heels really the best choice for the beach?"

She glanced down at her heels. No, they were a terrible choice for the beach. Wretched. But when she'd left the hotel earlier, Casey hadn't realized she'd be *going* to the beach. She'd thought that she would see Hayden Black at the sheriff's station. She'd known she'd be on camera, so she'd had to wear what she thought of as her full reporter getup.

She walked toward him and her high heels wobbled a bit on the uneven pavement of the parking lot. The lot was right in front of the dock—and the stretching, white sand beach waited to the right. The scent of the ocean teased her nose.

"I don't want to be your enemy," she said and she gave him what she hoped was a warm smile. She'd practiced that smile a lot when she first started reporting. That smile had taken her from a spot in small-town Illinois to the big-league fame of a prime-time show in New York City. Her smile was warm. Friendly. Approachable. That was her deal—her producer said she was relatable. That she came across as caring.

The truth was…she really did care. Often, far too much. She couldn't turn off the cases that she covered, and late at night, when she was alone, they haunted her. "I'm *not* the bad guy."

"Didn't say you were." His head cocked as she approached him.

"You just thought it." She inclined her head. "And you *did* say I was a vulture."

The other reporters were clearing out. The ME had left. The body had been transferred. The sheriff was gone.

Other than a few stragglers at the lot, she was left with Josh.

"I've seen your work before," Josh murmured. "I know plenty about you, Ms. Quinn."

"Cassandra," she corrected quickly. "Or—"

"Casey, right."

His expression was so hard and unyielding. He was a handsome man, but…tough. A dangerous vibe seemed to pulse just beneath his skin.

"You don't seem to have a lot of respect for reporters," she murmured, though she rather thought her words were a serious understatement.

He looked at her, considering, and then his gaze darted to the water behind her. He rolled back his wide shoulders and sighed. Some of the tension appeared to leave him. His face didn't soften but it seemed less… angry? "You know what? It's my baggage, and I'm sorry."

Wait—he was what?

"I'm being a jackass to you, and I apologize." He sounded as if he meant those words. "It's been a hell of a day, and when I find—"

He broke off, but she knew what he'd been about to say. *When I find a body…*

"I'm not at my best," Josh finished as he raked a hand over his face. "But I shouldn't be a jerk to you, and I apologize."

"Apology accepted," she said quietly.

He gave her a quick, searching glance. "May I tell you a story, Ms. Quinn?"

"Casey—"

He stepped toward her and her breath caught. He was…definitely strong. He wore a white T-shirt and shorts and she knew he'd changed out of his diving gear on the boat. The muscles of his arms and chest stretched the fabric of that T-shirt. He didn't look like the typical, straitlaced FBI agent.

Probably because he wasn't.

"A few months ago, I worked a real big case over in Fairhope, Alabama. We were after the Sorority Slasher…you remember that one?"

Her heart shoved into her throat. "Everyone remembers him."

"Another stupid serial killer name. Folks should have just said they were looking for Dr. Cameron Latham, the genius psychology professor who decided killing was just too much fun." His lips twisted into a bitter smile. "A reporter from that area was covering the case, trying to get all the headlines and make a name for herself."

The breath she took seemed to chill her lungs. "I—I know what happened to the reporter." *Everyone knows.* Because a story that terrible wasn't easily forgotten.

"No, you *know* what was reported. You *know* that Dr. Latham killed the reporter. He wanted to send a message, and she was the perfect target. That's what people know. But I was there." He edged even closer to her. His body brushed against hers as he lowered his head—and his voice. "I know exactly what he did to her. And everything I'm about to say is off the record."

She should back away. Put some distance between

them. But she just looked up into his eyes. *He's trying to intimidate me. I won't let him.*

"I saw the blood-soaked room. I saw the body. I saw the way he'd wrecked her. He enjoyed hurting her, and her last moments—they were just of terror and pain. He left her alive in that room, you see. He let her know that death was coming, and there was nothing she could do to stop it."

Casey licked her lips. Her mouth felt desert dry.

"So, yeah, I'm a little…sensitive to reporters right now. Because I think that reporter—Janice Beautfont— her death was a waste. She pushed herself into the spotlight, and he made her a victim. So when I see the reporters crowding around, wanting to spread the sick stories of *this* killer's crimes… I remember Janice, and I hate what happened to her. I hate that this guy is feeding off the attention he's getting, and I wish you would all just take a step back."

Her skin felt too cold. It was a summer day on the Florida coast. *Cold* was the last thing she should be feeling. "I'm not trying to be in the spotlight."

He raised one brow.

She swallowed the lump in her throat. "You don't know me. I get that. But you're *wrong* here. I want the focus on the victims. I want them to have justice."

"That's why I'm here," he murmured. "And it's always easier to do my job when I don't have a reporter dogging my steps."

So much for having a partnership with him. Desperate, she tried again as she said, "I can help you. I've been talking to the victims' family members and their friends. I know things about the victims. Maybe I can help build a profile—"

"We have agents from our Behavioral Analysis Unit who do that."

He was definitely shutting her down.

"Watch your step, Ms. Quinn," he said again, but she knew he wasn't talking about her high heels and the broken pavement in the parking lot. "Because you never know when a killer is close."

And the guy just turned and walked away from her.

Her right foot tapped on that uneven pavement. "Casey," she called after him. "My name is Casey. Remember it—because you'll be seeing me again." If he thought she was just going to give up, the guy needed to think again. She wasn't going to be scared away.

Giving up wasn't in her personality.

If Josh Duvane wouldn't help her, well, then she'd just go find someone else who'd be ready to talk. A good reporter never gave up.

And Casey didn't just want to be good at her job. She wanted to be great.

THEY'D FOUND TONYA. He'd watched as the reporters and the authorities slowly loaded into their vehicles and left the scene. They'd found her faster than they'd discovered his last victim.

But then, he hadn't taken Tonya as far out this time. He'd left her closer to the shore, a deliberate choice. He'd needed to dump her body quickly and then get ready for the next kill.

He already had a new victim in mind.

He could see his prey right then.

She stood in the middle of the parking lot, tapping one high heel. Her dark brown hair fell to her shoulders, a sleek style that even the humidity of Florida couldn't seem to muss. She had on a crisp white shirt and a formfitting black pencil skirt.

She was pretty...almost perfectly so with her fine-drawn features. He'd studied her often enough; he knew every detail of her face. Her wide-set, dark eyes, her bow-shaped mouth, her softly curved chin. He'd watched her on the news, marveling at the way she seemed to stare *right at him*.

As if she could see him.

I see you. He'd seen her all along. He'd seen everything she'd done. All the secrets she'd tried to keep. All the sins that she thought no one knew about...he'd seen everything.

She thought she was safe. She thought no one knew what she'd done.

But he knew.

He'd always known.

And before he was done with her, she'd be begging to tell the world her story.

They always begged.

And then they died.

Chapter Two

Casey sidled around the back of the sheriff's station. Sure, this wasn't exactly her best moment, sneaking up to the back of the building because she knew that the young deputy, Finn Patrick, was scheduled to get off work at eight o'clock that night. But Finn had been kind enough to share a little inside information with her before and she was hoping that he might feel similarly inclined again…

The back door squeaked open. It was a heavy metal door, and it led from the rear of the station to the small staff parking lot in the back.

Casey made sure her friendly smile was in place as that door opened. She stood in the shadows, waiting to see Finn's dark hair appear but—

Blond hair.

Her smile froze. She expected Sheriff Hayden Black to exit the building.

But the man who came out *wasn't* Hayden. The blond hair was a little too dark.

Josh Duvane shut the door behind him. He tensed and his gaze swept toward the right—toward the shadows. Toward her.

He'd changed his clothes again, and now the guy

looked more like an FBI agent. Khaki pants, button-down shirt and a holster. A holster that he was currently reaching for as he kept his narrow-eyed gaze in her direction.

"Wait!" Casey called out. She hurried forward with a clatter of her—yes, still wearing them—heels. "It's just me."

If anything, his expression became even darker. "Should have known you'd be skulking around."

"Skulking?" Casey repeated, not liking that particular word choice.

"Yeah, skulking. Hanging around, hoping for a weak link to appear so you can get another scoop." He put his hands on his lean hips. "I know Finn tipped you off last time." Josh gave a sad shake of his head. "You like preying on twenty-year-old deputies? The guy is green and you know it. You got him to spill confidential information to you that could jeopardize the case."

Furious, she kept marching toward him. "I didn't jeopardize anything! Finn just told me the number of stab wounds that the victims suffered—"

"And you immediately reported it, opening the door for copycats galore to come out and play."

Her breath heaved out. "You don't like me." Were they really back to that already?

"I don't know you, as you pointed out earlier." His gaze swept the dark lot. "And, lady, why would you want to be out here by yourself? You know you match the killer's victim profile, right?"

"I—" Yes, okay, maybe she did know that. But she was at the *sheriff's station*. Shouldn't that be the safest spot in town?

He grabbed her wrist, surprising her. It wasn't the

quick movement itself that surprised her. Rather, she was surprised by how gentle his touch was. His hand wrapped around her wrist, and she felt the faint caress of his fingertips against her pulse point.

A little shiver slid over her.

"Sheriff Black gave advice for folks to be vigilant. He gave that advice to *you*. And what do you do? You immediately run out and find the first dimly lit, empty parking lot that you can?"

"I know how to take care of myself."

"I'm sure the other victims thought that, too." His gaze slid around the lot. "Where the hell is your car?"

"My hotel is four blocks away. I just walked—"

"Because you have a death wish?"

She silently counted to ten, then said, "You are getting on my bad side."

He smiled at her, a quick flash that showed the dimple—no, not really dimple, more like a rough slant—in his right cheek. "When you get angry, your voice goes absolutely arctic."

Then she must be completely freezing him right then.

"Finn isn't coming out here. He's pulling a second shift and, even if he weren't, the sheriff just gave him orders not to speak to *any* reporter, including pretty brunettes who smell like candy."

Her eyes widened. "Smell like—candy?"

"Didn't realize that, huh? You do."

Her cheeks were burning.

He turned away, but kept his grip on her wrist and he pulled her toward the far side of the lot. A motorcycle waited there, a big black beast of a bike.

"I'll give you a lift to your hotel. See, I can be a *nice* guy."

He climbed onto the motorcycle and tried to tug her on after him. Casey locked her knees and refused to budge.

He sighed. He seemed to do that a lot around her. "Problem?"

"I don't like motorcycles." Yes, she sounded prim and disapproving. So what? She wasn't sure she liked him, either. She certainly didn't like his ride. "They go too fast. They flip too easily. They offer zero protection to the rider—"

"Not a risk taker, huh? Guess I pegged that part wrong about you." His gaze dropped down her body and stopped on her three-inch shoes. "It's the heels. When a woman wears sexy heels like that, it makes a guy think she may have an…adventurous side."

"Are you hitting on me? Or insulting me again?" She wanted to be clear. "Because earlier, you said I was a vulture. Now you're saying—"

He let go of her wrist, but only so that he could hand her a helmet. "This will protect your head and that pretty face of yours."

"You are hitting on me." She took the helmet. She did *not* get on the motorcycle. "Your routine needs work. A lot of it."

"I did a little research on you since our last meeting…"

Her hold tightened on the helmet. *Don't have dug too deep. Don't have found—*

"You've won a lot of awards, haven't you? Seems you're the investigative journalist to watch. And you make a habit of going after the darkest killers, don't you?"

Her heart was drumming too fast and hard in her chest. "I go where I'm needed. You might not like the work I do, but someone has to give the victims a voice."

Cynthia Eden25

"And that's what you do."

It's what she tried to do.

He revved the engine. The bike sounded like a giant, growling beast. "You said your hotel was four blocks away. Hardly far enough of a distance for me to go too fast on that short drive. And if you're with me…" He gave her that slow smile again, the one that made him look a little less dangerous. Only a little. "I'll be extra careful. I promise."

She looked around the parking lot. It *was* getting darker. A lot darker. And, yes, she did fit the victim profile; she knew it. She was the right age, a stranger, no close ties in Hope… "Don't go over the speed limit."

He laughed. It was a strangely warm sound that caught her off guard. "I'm FBI. Trust me—I've got this."

She climbed onto the motorcycle. Her skirt hiked up—up much higher than she'd anticipated—and she knew she was flashing thigh. Her heels settled along the bike, finding safe purchase. She put on the helmet and then her hands kind of fluttered in the air. Should she put them behind her? There was a bar back there. She should probably just grab on to it and hold tight.

"Hold on to me."

She'd been afraid he'd say that. Casey slowly wrapped her arms around him.

"Tighter."

Why? "I thought you said you weren't going fast."

"You still need to hold tight, Casey." It was the first time he'd said her name. It came out rumbly and sexy and she needed to *stop* thinking the guy was sexy.

He was an FBI agent working a case.

She was a reporter.

She might try to work *him* to get information, but

they were not going to have any sort of real, personal relationship. She didn't *do* personal relationships. She kept her distance from people for many, many reasons.

Fumbling a bit, her hands slid around his waist, but she didn't hold *that* tight.

"Tell me the name of your hotel."

There were several just up the road—a line of them that looked out over the beach. "West Winds."

She would *not* hold him tighter.

The motorcycle shot forward and her arms tightened around him, holding him in a death grip and smashing her body against his. He zipped through the town, not actually going too fast but…it was strange being on the motorcycle with him. The wind whipped at her, and the motorcycle vibrated beneath her. He was strong and solid in front of her, and Casey found herself thinking that…maybe, if it were a different time, if this were a different place…she and the FBI agent might not have found themselves being adversaries.

They might have been something a whole lot more fun.

Too soon, he was braking in front of her hotel. Other reporters were staying at the hotel, at least five she knew from previous jobs. And both her producer and her camerawoman were there—plenty of people that she knew. It was a safe place.

Josh killed the engine and put down the kickstand. She realized she was still holding him, and Casey let go quickly, nearly jumping from the motorcycle. Josh didn't move, but she could feel his gaze sweeping over her. A bit nervously, Casey pushed the helmet back at him. "Th-thank you." She hated that stutter. She *never* stuttered. Or at least, she worked hard to make sure she didn't. When she'd been younger, that stutter had always come out when she'd been afraid. Back then, she'd had plenty to fear. The nightmares had plagued her every night for a solid year during college.

He put the helmet on the back of the bike. He studied her a moment and the waves crashed in the distance.

Should she just walk away? Probably.

"You don't think it's odd?"

"What?" She wasn't sure she followed him.

"All of you reporters…" He gestured to the hotel behind her and she knew he'd realized other press personnel were staying in that same location. "You all came rushing down here weeks ago to cover the Theodore Anderson case."

Theodore Anderson. She crossed her arms over her chest. Yes, he'd been the reason she was first sent to Hope. He'd been arrested and linked to the abduction and disappearance of several young girls in the area. Many of the crimes had occurred *years* ago, but only recently had he been linked to the kills.

The saddest part of the case? At least to Casey? The man had killed his own daughter. Christy Anderson had been murdered by her father when she was just thirteen years old.

Theodore had made headlines when he was arrested, and, yes, the reporters had all flocked down to cover the case when he went to trial. He'd been found guilty on all counts, and Theodore Anderson would never see the light of day again. Originally, the press had focused on Theodore, but it hadn't been long before someone else started stealing the Front Page…

The Sandy Shore Killer.

"What are the odds," Josh continued in that deep

voice of his, "that in this sleepy little town, there would be not just one sadistic killer…but two?"

She licked her lips. "Considering how rare serial killers are… I'd say those odds should be astronomically low. But then…you're FBI. You should know better than I do."

"They *are* astronomically low. Coincidences like this one don't happen." Flat.

"But…it is happening."

"Something set this guy off. Something brought him here…" His head turned and he gazed at the hotel behind her. "Can't help but wonder…if it was you."

She backed up a step. *He knows. He dug into my past. He dug too deep. He found out what I did—*

"You and all the reporters," he continued as his hazel gaze slid back to her. "He didn't like the fame that Theodore Anderson was getting, so he decided to steal the spotlight. And you and your buddies—with your twenty-four-seven news coverage—you just fed his beast. You made him more determined to get the attention he wanted."

Casey shook her head. "You think this guy came here because of the reporters? Is *that* the theory the FBI is running with?"

His hand lifted and his fingers curved under her cheek. "We're off the record. Way, way off…"

His fingers were faintly callused, a little rough against her skin.

"As I said, it's highly unlikely we'd have *two* serial killers in the same town. That just doesn't happen. Serial killers are rare to begin with and this…it isn't by chance. Your 'Sandy Shore Killer' was drawn here for a reason."

"Have the victims been connected in any way?" She had to press for more details.

"You know about the victims already. Attractive women in their twenties, all single, all visiting the area—no close personal ties here. And that's all I will say about them now."

His hand dropped away from her cheek and curved back around his handlebar. He revved the engine again.

Right. He was leaving. "Thanks for the ride."

His gaze raked over her. She wondered... Did he feel that odd, thick tension between them? The heated attraction that seemed to fill the air?

His hazel stare burned.

He did.

"Good night, Casey."

He felt the attraction, but Josh just wasn't going to do anything about it. Those rule-following FBI guys. They weren't her type. Or at least, they shouldn't be.

"I'll wait until you're inside before I leave." He paused a beat. "A gentleman never leaves before a lady is safely inside."

"Is that what you are? A gentleman?"

He seemed to consider that. "Perhaps I could be whatever you want me to be."

Casey turned away and hurried up the steps that led to the hotel. When she was in the lobby, she glanced back at him. He was still sitting on the motorcycle, still staring at her. Still looking far too sexy.

She lifted her hand and waved.

He frowned, gave her a small wave back, then drove away.

A few people who she recognized filled the lobby, and she inclined her head toward them as she headed for the elevator. The doors dinged open and when she slipped inside, Casey immediately ditched her heels. *So much better.* When she reached her floor, she carried her shoes in one hand, letting them dangle and bump against her leg. She was on the top floor, one that gave her a great view of the beach. She used her key card and slipped inside. The room was dark and ice-cold because she'd left the air-conditioning unit on earlier that day.

Casey turned on the light by the door. The maid had been in to clean—the room was spotless. Her pillows were all fluffed. New towels were waiting and the room had a fresh, lemony scent. She dropped her shoes and headed for the balcony door. She flipped the lock on it and slipped outside. The crash of the waves hit her first. The sound, then the scent. Stars glittered in the distance and she could see a handful of people walking on the beach.

She stood there a moment, lost in the sight. It didn't seem right for something so beautiful to be linked to so much death. But if she'd learned anything in life... it was that beauty often hid darkness. A smile hid terror. Pain always waited. So did evil.

She turned from the view and reached for the balcony door. But...

Hadn't she turned on the light in her room? Because the interior was pitch-black. She could see the darkness through the glass.

I turned it on when I walked inside. I always do that.

At least, she thought she had. But maybe there was a short or some kind of electrical problem. She'd have to call the front desk if there was trouble.

She opened the door and slipped inside. A little light spilled in from behind her, providing enough illumination for her to make her way to the small table near the bed. There was a lamp waiting there. She'd turn it on and then—

Hard hands wrapped around her from behind just as a bitter, thick odor hit her. "Got you."

She opened her mouth to scream, but her attacker drove her forward, slamming her head into the wall just above the lamp. The impact was hard and she staggered. Casey didn't get to scream. She didn't even get to fight.

He rammed her head into the wall a second time.

Just like before...

No!

Her body was going limp. She was passing out.

His rough laughter was the last sound she heard.

Chapter Three

He drove for miles, just riding the motorcycle and letting the wind brush across his face. In his head, he kept reliving the day's dive. Sinking deep beneath the water, searching even as he hoped that he wouldn't find the body. He'd hoped that the victim was still alive. That she still had a chance.

Then he'd seen her hair. That was the way it often was on those dives. If he was searching for a woman, her hair would float up from her head. It would drift in the water around her, as if it were trying to reach out for the surface.

He'd seen Tonya's hair, then he'd seen her face. Not the pretty face from her picture—chalk white, bloated.

Dead.

He turned off his engine and sat near the edge of the beach, almost surprised to find himself so close to Casey's hotel. He hadn't meant to come back there, had he?

Casey Quinn.

He'd seen her news stories before, most folks had. She didn't work for some local channel—Casey was the big time. Prime-time TV on a major network. When he'd done some digging on her, he'd realized her pieces were always dark, focusing on the worst criminals out there. Not scare pieces, though, but reports that showed the broken lives that had been left in a monster's wake.

He knew she'd come down to Hope to cover Theodore Anderson's case—the sick freak had enjoyed kidnapping girls. Kidnapping them and killing them. He'd even killed his own daughter. Casey and the other reporters had been trying to interview both Theodore Anderson and the guy's son, Kurt. But Kurt hadn't talked to *any* reporters. Not yet. Josh was a bit surprised that Casey's charm hadn't worked on the guy. Her smile—yeah, he could see where she'd be able to get men to talk to her. That slow smile was pure sex appeal, and it did something to her eyes—made those dark chocolate eyes gleam. No wonder young Finn had overshared, but the deputy knew better now. Josh and Hayden had made *certain* the kid knew better.

He turned away from the beach and glanced up at her hotel. He'd touched her cheek and her skin had been like silk beneath his hand. She'd stood there, in those incredibly sexy heels, her skin a warm gold next to the white of her shirt, and that dark hair of hers had skimmed over her shoulders. She was small, built along delicate lines, but sure curved in every perfect place. When she'd been behind him on the bike—

Stop lusting, turn on the motorcycle and get out of here.

He wasn't going to cross any lines with the reporter. A sexy face and body weren't going to make him forget his job. He wasn't young Finn.

He rolled back his shoulders.

Get out of here.

But he couldn't help glancing at the hotel just one more time.

SHE HURT.

Casey groaned as she cracked open one eyelid. Her whole body ached and she was lying on something rough and hard. The hotel bed was normally soft, like falling into a cloud after a long day of work, but this—

I'm not at the hotel.

Both of her eyes flew open. She stared around, horrified. She wasn't in her hotel. She was... Where in the hell *was* she? She tried to move her body and realized that her hands and feet were tied. Her hands were behind her back and she could feel what felt like rough hemp rope cutting into her wrists. She twisted and her body slid over...over plastic?

Yes, she was on a big sheet of plastic. The smell of fresh wood filled the air, and her frantic glance took in the room around her. She was in a home...of some sort. One that appeared to be under construction. No Sheetrock was up on the walls yet. She could see the wooden framework all around her.

And I'm on plastic. Oh, God. Because she *knew* why an abductor would put his prey on plastic. *So there won't be a mess left behind when he's done with me.*

She wiggled and twisted and finally managed to sit up. When she did, she realized that light was pouring in through one of the windows to the right. Light, and she could also hear the thunder of waves. *I'm on the beach. In a house under construction. A house or some kind of condo complex or...*

No, it's a beach house. Because she remembered seeing about four houses that had been under construction on the west end of the beach. They'd been big, massive structures up on wooden stilts that screamed high-end real estate. But, if the place was under construction, where were the construction workers? Where was the crew? Where was someone who could— "Help!" Casey called out. Her voice was oddly weak, so she tried again, screaming, *"Help!"* with all of her strength.

She fought to remember what had happened to her. She'd been in her hotel room and then…*someone* had been there. He'd grabbed her. Rammed her head into the wall—jabbed her? Injected her with something? And she'd fallen. Everything had gone dark. But she thought that she remembered him…laughing.

The waves kept thundering. Her gaze narrowed on the window. There was only a little light coming in. Maybe dawn hadn't fully arrived yet. Since it wasn't dawn, that meant the work crew wouldn't be coming for a while and—

It's Sunday. Her eyes squeezed closed. No, the work crew wouldn't be arriving anytime soon.

She jerked and twisted her way across the room. The plastic slid beneath her, bunching up, and she tried not to think about it—or about the man who'd taken her. The man who could appear any moment. The man who—

"I heard you screaming, Casey Quinn."

She froze. Casey didn't want to look over her shoulder. *He* was back there. If she looked at him, if she saw his face—

"Guess your screams mean…it's time to get started."

And she had to look back. Her head jerked toward him. He stood in the framed doorway. Dressed head to toe in black—complete with a black ski mask that covered his face. She couldn't even see his eyes because there was some kind of weird mesh over them. "Stay away from me," she ordered, hating that her voice shook.

He laughed—the laugh that she remembered—and he pulled out a knife.

The plastic beneath me...it's to catch all of the blood.

"Can't stay away," he told her. "I have work to do."

"Y-you're going to stab me...five times?" Because that was what he did. With all of his victims, he stabbed them. And then he slit their throats and dumped the bodies in the ocean.

I fit his profile. Josh even said... No, no, this couldn't happen!

He came toward her, moving slowly. He bent and brought the knife toward her. She heaved and strained against the ropes, but they wouldn't give. He put the knife to her cheek. Pressed just enough that a drop of blood slid down her face. "Don't rush me," he murmured. "I've been waiting for this moment a long time."

What?

"You and I are going to talk. You're going to tell me all of your secrets."

No, she wasn't.

"Or I will cut you open."

He lifted the blade away from her face—the moment she'd been waiting for. He was crouched close to her— his mistake. He thought that just because she was tied up, she was helpless.

He was wrong.

She lifted her feet—*wish I still had on my heels, those spikes would have come in handy*—and she slammed them right into his crotch, as hard as she could. He gave a grunt and staggered back. The knife fell from his fingers. She grabbed it, rolling and slamming her body harder into the plastic. The blade cut her fingers, but she didn't care. She started sawing at the ropes that bound her wrists together and—

He drove his fist into her cheek, so hard that she saw stars. The knife fell from her fingers as her head slammed back and hit the plastic—and the hard wood beneath it.

He swore and grabbed her by the hair, yanking her toward him. As he hauled her up, her hands fumbled across the floor and something sliced into her pinky finger…something sharp and narrow.

A nail. A nail was sticking up through the wood.

"Don't go passing out on me. We have to make a phone call. That's step one for us. Got to let folks know who has the power here."

She kept her hands near that nail and started to slide the rope against it. Was it making a grinding noise as she sawed? Could he hear her? The knife's blade had almost cut all the way through the rope, and if the nail could just finish the job, then she'd have a chance.

He left her there, sagging on the floor, her hands behind her and working slowly with that nail as he yanked a phone out of his back pocket. Her gaze darted to his hands. He was wearing gloves, but she could see a little bit of tanned skin where the gloves ended near his wrists. The guy was Caucasian, a little over six feet, probably close to one hundred and eighty pounds, and he—

"I've got someone new," he rasped into the phone.

"Pretty soon, Sheriff Black, it will be time for you to find her."

He'd called the sheriff. Did he always do that? Always call while the victim was still alive? The authorities hadn't revealed that detail to the press, and if this was part of the guy's MO, then no wonder Hayden Black had looked increasingly worn. He'd been fighting to find the victims alive, but he kept turning up dead bodies.

His finger slid over the phone—she realized he must be wearing those smart gloves that allowed him to still work a phone screen—and she heard Hayden's voice fill the room.

"Give me proof of life," Hayden barked.

Her abductor laughed. She tensed and almost stopped cutting on that nail. *Almost.* She knew his laughter wasn't a good sign. Hayden wanted proof of life, so that probably meant the jerk in the ski mask was about to make her scream. He was going to hurt her again—

"It's Casey Quinn!" she screamed. *"He's got me in one of the houses under construction on the west end—help—"*

Her abductor threw the phone down and slapped his hand over her mouth. What? Had he believed she didn't realize where she was? When she'd arrived in Hope, she'd made a point of checking out the entire town. A good reporter learned her territory.

She glared up at him.

"Think you're clever?"

She thought she had a chance. Hayden would come racing to the scene. And maybe…maybe he'd get there fast enough to save her.

"Your mistake. You're just dead."

No, she wasn't. Not yet. Did he think she was too afraid to fight back?

She felt the ropes give way around her wrists. Her hands were free. Now she needed to get rid of the ropes around her ankles. She stared up at him, just seeing the mesh over his eyes. Her heartbeat thundered in her chest.

His hand slowly fell from her mouth.

"You should run," she whispered. "The sheriff will be here soon."

"I'm not going anywhere…" He turned away from her. Bent and picked up his phone. She could see the smashed screen. "Not yet." His back was to her.

The knife was on the floor. He hadn't picked it up after he'd punched her. Her hand flew out and grabbed it and she immediately tucked it behind her body, resuming her position as he turned back toward her so it would appear as if her hands were still bound behind her.

"I've waited too long to get you, Casey." His voice was rougher and his tone was almost intimate. "It won't end like this."

It's not going to end at all. She hadn't fought her way back from the darkness before to die this way.

He rolled back his shoulders and he moved a few feet away, his head tilted toward the floor. He lifted up a piece of plastic. *What are you looking for? The knife? Did you just realize it's gone?*

His head swiveled back toward her.

She lifted her chin.

He smiled. "Give it to me." He took a step toward her.

Since he asked…

He grabbed for her arm.

She stabbed him.

THE SOB HAD taken Casey.

Fear was a cold knot in Josh's stomach. Hayden had called him and told him the news, and he'd driven fast as hell to get to the line of houses under construction on the west end of the beach. The motorcycle howled as he raced down the road. He was ahead of the sheriff and his deputies—he'd been closer to the scene. And he was breaking every traffic law out there as he cut across roads and ran through lights to get to Casey.

I shouldn't have left her. He could still see her, standing in front of the hotel, wearing those high heels as her dark hair tossed around her cheeks. He'd even told her that he'd wanted her to be safe because that perp was still out there. The guy was hunting women like her.

He'd been hunting her.

Josh spun around a tight corner and saw the row of partially built houses up ahead. Which house was she in? He barely braked his bike—just jumped off the motorcycle and ran for the first house. "Casey!" Josh roared her name. He yanked his gun from the holster. "Casey, where are you?" *Be alive. Be alive, Casey. Answer me!*

Because in his mind, he still saw Tonya Myers. She was in the water and her dark hair drifted up around her face. *That can't happen to Casey.*

He rushed through the first house, shoving plastic out of his way. Construction debris was everywhere, but the rooms were empty. No sign of Casey.

Josh ran back outside. The light from dawn swept out over the water. *"Casey!"*

How long had it been since the perp had called Hayden? Ten minutes? Fifteen? Twenty?

It only took a moment to die. One moment.

He rushed toward the second house.

"H-help..."

He froze. That call—it had come from the house before him. A temporary door was in place, one without a doorknob, and he just kicked that damn thing in. "Casey!" His bellow seemed to echo around him.

And then he saw her.

She was holding on to the makeshift banister that had been put in place on the stairs. She was trying to come down to him. A red imprint marked the left side of her beautiful face. There was blood on her cheek. She was too pale and she was shaking and—

He bounded toward her.

Her eyes widened when she saw him. She lifted her hand toward him, and he saw that she was gripping a blood-covered knife.

"J-Josh?"

"You're safe." He wanted to scoop her into his arms. Wanted to hold her tight and make sure she was okay. "Where is he?"

She blinked. She looked lost. Scared. And...

Hurt. He hurt her.

Josh wanted to kill the guy.

"I—I don't know." She looked around, her hand shaking but not letting go of that knife. "He... I stabbed him and he ran out of the room. He...left me."

Grim pride swelled inside of him.

"Get me out of here," she whispered. A tear leaked down her cheek. "It's too much...like before. Get me out."

He didn't know what she was talking about, but he had to touch her. Josh curled his left arm around her as he pulled her against his body. She didn't let go of the knife. He kept a solid grip on his gun. If the perp had run from the room on the upper floor, he could still be hiding in that house. Josh wanted to search every inch of the place, but getting Casey to safety was his priority.

She felt so delicate against him. And each time her body trembled, the rage he felt grew.

I will find you, you bastard. I will make you pay.

He led her past the broken front door and outside. He didn't stop walking, not until they were near his motorcycle. Then he slid his hand under her chin. "Where are you hurt?" His voice was a rough growl. Her cheek was already darkening, the pink giving way to a bruise.

"I'm...okay." Her eyes said the words were a lie. Her head turned, and she looked around the scene. Her voice became a whisper as she said, "Where did he go?"

Josh intended to find out.

Before he could speak, he heard the approaching wail of a siren. The local sheriff and his deputies—about time. They'd search every inch of those houses. They'd find that perp.

He started to step away from Casey but her hand grabbed his wrist. Her fingers curled around him, holding tight. "He's going to kill me."

The hell he will.

"He said...he won't stop. He *will* kill me."

The siren was louder. Closer.

Another tear slid down her cheek. "He said he'd been waiting for me...that the waiting was over."

His body brushed against hers. "He's not going to ever touch you again." Josh intended to make sure of that. "You're safe."

But she shook her head, and Josh knew that she didn't believe him.

The sheriff's patrol car whipped around the corner. The lights flashed from the top of the car.

Casey's hold tightened on Josh even more.

"You're safe," he said again, but Josh didn't think she believed him.

Chapter Four

She was the story.

Casey hunched her shoulders as she sat in the back of the ambulance. The EMT had checked her out thoroughly, over her protests. The guy wanted her to go to the hospital, and she figured he'd be forcing her there soon enough. After all, she knew the routine. She'd have to be examined, evidence would have to be taken from her. They'd clean beneath her nails, they'd take her clothes, they'd—

"Tell me what happened."

Her gaze lifted and she saw Hayden standing at the back of the ambulance. The doors were open and the fury on his face was undeniable. The sheriff was definitely not so controlled any longer.

And neither was Josh. Josh stood beside Hayden, and the FBI agent's face appeared carved from stone. His eyes blazed as he stared at her.

The FBI and the local authorities had been searching the scene, but they hadn't found the man who'd taken her. He'd just…vanished.

She saw a coast guard ship out on the water, darting around. Did they think the perp had escaped by sea? She didn't remember hearing the roar of a boat. She'd just heard the growl of a motorcycle—Josh, rushing to the scene. *I will never fear motorcycles again.*

"Casey," Josh said her name softly. "Look at me."

Her gaze slid back to him. She was sitting on the stretcher in the ambulance. The space was too small. There were too many little machines and the place smelled of antiseptic.

"Tell us what happened."

She already had, hadn't she? At least once? Maybe twice. But if they wanted to hear the story again... Casey pushed back her hair with a weary hand.

Josh swore and he bounded into the ambulance with her.

"Your wrists..."

Oh, right. Those were bandaged, too.

His hands caught hers, his touch incredibly gentle. His tenderness kept surprising her. He seemed so rough. Not a guy who could use such care, but when he touched her, he always seemed to handle her as if she were delicate glass.

She wasn't, though. Far from it. Her gaze darted to her bandaged wrists. "The rope was tight and when I cut myself free, I sliced the skin a bit." She hadn't even felt the pain at the time. Her gaze shifted back to his face. Her shoulders rolled back in a shrug, as if to say... *Doesn't matter.*

Josh glanced at the watchful EMT. "Give us a minute."

The EMT hurried out, but stopped to say, "I'm ready to take her to the hospital and—"

"And I'm not done with my witness," Hayden cut in. "You heard the agent. We need a minute."

The EMT nodded, ducking his head as he backed away.

Josh's fingers slid carefully over her hand. "Start at the beginning."

The beginning? She didn't want to go back there. "He got away."

Josh just stared at her.

"That means he'll kill again." She had to say those words. Her chest seemed to burn. "It's what he does, right?"

"*You* got away," Josh pointed out. "You're the first one, Casey. The only one who got away from this perp."

Because he'd killed the others. Dumped them in the ocean and hunted again. A shiver slid over her. "He said he'd been waiting for me."

Josh shot a quick glance at Hayden. The sheriff didn't speak.

"Is that what he always says?" Casey wondered. "Does he tell his victims that he's been waiting for them? Because he…he acted as if I were special, somehow. Like he'd been…he'd been trying to get me for a while." Nausea rose within her as she realized that, of course, they didn't know what he always said. As Josh had just told her…she was…

The only one who got away.

"Go back to the beginning," Hayden instructed her quietly. "I need to know everything about this guy."

She shivered. How was it so cold? "I was at my hotel. I'd just… I'd just gone inside after you dropped me off." She nodded toward Josh and his jaw hardened. "I went onto the balcony for a moment." Her gaze dropped to her feet. Her bare feet. "When I went back inside, the lights were off, and that was wrong because—" her head was pounding "—I'd turned on the light. It should have been on. I thought maybe there was a short, and I was going to call the front desk but..." Her gaze rose once more to meet Josh's. She swallowed the heavy lump that had risen in her throat. "He was already in the room. He grabbed me." Her fingers fluttered over her head. It was aching. Pounding. "He slammed me into the wall. At least twice, I think. I blacked out."

Josh swore, the words long and low and vicious.

"I don't remember how I got out here. I just woke up, and I was on the floor."

"I already sent a crime scene analysis team to your hotel," Josh said, his voice flat. "Maybe the guy left evidence behind that we can use."

The FBI and the local authorities were already working closely together, so she wasn't surprised that a team was already combing over her room. There was also a team at the scene there, going into the partially constructed houses, checking them one by one—starting with the house she'd been inside. Her chill got worse. "Do you think... Did he kill them all in that house?"

Josh and Hayden shared another hard look.

Maybe that look was answer enough.

"There was plastic on the floor," she whispered. "When I woke up, he had me in that upstairs room, tied up, and there was plastic beneath me." Just like a scene from a horror show.

"Are you *sure* you didn't see his face?" Josh pressed.

The pounding in her head grew worse. "He had on a ski mask. And the eyes—where the ski mask holes should have been, something like mesh covered his eyes so I couldn't see them. I didn't see his face. Didn't see his eyes, but I—I did see his hands." She eased out a slow breath. "He's Caucasian. Big—over six feet. Strong. Not heavy, but muscled." A killer in his prime.

"His voice was rasping and low." Her body swayed as the nausea rolled within her again. For a moment, she thought she might vomit right then and there.

"Casey?" Josh's hand closed over her shoulder.

"She needs to get to a hospital!" The EMT was back. "The woman suffered head trauma. She needs medical attention and I am *insisting*, Sheriff, that you let her go."

Hayden nodded. "I'll talk to you again, Ms. Quinn."

Josh started to back away. She tensed and actually thought about grabbing him and *making* him stay with her.

But she didn't. Casey let him go. Josh jumped out of the ambulance. The EMT hurried back in to her side.

"You okay, miss?" he asked.

She was so far beyond okay.

Other reporters had already made it to the area. She saw Deputy Finn Patrick trying to hold some of them back so they didn't contaminate the crime scene. His dark hair was mussed and he appeared shaken. Cameras were rolling. Cameras that would focus on her.

I am the story.

Would her past come to light now? Probably. When the right people went digging, it was easy enough to find secrets.

But maybe…maybe someone already knew her secrets.

The man who'd taken her. The man who'd gotten away.

Josh stared at Casey a moment longer, then he slammed the ambulance doors shut. The siren screamed on.

Her eyes closed.

"You're safe now," the EMT assured her. Josh had pretty much said the same words.

But she wasn't so sure that she *was* safe.

I think he'll come after me again.

JOSH WATCHED THE ambulance drive away—the reporters had to clear a path so the vehicle could get by. The reporters were definitely already swarming the scene. Casey's story would be huge.

A survivor.

His hands fisted. He'd wanted to stay in that ambulance with her. "Make sure that a deputy remains with her at the hospital," he snapped to Hayden. "Someone needs to be with her every moment."

Hayden nodded. "Finn! Finn, get over here."

The young deputy rushed toward them. Sweat had already slickened the sides of his dark hair. "Sir?"

"Follow the ambulance. Make sure that Casey Quinn is guarded at all times."

Oh, hell, he was sending the kid after her? The deputy rushed to his patrol car, and Josh muttered, "You think that's the best plan? A woman survives a serial killer attack and gets the junior ranger for a guard?"

Hayden lifted a brow. "You got a problem with Finn?"

Yeah, he did.

"He's young, but he's good at his job. Protecting her will be his priority—"

"Sorry, Sheriff," Josh said curtly. "But the FBI has ranking jurisdiction here." The instant they'd confirmed the presence of a serial killer, the FBI had assumed control of the investigation. "And I'll be taking Casey Quinn into protective custody."

Hayden's eyes widened. "Will you now." Not a question, not really.

The ambulance was gone. And Josh didn't like having Casey out of his sight. There were some local FBI agents on the scene and he knew he could leave them in the area to help with the search. "I'm going after her." *I should have been in the ambulance with her.*

"You think the killer will go after Casey Quinn again?"

"I don't know what he'll do, not yet. This is the first time one of his victims has gotten away." At least, the only victim they *knew* of escaping. "For all we know, he'll immediately go gunning for her again, and if that happens, I want more than just Deputy Patrick standing between her and danger." The kid was still green behind the ears.

"*You* want to be standing between her and the threat."

Josh's chin notched up. "She stabbed her attacker. I think that shows that she's capable of protecting herself... But her attack...it could very well have enraged the perp." *No doubt about that... My money says the guy is somewhere, choking on his rage.* "That means he could fixate on her. He could come at her with all he's got or..." His sentence trailed off.

"Or...?" Hayden prompted.

Josh glanced at the line of unfinished houses. "Or he will grab the next available victim who matches his profile. He'll let his rage out on her." Which meant they needed to be on guard—all of them.

"For someone who said he wasn't a profiler, you seem to know your killers pretty well."

He definitely wasn't a profiler. "I work on evidence collection. I don't poke into the heads of killers." His buddy Tucker did that. And Tucker Frost was scheduled to arrive in town any moment. The guy had just finished up a case in Colorado and now he was working on the profile for the killer in Hope. The FBI brass hadn't been satisfied with the work of the other profiler who'd been in town, and when Tucker finished his last case—he'd been immediately reassigned to Hope. When Tucker arrived, Josh knew the guy would want to speak with Casey right away. She would be key to the investigation.

"I have to make sure she doesn't say too much to the media." Another problem. Since she was a reporter, Casey would no doubt want to run live with her story. That wasn't going to happen.

He turned on his heel and headed for his motorcycle.

"Duvane!" Hayden's voice thundered after him.

He glanced over his shoulder. He liked Hayden—the guy was tough, smart and didn't generally take crap from anyone. But then again, Hayden was a former SEAL, and most folks knew better than to mess with SEALs.

"Is this personal?" Hayden asked him, voice quieter. Personal?

Hayden eased toward him. "You dropped the reporter off at her hotel last night?"

Josh nodded.

Hayden's head cocked to the right. "Didn't realize you two knew each other so well."

They didn't know each other well. So his reaction to her shouldn't be as intense as it was. But… "She's a victim. And my job is to protect victims." Lately, it seemed as if all he'd done had been to discover the dead. Casey wasn't dead, and he damn well wasn't going to let anything else happen to her.

Hayden's stare was assessing. "Better watch your-self. Once emotions get involved, the cases become even harder." His lips twisted in a humorless smile. "Trust me—I know exactly what I'm talking about."

Josh knew the guy was speaking from experience because the woman Hayden loved, Jill West, had been targeted by Theodore Anderson. Theodore had first kidnapped Jill when she was just a kid, but Jill had managed to escape him. Years later, she'd returned to Hope, determined to finally solve the mystery of her past. But her return had set off a deadly chain of reactions... In the end, Jill and Hayden had both been fighting for their lives.

They'd won, though. They'd stopped the killer. They'd unmasked Theodore Anderson. And now Jill and Hayden were finally free to work on their future together.

But Josh *wasn't* Hayden, and Casey…she wasn't Jill. They didn't have a past that linked them, and as far as how he felt about her… "Emotions aren't an issue for me. She's just a case." Simple words. Emotions didn't get to him. He did his job, and he moved on. Simple.

"Keep telling yourself that," Hayden mumbled.

Josh climbed onto the motorcycle. He glanced over at the house and saw the yellow line of crime scene tape.

Casey could have died in that house.

His jaw clenched. The killer wouldn't get close to her again. Not on his watch.

SHE'D BEEN POKED and prodded for hours. *Hours.* And Casey was not a happy woman. Her control was barely holding on, and any moment, she was afraid she might just break apart.

She didn't want to break in front of the too friendly nurses. Or the steely-eyed doctors. Or *anyone.*

"Are we done yet?" Casey asked, fighting to keep her voice calm.

Dr. Abernathy, a young African American woman with small, wire-framed glasses and a no-nonsense manner, looked up from Casey's charts. "You are a very lucky woman, Ms. Quinn."

She had to swallow three times before she could manage to speak again. "Luckier than the other victims."

A faint furrow appeared between the doctor's eyes.

"I don't feel sick any longer. I don't have the headache—"

"It's good that you're feeling better, but I'd like to keep you for observation a bit longer. You took a severe blow to the head—"

"I just told you my head felt fine now." Only a tiny lie. Her head still ached a bit, but it was nothing she couldn't handle.

"In concussion cases, the victim may suffer from seizures or convulsions. It's possible that you could become confused and agitated—"

"I feel plenty agitated right now," Casey muttered as she fiddled with the paper hospital gown that she was wearing. Her clothes had been taken, confiscated as evidence by the authorities. "Thank you for all that you've done. Really, thank you. But I want to get out of here, okay? I don't have nausea, no blurred vision, no memory lapses. I know our president. I know my birthday. I know—"

The curtain on the side of her bed swung back. "You know that you're causing trouble."

Her breath left in a quick rush. Josh. "I—I thought you were at the crime scene." She pulled up her covers—or rather, the thin sheet that was her only cover, other than the paper gown. "How long have you been here?" Had he just been hanging around, eavesdropping on her talk with the doctor? Didn't he get there was a whole patient privacy issue going on?

He stepped closer to the bed. A line of stubble coated his hard jaw. "Been here long enough to know that you're pushing yourself too hard."

"No, I'm not. I let the doctors check me out. I did everything they wanted." Her shoulders straightened. "Now, I *want* to go back to my hotel—" But even as she said the words, she stopped. No, she didn't want to go back to the hotel. She didn't want to return to that dark room and remember what it had been like when the attacker grabbed her.

"Your room isn't an option."

Because a crime scene team was still there? "I'm sure I can get another hotel room."

His jaw hardened. "What you're getting is a safe house."

A what?

"Um, excuse me," the doctor began.

Josh flashed his ID at her. "FBI. I'm Josh Duvane, and I'll be seeing to Ms. Quinn's security."

"I told you to call me Casey," she reminded him, again.

He flashed her a hard look.

Fine. Enough of this. Casey shoved back her thin cover. If need be, she'd leave that place in her paper gown. She swung her legs over the side of the bed. She started to rise—

Josh locked his hands around her shoulders and pushed her back down. "You aren't going anywhere."

Her eyes narrowed on him. "Yes, *I* am going some-place. I'm getting out of here. Because I don't like hospitals. I don't like getting poked and prodded, and since nothing is wrong with me, there's no reason I can't just walk right out of that door."

There was more to it than that. She had a very specific reason for not liking hospitals. Once, she'd spent far too much time in a hospital. She'd grown to hate those white walls and the scent of antiseptic. That scent was like death to her.

He glanced at the doctor.

"She needs someone to stay with her," Dr. Abernathy said. "In case she has any issues—blurred vision, slurred speech, convulsions…"

Oh, yes, that lovely list again. "I'll bunk with my camerawoman. Katrina can make sure I'm okay." Speaking of Katrina, the woman was probably freaking out. Casey needed to talk with her immediately but no one had let her have a phone.

Not helpful.

"If I make sure she isn't alone," Josh said, his hands still around her shoulders, "will she be able to leave?"

Dr. Abernathy nodded. "Yes, but if she displays any of those symptoms, she has to return to the hospital right away."

He nodded. "Done."

Done?

"I'll get an orderly to help Ms. Quinn to the car," Dr. Abernathy stated briskly. "Patient pickup is located at the front side of the building—"

"And that side is covered by reporters. I'll be getting Casey out, don't worry about that."

The doctor blinked. "Uh, right. Okay, then. I'll go

prepare the discharge paperwork." She exited the room. Josh didn't move.

Casey stared up at him. "Safe house?"

"Yes, it's a place we put victims or potential witnesses so we can be sure that—"

"I *know* what a safe house is," she said. "But since when am I going to one?"

"Since you escaped a killer?"

"Josh—"

"I'm afraid you're being taken into protective custody for the time being." His hands slid away from her. He turned and paced toward the door—and he picked up a small duffel bag that she hadn't even noticed before. "And while you're under protective custody, I have to ask that you refrain from speaking with reporters."

"I *am* a reporter."

He brought the bag to her. She glanced inside and relief filled her. Clothes. The guy had stopped and picked up some of her clothes. "I could kiss you," she mumbled.

"If you want…"

Her gaze jerked up to his.

He stared at her. The tension between them mounted. She hadn't even been thinking when she'd spoken. It had just been an expression but now…

She swallowed. "You're not…you're not like other FBI agents, are you?"

"You've met a lot of us?"

"My fair share." She felt too exposed. Being in front of him, just that thin gown covering her skin, made her feel too vulnerable. "Side effect of my job, you know? I tend to cross paths with the authorities a lot." She was rambling. Casey clamped her lips shut.

His hand lifted and he touched her cheek.

Casey flinched.

"Easy…"

"There is nothing easy about how I feel right now." Her whole life was out of control.

His gaze was on her cheek. "Does it hurt?"

"The cut or the bruise?" Then she shook her head. "Doesn't matter. Josh, get me *out* of here."

"It matters." His voice was rough, his gaze gleaming. "It matters one hell of a lot to me." He stepped away. "Do you need help changing?"

Help… Ah, him? Seeing her naked? "No, I…have it."

He pulled the curtain back into place.

"You're just…standing there?" On the other side of that thin curtain?

"I can't see you."

She slid off the bed and dressed—slowly. She didn't want to fall and have him rushing back in to pick her nearly naked self off the floor. After sliding into the underwear and bra, she put on jeans and pulled on a T-shirt. He'd even brought her some tennis shoes. He'd covered all the bases. What a guy.

"Casey?"

She left the gown on the bed. "I'm done."

He shoved back the curtain. His gaze raked her.

Her hands twisted. "So…a safe house, huh?" Crap. She'd said that before. "Just how long will I be staying there?"

He caught one of her twisting hands in his and led her to the door. "I don't know yet."

That wasn't good. Not knowing implied it could be days. Weeks? No, absolutely not. She had a job. She had a story to cover.

I am the story. Her stomach twisted.

"Who'll be staying with me?" They were walking down the polished hallway of the hospital. He kept his grip on her hand and he stayed firmly at her side. He'd probably drop her at the safe house and vanish. After all, his work was in the water—

"For the time being, I am."

She stopped. "You. But…why?"

He turned toward her. His gaze wasn't gleaming now. It was burning with emotion that she couldn't read. "Because I *can* keep you safe. No threat will come to you when I'm near."

She wanted to believe him. He sounded so confident, and right then, she was feeling…scared. Casey didn't let herself fear much, but after her night from hell? She figured she was entitled to some good, old-fashioned terror.

He was going to kill me.

"You fought him off. You survived." Josh's voice was so deep and dark. "Now my job is to make sure you *keep* surviving."

"But… I thought you were the USERT lead—"

"I am, and I'll keep working with USERT. But right now, I don't have a body to search for."

Because she'd survived.

He started walking again. He stopped near the elevator and pressed the button to bring it up. A moment later, the door dinged. They stepped inside, and he hit the button to take them down to the basement. No, to the parking garage.

When the doors closed, they seemed to immediately be wrapped in intimacy. Why did the elevator feel so small? Or maybe he just seemed too big.

"Are we using your motorcycle?" Casey bit her lip. "Because I'd really prefer a different ride."

His lips quirked. "Already ahead of you. Got a rental waiting for us."

Again, he'd covered all the bases. He must have been a Boy Scout back in the day.

"When we get to the safe house, another agent will be waiting for us. He's going to need to hear your story again."

The doors dinged open. The parking garage waited. She started to step out, but Josh caught her arm and pulled her back. Then *he* went out first, and his gaze swept the scene.

"You really think he's coming after me again, don't you?"

He kept a tight hold on her arm as he led her to a dark SUV. His rental. He put her in the passenger side and didn't speak until he'd slid in behind the steering wheel. He locked the doors, turned on the engine then glanced over at her. His gaze was hooded as he said, "I think we have two options with a killer like him."

A serial killer. A sadistic—

"You're the first victim—that we know of—who has gotten away. He may look at you as unfinished business. He may focus on you. Fixate."

That sounded very, very *not* good.

"Or he may immediately pick a new victim to replace you."

Someone to die while she lived? Casey shook her head. "I don't like either option." Her voice came out sounding very small.

"Neither do I." He drove them out of the garage. She looked to the side as they left the hospital, and saw plenty of familiar faces in the crowd of reporters. "That's why Hayden has his men and the local Bureau agents combing this town. We have to find the perp before anyone else is hurt."

Before he attacked someone else…

Or before he comes for me again.

I SEE YOU, CASEY.

He stood at the back of the pack of reporters. They were all staring at the main entrance to the hospital, hoping to get a glimpse of Casey Quinn. One of their own had just become the center of their attention.

But they should have focused their attention elsewhere. He'd been glancing toward the parking garage exit, and he'd just seen the SUV slip away. For a moment, Casey had glanced back, almost seeming to look right at him. She'd been in the passenger seat, and her hand had risen to press against the window.

I see you.

He noted the license plate for that vehicle. He hadn't been able to glimpse the driver, but with all the Feds running around town, he was betting Casey had just gotten herself some protection. Not that protection would do her any good.

He eased away from the crowd and slipped into his car. The dark SUV—Casey's getaway SUV—was stopped at a red light just ahead. Simple enough to spot. Easy enough to follow.

He'd just see where Casey was going because he wasn't done with her. Not by a long shot.

He and Casey were just getting started.

Chapter Five

She had a bruise on her cheek and fear in her eyes.
Josh didn't like that—didn't like the bruise, didn't like
the small cut on top of the bruise and he didn't like
the way her body trembled as she walked into the safe
house that he'd secured for her. They'd traveled to the
newest condominium complex in Hope and they were
in the penthouse unit, a unit that provided them with
maximum security. There were video cameras positioned in the hallway, and a guard stationed to review
IDs in the lobby.

He'd checked out the small town of Hope and figured
this place was Casey's best bet. It was the most secure
building in the area.

"The place has a killer view," Casey murmured. She
stood in front of the floor-to-ceiling windows that overlooked the beach. Her arms were wrapped around her
stomach. She glanced back at him and raised her brows.
"The FBI must be spending a ton of money on me."

He strode toward her. Her scent—light, and still re-
minding him of candy—drifted to him. "Don't worry
about the money." Her safety was what mattered.

"I thought you said there was going to be another
FBI agent here."

"Tucker will be arriving any moment." He'd gotten a text from Tucker right when they arrived. The other agent had been delayed because he had to meet with Hayden. Special Agent Tucker Frost was the behavioral specialist who'd been sent to figure out the killer—and to replace the guy who hadn't made any progress on the case for the past three weeks. FBI brass had wanted a change, a fresh perspective—so Tucker had been shipped down to Florida. "There's a new… team working within the FBI," he said. "Tucker is part of that team."

Her head cocked.

"A few agents have been hand selected for this group. Their job is to specifically track and apprehend serials." He was being very careful with what he shared—after all, Casey was a reporter.

"And you didn't want to be part of this group?" She turned away from the windows and focused completely on him. Her arms were still around her stomach, as if she were trying to warm herself. Or shield herself.

He took another step toward her even as he gave a slow shake of his head. "I don't like climbing into a killer's mind." That wasn't for him. Figuring out what made those monsters tick? Looking into the darkness and having it try to swallow you whole? No, he'd come too close to that before. "I work with the victims."

Her lips parted. "You bring them home."

"I find them…and I find the evidence we need to lock the killers away. That's the job I like—making sure that no one gets away with murder."

She studied him a moment, seeming to consider his words, then she said, "I—I should call my boss, Tom.

I should talk to Katrina, too. Let them know what happened. They must be worried sick about me."

Her voice had softened a bit when she mentioned her boss's name. "I already contacted Katrina and told her you were all right. She said she was calling your producer."

"That's Tom. Tom Warren. He's the producer of the show—and the guy pretty much controls *everything* that happens on the show. He'll want to talk to me." Her hands dropped. "I don't have my phone, though. When I was, um, taken from the hotel room, I didn't exactly get a chance to grab it and—"

His hands closed around her shoulders. "Stop." Because her words were too brittle. Her expression too guarded. "You're safe, Casey. Do you hear me? *Safe.* I'm not going to let anyone hurt you."

And…he saw the change in her expression. The fear that couldn't be denied as it swept over her face. "I've heard that promise before."

What?

"It wasn't true then." Tears gleamed in her eyes but she blinked quickly, not letting those tears fall. "And I'm scared it won't be true now."

What was she talking about? "You were attacked before?" The rage he'd tried to control grew like a fire in his blood. "Casey, what in the hell—"

She jerked away from him and her eyes had flashed wide. "It's going to come back, isn't it? *I'm the story…* just like I thought, and it will all come back again." She frantically shook her head, then her hand rose to press to her temple. "I didn't want it back. I worked too hard to bury the truth."

He caught her fingers in his hand. "Casey."

She blinked at him.

"What truth?" The gnawing in his gut told him this was bad.

"I should call Katrina," she said again. "Just to check in. I don't have any family members who will worry, but I need to tell her—"

His hold tightened on her hand. "She knows you're okay. But I'll make sure you talk to her, okay? Right after we finish with Tucker, you can call her."

She pulled in a deep breath. "Thank you."

His chest felt too tight. "Casey—"

But there was a sharp knock at the door. She stiffened, and he wanted to pull her against him. Wanted to hold her tight and tell her that everything was all right.

It wasn't all right, though. Not with the killer still out there.

"Stay here." He headed for the door, and his gaze swept to the laptop he'd opened on the table near the entrance. He'd already set up a feed so that he could see the security cameras in the building. There were four images displayed on his screen, and in one of those images, he saw a man standing just outside the penthouse.

The guy turned toward the camera and inclined his dark head.

"Tucker." Josh unlocked the door and offered his hand to the other agent. "Good to see you again."

Tucker's shake was firm. "Wish it were under better circumstances." His bright blue stare held Josh's. "I've got a key to the place, but I thought the vic might appreciate a heads-up before I came in."

Josh heard the faint tread of footsteps behind him. "The *vic*," Casey said, her voice flat and her emotions once more seemingly locked down, "has a name."

Tucker's brows climbed. "Casey Quinn, I presume."

Josh backed away so that Tucker could march past him. Josh shut and locked the door and his gaze swept to the security feed. No other activity.

Tucker offered his hand to Casey. "I'm FBI Special Agent Tucker Frost."

She backed up a step and didn't take his offered hand. "Frost." Casey seemed to taste the name, and Josh knew it instantly clicked for her when her gaze sharpened. "I remember you…and your brother." Her head cocked and then her hand was rising. Her delicate fingers were swallowed by Tucker's much bigger hand. "I'm sorry."

"Sorry?" Tucker murmured. He didn't let her hand go. "That's not the response most people have to me— or to my brother."

"I'm not most people."

The guy could let go of her hand at any point. Josh cleared his throat. They were just standing there, staring at each other. "Casey's been through a hell of a lot— why don't we let her sit down while she tells you what happened? The doc warned me to keep an eye on her."

Tucker finally let go of her hand. About time, Josh figured. Concern shadowed Tucker's eyes as his gaze swept over her. "I'm sorry about the attack." His fingers lifted to brush her cheek. "Are you—"

Josh pulled Casey back. "No, she's not okay. She's not going to be okay until we catch the jerk who's out there." He normally liked Tucker. The guy was a good agent. But right then…

I'm jealous. The emotion caught him by surprise. He was never jealous—and he and Casey had just met. She was a witness. A victim. Nothing more.

Maybe I just feel protective of her. Maybe that's it.

He steered her toward the couch. She sat down, but didn't relax. Instead, Casey perched on the edge of the sofa.

Tucker looked at her, then at Josh. "Something I need to know about?"

"Yeah." Josh kept standing at her side. "You need to know about the freak who came into her hotel room, knocked her out and dragged her away to kill her. Let's focus on him for a bit." The anger in him was getting worse. Josh raked a hand through his hair. "Because he's still out there. I need something to guide the team toward him. We need to *stop* him because he got away clean at the scene."

"Not completely clean," Casey said, her voice husky. "I stabbed him. He was coming at me, and I had to stop him."

Right. She'd told him that back at the beach house. "The evidence unit collected the blade—they'll be running checks on the blood. Maybe we'll get a hit on him in the system."

"You stabbed him?" Admiration deepened Tucker's voice. "I'm impressed."

"I wasn't going to die in that room. He'd set the stage, but that wasn't how things were going to end for me." Her hands fisted in her lap. "Where do you want me to start? When I woke up on the plastic or—"

"Your hotel room." Tucker sat down next to her. "Start there. Tell me everything you remember, big and small. Those pieces will help me to understand the man we're after."

They already did understand him, to a certain degree. They were after what the behavioral analysts called an "organized" killer—a killer who carefully planned his crimes. Who didn't leave evidence behind. Casey had already told Josh that the man had worn gloves and a mask to cover his face. He'd had the plastic spread out beneath her—a clever touch—so that the scene would be easy to contain.

She let out a low sigh. "I was on my balcony and when I turned to go back inside, I noticed that the lights were out. I—I'd left one light on before I went outside—"

"You're sure about that?" Tucker broke in.

"Yes." Her voice was certain. "But I just thought maybe the bulb had blown or there was a problem with the fuse. Something like that. I was going to call the front desk when he grabbed me and slammed my head into the wall."

"How did he grab you?" Tucker asked.

She swallowed. "From behind. I didn't even see him, didn't hear him. He was suddenly just there and he shoved me forward into the wall."

The fury was still thickening in Josh's blood. "You told me you heard his laughter."

She glanced toward him. "I did. I remember him laughing right before I passed out."

His muscles were tight, his body thick with tension.

"When I woke up, my hands were tied behind me and my feet were tied." Her gaze slid back to Tucker. "I was lying on the plastic, and I could smell the ocean. I could hear it. There was just enough light for me to see the room around me, and I realized I was in one of the houses under construction. Katrina and I had recorded some footage near them just the week before."

She licked her lips. Once more, her gaze darted to Josh. "Did he kill them all in that beach house?"

"The techs used luminol and found traces of latent blood." So, yes…he thought the other victims had been killed there but it would be a while before they received any sort of conclusive results on the blood evidence that had been collected at the scene. The homes under construction were isolated, and on the weekend, no workers came out to them. It would have been an ideal spot for a killer and his victim. "We'll know more once we get additional reports." Once the samples collected had been compared to their victims. "There wasn't a lot of blood found. The guy was probably trying to keep the scene clean with his plastic, but with these kinds of attacks, there can be a great deal of—" He stopped, hating to say more.

"Blood spatter?" Casey asked softly. "Yes, I know."

Of course, she would. Casey wasn't an ordinary civilian. So why was he treating her with kid gloves?

Because she's wounded. She's fragile. She's frightened.

She's…different. Something about her was calling to him.

"Where was he, when you woke up?" Tucker asked.

"Outside the room. I didn't see him at all and I screamed for help." Her breath whispered out. "My scream brought him to me."

"Describe every detail of him that you remember." Tucker was focused completely on her. He'd taken his laptop from his bag and he had it open in his lap as he listened to her.

"He was…tall, like you and Josh. Probably almost the same height, I would guess a little over six feet.

Muscled. Broad shoulders." Again, she nodded toward Josh. "He had on a ski mask with some kind of mesh over the eyes, so I don't know his eye color. I can't describe his face. But he was Caucasian, I know that. He was wearing gloves, but I saw his wrist. It was tanned, like he'd spent time outdoors."

The town of Hope was right on the beach. Nearly every Caucasian male in the area was sporting at least a light tan.

"When he came in…he said he'd heard me screaming. And that meant it was time to *get started*."

Bastard. "Did he have any accent?" Josh demanded. "Did anything about his voice stand out to you?"

She shook her head. "He was…rasping. I don't think that was his normal voice."

Tucker shot Josh a fast, hard glance. Josh nodded. *The guy is hiding his identity. Odd, since he planned to kill Casey. Usually when the perps think there is no hope for their prey, they'll show their faces.*

But this time…

"He…he said I was going to tell him all of my secrets." She licked her lips. "And that if I didn't, he would cut me open."

Josh surged away from the couch. *I will find you. I will make you pay.*

"I don't think…he expected me to fight back. I mean, I was tied up, so maybe he thought I'd be helpless. Or too afraid to fight back. But I wasn't going to die there."

She's strong. Strong and brave. He locked his legs and stared down at her.

"I kicked him with my bound feet. He fell back and lost his knife. I got it and used it on the ropes around my wrists, but he hit me before I could get free." Her hand rose to her dark cheek.

He will pay.

"H-he said he had to do step one."

Silence. Josh's heavy heartbeat drummed in his ears.

"What was step one?" Tucker asked.

"Making a phone call. To Sheriff Black. The guy said…he said we had to let people know who had the power." Her hand fell back to her lap. "But the sheriff wanted proof of life, and when the guy in the mask turned back to me—I think he was going to try to make me scream—I shouted at the sheriff, telling him where I thought I was. I was hoping he'd come for me in time."

Josh rolled back his shoulders. Casey had told him this story before, at the crime scene. She'd told him how, after the phone call, she'd stabbed the attacker. He'd fled and she'd been left alone in that house.

"I forgot." Her voice was low. "I forgot what he said…"

Josh stalked toward her.

Her head snapped up and she stared straight at him. "I didn't tell you before… I forgot…but he said, *I've waited too long to get you, Casey.* Those were his words. As if he'd always intended to take me."

Tucker had gone still beside her.

"But he was just talking, just scaring me, right?" Her gaze swung between the two men. "I mean, he picked me after his last victim was dead. It's not like the guy has been after me for a long time or anything."

The killings started after all the reporters came to town to cover Theodore Anderson's case and sentencing.

"Josh?" She rose to her feet and came toward him.

"He hasn't been after me for a long time. I was just—just his next victim, right? Like you said, I fit the victim profile. Right age, right sex. From out of town. No close ties here…"

Tucker cleared his throat when Josh remained silent. "There could be more to our profile," he said carefully. "It changes and adjusts as we gather additional information about our perp."

She was standing in front of Josh. Her body trembled. He'd never forget seeing her in that beach house, holding that bloody knife.

"Was there anything about him that seemed familiar to you?" Josh asked her because the knot in his stomach told him where Tucker's profile was heading. He didn't like getting into the heads of killers but in this case… with her…*for* her, he'd do it.

"Familiar?" Her laughter was bitter. "No, a man in a black ski mask who wants to cut me up and learn my secrets isn't exactly familiar to me."

Tucker had risen, too. "Since you've been in town, have you been seeing anyone romantically, started dating any locals or any other reporters or—"

She didn't look away from Josh. "I'm not dating anyone."

"What about in the past…maybe when you were in New York?" Tucker added. "Could you give us a list of the men you were seeing back home?"

Her chin notched up. "You want a list of my lovers, is that what you're saying?"

Tucker cleared his throat. "I think that might be helpful, yes."

Her eyes were on Josh. "Because you think one of them—one of the men I've slept with in the past—

came all the way down here, killed three other women, dumped their bodies in the ocean and then came after *me*. That's what you think?"

Josh wanted to touch her. To smooth away the line between her brows. "Based on what he said, it seems that this perp was focusing on you, Casey. By looking at those close to you, we may be able to find out why."

"Maybe he said the same thing to every woman he took." Now she glanced over at Tucker. "That's what killers like him do, right? They follow their rituals, their rules. Like step one…calling the sheriff—taunting him. Then step two…was learning the secrets of his victims. Maybe he said the same crap to us all. There's nothing personal there between us. I don't know him."

"He had on a mask," Tucker pointed out. "And you said he even disguised his voice. Maybe you *do* know him. And…you're a celebrity, Casey. Even if you don't personally know him, he may feel that he knows you. You're on his TV every week. That could have led to a fixation. It could have led—"

"To him kidnapping me and trying to kill me? To killing all of those other women?"

Tucker just stared at her. "I'll need the names of your lovers, ma'am. I need the names of any close friends you have down here *and* back in New York. On a case like this, every angle must be explored."

Her cheeks had flushed a dark pink. "The list is short, okay? I haven't had a boyfriend in two years, so there isn't anyone back home who needs to make your list. As far as friends—yes, I have a lot of those, but they're mostly superficial. I don't exactly let a lot of people close." She exhaled. "But I'll still make you the list. I just… Can I rest first? My head is aching again and I just—I need a minute." She brushed past Josh.

No, she *tried* to brush past him. He caught her arms and forced her to look at him. "You okay?"

Her laugh sounded bitter and rough. "I am very far from okay." Her eyes were filled with moisture but, just like before, she blinked before any teardrops could fall. "Where's my room?"

"Down the hallway. Second door on the right." His was the first door. He let her go. Josh watched as she hurried down the hallway and slipped into the second room on the right. When the door closed behind her, he turned back to focus on Tucker.

Tucker Frost. Like Josh, the guy had a dangerous past. When it came to killers, things were very, very personal for Tucker. No wonder his name had clicked for Casey. Being a reporter, there would have been no way for her to miss the sensational story that had been Tucker's life, even if that bloody hell had made the news years ago. Some stories were never forgotten.

"She has secrets," Josh said flatly. For some reason, when he said those words, he felt as if he were almost betraying her. Ridiculous, of course. He was just doing his job. But…

Tucker lifted a brow. "You seem to be very close to our victim."

She's more than a victim. "I'm the one who took her to the hotel right before she was abducted." *I'm the one who will never leave her alone like that again.*

"And here I thought Ms. Quinn said she didn't have a lover in the area."

He took a step toward the other agent, but caught himself. "*Not* like that," he gritted out. He'd known

Tucker for a long time…way before they'd joined the FBI. Back when they'd been two lost men trying to save the world, one bloody battle at a time. Tucker had been the one to actually convince him to join the FBI. Tucker had been the one to tell him that there was a place for Josh at the Bureau.

Tucker had wanted to focus on the killers. He'd been obsessed with finding out how to get in their heads. With Tucker's past, Josh certainly understood why. But…

For me, it's always been about the victims.

"She was waiting outside the sheriff's station. I gave her a ride back to her place. That is *all*."

Tucker rolled back his shoulders. "Then how do you know about the secrets?"

"I can tell when a woman is hiding something. She admitted it herself—no close friends, no lovers that she lets in. She's protecting herself."

"Which one of us is building the profile?" Tucker mused.

Josh raked a hand through his hair. "You know I don't go for that. I don't want in their heads." Too much darkness lived there. Once, the darkness had tried to swallow him alive. After a mission gone horribly wrong. "I'm going to dig into her past. I'll find out what she's hiding."

"Her past could be tied to the killer."

That was what he feared. "We both know that two killers of this caliber—Theodore Anderson and the perp who attacked her—there is no way they should both have been hunting in this town." The odds were just against that ever occurring.

Only it *had* occurred.

"We need to talk with Theodore Anderson," Tucker said. The faint lines near his mouth deepened. "Right now, Sheriff Black is operating under the assumption that Anderson committed his crimes alone. But maybe that's not the case. Maybe there was always someone else in the background."

Josh swore. "Someone who isn't content to stay in the background any longer? Not with Anderson out of the way?" When Anderson's sentencing had come down a few weeks ago, everyone had known that the man would never step foot outside those prison walls.

Tucker nodded. "That's one possibility. Option two…" His gaze slid toward the hallway. "Option two is that this killer was drawn to this town. Drawn to the crowd of reporters and the attention that Anderson received. He wanted his own spotlight so—"

"What better way to get in the spotlight than by taking a star reporter?" Talk about a victim that would grab headlines.

His friend exhaled. "Then we have our third option. It's the one I like least of all."

Josh knew this option. It was—

"Personal," Tucker said. "The killer went after Casey Quinn specifically. He targeted the other women, but only because he was working up to her. If he hadn't ever killed before these attacks in Hope, then he would have wanted to perfect his craft before getting to his real goal. His main prey."

And that prey? It could be Casey.

Chapter Six

"Are you sure you're all right?" Katrina demanded, her sharp voice showing her worry. "I mean…the killer took you, Casey. He *took* you."

Her hold tightened on the phone. Josh had brought the phone to her a few moments before, and then he'd urged her to be very, very careful with the facts she shared with her friend. He'd also told Casey that she wouldn't be getting her own phone back anytime soon—it had been bagged as evidence at her hotel.

As soon as he'd slipped out to go and join his FBI buddy again, she'd been calling Katrina. "I'm okay. I promise. Nothing that won't heal."

"Where are you? The FBI has been giving me some bull story about you being in protective custody—"

"It's not bull." She turned and glanced at the closed door. "I'm in a safe house, for the moment."

"What?"

That cry nearly split Casey's eardrum. "It's just temporary, okay? Agent Duvane got me out of the hospital and brought me here so I could rest. I think my hotel room is still crime scene central—"

"Tom moved us out of that hotel," Katrina said quickly. "We all have rooms at a new place. Way better security, I promise. So you don't need to stay with the FBI. You can come over here. Tom is right next door, and seriously, the guy is about to go out of his head. He wants to talk to you. You know, I don't think he's over that crush he had on you—"

"Tom doesn't have a crush on me. Tom just wants a story. A big story. Having his reporter escape death is going to give him huge ratings, and he knows it." Ratings on TV. Hits on the web. Everything a producer could desire. "But tell him he has to wait. The FBI said I couldn't talk to the media yet."

"You *are* the media."

"And I'm the victim." She dropped onto the edge of the bed. The mattress sagged a bit beneath her. "They've got me talking to some kind of profiler now." Though profiler wouldn't be his technical term. Profilers didn't actually exist in the FBI. The guy—Tucker Frost—she figured he was working for the Behavioral Analysis Unit.

A man who understood killers.

With what she knew of Tucker's past, she figured he would understand them very, very well.

"Is that her?" A man's voice sounded in the background and she knew Tom had come into Katrina's room. Not surprising, really, since she knew Katrina and Tom hooked up frequently. *And yet another reason why the man is not interested in me at all.*

"Let me talk to Casey," Tom continued.

Casey's heels kicked against the side of the bed as she swung her feet and waited.

"Casey," his deep voice boomed over the line. "Tell me where you are and I will come get you right now."

"That's not an option, Tom. I'm at a safe house.

Places like this stay safe because you don't tell people where they are."

*"Casey…*you're the lead story on every television in the US right now. You have to give me something. Tell me about the man who took you. Tell me what he looked like. What he said. Tell me—"

Her bedroom door opened. Josh seemed to fill the doorway.

"Casey?" Tom called in her ear. "Say something! I need *something*—"

"I'm okay, Tom. I survived." Her words sounded brittle even to her own ears. "Thanks for worrying."

"Wait, I *do* worry, I—"

Josh closed the door behind him and paced toward her. "End the call, Casey."

Had he been eavesdropping on her? That was such a terrible habit. She couldn't look away from him. "Got to go, Tom. I'll check in again soon."

"But I need a quote—"

Her fingers swiped over the screen, ending the call.

Josh stood just over her. His gaze seemed hooded as he stared at her. She tipped back her head, looking up at him. "Don't worry, I didn't tell Tom or Katrina anything about this place." She glanced around the room. "I left out the fact that I was staying in the lap of luxury." She tossed the phone onto the bed beside her. "I just assured my friends that I was still in the land of the living."

His jaw hardened. "How's the head?"

"It—" She started to lie and say that it was perfectly fine, but there was just something about his gaze. So deep and dark. "It aches."

His hand lifted and his fingers feathered over her temple. "You should have stayed in the hospital."

She immediately tensed. "No, that was the last place I wanted to be."

He studied her a moment in silence, then turned on his heel and headed into the bathroom. A moment later, he was back, carrying a cloth that he put to her forehead, then swept over her temple. It was a cool, soft cloth, and it immediately made her feel better.

"Any blurred vision? Nausea?"

"Nothing. Just an aching head...because it collided too hard with a wall."

He slid the cloth over her temple again in a gentle caress. "I—I didn't expect gentleness from you."

"What did you expect?"

"Danger. Arrogance. Maybe some adrenaline-junkie personality traits."

"Just because I was a SEAL, it doesn't mean I was addicted to the high of battle."

No, it didn't. "Why were you a SEAL?"

He still towered over her, but, after a moment of silence, Josh moved to sit on the bed beside her, and suddenly, it was harder to breathe. Maybe because every breath brought her his rich, masculine scent.

"My father was a navy man, spent his whole life serving. When I was a kid, I bounced around, living all over the world as we headed to new bases. My mom and I—she always said it was an adventure. I liked that adventure."

Wanderlust...that was why he'd been a SEAL? No, she didn't buy it. "There's more to your story."

His lips twisted in a faint smile. "Going to feature me on your show? Trying to figure me out?"

"Not everything is about the show." She pushed away the cloth and her fingers tangled with his. Whenever

they touched, she felt that contact straight to her soul.
Crazy. Ridiculous. Just a product of her overwrought
emotions.

Except…even before her attack, when he'd taken her
on that motorcycle ride, his touch had burned straight
to her soul.

"You want to know about me?" His faint smile stayed
in place. "Well, I want to know about you, Casey Quinn.
How about we trade secrets? I'll tell you my past, and
you tell me yours."

Her hand lowered. Their fingers stayed intertwined.
She couldn't look away from the sight of them. "You're
going to dig into my past, anyway. You think I don't
know that? Your buddy Tucker is probably already calling the FBI. He's telling them to pull up every single
file they can find on Cassandra, AKA Casey, Quinn."
She leaned toward him, putting her lips right next to
his ear. "But here's the first secret, Josh. He won't find
anything on Casey." Her lips brushed his ear. A deliberate move on her part. She was feeling too much—and
her normal control wasn't in place. She was playing a
dangerous game with him because playing made her
feel alive. And she wanted to be alive.

She'd come too close to death.

"Why not? Why won't we find you?"

Was it her imagination or had his voice gone deeper?
Darker?

"Because Casey Quinn didn't exist until seven years
ago." When she'd turned eighteen, Casey had been born.
Once more, her lips brushed against his ear. "I'm not
real." Her secret, the truth she held so close, but she
knew he'd find out. And it almost felt good to have her
cards on the table. To not pretend, for once.

"If you're not Casey—" his voice was a little more than a growl now "—then who are you?"

Her heart ached as she trailed her finger down the column of his neck. "I'm the girl who should have died. Everyone else died, but I didn't."

His head turned toward her. His gaze blazed. "Casey—"

"Your turn." She had to force those words out. "No more from me. Tell me a truth, and don't say you're a former SEAL because you liked traveling to new places. I won't buy that. Do better."

"Fine." The word was nearly a snarl. "I'm good at hunting. A damn deadly weapon."

She shook her head. "Lie."

His eyes widened. "What?"

"Oh, I don't doubt that you're very good at hunting, and I'm sure you're a perfectly timed killing machine when the need arises, but that's still not the reason you were a SEAL." Her heart pounded hard in her chest. "Have I told you… I'm good at seeing lies? You can see lies in the way a person's eyes change." Her hand lifted and her fingers feathered near the corner of his eye. "When you look away from me or when you focus just beyond my gaze…dead giveaway." Her hand dropped to his chest. "When your breath comes faster, when your heart pounds… I can see the lie. I've interviewed hundreds of witnesses in my time. I *had* to know who was telling me the truth, and who was just trying to lie to me."

"I'm a federal agent. I *know* how to control my responses. You don't see anything when I lie—"

"Got you," she whispered.

A furrow appeared between his heavy brows.

"You just confessed. You are lying. And here I was, telling you the truth." Disappointment rushed through her. "If this is going to work, I need you to be honest with me."

He edged ever closer to her. "And you'll be honest with me?"

She had been, so far.

"I wanted to make a difference. Be all I could be… just like my old man. When I got out there in the field, I found out that I did like the job. I liked the rush. But I was away on a mission when my mother *and* my father both died in a robbery. Some jerk held them up at gunpoint, stole one hundred dollars from my father. *One hundred dollars.* Like that's worth someone's life. He shot my father, and he shot my mother, and when I came home, all I had waiting for me were two coffins."

Her hand wrapped around his. "I'm sorry."

"Tucker is the one who came to me then. Telling me my skills could be put to use. Telling me there was a way to help right here at home. My family was gone, and I didn't want to ship out again. So I listened. I became part of the FBI and found my way to USERT." His lips twisted. "The water has always been part of me, so using my skills there again, yeah, I liked that."

He'd shared more secrets than she'd expected. "I'm sorry about your parents." She knew just how deep of a blow losing them must have been. "I…lost mine, too. When I was seventeen." *Just a month away from my eighteenth birthday.*

"What happened?"

It was better to tell him now, so he could hear her side, and not just read the cold facts on a computer screen later. "Sometimes, people can't let you go."

His eyes narrowed.

"I had a boyfriend back then. Smart, super smart guy. And intense. But he…he started planning out my life for me. *Our* life. Only it wasn't a life I wanted. I had my own plans. A different college that I wanted to attend. A whole different life that waited for me." She pulled in a slow breath that seemed to chill her lungs. "Benjamin didn't understand that. He thought someone else was pressuring me. That my parents were trying to pull us apart."

"Casey…"

"So one night, he broke into my house and he killed them."

She saw the shock flash on his face.

"I heard the gunshots and that was what woke me up. I ran downstairs and found them, and he was still standing over them. He *smiled* at me and lifted his hand up, telling me that it was time for us to go."

His eyes had widened. "What did you do?"

"My mother was still alive. I could see her breathing. I ran to her and I screamed for him to get away. I put my hands on her chest, trying to stop that blood from pumping out of her." She lifted her hand away from him. Sometimes, she could swear that she still saw blood on her. "He grabbed me, yanked me up. Told me we were leaving."

The room was so quiet.

"I wasn't going to leave them. I told him that…and he put the gun to my head."

His hands flew up and curled around her shoulders. *"Casey."*

That hadn't been her name, not back then. Back then, she'd been Cassidy.

Cassidy, I did this for you! All for you! We can have everything now! We can be together now!

"He said if I didn't leave with him, he was going to kill me."

Josh's fingers bit into her skin.

"I knew he meant those words, too. We'd been dating for six months, and I'd never seen him for what he really was, not until that terrible night. He was going to kill me. My mom couldn't even pull in a full breath. Her blood was everywhere. My dad was *gone*, and if I didn't walk out of that house with Benjamin, I was going to die, too." Her voice was brittle, as if she were on the verge of breaking. She wasn't, though. She hadn't broken back then…

I won't break now.

"The neighbors must have heard the gunshots. The police came swarming up just as we stepped outside. Benjamin fired at them and I ran…"

She could never forget that night.

"I felt the bullet hit me in the back. I slammed down into the ground. I tried to look back and I saw that Benjamin was getting ready to shoot at me again. He was aiming for me. He wasn't letting me go."

Bam! Bam! Bam!

"But the cops fired—they kept firing until they took him down. Benjamin died on my front porch."

Josh's face seemed carved from granite. A hard, stone mask, but his eyes blazed with emotion.

"I stayed in the hospital afterward. I was lucky—the bullet had missed my spine. Lucky… I was alive and everyone else was gone. I stayed in the hospital, and I hated that place. I *hated* what had become of my life." Just as she'd hated Benjamin. It was easy to hate the dead.

"No wonder you wanted out of the hospital."

Her lips twisted. "And that's the same reason I don't have any current lovers to give your FBI buddy. I don't trust easy. Relationships aren't really my thing."

"Victims are." His fingers stroked down her arms. "That's why you're a reporter, isn't it? You're doing the profiles on the victims in your stories."

"I try to make sure they get the justice they need." Because there had been no justice for her—her family had just been gone. "I changed my name because I wanted to put the past behind me. I'd always wanted to be a reporter, and I wasn't going to let him take that from me. But I didn't want everyone seeing *me* as the victim. I didn't want it to be about me. I didn't…" Her breath expelled on a sigh. "I didn't want to be the story."

But she was. Again.

His touch was so careful on her skin. "I had you all wrong."

She swallowed. "You mean…when you called me a vulture?"

"Did I apologize for that yet?" Josh winced. "Because I am sorry. And I think we need to start over. Way over."

But Casey shook her head. "I don't want to do that. You're the guy who came rushing to my rescue. I'm not forgetting that."

"Bull. You saved yourself."

"I won't be destroyed again." When you had nothing left, you learned to fight. She'd learned and she would never forget.

His hand slid under her chin. "I don't think anything can destroy you."

He had no clue. When she'd been in that hospital, everyone else gone, she'd felt utterly destroyed. The machines had beeped around her, the nurses had slipped in and out of her room, and she'd felt like a ghost. Everything had been surreal. And the days had just passed— the world had kept going—while she was alone in her bed.

His face was so close to hers. Their lips were close. She'd just bared her soul to him. But it was better that way, right? Better for her to tell him instead of him reading those dark details without her in some neat little file at the FBI. "It's your turn." Her voice had grown husky. "You have to tell me something…"

"I want you."

Her eyes widened. That was *not* what she'd expected.

"I think you're the most beautiful woman I've ever seen, and I know I should be keeping my hands off you."

His hands weren't off. They were on.

"You need comfort right now. You need sympathy. You need care."

Maybe what I need…is you.

She'd had too much sympathy. Didn't he get that? She'd changed her name, changed everything so that she could be stronger. So people would stop looking at her with pity in their eyes.

"I'm not an easy guy, Casey."

No, she didn't think he was.

"I like danger. I take risks. Emotions haven't been a big part of my life. Usually, when I see something I want, I go after it."

And he wanted her.

But he wasn't moving. A few more inches, and his mouth would be on hers. He was staring at her with his intense gaze. She licked her lips. His stare heated even more. "Why…why aren't you kissing me?" Casey asked.

His pupils seemed to double in size as the darkness spread in his stare. His nostrils flared. "Because I'm trying to be different…with you. You deserve different."

He let her go. He stood up. Headed for the door.

That was it? He was…leaving?

"I don't want pity from you." She rose to her feet. Her hands fisted at her sides. "I told you my story because I knew you'd figure out the truth. But now you're acting like I'm different. You're acting like—"

"You matter." His back was to her. His words came out sounding rough. "So I'm trying not to mess this up. I didn't expect you." He looked back at her. "But I'm trying to do this *right*. You confessed your darkest pain to me, and I'm *not* going to pounce on you. I'm going to give you space. I'm going to give you whatever you need—"

Because he was a protector, straight to his core. Did he even get that? She'd asked why he'd been a SEAL, why he'd joined the FBI…and the truth was right there.

To protect.

She closed the distance between them and put her hand on his shoulder. "Neither one of us has exactly had an easy life." But no one was guaranteed easy. "Sometimes right doesn't matter. Sometimes there isn't a wrong." In that moment, there was only one thing she wanted. "Kiss me."

A muscle flexed along the hard line of his jaw. "Casey…"

"If I'm really what you want, then kiss—"

He pulled her into his arms. His mouth took hers. She'd expected some passion. Some excitement. What she didn't expect was the absolute explosion of feeling that she experienced when his mouth took hers.

The kiss rocked Casey straight to her core. Every cell in her body seemed to ignite. Her hands grabbed on to his arms, her nails sank into his shirt and she pulled him closer. He'd crushed her to his body, and his hard strength pressed against her. He kissed her with a hunger that she couldn't deny, with a need that called to her. Her lips parted even more for him, and his tongue thrust into her mouth. She moaned and her body rubbed against his. Her skin felt so sensitive, primed, and the way the man kissed…

His mouth pulled from hers. She immediately bit back a protest.

"I…shouldn't have done that."

No, he should have done a whole lot more.

"My job is to keep you safe." He stepped back and let her go.

She stared at him. Her heart was racing. Her breath came in quick pants.

His heated stare swept over her. "But I'm not apologizing."

Good. She hadn't asked for an apology.

"And it's probably going to happen again."

Probably? "Count on it," she said.

His lips kicked into a half smile. "But it will *not* happen until your twenty-four-hour concussion watch is over."

"Josh—"

He held up a hand, stopping her when she stepped toward him. "I don't think you understand how much

I want you." His smile vanished. "And how fragile my control is where you're concerned."

She could still taste him.

"Stay in here and relax a while," he said. "I need to… talk a few things over with Tucker."

Translation—he needed to go and tell Tucker about her past. Some of that wonderful warmth she'd felt faded.

"Benjamin is dead," she said quietly. "He was an only child. His mother passed away last year, and his father—he died a few years ago. There is no one in his family who would be seeking any kind of crazed vengeance against me." Her shoulders straightened. "And there is no one that I've let get close since then."

"I guess that depends on your definition of close."

She wasn't sure she followed.

"For some guys, it's all about the fantasy. You don't realize you're starring in that fantasy until it's too late." He reached for the doorknob. "I'll be right outside if you need me, okay? I have to talk with Tucker and check in with the rest of the team." His gaze slid to the phone on the bed. "No more phone calls, okay? Not today."

Then he was gone. Maybe she should have felt like a prisoner, locked away but…she felt safe—for the moment, anyway.

HE'D MISREAD CASEY. Totally judged her wrong. He'd let his past interactions with reporters get to him, and Josh hadn't seen her for the woman she was.

His blinders were off. He saw her now. He always would.

He marched back into the den.

Tucker was tapping away at his laptop, but when

he saw Josh, he put down the computer and raised his brows. "How'd that chat go?"

"Her past isn't pretty." Talk about an understatement. "But it might be a lead we can use." He headed toward Tucker. There were a few details about the recent murders that hadn't made it to the press. A deliberate move.

"She's linked, just like the other victims," he said, making sure to keep his voice low. "She was the victim of a violent crime, too."

Tucker's jaw hardened. "He definitely has a victim type, doesn't he?"

Yes, he did… The perp liked a survivor. The first victim, Kylie Shane, had been attacked when she was sixteen years old. She'd been stabbed twice, but had managed to get away from her attacker. During the exam of her body, the ME had found those old scars.

The second victim, Bridget Donaldson, had been the victim of a hit and run when she'd been just fifteen. She'd been walking home from school and the driver hadn't even slowed when he hit her. Bridget had spent four weeks in the hospital. But she'd survived.

Just as Kylie had survived.

And Tonya Myers? An arsonist had set her home on fire, while Tonya and her sister had been inside. The sister had died, but Tonya escaped. She'd suffered second-degree burns on her legs, but she'd *survived*.

As Casey had survived.

"Casey's high school boyfriend killed her family and tried to kill her." Rage boiled inside him, a hot blackness that wanted to consume Josh. "She even changed her name after the attack, tried to become someone new."

Tucker's gaze was considering. "But our perp found out her secrets."

Tell me all of your secrets.

Tucker tapped his hand on the side of the couch. "It's not just about the victims being attractive women in their twenties, not about them being outsiders. These women were survivors."

"Were," Josh pointed out darkly. Because that was the point to note. "They survived until he got hold of them." And then the killer had made sure that they didn't escape death. He'd made so sure…he'd given Kylie, Bridget and Tonya a watery grave.

No escape.

"Your Casey survived," Tucker noted.

She isn't mine. But he wished that she were.

Tucker's face became grim. "He isn't going to let her walk away. If he's choosing these women specifically because of their past, he isn't going to find an easy replacement for Casey. And her escaping him…he'll take it as a personal attack. She *survived* what he did to her. He can't let that happen."

"He'll come after her again." Even as he said it, Josh hated those words.

"Yes." Tucker wasn't the sugarcoating type. With his life, Josh knew he couldn't be. Neither of them could be. "We have to be ready."

They would be. Because Josh was not going to let Casey be hurt. He'd stand between her and any threat that came.

Chapter Seven

The sun was shining. The waves were pounding against the shore—she could hear them through the open balcony door in her room. And Casey didn't feel so safe any longer.

She opened the bedroom door and marched down the hallway. She headed into the kitchen and spotted Josh's back as he leaned inside the open refrigerator.

"I can't do this. I can't just…stay here, indefinitely. It's been over twenty-four hours since you brought me here, and I'm already going crazy." Her words tumbled out too fast. *Twenty-four hours.* Twenty-four very slow hours had elapsed while she'd been in that penthouse. "I need to talk to Katrina again. I need to do *something* to help find that freak who attacked me. And just staying in here while that guy is out there, possibly lining up someone else in his sights—that isn't *me*."

The man rose and she saw his dark hair. Hair that didn't belong to Josh. Her mouth dropped open a bit. She'd been so sure—

Tucker Frost stared at her, one brow raised. "I told him we'd be lucky if you lasted a day." He shut the refrigerator door behind him.

She glanced around the quiet penthouse. "Where is Josh?"

"At the sheriff's station. He needed to talk with Hayden Black."

He'd left without telling her. Just…left? Why did that make her angry?

"He'll be back soon—don't worry."

"I'm not worried," she immediately replied. She wasn't. She— "The disposable phone vanished from my room."

"Right. Yes. Josh took it. With him leaving, he wanted to make sure you didn't get the urge to call your news buddies in his absence."

So Josh hadn't trusted her. "I can't keep staying here." Each word was snapped. *Take a breath, Casey. Calm down.* But she was going stir crazy. She hadn't been outside in a day and staying cooped up, with nothing to do…it just gave her time to think about her attack. Over and over again. "I want to help."

"You're the only witness, the only survivor. Trust me, you *are* helping."

"No, I'm hiding—there's a difference." And she'd come to a hard realization during the long hours that had passed. "If someone else dies while I'm here, that death will be on me."

"No," Tucker said flatly. "That will be on the killer out there. He's the one who takes the life—he's the one who has the responsibility." His hand raked over his face. "No matter what anyone else will tell you."

"I came here yesterday because the doctor said that in order for me to be released from the hospital, I needed someone to watch me. Josh said he'd take that job. And I—I wasn't quite myself." She'd wanted a safe harbor.

"But there has to be more than just…*this*. If I don't contact my boss again, I may not have a job. I can't just sit here, waiting forever."

The door opened behind her. She whirled around and saw Josh standing in the entranceway. His gaze slid from her to Tucker.

"Happened just like I said," Tucker murmured. "Barely a day and she wants out."

"What *she* wants," Casey stressed, "is to help. To be of use. Not to be hidden away." She hurriedly crossed the room and stood in front of Josh. "I want to help the investigation. I'll keep a guard with me—I'll play by the FBI's rules, but staying here indefinitely just can't happen."

He shut the door and secured the lock. "Your face is currently on every TV in the area. Your story is showing constantly."

She'd rather expected as much.

"You go out into the city, and you won't be helping. You'll be swarmed by your fellow reporters. They'll close in like sharks."

"But—"

"I need you."

She blinked. Those hadn't been the words she expected.

"Sheriff Black called me to his office today because there's been a…development."

A development?

"Before the attack, you'd been working to get an interview with Theodore Anderson."

"Yes." She nodded. "He hasn't spoken to any reporters, and I wanted to interview him. I know it was a long shot, and his lawyer kept denying my request but—"

"He's not denying it anymore. Theodore Anderson wants to talk. But only to you."

Her eyes widened. "You aren't serious."

"Dead serious. *That's* why I was talking to Sheriff Black. Anderson has been completely shut down since his trial, but suddenly, the guy is saying he'll speak freely…to you. He doesn't want his attorney present—he said he didn't give a damn about his rights. He just wants to see…you."

She tucked a lock of hair behind her ear. "My producer must be freaking out."

"Yeah, I met him. Dear *Tom* was camped out at the sheriff's station, demanding to see you. He wants to make certain you're all right, and he wants his star reporter going in for that interview."

She couldn't miss that opportunity. "Theodore Anderson could have killed other victims. He hasn't said a word to the cops—if he will really speak freely, there is so much I could learn from him."

Tucker had come up to stand at her side. "The FBI has been wanting him to talk…"

"Yeah." Josh rubbed the back of his neck. "And he's said jack to everyone so far. But this could be a chance…"

Excitement had her rising onto the balls of her feet. "You're going to let me out of here so I can see him?"

His hand fell. His eyes glittered. "*We're* going to see him."

"I don't—"

"You just agreed to keep a guard with you. I'm that guard. And I'll be going with you on the little visit with Anderson. Consider me your new assistant."

"But…" But she didn't know what to say.

"I don't trust Anderson," Tucker said quietly.

"Neither do I," Josh immediately agreed.

It was hard to trust a convicted murderer.

"And for him to want to see you, Casey, right after your attack…" Josh whistled. "I don't like it, not at all. Despite being locked up, he would still have access to the news in prison. He'll know what happened to you."

Her mind was spinning and there was a dark suspicion that she couldn't ignore. For Anderson to want to talk with her *now*, after she'd escaped that creep with the knife… "There's more here."

Tucker cleared his throat. "There's an…option we may need to explore."

Her head tilted toward him.

"Two serials of this nature, both hunting in Hope… perhaps they are connected."

Her lips parted. "You think the guy who took me *knows* Theodore Anderson?"

Tucker shrugged. *Not* an answer. "I think we can't overlook any possible connections. At this time, everyone has been operating under the idea that Anderson committed his crimes on his own."

"But what if he didn't?" she whispered.

"What if," Tucker continued, "there was always someone in the background?"

She understood exactly what Tucker and Josh wanted. "You need me to talk to Anderson and see if he'll reveal anything about this perp."

Josh didn't look happy, but he said, "It's too coincidental that he wants to see you now. We can't let this chance pass us by. We need to go in and see what the guy will reveal." But he seemed hesitant. "Are you up for this? Be sure…"

She'd interviewed killers before. She'd stared straight into eyes that she knew were pure evil. Casey's chin lifted. "I'm up for this."

"I'll be with you every step of the way," he promised.

THEODORE ANDERSON WAS being held in a maximum security facility. Getting in to see him took some time, and Josh made sure he stayed with Casey every moment. Once they finally cleared security, he led the way into the small conference room that they would use for their session. A table waited inside, and a video camera had already been set up for the talk. As part of the deal for that little one-on-one, the FBI would be getting the video footage. Later, once they'd reviewed it thoroughly, the Bureau would turn over the video to Casey and her producer, Tom Warren.

That was the deal.

He glanced toward the one-way mirror that lined the wall on the right. Tucker was behind that mirror, watching and getting ready to make his observations. Hayden Black was in there, too. Hayden had to be kept away from the prisoner. Things were too personal between them. Anderson had gone after the woman Black loved, a woman who happened to be an FBI agent herself.

And Hayden wasn't exactly the forgiving sort.

Don't blame him a bit.

"You know the questions to ask?" Josh asked as he paced the room. Anderson would be arriving any moment.

Casey shot him a slightly annoyed look. The bruising on her cheek had faded a bit today. He still hated the reminder of her pain. And he couldn't wait to find the jerk who'd hurt her.

"I'm a professional," she told him, a crisp edge to her voice. "I really don't need my questions hand-fed to me."

No, she didn't. But those prepared questions had come straight from Tucker because the guy was trying to get into Anderson's head.

She pulled out a chair at the table. She sat, with her back perfectly straight, right before the door opened. A guard entered first—young, with dark brown hair and dark eyes.

The prisoner came in after him. The man was tall, fit and wore the garish orange of a prison jumpsuit. The lines on Theodore Anderson's face were deep, and his blond hair had thinned. His tan complexion had turned pallid since he'd been locked up. He shuffled forward, and Josh saw the shackles that connected from the lock around the prisoner's ankles to his bound wrists.

Another guard followed Theodore inside. The two guards kept their attention on Theodore, obviously worried he might lunge at the pretty reporter as they steered him toward the table. But he didn't lunge. Theodore just kept moving with those slow, shuffling steps.

A few moments later, he'd taken the seat across from Casey. His gaze swept over her, narrowing a bit when he saw the swelling and bruising on her cheek.

Josh rolled back his shoulders. He was standing to the side, his back against the wall as he stared at the prisoner—and at Casey. One wrong move from the prisoner, and the guards wouldn't have to attack because Josh would be on the guy.

"Mr. Anderson." Casey's voice was smooth, calm. "Just why did you agree to see me today?"

He was silent—a silence that stretched a bit too long.

Tucker had coached a disgruntled Casey before she went into the prison—trying to tell her how to use interrogation techniques. Casey had been adamant that she already knew plenty of techniques to use. And as she'd told Tucker and Josh, it wasn't her first time interviewing a murderer. Not her first time, not even her fifth.

"Sorry about what he did to you," Theodore said, hitching his head forward. His eyes were bright in his pale face. "Such a shame…"

"He?" Casey prompted.

Theodore smiled. Josh didn't like that smile. Too cold. Too calculating. A monster's smile. But then, he was staring at a man who'd killed his own daughter. Was there a worse monster?

"I heard the guards talking about what happened to you." With his bound hands, Theodore gestured to the men beside him. "Seems the good people of Hope have more to fear than just me these days."

"The people of Hope feared you for a very long time. A killer living right among them—someone they never suspected." Her voice was still low and unemotional. "They felt sympathy for you, pity, because you lost your daughter." She gave a brief pause. "They never realized that you were the one who'd murdered her."

Theodore's hands slammed down onto the table. *"That wasn't my fault!"*

Josh—and the guards—immediately surged forward, but Casey waved them back. "Then whose fault was it?"

"Christy was never supposed to die! You think I'd go after my own daughter? No, *no*. I had a victim. Jill… sweet little Jill, but she got away. She got away and she messed *everything* up for me."

Jill… Jillian West. The woman Hayden loved. The

FBI agent who'd finally learned the truth about Theodore Anderson.

"Christy was the one good thing in my life." Theodore's shoulders slumped forward. "After she was gone… I was only left with…*him*."

"Him?" Casey prompted.

Theodore looked up at her, squinting. "You ever stare straight at evil, Casey Quinn?"

She's staring at it right now. So was Josh. He knew evil when he saw it. But Casey didn't speak, she just waited.

The woman does know how to work an interrogation. She would have made a good FBI agent.

"I have. I saw it…in his eyes." Theodore licked his lower lip. "He's the one who took you. He's the one who hurt you. Who hurt the others… I tried to keep him in check all those years, but now that I'm locked up in here…there's nothing to stop him."

Every muscle in Josh's body locked down.

"You know the identity of the man who abducted me?" Casey asked, leaning forward.

Josh didn't like that. He didn't want her getting so much as another inch closer to Theodore Anderson.

The prisoner nodded. "He took you…and I heard what he did to those other women, too. He killed them. Always knew he'd be a killer."

"Who is he?" Casey's voice was strained now.

"Guess sometimes, it *is* in the blood, huh?" He expelled a long sigh, then looked regretful as he said, "The apple didn't fall so far away, now did it?"

And Josh knew what the guy was going to say, even before Theodore Anderson smiled.

"The man who took you," Theodore said, "the man who killed those others…it's my son, Kurt."

JOSH KEPT HIS body next to Casey's as they exited the interrogation room. After his big reveal, Theodore Anderson had locked down, refusing to say another word. Apparently, he'd wanted to point the finger at his son.

And he had.

Josh opened the door to the right and led Casey inside the observation room. Tucker was on the phone.

"Yeah, that's right," Tucker barked into the phone. "I want to know where Kurt Anderson is right now. Find the guy and bring him to the sheriff's station. I want to talk to him… Yes, yes, get him there, and I'll meet you." He hung up and swung to face Casey. "Good job, Ms. Quinn—"

"Casey," she cut in. "Just… Casey, okay?" she slid away from Josh and moved toward the observation window. The glass showed them the now empty interrogation room. "Do we believe the guy? I've talked to Kurt Anderson a few times since coming to town."

Behind her back, Josh and Tucker shared a long look.

"Kurt struck me as someone who was fighting a lot of grief and anger. He'd just found out that his own father murdered his sister years ago…and that he'd *lived* with that killer. He was hurting, but for him to suddenly start killing…" One shoulder lifted in a weak shrug. "Does that fit?" She looked back at Tucker, then at Josh.

"It *could* fit," Tucker allowed. But he didn't say more.

Josh just watched Casey. He was worried she was pushing herself too hard.

Her full lips pressed together. "You are *not* shutting me out now."

"We should get going," Josh announced. "It's a drive back to—"

"*I* did this interview for you both. I got the guy to talk. Now you're trying to pull some FBI rank and not share with me?" Her cheeks flushed. "Not cool, gentlemen."

"You're a reporter," Tucker gently reminded her. When her eyes turned to slits, Josh figured she didn't like—or need—that reminder. "And this is an active investigation. There's only so much we *can* say to you."

"I want the guy who attacked me caught! I want Kylie, Bridget and Tonya to have justice! I'm *helping* here. What happened to us being a team? What happened to that?" Her gaze raked them. "Or are we only a team when the two of you want to use me?"

"You're the one who insisted on doing this," Tucker replied, voice quiet. "And you're the one who'll get to air the footage later. You'll have the scoop of the century, won't you? So I think it's a win for you."

Her expression hardened.

No, it wasn't a win. Tucker was misjudging her, the same way Josh had. Josh crossed to her side. "We should get going."

Her gaze jumped to his face. "Do you think it's Kurt?"

He thought it was possible, but his stare slid to Tucker and he replied, very carefully, "Just because a killer's in the family, it doesn't mean you have bad blood. Each person makes his or her own choices."

"I'm going to find Kurt," Tucker stated. "Josh, we'll talk later." Then he turned on his heel and marched out.

"It's hitting too close to home for him," she murmured. "Isn't it?"

Yes, the case was. Because Tucker had a killer in the family, too. One who'd come far too close to destroying everything that Tucker loved.

Josh caught Casey's hand in his. His fingers slid over her wrist, and he felt the quick jump of her pulse. "Let's get out of here."

"You still didn't tell me whether or not you think the killer could be Kurt Anderson."

No, he hadn't told her, not yet. "Just how many times did you talk to Kurt?"

"Three times." They walked down the narrow corridor, past the guards. The security doors were opened for them, one after the other. Soon they had cleared the checkpoints. Josh took his gun back and adjusted his holster.

"The last time I saw him…" She'd been quiet as they passed the guards. "We had a brief dinner on Friday night."

She'd gone to dinner with the guy? Dinner…the night before she'd been abducted.

"I wanted to hear his side of things." They walked out of the facility. The sun was bright, beating down on them. "He lost his sister. He was just as much of a victim as—"

"Casey!" a man's voice boomed.

Josh tensed and his body immediately moved in front of Casey's. His hand went to his weapon.

A man with black hair and thin-framed glasses rushed forward. He wore a suit and had a flashy watch around his wrist. A short-haired woman was behind him—Josh recognized Katrina, Casey's camerawoman. And, unfortunately, he recognized the man, too. Tom Warren. Casey's producer.

"Knew you'd get the exclusive!" Tom cried out. He tried to reach out and touch Casey. Josh just moved his body and prevented that touch. "Wait—what the hell are you doing?"

Protecting Casey.

Tom's gaze sharpened on him. "Look, Agent Duvane, I get that you saved Casey, and I'm grateful, but you can relax. I'm not any threat to her."

Josh didn't relax.

A trickle of sweat slid down Tom's temple. "Hey… I've got an idea." He flashed a smile. "It would be great if we could get you both on camera. You know, some footage of Casey and the agent who saved her." He motioned to Katrina. "Get the gear from the van."

"Not happening," Josh said flatly. "And for the record, Casey saved herself."

"Right, right, yes, but I haven't gotten all of those *details* yet." Tom's smile slipped. "Because I kept being told that I can't speak to my own employee."

Josh didn't want the guy talking to Casey. And the other woman, Katrina, was shifting nervously from foot to foot. Obviously, she was wondering if she should follow Tom's orders and rush to get the camera or if she should stay put.

"Casey." Tom's voice deepened. It took on a personal, almost possessive edge as he said her name. "I've been worried about you."

Katrina slanted a quick, hard stare toward her boss.

Casey slid closer to Josh's side. "I'm okay."

"Your face." His eyes were absolutely horrified as he stared at her cheek. "Katrina, get the camera." He stepped toward Casey, lifting his hand to touch her cheek. "People need to see—"

Josh caught the guy's wrist before Tom could touch Casey. "See what? Her pain?"

Tom's pale blue eyes narrowed. "They need to see the damage that the monster did to her. When people see real pain, up close and personal, they have a more visceral reaction. The public loves Casey. They relate to her. We show the world what that SOB did to her, and everyone will be hunting for him."

"Everyone is hunting for him now," Casey said and her shoulder brushed against Josh's arm. "But it's hard to find a killer when no one knows what he looks like."

Josh let go of Tom's hand.

"You didn't get a look at his face?" Now Tom sounded disappointed.

She shook her head.

"You must have noted *something* about him. Something distinct that we can lead with. His voice. Mannerisms. A stutter—"

"You aren't leading with anything," Josh said flatly. "Casey is leaving with me, right now."

Tom's mouth opened, closed and then opened again. Finally, he sputtered, "She works for me!"

Josh really didn't like the producer. "And she's in *my* protective custody. For the moment, I need her to stay off the radar. By going on-air again, she might just make the killer focus even more on her."

Casey sighed. "He's already come for me once. I don't know that there can be *more* of a focus."

Josh turned toward her. "Going on camera would be like shining a spotlight on yourself right now." He didn't want that danger gathering around her again. "Give me a little more time." Time for them to find Kurt. To bring him in for questioning. Time to analyze the situation more. "Just— I'm not asking for forever. I'm just asking for you to stay off the air a little longer, let the agents and Sheriff Black do their jobs. Give us a little more time."

"You can't hold Casey prisoner," Tom huffed. "You can't keep her trapped in protective custody. I'm her boss, but I'm her friend, too. And I'm not going to let you trample over her rights!"

He wasn't trampling over anything. He was trying to keep her alive.

"We're both her friends," Katrina muttered, her lips curving down.

Tom nodded. "Kat and I will stay with Casey. We'll make sure she's safe." He waved toward Casey, as if expecting her to just walk toward him. "You really think I'd leave my top reporter without a guard under these circumstances? One phone call, and I'll have *two* bodyguards at her side at all times. I mean, I appreciate your efforts, Agent Duvane, but isn't your focus more on diving into the water? Evidence retrieval? Perhaps you're just not suited to this role at all."

He would so enjoy driving his fist into that guy's face. But an FBI agent wasn't supposed to do stuff like that. He wasn't supposed to *want* to hurt a civilian. "My focus right now is on Casey. Her safety is the priority for me."

Tom's lips thinned. "Casey? Come on, you know I can get you the best protection money can buy. I can get—"

She slowly exhaled. "Thank you, Tom, but I'm going with the FBI right now. They've promised me an exclusive regarding new developments in this case, and the closer I stay to Agent Duvane, the better chance I have of being on scene when the killer is apprehended."

A gleam lit Tom's eyes. "They're that close to catching him?"

No, they weren't. And he didn't remember making the promise Casey was talking about.

"I'm going to stay with Agent Duvane for at least the next twenty-four hours," Casey continued, her voice brisk, as if she'd reached a decision and that was all there was to it. "Then I'll be ready to go on-air again."

Twenty-four hours. Well, that was better than nothing.

But Tom shook his head. "I need a report *sooner* than that. You have people waiting for you—you have—"

"Twenty-four hours," Josh said flatly. "You heard the lady." And if he had twenty-four more hours without that Tom jerk breathing down their necks, that would sure be a sweet deal to him.

"Everyone will tune in for the story, Tom," Casey promised. "You know they will."

And he could tell by Tom's expression that, yeah, the guy knew she was telling the truth.

"I'm hoping you got something good in that place," Tom said as he dragged his hand across his jaw. "Theodore freaking Anderson—can't believe he finally agreed to an interview with you. I've been after that guy for ages. Casey, you are the queen."

"We're leaving." Josh didn't like standing out in the open with Casey, not even in a scene where dozens of guards were patrolling the grounds. He wanted her away from there—or maybe, maybe he just wanted her away from Tom.

"Here, take this." Tom pulled a phone from his

pocket and pushed it into Casey's hand. "I think the cops took yours from the hotel, and I wanted to make sure you could contact me, whenever you needed me." He slanted a hard stare toward Josh. "I got the feeling the last call was made on someone else's phone, and I wanted you to have the freedom to call me anytime."

The guy just seriously didn't understand what protective custody actually meant.

Then Tom pulled Casey in for a hard, tight hug. "I was worried." His voice had turned gruff. "You scared me. You're too important to the show—to me. Nothing can happen to you."

Josh saw Katrina's face harden. She quickly glanced away from Casey and Tom.

"Agent Duvane will make sure I stay safe." Casey eased from Tom's hold. "And thanks for the phone." She slid it into her pocket. Then she reached for Josh's hand. "Ready?"

Hell, yes. He curled his fingers around hers and stalked toward the waiting SUV. He opened her door, made sure she was in securely, then he slammed the door shut. He glanced back and saw that Tom was still watching them.

Or maybe the guy is just watching her. Tom certainly seemed to have a personal interest in Casey. Josh headed around the vehicle and yanked his door shut after he'd jumped inside. He cranked the engine. Tom was still watching. "Your boss wants you."

Her laugh was startled. "What? No, I told you already…he's involved with Katrina. One of those friends-with-benefits type deals."

Not really friends if the guy was her boss.

"He wants you," Josh said flatly. He'd read the guy's expression too clearly.

"Well, I'm not into him. Sleeping my way to the top has never been on my agenda. And I can't do the with-benefits routine because—" But she broke off, not saying more.

He drove them out of there. "Because of your past."

"Trust is hard. Being that intimate with someone… I don't like to take risks."

No, he got that. But what he didn't get… "Why didn't you go with them?" Tom had given her an out right then and there, but Casey hadn't taken it.

"Because I wanted to stay with you."

"I didn't promise you an exclusive." The Bureau brass would freak if they thought he'd been making any side deal with her. "The only thing on the table was your access to the footage from that little sit-down with Anderson." A sit-down that had not gone the way he expected.

Kurt Anderson. He'd met the guy before, too. The man had seemed shaken, grief-stricken. And he'd been filled with a lot of rage. But Josh had thought all of that rage was directed at Kurt's father.

Had he been wrong?

"I know, Josh." Her soft sigh filled the car. "I lied," Casey admitted without even a hint of guilt.

He cast a quick glance toward her.

"I wanted to stay with you," Casey said again. "I… feel safe with you, okay? I mean, I've already told you the deepest, darkest secret that I have. You pretty much know me better right now than anyone else has known me in years."

Why did that make him feel good?

"Even though you didn't do an even secret exchange," she added.

Maybe he'd make that up to her.

"Tom can hire bodyguards, I know that. *I* can hire my own guards. But right now, I'm where I want to be." She paused. "But I do want a favor."

A favor?

"In return for agreeing to stay in federal custody a bit longer, in return for the solid I did you by interviewing Anderson, I want you to take me back to the scene of the crime."

He braked hard at the red light. *"What?"*

"I need to go back," she said. "I think if I go back, I might remember something. It's a technique I've had psychologists use with victims on my show before. I want to try. I want to go back to my hotel room, and then I want you to take me back to the beach house."

Someone honked behind him. He didn't move. "You know you can only get access to those locations if you're with me…or with another federal agent." Was that the real reason why she'd agreed to stay with him? "You realized that all along, though, didn't you?"

She gave a disappointed sigh. "Do you always see the bad in people first? Or do you—sometimes—stop to see any good?"

There wasn't always a lot of good in the world. The car behind him honked again, and Josh slowly accelerated.

"Come on, you know it's in your best interest for me to remember more, too. So why not just take me to the scene? I'll still be in protective custody. Your custody. And maybe I'll see something that jars my memory.

Maybe I'll be able to find some clue that was overlooked before. There is nothing to lose by trying."

No, there wasn't. And while he took her back to the hotel and to the crime scene, he knew Tucker and the sheriff would be hunting Kurt Anderson. Soon, the case could be over. The killer could be caught.

And Casey would be free to go back to her old life.

The thought should have made him feel better. Oddly, it didn't.

"I DON'T LIKE that agent." Tom Warren stood with his hands on his hips, glaring after the SUV. "He's acting like he's in control of Casey."

Right. Katrina barely controlled an eye roll. *That* was why the guy didn't like Agent Duvane. "He *is* in control of her, right? I mean, the guy has her in protective custody."

Tom marched toward his car—not just any rental. A Benz. Nothing but the best for Tom. Always. "Protective custody is a joke. I'll make some calls and get the best bodyguards in the business down here for her. You think I'm going to lose my star to the FBI?"

His star? Did the guy even realize how possessive he sounded when he talked about Casey? Not that she was jealous. Katrina didn't care enough to be jealous. Tom was fun—every now and then, anyway—but the guy could also be a Grade A jerk.

"I made Casey," Tom continued grimly. "I'm not about to lose her this way." He stopped by the car and pulled out his phone. His finger swiped across the screen and a slow smile stretched across his face. "Got you."

Unease coiled through her. Just who did the guy have?

"Come on. Get in the car." Now his words were clipped. "I'll drop you off in town and then take care of business." Impatience gritted beneath each word.

"You don't want me to get some scene shots of this place? For the show later?"

He huffed out a breath. "Yeah, yeah, just hurry, okay?"

She took out her equipment from the backseat. She turned away so that she could eye the buildings and the guards—

"Do you think they're sleeping together?"

Katrina almost dropped her bag. "What?"

"Casey and the agent. I noticed the way he touched her—and the way she touched him. Casey doesn't touch anyone, not as a rule."

No, she didn't. Katrina was just surprised that Tom had noticed that. Casey was always very careful with everyone. She kept them all at the same distance.

"She just met him," Katrina replied, trying to choose the right words. "Casey never gets involved with anyone that way—not right after they meet." Not the other woman's style. But then—Casey's style wasn't for attachments. She lived for her work. The woman was dedicated, tireless, and Katrina actually admired the hell out of her. Casey didn't take crap from anyone.

Good for her.

"You're right." He gave her an absent smile. "Still, it would have made for a good angle, right? The victim falling for the FBI agent."

She stiffened. "Casey's more than just a victim."

"Not right now, she isn't." He waved a hand toward her bag. "Get the shots. I don't have long." He looked back down at his phone. "I can't let her go."

That whisper of unease blew through her again as she turned back to the prison. So many guards—and such big, thick walls. *No escape.* And the idea of being locked away in a place like that…it chilled Katrina's blood.

Chapter Eight

Josh shut the hotel room door with a soft click. He looked around the darkened room, his body tense. Getting Casey into her old room had been easy enough. He'd just flashed his badge and gotten a personal escort up from the manager on duty. A manager who'd spent the whole elevator ride apologizing to Casey.

The security cameras at the hotel had *mysteriously* gone down the night she'd been taken. A glitch, or so the manager said. Josh wasn't ready to buy that line. Knowing the killer they were after, the way the guy left nothing to chance, Josh figured the perp had made sure the security feed wasn't working. The guy's bit of sabotage had protected him.

"Walk me back through the night," Josh instructed. Casey was standing in front of the balcony door. She looked hesitant, so uncertain. Not at all the way he was coming to view her.

Casey looked over her shoulder at him. "I was on the balcony, getting some air—"

"How long were you out there?" Josh asked.

"Just a few minutes. I was—I was thinking about everything that had happened that day."

Her voice had stumbled, just a bit. "Now who's lying?"

"Fine." She rolled back her shoulders. "I was out there, thinking about you, okay?"

His brows climbed. "Okay." She'd surprised him, again.

"I could hear the waves crashing, but I didn't hear anything from the hotel room. So when I turned around and the light was off, I had no idea that anyone was in here." She walked toward the phone that waited on the bedside table. "I was going to call the front desk, but he caught me from behind."

His gaze scanned the room. There weren't a whole lot of places for someone to hide in there, but if the room had been in total darkness, the perp would have just needed to find a corner, to stay still, to wait for her to come back... He walked toward her. The thick carpet swallowed his footsteps. "You turned on the lights before you left. *No one* was here?"

She turned to face him. "I didn't see anyone. Didn't hear anyone."

He stopped right in front of her. He *hated* that she'd been hurt. To think of that creep slamming her head into the wall, carrying her out of there... "I noticed the emergency exit is just one door down from your room. It would have been easy for him to take you out that way—no one would see you. The stairs there lead straight down to the parking lot below."

She swallowed. "And it's not like I was able to call out for help. I mean, Katrina was in the adjoining room—" Casey motioned to the door that connected the two rooms. "But I never even had a chance to scream for her."

He looked back at that door. He'd already known that Katrina had been in the room beside hers. The sheriff had interviewed the camerawoman—she hadn't been in her room that night. "It wouldn't have mattered if you *had* screamed for her," he said. "Katrina wasn't there."

"She— Oh. Right. Staying with Tom?"

"No. She said she was at a club down the road. Just dancing. I don't think she even realized you were gone until the next day." At least, that was what Katrina had told Hayden.

Casey tucked her hair behind her ear.

"But if Katrina wasn't here," Josh continued as he tilted his head. "Then maybe the perp used her room. Maybe he was in there, waiting for you to get back. He could have come straight in through the connecting door." He headed for that door now, wanting to test the lock. It was still secure but…if the guy had been on the other side, it would have been easy enough to gain entrance to Casey's room. And a perp who knew what he was doing? He wouldn't have left so much as a scratch on any of the doors.

"Is that what the FBI thinks happened? I mean, I'm sure you've gotten together with your team and talked about it." There was an edge to her voice that had him glancing back. "Why don't *you* walk me through things and show me what happened. You be the perp. Show me what he did. Help me to re-create it all."

He locked his jaw. Yeah, the FBI had theories—and that was one of them. But for him to re-create things with her… *I don't want to scare Casey.* "Are you certain about that?"

She nodded once. "It's getting late. The sun is setting. It's dark enough in here that…it will be the same."

"It *won't* be the same." She needed to understand

that. "You're safe with me. Nothing is going to happen to you."

"So…you *do* think he was in Katrina's room? That's what the FBI is going with?"

Treading carefully he said, "We believe the perp had been watching you for a few days. The night he attacked you, the guy knew that your camerawoman hadn't come back here. So, yes, we think it's possible that he was able to come inside, and he just waited…he could have even been out on the balcony next door, listening to see what you were doing while you stared down at the ocean. He could have been right there. Making sure you were alone."

"Then I guess you should have come up with me." Her words were said flippantly, and her tone was too brittle. "Then I wouldn't have been alone."

She turned away from him, but Josh grabbed her wrist. "I sure as hell wish I'd come up with you."

"I—I didn't mean that. You know, I—"

"I wish I'd been here. I wish I'd stopped the bastard."

She looked down at his hand as it gripped her wrist. Her wrist felt so small and fragile in his grasp. He wanted to pull her closer. Wanted to take her mouth beneath his once again. Would the need explode like wildfire in his veins when he kissed her once more? Had it been a fluke before?

Would it be even better this time?

The job. The case. Don't do this. Don't cross that line. He let her go. "You want to re-create the scene, then we'll recreate it." He motioned toward the balcony. "Go out and come back inside. I'll turn out the lights and we'll see if anything jars your memory." He paused. "If you're *sure*."

"I'm sure." But she licked her lips, a quick giveaway of her nerves. "Will you…will you come up behind me like he did?"

"Is that what you want?"

"I want to learn something new. I want to remember *something* else that can help us." She squared her shoulders. "Come up behind me. Grab me, just like he did. But, ah, don't do anything else, okay?"

"I won't." He kept his voice gentle for her. "If you get scared, just say stop and I will."

Casey gave a jerky nod. "Right. Got it." With brisk steps, she headed for the balcony. She opened the door and stepped outside.

Josh turned off the lights.

THEY'D LOCATED KURT ANDERSON.

Tucker Frost jumped onto the coast guard vessel with Hayden Black. As soon as Theodore Anderson had identified his son as a suspect, Tucker had been on the phone and getting an APB out on the guy. Then Tucker had gotten lucky. A deputy at the marina remembered seeing Kurt head out on a boat.

"I talked to the guy who owns the boat rental company," Hayden said as the vessel shot away from the dock. "Apparently, Kurt has been taking out a rental a few days each week…and heading out into the Gulf of Mexico. Every time, he goes out alone."

Interesting, especially considering that the Sandy Shore Killer had a habit of heading into the Gulf, too… and dumping bodies. "He's sure Kurt goes out alone?"

"Yeah, Chaz—that's the guy's name, Chaz Fontel— Chaz said that Kurt told him that he needed time away."

Time away—or time to get rid of his victims?

The boat flew across the water. "Kurt almost killed his father." Hayden's voice was pitched to carry over the roar of the waves and the engine. "You probably read that in the files but…"

Tucker had. "But there are some details that don't make it into the files," Tucker finished. He knew that truth firsthand.

"I saw the grief in his eyes. He was broken. Kurt loved his little sister, and to find out that his own father killed her—that shattered something in him." Hayden stared out at the water. "He was filled with anger and pain, but the grief was stronger than anything else. Jill and I—we stopped him before he could kill Theodore. We convinced Kurt that he wasn't like his old man. He wasn't a killer."

"He may not be," Tucker said. Blood didn't always tell. He was living proof of that. Or at least, he hoped he was. "We're just going by his father's words. Just following up with some questions. We don't have any evidence that directly ties him to the crimes." Not yet, they didn't.

Hayden's laugh was bitter. "We don't marshal a hunt like this just to ask a guy some questions. You and I are both thinking the same thing—he fits."

Kurt Anderson did match the profile that Tucker had been working up. He'd been building that profile slowly, not wanting to make any mistakes. Once upon a time, he'd been dead set on getting into the minds of killers. *Into proving that I wasn't one of them.* But then he'd backed off… Tucker had gotten more involved in the Violent Crimes Section at the Bureau. He'd worked Violent Crimes for a few years, but, recently, things had changed for him.

A new opportunity had developed at the Bureau, one that had come courtesy of the best damn behavioral analysis specialist he'd ever met... Samantha Dark.

This case, the Sandy Shore Killer, was Tucker's chance to prove that he could get back into the work. His chance to prove that he could belong on the elite team that Samantha Dark was leading.

He wouldn't screw up. And he *would* investigate every viable suspect. Right then, Kurt Anderson appeared very, very viable.

"Why would he want to go out at night?" Tucker mused. The sun had sunk beneath the sky. "Seems to me that a person only does that if he has something to hide."

"I hope to God he isn't dumping a body." Hayden exhaled then he glanced over at the man steering the vessel. "Can you go faster?"

They were already going awfully fast.

"Kurt might not realize that the Chaz has a GPS tracking device on every boat that he rents out. The guy wasn't about to risk someone stealing his vessels."

Tucker considered that. "Does Kurt always take the same boat out?"

"Always, according to Chaz. Kurt requests the exact same one."

"Then when we get him, we can check his log—we can check his GPS and see exactly where he's been going each time."

And if the guy had been going to the same locations where the bodies had been found... *We've got you.*

CASEY COULD HEAR the crash of the waves. She could smell the salty breeze. And she could feel her knees shaking. It was ridiculous to be so afraid but...

She was.

It's Josh. He won't hurt me. It's just Josh.

She opened the balcony door. Darkness waited inside. Josh had turned out the lights. Just like the perp had done. She took a step forward and hesitated.

It's Josh.

She should go toward the bedside table. That was what she'd done before. She'd gone to the table and reached for the phone. Casey tiptoed inside. But then she stilled. Where was Josh? She glanced around, but it was so dark. The light from the balcony just spilled inside a small bit, pooling near the sliding glass door. It was darkest in the room near the door that led to the hallway and…near the connecting door. The shadows were actually *the* thickest there. "Josh?" His name slipped from her.

"I'm here."

Her heart drummed too fast. His voice had come from those thick shadows near the connecting door.

She moved toward the phone. She reached for it—

His arms closed around her, holding her tightly. Fear stole her breath even as she opened her mouth to scream.

"It's okay." His whisper filled her ear. "I've got you." His lips brushed lightly against the shell of her ear. His scent hit her—the rich, masculine scent that seemed to surround him. It wasn't the bitter odor of oil that had tinted the air before and—

"I remember!" She spun in his arms. Grabbed his shoulders. "I remember…he smelled like oil! It was a bitter scent, and I caught it right before he…he shoved my head into that wall."

Darkness still surrounded them.

"You're sure it was oil?" Josh pressed.

"Absolutely! My dad—he used to have an old '66 Chevy that he restored on the weekends. I helped him, and nearly every Saturday we'd come back into the house with our hands stained with oil. I know that smell. I *remember* it." Joy filled her. It had worked. She'd remembered something new. Maybe something else would come to her. She was so excited that she pulled Josh toward her. She rose onto her toes, and her mouth pressed to his.

His body tensed. She felt his muscles go rock hard beneath her hands, and Casey started to pull away. She—

His hands locked around her, holding her tightly against him. His mouth opened, and his tongue thrust past her lips. He kissed her with a ferocious, consuming need. Kissed her with a dark desperation.

Kissed her the way only he could.

Desire burned through her blood. She'd known only fear moments before, but the touch of his mouth against hers had ignited a firestorm inside her.

She wanted him.

And she was going to have him.

She'd spent years playing it safe in life—and what had that gotten her, exactly? She'd attracted the attention of another killer. She'd been targeted again. Maybe there was no safety. Maybe there was just the moment— the present. Maybe she should grab on tight to what she wanted and not let go.

She wanted him.

A moan built in her throat. His hands had slid down her back, and now they rested right over the curve of her hips. She wanted him to touch her, skin to skin.

The barriers should be out of the way. They should both just let go.

And never look back.

But—

Josh slowly lifted his lips from hers. She heard the rasp of his breath and then he took a step away from her. Immediately, she missed his touch.

"You're playing a dangerous game," he said.

She touched her lips. Then her hand fell back to her side. "It's no game." She wasn't going to lie or pretend or be coy. Why waste time? "I want you, Josh."

"Casey…"

"You know I have trouble trusting the men in my life. But there is something about *you*." She didn't want to say that she was falling for him. It was too fast, too soon, but…

He's getting to me. I know it.

Casey swallowed. "I'm not playing games. We don't have time for games, and I don't like them, anyway. I want you. And you want me."

The darkness was around them, but all of her fear was gone.

"The question is," Casey continued quietly, "what do we do about that desire?"

THE SPOTLIGHT HIT the other boat. They'd found him. Tucker tensed.

"Kurt Anderson!" Hayden called out. "We need you to step forward so that we can see you—and put your hands up!"

Up…just in case the guy had a weapon. Up…just in case they were confronting an armed, desperate man.

It took a moment, but Kurt Anderson appeared.

His hair was disheveled, his face covered by the thick growth of a beard, and in his right hand he held a beer can. His tall body wobbled a bit as he stood on the boat.

"What the hell? Hayden?" Kurt squinted against the bright light. "What's happening? Why are you out here?"

Tucker knew that Kurt and Hayden had once gone to school together. They'd been friends, a lifetime ago. Murder could change so much about a person.

"We're out here because we need to talk to you." Hayden's voice carried easily. "Is anyone else on your vessel?"

"No…" But Kurt looked back, at the cabin entrance behind him. "Just me."

Was the guy lying? "Mind if we take a look?" Tucker asked him. Even if the guy did mind, they'd be getting on that boat.

"Why would I care?" Kurt started to lower his hands.

"Keep them up, buddy," Tucker ordered. The guy could have a knife hidden on him. A gun. Any weapon that he could pull in a moment's notice, and Tucker wasn't in the mood for an attack.

He and Hayden boarded the other vessel. As they approached Kurt—

"What the hell?" Hayden demanded. "How many beers have you had?"

The scent of alcohol clung to the man, and Tucker had to kick a rolling beer can out of his way. He glanced around and counted at least seven empty beer cars on the deck.

"Just a few," Kurt said. His voice was slurred. "Makes it…easier, you know? Easier to forget…"

Hayden gave the man a pat down, then nodded toward Tucker. "He's clean."

"Damn right!" Kurt laughed. "Clean… Clean and my old man is dirty. A dirty killer. He killed and killed, and I just let it happen. Let it…happen…" He stumbled a bit.

Hayden righted the guy.

Tucker slipped below deck. He searched the boat and he saw…blood. A bloody shirt was tossed on the back of the small couch below deck. He didn't want to touch the shirt. There was no way he wanted to be responsible for contaminating evidence. Right next to that shirt, he saw a knife with a long, flat blade. Blood had dried on the tip of the blade. Pulling his gun, he headed back up the small flight of stairs.

"Where did that blood come from?" Tucker asked Kurt.

Kurt swung his head toward him. "Do I know you?" The fellow squinted at Tucker. The spotlight from the coast guard vessel still illuminated the scene.

"I'm Special Agent Tucker Frost." He stared at the suspect. "And, again, I'm asking you…where did the blood come from?"

Kurt didn't answer.

"There's a bloody shirt below deck," Tucker explained to Hayden.

And Casey stabbed her attacker.

"What happened?" Hayden demanded, his voice sharp.

"I was cutting some tangled fishing line and the knife slipped. I cut myself. No big deal." The last words came out together—fast, stumbling. Drunk. *Nobigdeal.*

It was a big deal. A very big deal.

"You know boating under the influence is against the law, don't you, Kurt?" Hayden's voice was hard.

"Not drunk. Just had…six. No, seven beers. Got to forget. Got to forget Christy. Makes it so much easier…"

"No, it just seems easier," Tucker responded. "When the haze of booze clears away, it will be even harder." He knew Hayden was going to arrest Kurt—the guy had given them the perfect reason to take him into the station. Once Kurt sobered up, they'd question him. They'd search the boat. They'd tear into his life.

And if he was guilty, he would pay.

He paced around the boat, heading back toward the motor. His nostrils flared. "You got yourself a leak, Kurt." The stench of oil was strong.

"That's why I stopped out here," Kurt muttered. "Boat's been giving me trouble. Every time I take it out… I told Chaz at the shop. Still not fixed…"

He gave the man a small smile. "I find myself very curious about your trips. Want to tell me…just where have you been going?"

Kurt blinked, and for the first time since they'd boarded his boat, worry flashed on his face. "What's going on? Why—why'd you come all the way out here after me? I haven't even had the chance to call in my Mayday yet."

No, he hadn't.

"We came looking for you," Tucker said, watching him closely. "Because your father sent us to find you…"

Chapter Nine

He should keep his hands off her. Josh *knew* that he should keep his distance from Casey. So why was he so desperate to get closer to her?

He secured the penthouse door behind them. The alarms were set. The cameras rolling. They were safe for the night.

"I wish we'd gone to the beach house." She stood a few feet away, gazing out at the darkness below her.

He shook his head, even though Casey couldn't see the movement. "Too dark. You wouldn't be able to see anything out there. You really want to re-create the scene, then we'll do it first thing tomorrow. We'll go back at dawn."

She looked back at him, a sad smile on her full lips. "Because that's when you found me."

A scene he'd never forget.

"You should go get some rest. I know it's been a long day for you." He glanced down at his phone. On their way to the penthouse, he'd tried calling Tucker, wanting to tell him about the oil scent, but he'd just gotten the guy's voice mail.

"Today wasn't as bad as yesterday. I didn't get at-

tacked in my hotel room tonight. I consider that a win."
She paused. "But I did get rejected."

His head snapped up.

That faint smile was still on her lips—a smile that
didn't reach her dark, gorgeous eyes. "I get it," Casey
added. "I'm not your type. I misread the situation. It
won't happen again. I apologize if I…made you uncomfortable." She turned, obviously heading for the
hallway—and her room. "I'll see you in the morning,
okay?"

He should let her go. He should keep his mouth shut.
He should— "You're not the only one with trust issues."

Casey stilled.

"You wanted to know my secrets? You wanted that
fair exchange. Fine. Here goes." Josh released a long
breath. "I trusted the wrong person, too. With fatal consequences."

Slowly, she turned back to face him. "Josh?"

"He was a man on my SEAL team. I thought he had
my back. I thought he was a friend. In an instant, he
turned on me—on us all. I lost two good men that day.
And every day since, I've asked myself why I didn't see
the truth about him sooner."

Her lips parted. "I've asked myself…why I didn't see
the truth about Benjamin."

He understood her, and he knew—Casey understood
him, too.

"I'm sorry," she whispered.

He didn't want her pity but—when he looked into
her eyes, he realized she wasn't staring at him with pity.
Just a kind of shared pain.

He'd never really thought about a future with anyone,
but when he looked at Casey, he found himself imag-

ining all kinds of things that he *shouldn't* be thinking. "My job is to keep you safe."

"I can hire a bodyguard for that. Tom was right on that point."

He was better than any bodyguard out there. "I'm an FBI agent," he tried again. "And you're—" But he broke off because he was staring into her eyes and he couldn't look away. He didn't want to look away. Her gaze was so deep and rich, and her lips were red and full. He loved her mouth. Josh was pretty sure her mouth was the sexiest thing he'd ever seen. That lower lip of hers was plumper than the top, and he kept having the urge to bite it.

He wanted his mouth all over her. He wanted to make sure that fear was the last emotion he would see in her gaze.

He. Wanted. Her.

So why was he fighting himself?

"I'm what, Josh?"

"You're the woman I want too much." She'd been honest with him. He'd give her the same in turn.

He heard her take a quick draw of breath. "How can you want someone too much?" Casey took a step toward him. Then another.

If she kept coming to him, if she got close enough to touch…

He'd touch. He'd take. He wouldn't stop.

"I don't think once would be enough for me." He was trying to warn her. There was just something about Casey. From the moment he'd met her, Josh had been on high alert. Every muscle in his body had tensed. His focus had sharpened on her. "You're looking to escape aren't you? To get away from the darkness for a moment, but being with me won't take you away from the darkness." Too much darkness surrounded him. "I'm not the safe lover you want."

Another step. Her scent reached him. Sweet. Sexy. Casey. "You're an FBI agent. I think that probably makes you the safest lover I've ever had."

Carrying the badge, working on the right side of the law...she didn't get it. There were different kinds of safety. "I'd never hurt you." And he knew, even as he spoke, that he was setting out the terms. Because it *was* going to happen. They were going to happen. "I'd never hurt you physically, you have my word on that. I'd put myself between you and a threat any day of the week." He meant that. When he was with Casey, no threat would touch her. He'd make sure of it. And because of her past, he had to say, "You would never need to fear me."

She took another step. If he lifted his hands, he'd be able to touch her. But he didn't lift them, not yet. They needed to be very, very clear before they crossed this line. "There won't be any going back. No pretending in the morning that this didn't happen. Once won't be enough..." It was what he'd said before because he already knew he would want more. He wasn't sure he'd ever get enough of her. "I'm not an easy lover. But I'll give you so much pleasure you can't stand it."

Her eyes gleamed. "Promises, promises..."

"Yes." That was all he said.

She caught her lower lip between her teeth.

Josh wanted to be the one taking that bite.

"My turn," Casey said. "Only fair, right?"

Absolutely.

"I'm not looking for easy. I'm looking for someone

who wants me so much that he can't hold back. That he won't hold back. I want us to both get lost—so lost we forget to come up for air. I don't want you treating me like a victim. I don't want you pulling back when the light of dawn is here. I'll never be anyone's dirty little secret, and I don't expect you to be mine, either. I want you—and I have, even before that crazy jerk abducted me. So this isn't about fear or adrenaline or anything like that. I wanted to kiss you when we were on that motorcycle. I wanted to see where the desire would go."

He knew exactly where it would go.

"So I guess…we have a deal?" She held out her hand and gave a little, self-conscious laugh. "This seems so odd. I mean, where's the romance and—"

His fingers curled around hers. "No deal."

Her eyes widened.

"Pleasure, sweetheart. What we have is a whole lot of pleasure." *And no regrets.* He used his grip on her hand to pull her closer. He'd known what would happen if he got his hands on her, and now, he wouldn't be letting her go.

His mouth took hers. A careful kiss, at first. Then he caught her lower lip between his teeth. He nibbled, he sucked and he gave in to the need he'd been feeling. Then he was kissing her, harder, deeper, letting go of his control. As she'd said…no holding back.

She gave a little moan in the back of her throat, and that husky sound just amped up his desire. He wanted to make her moan again. He wanted to make her scream. He wanted to make her go wild, as wild as he planned to get.

He pinned her against the door with his body. His hands caught hers and he curled his fingers around her wrists. He pushed her hands back against the wood as his mouth trailed down her neck. That little moan came again and he knew that he'd found her sweet spot. He licked and kissed, enjoying the way her body arched up against him. His arousal shoved against the front of his pants. His need was quick and fierce, but Josh was determined to take his time. To explore every inch of her. Some things shouldn't be rushed. Some people should be savored.

Casey should be savored.

He pulled back so that he could stare into her eyes. The desire he saw there was like a punch straight to his gut. Did the woman have any idea what she was doing to him?

He let her hands go and she immediately reached for him. She grabbed his shirt and yanked and he was pretty sure buttons went flying. Josh blinked at her.

She smiled. The sexiest smile he'd ever seen.

"I told you." Her voice was the softest temptation. "I didn't do easy, either. Give me everything that you've got, Josh. I can handle it."

No doubt.

Her fingers slid down his chest, skating over his abs and down to his stomach. She touched the button on his pants—

He caught her hand. "I get to take care of you first."

She smiled. Again…he was lost.

Josh scooped Casey up into his arms. She was so light. Her scent surrounded him as he carried her to the bedroom—not her room, but his. He put her on her feet near his bed, and then he stripped her. Carefully. He started with her T-shirt. He pulled it over her head, making sure not to so much as jar her injuries. Then she was clad in her bra and her jeans. She'd kicked off her shoes, he wasn't sure where they were, and his fingers went to the snap of her jeans. In seconds, he was shoving those jeans down her legs, revealing the black panties that matched her bra. Sexy. So insanely sexy. Her breasts thrust against the cups of the bra. The panties barely shielded her secrets...

And he was about to explode.

Josh lowered her onto the bed and he followed her. His fingers slid over her, touching, stroking, driving her to a fever pitch. Then his mouth followed his fingers. He shoved the bra out of the way and kissed her breasts, loving her tight nipples. *Sweeter than candy.* He hadn't even realized he had a sweet tooth, not until that moment. He was sure he'd always crave her taste now.

He reached between her legs, felt her sexy core. Her nails sank into his shirt—he was still dressed. He'd ditched his shoes, but he still wore his pants and his shirt hung open.

"Get rid of your clothes," Casey said. "I want to feel you, *all* of you."

He'd give her exactly what she wanted.

He shrugged out of his shirt and tossed it across the room. He stood at the edge of the bed, moving away from her just long enough to strip. She watched him, her gaze drifting over his body and he wondered what she saw... He had scars. Scars from bullet wounds he'd taken while protecting his country. Scars from attacks he'd survived while being in the FBI. His body was rough, hard, and she was soft and silky. She was sensual, his every fantasy—and he hadn't even realized he'd been fantasizing about her. She was—

"You are so sexy," she murmured. Her hand reached

out to him. Then she was rising, moving to her knees and reaching for him. Her fingers slid over his chest and his muscles locked down. His arousal jerked toward her. Her fingers trailed over his nipples and then her head bent. She licked his nipple, she sucked, and her hair slid over his skin. His hands curled around her shoulders, the desire beat in his blood and then Josh tumbled her back on the bed.

Can't wait. Need her. Want her. Take her.

She gave a little laugh and his heart lurched. He grabbed the protection from his nightstand drawer before he went back to her. Her legs parted. She reached up to him—

No going back. No pretending this didn't happen in the morning. She'd never forget what they did this night. Neither would he.

Josh drove into her. He sank deep, then stilled for a moment as he stared into her eyes. Her gaze had gone even darker. Her cheeks were a rosy pink. She lifted her hips.

"Give me more."

He did. Josh withdrew, then thrust. His hips jerked against her. He lifted her up, then surged down, knowing he'd stroke across her most sensitive spot. She gave another moan, but that wasn't enough for him. Not nearly enough. His fingers pushed between them. Even as he thrust, he found the spot he wanted. He caressed and stroked until she came apart for him.

He loved the sound of her scream.

Josh followed her, driving harder, his pace nearly frantic now. Again and again, he sank into her. The bed squeaked beneath them, his breath heaved from his lungs, and then the pleasure hit—crashing over him and obliterating everything else.

Only Casey.

Only Casey mattered.

HER EYES OPENED in the darkness. Casey's heart was racing, and fear held her in a tight grip. She lifted up her hands, afraid that she'd find them tied together with rough rope.

But her hands were free. She was free.

She just wasn't alone.

She could feel him against her body. They were still in his bed. She was still naked. Casey bet Josh was, too. They'd fallen asleep together. She couldn't remember the last time she'd stayed with a lover.

Part of her wanted to slip away right then, to go back to her bedroom. Another part of her wanted to stay exactly where she was. But...

What had woken her?

Then she heard the sound again—a vibration that pulsed. Quietly. From the floor? She slipped from the bed, trying hard not to wake Josh. She pulled a sheet with her, curling it around her body. The lights were out, but now that she was at the side of the bed, she could see a glow on the floor.

Her phone? Yes, it was the phone that Tom had given her. Vibrating. Ringing. So low and quiet—she picked it up and her finger slid across the screen.

"Hello?" Her voice was hushed.

"Casey?" Tom demanded. "Casey, what's wrong?"

Nothing. I'm just trying to be quiet so I don't wake my lover. "This isn't a good time." What time was it? Had to be nearing midnight. Why was Tom calling her so late? She edged toward the bathroom, still keeping her voice whisper-soft. She opened the door, eased inside and then shut that door firmly behind her. She hadn't woken Josh, at least, she didn't think she had.

"You didn't call me."

What? Seriously?

"I was worried," Tom continued, and he actually did sound worried. "I'm outside the sheriff's station. They just brought in Kurt Anderson."

Her heart jerked.

"They sneaked him in through the back door. They think no one knows what they're doing, but after your little visit to the prison today, Katrina and I were on stakeout here. We got footage of him going into the station. Now I'm going to need you to go on-air in the morning—be here at dawn. We'll get the sheriff to talk. You can get some quote from that FBI buddy of yours—"

"He's not my buddy." He was her lover. She could still feel his touch on her body.

"Whatever," Tom growled. "Get him or Sheriff Black to give us a sound bite. Use Duvane to find out what Kurt Anderson is saying to the authorities. Is the guy guilty? Did they find evidence on him? You're the star reporter—break this case like I know you can."

It was one thing to report on the story. It was another thing to wake up, hands and feet tied, as a madman in a mask prepared to slice you with his knife. "I'm not using Josh." She wanted to be clear on that. "It's not happening."

"Are you kidding me? Work that Casey Quinn charm on him—the way you always use it on those law enforcement guys. You can get him to tell you anything."

She didn't speak. Had she just heard a rustle of sound from the bedroom? Was Josh awake? Was he listening? *I won't use him.*

"I get that you're going through a lot." His tone had changed. That was Tom. Always working the angles. Now he sounded sympathetic. "And if you can't handle this story—if you're too close now—I can bring someone else in."

Ah, his ultimate threat—replace her. He'd tried that technique in the past. With her. With other reporters. That was the nature of the beast—in their business, there was always someone younger and hungrier waiting in the wings.

"I can do that," he continued carefully, "but I don't want to do it. I want you, Casey. You're my star. You're the one the public wants to see. Come back to me. Do this story like I know you can. I mean, seriously, this is *the* story of your career. You were a victim, so you'd be covering the case from an angle no one else could match. This would make us both."

She heard a creak from behind the door. Her shoulders stiffened. "I have to go."

"Casey." Worry sharpened Tom's tone. "Casey, are you okay?"

"I'm fine. It's just the middle of the night, and I'm going back to bed." It was easy to lie—to Tom, anyway.

"Be there at dawn. Katrina and I will be waiting for you at the station."

He hung up.

She exhaled slowly and opened the door. She expected Josh to be standing right there—only he wasn't. She inched forward, but Casey didn't see him in bed, either. "Josh?"

The bedroom door was open. She put the phone down on the nightstand and slipped out of the bedroom. She padded down the hallway and found him in the den—standing in front of those big glass windows. He stared out at the darkness.

"Glad to know you aren't using me."

He *had* heard that part. "Eavesdropping at bathroom doors, huh?" She swallowed. "I didn't mean to wake you."

He turned toward her. She realized that she was still just wearing the sheet. She'd hurried after him and dragged it with her. Maybe she should have stopped to grab a robe or something.

He was wearing a pair of loose sweatpants. They hung low on his hips. A lamp was on near the sofa, spilling soft light into the room so that she could see him. *His disheveled hair.* She'd run her fingers through that hair. *The line of dark stubble on his jaw.* That stubble had rasped over her body. *His powerful build.* She'd touched every inch of him when they'd made love.

But he was standing there, his body stiff, his gaze locked on her. And something was just *off.*

"I can't figure you out."

She walked toward him and the thick carpeting swallowed her steps. "What's to figure out?" His voice had been tense, and she hated that. Hadn't they already covered the part where she said she *wouldn't* use him?

"I think you're a dangerous woman, Casey Quinn."

"That's only fair. I think you're a dangerous man."

His head inclined—in acknowledgment?

"That was Tom on the phone." Though she was betting he'd already figured out the identity of her caller. "He said that Sheriff Black and Agent Frost brought

Kurt Anderson into the station. They sneaked him in through the back door. I thought you'd want to know—"

"I know. Tucker texted me earlier. You were asleep next to me, so I didn't wake you to tell you that they'd found him out on the water. They found him…and the boat he was on had an oil leak. Tucker smelled the oil all over the place."

Her heart lurched in her chest. "It's…him?"

He wasn't touching her. "We don't know that yet. The guy is drunk, way over the legal limit, so the sheriff brought him in for boating under the influence. That buys us time to question him, to thoroughly search the boat and to see just what secrets he's been hiding." His shoulders rolled back. "There's more, though. The guy…he had a bloody knife in the cabin on the boat. He said he'd cut himself while trying to slice through a tangled fishing wire."

"I stabbed my attacker." But she'd kept the knife, so there shouldn't be any bloody knife to find on Kurt's boat. Unless…

Unless he's already taken another victim.

Josh's head inclined. "All the angles are being investigated, I promise you that. And at first light, I'm going out. Tucker has pulled up all the GPS data from the boat Kurt used. I'm going diving to check out all the stops he's made. Just in case…" His words trailed away.

"In case there's another victim out there?" In case he'd grabbed someone else after Casey had gotten away.

"Just in case," he said flatly.

Her hands clenched around the sheet she wore, sinking into the material. "I'm guessing all of this is off the record?"

"This is for you to know…because you've got the

biggest stake in this case. As far as the public and the press are concerned, the FBI and the local authorities are investigating a person of interest in the investigation. If we find evidence to conclusively link Kurt to the crime, we'll immediately call a press conference."

"You trust me to keep this quiet?"

He laughed, and the sound was a deep rumble. "Yeah, I actually *do* trust you, Casey."

That made her feel…warm. Good. "I trust you, too." As soon as the words slipped out, she felt her eyes widen. She hadn't meant to say that, had she? No, no, it was just… She cleared her throat. "You're FBI. Your whole bit is that you uphold the law and you keep the world safe. If I can't trust you, then I really can't trust anyone, can I?" Though wasn't that the way she'd played it for years, never trusting anyone? Always worrying, always being afraid? And what had playing it safe really gotten her?

She'd still been attacked again.

But I got away. I fought back.

"You should go back to sleep," Josh said, his voice still a dark rumble. "You've been through a lot, and you need to rest."

That was one idea. Certainly. Rest. He seemed to like that idea because he pushed it to her a lot. She nodded and turned away from him. She could feel Josh's gaze on her. Casey paced toward the couch, and then she turned off the light. Instantly, the room plunged into darkness.

"Casey?"

She let the sheet fall to the floor. "I don't want to rest." She turned back toward him. He still stood in front of that floor-to-ceiling window. He was a dark shadow and behind him, she could see the glittering stars. So many stars. "I want you." Because she could feel them running out of time. If he and Tucker found evidence to tie Kurt Anderson to the crimes, it would be great—they'd lock the killer away.

And then she'd report on the story and fly back home.

Josh would tie up loose ends and he'd head off to tackle another case.

The thought made her feel lost, sad. And she didn't want to face what was coming—not yet. Dawn would be there soon enough. She wanted to stay in the moment—with him. She wanted to hold the night close and pretend that nothing bad was waiting.

Just the moment. Just them.

She lifted her hands and pressed her body to him. Casey rose on her toes and her mouth brushed across his throat. She wasn't the only one with a sensitive spot. His hands clamped around her hips as he gave a ragged groan.

"Casey…"

"It's okay, being up here, near the windows…it's dark inside and only the ocean is out there to see us." She wanted him right there—then and there. She gave him a little nip and her hands slid down his chest. He was built—she loved his muscles. His strength and his heat. Loved the way he surrounded her and the way he made her *feel*.

She—

He lifted her up, holding her easily, and Casey gave a little laugh as her legs wrapped around his hips. His desire pressed against her. He wanted her just as much as she wanted him. Right there. Right then. As if nothing else mattered.

In that moment, nothing else did.

He kissed her, and she savored him. Her breasts pressed to his chest, his hands curled around her hips, and he turned, not pressing her to the glass of the window, but instead pushing her back against the wall to the right. He held her there, using his easy strength, kissing her and driving her out of her mind.

They could have built passion up slowly—with the sensual foreplay he'd shown her before. But Casey wasn't in the mood for slow. She wasn't in the mood for anything but him.

"Now," Casey whispered. "Right now."

His hand eased between their bodies. He stroked her and had her gasping and arching toward him. His fingers slid into her. Casey's eyes squeezed closed. He knew just how to touch her, exactly what she wanted, as if they'd been lovers for years instead of—

Just one night.

He caressed the center of her need—the spot that made her gasp again and press harder to him. His fingers filled her and her whole body shuddered as the first wave of release hit her.

"So beautiful," he rasped.

Her breath heaved out of her chest.

He kissed her again, softly, and, still holding her tightly, he went back into the bedroom. He put her on the bed, and she heard the rustle as he grabbed for the protection. He returned to her seconds later, and she was the one to push him down so that he lay on the bed. Casey rose above him, her knees on either side of his hips. She lowered herself onto him, and he filled her so completely. When he was fully inside her, she stilled. In the darkness, she tried to see his eyes.

She wanted to see him.

But his fierce hold lifted her up, and she sank back down onto him. The passion swept through her and she could only move, faster, rougher, and her hands slammed against his chest. Nothing else mattered— just them. Just that moment.

Again and again, her body lifted and her hips pushed back down on him.

The pleasure hit her, a climax so intense that her whole body was engulfed by the release, and he was moving—tumbling her onto her back, thrusting deep and then exploding within her.

In the aftermath, the only sound was their ragged breathing.

And…

He kissed her.

IT WASN'T OVER. The cops and the FBI might think they were so smart, but they had no clue. They weren't going to defeat him. He'd been too careful. There was no evidence, nothing to tie him to any of the crimes.

They didn't have their killer. They wouldn't have him.

They'd look ridiculous in front of the media. They'd turn up *nothing*.

And he would continue his hunt.

He knew exactly where Casey Quinn was hiding. Did she think that she was safe? That she'd gotten away from him? No, no, she'd just made him angrier.

It was time to finish what he'd started. This time, she wouldn't slip away.

This time, she'd be the one who bled.

She wasn't going to end this tale as a survivor. That wasn't the way she got to escape. That wasn't her final story.

She'd be a victim. A footnote. And he'd be the lead.

Chapter Ten

"Why the hell am I here?" Kurt Anderson let out a loud, long groan. "And why does my head feel like a jackhammer is inside it?" He sat up, hunching on the cot in the jail cell—the holding cell was in the back of the sheriff's station.

Josh slanted a glance at Tucker. The other FBI agent stood just a few feet away from him. They were both outside the cell, ready to see just what Kurt had to say. Dawn had finally come to Hope. Josh had stopped at the sheriff's station so that he could check in with Tucker before he went out on the water to begin searching.

Tucker's gaze was considering as it swept over the prisoner. Did the guy buy Kurt as the killer they were after?

"You're here," Tucker explained quietly, "because last night when Sheriff Black and I approached you on your rented vessel, you were so stinking drunk you could barely walk, much less drive a boat. So we brought you in both for your safety and for everyone else's. That whole stinking drunk bit? That's also why you feel as if a jackhammer is going off in your head."

Kurt squinted at him. "Do I know you?" His squinty gaze darted to Josh. "You both look liked Feds."

"We are Feds," Josh answered. "And, yeah, you know me. I'm Agent Josh Duvane." He inclined his head toward Tucker. "And this is Special Agent Tucker Frost." He paused for a moment. "And we need to discuss something your father recently said."

At that magic word, *father*, Kurt's whole face hardened. "I've already talked to so many suits about him… Questions come constantly. For the last time—" he surged off the cot and lurched toward the bars, his face twisted in angry lines "—I didn't know what that sick freak was doing. I had no idea that he'd killed my sister. I had no idea that he'd hurt anyone. I wasn't a part of anything that he'd done—"

"We actually aren't here to talk to you about what *he* did," Tucker interrupted smoothly. "His actions are his own. It's you that we want to talk about."

Kurt was pale, but two angry splotches of color appeared on his cheeks. "Me? You want to talk about me?"

"You are aware of the recent murders in this town, correct?" Tucker pushed.

Kurt blinked.

"Kylie Shane, Bridget Donaldson and Tonya Myers," Josh supplied curtly.

"Right, yeah, so what?" Then Kurt shook his head. "Wait, I don't mean that. I mean…what do their deaths have to do with me?"

"Your father said you were responsible for those crimes." Josh delivered this news quietly.

Kurt's jaw dropped. *"What?"*

"Do you know Casey Quinn?" Tucker asked. It was an old technique—keep firing at the suspect, keep him off guard. If they both went in with questions, the guy would be confused. And he might slip up.

"Casey—the reporter? Yeah, yeah, I know her. I talked to her a few times. She's not like the others— she wanted to tell *my* side and—" He stopped. "She was taken. I—I saw that on the news."

"Casey stabbed the man who abducted her." Tucker pointed to the guy's arm. "Can't help but notice that ragged cut you've got there."

"I cut myself trying to untangle stupid fishing wire!" Those dark spots of color on Kurt's cheeks darkened. "I'm not the killer! I didn't hurt those women! I haven't hurt *anyone*!" Then he gave a ragged laugh. "Though I wanted to hurt someone… I wanted to kill my old man. I wanted to wipe him off the face of the earth. I didn't. Hayden stopped me. Said I was better than my father…" Again, that ragged laughter came. "If only he knew…"

Josh didn't look away from the man before him. "Knew what—exactly?"

Kurt swallowed. His hands rose and curled around the bars. "I want out of here."

"What is it that you wish Hayden Black knew?" Tucker's gaze was fixed on the prisoner.

"Don't I get a lawyer or something?" Kurt's confusion that he'd suffered after waking was vanishing. "I want a lawyer. I want out of here. And I don't care what kind of BS story my crazy father is telling you—I didn't hurt those women. I wouldn't do that. *I'm not him.*"

Tucker took a step back from the bars. "We'll get you that lawyer." He jerked his head toward Josh. "Let's go." He turned on his heel, marching away.

"I wouldn't do that!" Kurt yelled after him.

Josh stared at the prisoner a moment longer, then he turned and followed his friend out of the holding area.

As soon as they were clear, Tucker stopped. He stared straight ahead.

"Uh, buddy?" Josh gazed at him with worry. "You okay?"

Tucker glanced back at him. "I want him to be telling the truth."

Josh wasn't so sure the guy *was* telling the truth, though, and—

"I want it for personal reasons. I want it because— damn, just because you have a killer in the family, it doesn't mean you're screwed to hell and back, too, right? We can be different." He blew out a hard breath and shook his head. "I'm losing my perspective on this case. This one was supposed to be my proving ground, and I'm letting my own past blind me."

"Why'd the father point the finger at him?" Josh demanded. "Why shove the guy down our throats? Because nothing I know about Theodore Anderson indicates the guy is the kind, concerned citizen type."

"No, he isn't concerned. He was all too ready to throw his son under the bus."

"Considering that Kurt had to be persuaded by the sheriff not to kill his father, I'm guessing it's clear their relationship is shot to hell and back. So maybe the father had decided to get a little last-minute revenge by trying to take his son's freedom away."

"We need evidence." Tucker's chin notched up. "You ready to dive?"

"Always."

They filed out of the hallway and headed back to the sheriff's office. Casey was in there, sitting across from Hayden. When Josh opened the door to the office, she immediately jumped to her feet and came toward him.

Why did that make him feel good? No, *she* made him feel good.

And that could be dangerous. *Be careful with her.* Josh knew he had to tread very, very carefully. "The guy wants a lawyer," he said, making sure his voice was flat. "Kurt isn't going to talk anymore. He's done. And I'm heading out with my team for the dives." He knew he'd be diving for most of the day, and he hated to leave Casey on her own. He'd tried to convince her to stay at the penthouse. Local FBI agents would have been there to protect her in his absence but...

She'd been adamant. She wasn't going to hide, not anymore. His promised twenty-four hours weren't even up. But he couldn't *force* her back into protection. At least, not yet he couldn't.

"There have been no missing persons cases filed lately," Hayden said as he rose from his chair. "And the perp we're after—he always calls to tell us when he has a victim. The guy acts like it is some kind of game. Can we find him before the victim dies? That's his taunt."

Casey flinched. "Only the game didn't work out the way he expected last time."

No, it hadn't.

"If he picked another victim with no close ties, then it's possible her disappearance just hasn't been reported." Josh couldn't overlook that possibility. "So I'll dive down to every spot on that boat's navigation record. If a victim is there, I'll find her." His gaze slid back to Casey. Before he left, he needed to know that she was safe. He needed to know—

There was as sharp knock at the door behind him. He glanced back and saw Deputy Finn Patrick open the door. Finn's face showed his worry. "Sheriff Black, the reporters are out front again. They got tipped off that we may have a suspect in custody."

"And the circus never ends," Hayden muttered. "Thanks, Finn, I'll handle them."

But Finn didn't leave. His stare shifted to Casey. "Guy out there…said he's her producer. He's demanding to see Ms. Quinn."

"He can demand all he wants," Hayden began, "I don't—"

"I'll handle him." Her voice was soft. Her stare was certain. "My producer, my job. I've got this." She started to walk toward Finn, but Josh stepped into her path.

His hand curled around her shoulder. "Are you sure about this?" Sure that she wanted to give up federal protection? Sure that she wanted to walk back into the fire?

"I know Tom. By now, he'll have bodyguards for me. I'll be protected. And you…you and the other agents have other things to do. You can't watch me forever."

But he wanted to.

His hand fell away.

There was so much more he wanted to say to Casey, but with everyone else watching them…he just let her go. Josh watched as she walked away.

"It's hard when emotions get involved," Hayden said quietly, and Josh wondered just how much he'd already given away. He looked back at the sheriff, but Hayden wasn't staring at him. He was looking at a framed photo on his desk. "I'm glad Jill is out of town right now. Going through all of this again—seeing Kurt brought in for questions relating to all these murders—it would just stir up the pain from her past again." His jaw locked. "And I can't stand to see Jill's pain."

Jill West worked on the FBI's Child Abduction Rapid

Deployment Team—and Josh knew she'd taken that job because of her own painful past. Jill was currently training a new crop of agents up in Quantico, and, like Hayden, he thought that might be for the best.

"When emotions are involved," Hayden continued and his gaze lifted from the photo to lock on Josh. "You can lose perspective and that loss can lead to deadly consequences."

Josh didn't intend to lose *anything*. "I need to check in with my team. We've got a lot of work to do on the water."

Tucker followed him out, and they stopped near the check-in desk to go over their files. He caught a glimpse of Casey—she'd paused right before the glass doors that would take her out of the station.

She looked back at him. She gave him a smile that made his chest ache, then she opened the door and stepped outside. He saw Tom's face as the guy rushed toward her. Katrina was there. A half-dozen other reporters closed in on Casey.

"We could have forced her to stay in custody," Tucker said, his voice careful.

If only. But things were more complex than they seemed. "I got word from the FBI brass that we had to let her go." He hadn't told Casey about that, not yet. "Seems her *producer* has some powerful friends, and he didn't like the way we were 'imprisoning' his reporter."

Tucker swore.

"Yeah, exactly how I feel. Tom promised she'd have the best bodyguards on her while she was still down here. And I was told that unless we wanted a media relations nightmare on our hands, then Casey got to walk."

And she'd just walked away.

His fingers drummed on the countertop. He couldn't see her any longer.

"Things between you two…they got personal, didn't they?"

Did *everyone* notice? "She was a victim." He straightened his shoulders. Finn was nearby, watching and listening too closely. "And I'm the guy who needs to dive into the water. You coming on the boat?"

"Yeah, yeah, I'll be right with you."

Time to get back to business.

Tom had better hold up his end of the deal. He'd better keep those guards on Casey. If he didn't…

If anything happens to Casey, I'll destroy him.

THE QUESTIONS WERE battering at her, nonstop. She'd been in a crowd of reporters, just like this one—too many times. Casey knew better than to try answering any of the barrage of questions being fired at her. She would handle the press her way, in her time. And right then… they weren't getting any comments from her.

Tom grabbed her hand and steered her toward the SUV that waited. It was a massive beast of a vehicle. She jumped into the back, and he followed behind her. Katrina jumped in the front passenger seat.

As soon as Casey got inside the vehicle, she saw that two men were already waiting there. A quiet, intense-looking African American male sat to the left. The driver—a redheaded guy—immediately took off as soon as they were all in the vehicle.

"Hello," Casey said to the man in the back with her. He inclined his head. "Ms. Quinn."

"Just call me—"

"Didn't expect the full crowd to be there," Tom

grumbled as he shoved in next to her. "Hard for us to get any footage when they were blocking the place. No matter, we'll come back and do the shots then. For now, we'll go to the beach—maybe down to the dock—and get some scene recordings there. You can tell your story while the waves pound behind you. Very moving…especially considering the other women were found in the gulf."

"Do you mean to be an unsympathetic jerk?"

He blinked. "What?"

"Do you mean to come across that way…or do you just not even hear the words coming out of your mouth?"

He blinked again.

There was a smothered laugh from the driver.

Tom's eyes narrowed. "Did you seriously just speak to your boss that way?"

"Yes, I did. And did you seriously just act as if those victims were props to use in your video footage?"

His lips compressed.

"Ah… Casey, it's good to have you back," Katrina said.

Casey's gaze slid to her. Katrina had turned to give her a weak smile.

"Have you met your protection? That's Andrew to your left."

"Just call me Drew," the guy rumbled.

"And you call me Casey."

Katrina pointed to the driver. "That's Shamus. They both came very highly recommended."

"We'll be your shadows," Drew told her. "You won't have to worry about a thing. We guarantee your safety."

If Kurt Anderson was the killer, then she didn't have

to worry—he was locked up. Everyone would be safe again. But if he wasn't the perp...

Then the man who wants me dead is still out there.

"So...DO YOU think he was dumping bodies out there?" Chaz Fontel shook his head. A tribal tattoo circled his upper arm and his long hair brushed across the collar of his shirt. "I can't believe that guy—I mean, I felt *sorry* for him, you know?"

Chaz was the owner of the boat rental shop, and he was also the guy who seemed more than eager to cooperate with the Feds. He'd already provided them with all the information they needed to go back and retrace all the stops that Kurt Anderson had made on his trips.

And the guy had made a *lot* of trips. But none of the trips taken from the boat he'd used matched up with the spots where they'd found their other three victims.

Did that mean Kurt was innocent? Or that he'd just used another vessel when he disposed of the bodies? Josh knew Tucker already had agents canvasing the other boat rental shops in the area, just in case Kurt *had* used another vessel. But he might not have rented another boat. Half the people in that town owned boats. He could have borrowed one, could have taken—

"Did Kurt Anderson ever say anything to you about his father's crimes?" Tucker asked.

Chaz gave a low whistle. "No, man, and it's not like I'd ask, you know? Talk about a painful subject. I just rented him the boat. That's it."

A dark SUV pulled up near the dock. Josh's gaze narrowed as the doors to that vehicle opened.

Katrina. Tom.

Casey...

He stiffened.

He saw the two guys who exited the vehicle, too, and instantly pegged them as the protection that she'd been promised.

"Oh, man, is that Casey Quinn?" Chaz asked, excitement in his tone. "I love her."

Josh's gaze cut back to him, but Chaz wasn't paying him—or Tucker—any attention. His focus was entirely on Casey.

"Heard about what happened to her." Chaz's hands fisted. "So glad she's okay. I watch her all the time."

"Do you now…" Josh muttered. Not a question.

"Maybe she'll want to interview me." Chaz's shoulders straightened. "I mean, I'm the one who rented Kurt the boat. Bet she'll want to talk to me. I bet—"

Josh stepped in front of the guy, blocking his view of Casey. "We're talking to you right now."

"Uh, yeah. Right. He, uh, never mentioned his old man. Never mentioned anything. Just came on board with his gear—his bags and the coolers and he left. Figured the guy just wanted some time by himself. Water can heal the soul, you know? That's what the ocean does."

It healed—or the ocean became a grave for the dead.

Josh cast one last look over at Casey. He found her staring back at him.

"Your agent is going out on the water?" Katrina sidled closer to Casey and kept her voice low. "What is he trying to find out there?"

Casey tried to drag her eyes off Josh. Why was she reacting this way to him? "USERT is his primary job with the FBI. You know that."

"Yeah, but I mean…who is he going to rescue down there? Is another victim in the water?"

"USERT stands for Underwater Search *and* Evidence Response Team. He's searching." For clues. For evidence.

And, yes, for a body. But she really hoped he didn't find one.

Tom was talking to the two men who were her new guards.

"If he's USERT, then why did he spend so much time looking after you?" Katrina wanted to know. "Weren't there other agents—"

"They didn't need him in the water then. So he thought it would be good for me to have an agent… with me."

"Hmm."

What was that supposed to mean?

Katrina smiled at her. "I think he likes you."

I think I like him. "He was doing his job. With this many agents in the area, everyone is assigned a task. I was his task."

Katrina lifted a brow. "You really think you were just a task to him?"

She hoped that she'd been more but…

He was climbing onto a boat. Pulling tanks on after him. She knew he'd be heading out for his dive. When he got back, would he come and find her?

Should she find him?

"I can keep a secret, you know," Katrina added. Her voice had become even softer. "You…you fell for the agent, didn't you? I mean, I've worked with you a long time, and I've never seen you look at anyone the way you're looking at him right now."

"We just met." She tried to brush Katrina's words aside even though she knew she'd given too much away. *The way you're looking at him right now.* "He was doing his job. And I was barely holding things together."

"Let's get her wired up!" Tom called out.

Tom, ready for business. She needed to get ready, too. This *was* her job, after all.

Casey squared her shoulders. The waves crashed behind her.

HE LEFT THE wet suit at his waist. Josh would finish getting it into position when they were closer to the first dive site. The boat shot away from the dock, and his gaze once more slid to Casey. He could barely see her now.

"You think we can trust her?" Tucker asked him. "Just how much did you share with her while they two of you were in that penthouse?"

Josh turned his head and met the other man's gaze. "I trust her."

"She's a reporter, going live right now from the looks of things. If she reveals too much—"

"She won't."

"For both our sakes, I hope so." Tucker wasn't wearing a dive suit. Josh and his team were going down, but Tucker was staying on the boat. The water splashed around them as they flew across the waves.

"Do you think there's another victim out there?" Josh asked Tucker.

His friend's jaw hardened. "If there isn't—" he rolled back his shoulders "—I'm afraid there will be one very, very soon."

That was Josh's fear, too.

They didn't speak again, not until they were at the first dive site. Josh pulled his wet suit into position. He secured his mask and slid the tank on his back. He had his dive knife ready—the way he always did. He *never* went down without a dive knife strapped to his ankle. He'd once had to use his knife on a blacktip shark that had gotten too curious—and aggressive. He checked his BCD. The buoyancy control device was absolutely essential for diving. He put his mouthpiece in, then sat on the edge of the boat. Two of his team members were in position near him. Josh put his thumb and forefinger together in the Okay signal, and then he fell backward, tumbling into the water below.

"CASEY! *CASEY QUINN!*"

She turned at the shout. She'd just finished her first segment. Tom was a few feet away, Katrina was filming and her guards—they sure tensed fast at that yell.

A man with sun-streaked hair jogged toward her. He was waving.

Her guards immediately moved to intercept him.

"Hey, no, wait! I'm a witness! I think Casey wants to talk with me!"

"A witness?" Tom's brows shot up. "Let the guy through."

The two guards hesitated. Especially Drew. He looked seriously unhappy, but he finally stepped back.

And Casey got a good look at the guy approaching her. He had a tribal tattoo around his upper arm. A golden tan was on his body and he wore a T-shirt with Chaz's Rentals on the front.

"Just talked to the FBI." His chest puffed out. "Thought you might want to talk to me, too."

He was the boat rental manager. Right.

"Chaz Fontel," he said, offering her his hand. "I'm a *big* fan, Casey."

Her fingers curled around his. She looked down and saw his wrist—a strong wrist. Tanned.

For an instant, she was back in that cabin, tied up, and her attacker's glove had come down just enough for her to see his wrist…

"I'm so sorry you were hurt."

Her gaze slid back up to his face. Sympathy was there but…his eyes seemed a little too bright. *He's excited.* Excited because he'd been working with the FBI? Because he thought he was helping to crack the case or—

"They're looking for bodies." His voice was a whisper. Chaz still hadn't let go of her hand. "More women, lost beneath the waves." He was still holding her hand. "Such a crying shame. For something so beautiful…to just become a grave."

A chill skated down her spine. She pulled her hand away from Chaz and backed up a step. Her shoulder bumped into Drew's. Immediately, he was pushing her behind him and putting himself between her and Chaz.

"Hold on!" Tom's voice called out. "I think we need to hear more from Mr. Fontel."

Chaz glanced at him, frowning. "What do you want to hear?"

Tom smiled at him. He motioned for Katrina to get her camera filming. "Everything."

Chapter Eleven

He hit pay dirt at the second dive site. Josh saw the bag, a big, thick, black bag that had been weighed down and tossed into the water. It had sunk to the bottom, hit the sand and stayed trapped there.

It was a large bag—easily big enough to cover a body. And it was long—bulky with its contents.

He didn't want a woman to be in that bag.

His team worked as bubbles drifted up from their tanks. They were trying to protect the evidence, not destroy anything. The bag was heavy—*so heavy that a victim could be inside*. His thoughts stayed dark as they worked.

He was too used to finding the dead.

It took time, but Josh and his crew got the bag back to the boat. Water streamed from it as they set the bag on the deck. Josh dropped his equipment. He stored his tank.

Then the team gathered around that bag.

Josh exhaled as he pulled out his dive knife. He cut through the hemp rope that bound the top of the bag, and the bag opened. He reached inside and—

His fingers touched something soft.

Damn it.

CASEY WAS WAITING at the station when Josh came back with his team. Her guards were with her—they'd stayed close all day long. And when she saw Josh's team head to the back of the station, she knew something big had happened.

"Did they find another body?" Katrina whispered. "Is that what happened?"

There was only one way to find out. Other reporters were at the front of the station. She'd been staying out of their line of sight. She'd given a few other interviews during the day—enough to make most of those reporters happy, but she hadn't wanted to tempt fate by staying right in the mix with them.

"Did someone die in your place?" Katrina asked.

And Casey was chilled to the bone.

KURT ANDERSON HADN'T been released from custody. He was still at the station, only now his lawyer, Sarah Hastings, was at his side.

"My client has been held here entirely too long," she began as soon as Tucker and Josh stepped into the little conference room. The sheriff was already in there, his shoulders against the wall on the right. "He was brought in under a charge of boating under the influence but—"

"We found your bag," Josh cut in.

The woman frowned. "Bag? What bag?" Then she waved a hand dismissively. "You have no idea that anything you *may* have found is linked to my client in any—"

Josh pulled out an evidence bag and placed it on the table right in front of Kurt. "Does that look familiar to you?"

Kurt's shoulders hunched. A pink bear was in that plastic bag…a bear that was still soaking wet.

"Because we found that bear—and dolls and toys and clothes—at the bottom of the Gulf."

Kurt reached for the bag, but Tucker scooped it up before he could touch it.

"You're not supposed to have it," Kurt whispered. "I was giving it back to her." His Adam's apple bobbed as he swallowed. "Do you know…he kept everything…?"

"Stop taking, Kurt," his lawyer advised him sharply. *"Stop."*

But he just shook his head. "Her room was like a shrine. Her books were on her desk, and her clothes still hung in her closet. Stuffed animals—the ones she'd had when she was four and five—they were still in her closet. He kept everything, like it all mattered. Like she mattered. When all that time, he'd been the one to kill her."

Sarah shot to her feet. "All my client did was dispose of items that were no longer wanted at his home. So there *could* be an illegal dumping charge, but given the situation—"

"After his arrest, the cops and Feds took some stuff from Christy's rooms, but I didn't know what to do with the rest of her things. Christy always loved the water, so I took it all out there." He was staring at his fisted hands. "I let it sink. I told her goodbye."

Sarah's hand curled around his shoulder. "You don't need to answer any of their questions. They're just trying to trip you up. They're trying to pin *murders* on you, and you haven't done anything wrong." Her eyes glinted. "My client is grief stricken. He is trying to get through each day the best way that he can. So, yes, maybe he had too much to drink. That's on him. But he hasn't hurt anyone. He *isn't* his father, and this interview? It's over." She nodded once, decisively. "So either charge my client with something *other* than boating under the influence—or this illegal dumping joke—or let him walk. Because I think he's been through more than enough."

They didn't have any evidence to tie him to the murders. And the way the guy was shaking, the way he'd gone solid white when he saw that little stuffed animal, Josh wasn't so sure that Kurt was the killer they were after.

Kurt's father had killed his own daughter. It wasn't beyond the realm of possibility that he wanted to destroy his son's life, too. And a false allegation had been all it took to put Kurt under the microscope.

"He can go," Hayden said. "But...don't leave town, Kurt, okay? There will be more questions."

Not that there *could* be more questions. Just that there *will* be more.

Sarah kept her arm around Kurt as they headed out of the room. She was whispering to him, her voice oddly soothing. Her pose with him was almost...intimate.

The door closed quietly behind them.

"I don't want it to be him," Hayden said quietly. He raked a hand over his face. "I knew him when we were kids. The things his father did...the things he tried to do to my Jill—I hate Theodore Anderson for that. *But I don't want Kurt to be like him.*"

"Maybe he isn't," Tucker said. "But I still want to have eyes on him. Let's keep a tail behind the guy just so we know his movements."

Hayden nodded. "Already done. I gave the order right before I came in for this little sit-down."

Josh paced around the room. "If it's not Kurt Anderson, then we're back to square one. We need to take another look at our perp…"

"Male, Caucasian, fit," Tucker began as he ticked off the points they knew. "I'd say we're looking for an individual between twenty-five and thirty-five. He knows the area, and he knows his victims. By picking individuals who are all survivors, he's showing that he's done research on them. They aren't random. He's proving a point—"

"That no one can survive what he's done."

Tucker nodded. "Exactly. When Casey escaped, I wondered if the killer would immediately get another victim. Or if—"

"If he'd come after Casey again." Josh's body had tensed.

"But he didn't come after her," Hayden said. "And he hasn't taken anyone else, either."

He hasn't come after her yet. Josh wished Casey was still with him. He needed her close so that he could be sure she was safe.

He just… He wanted her close.

"Casey stabbed him," Hayden continued, his brows pulling low. "Is it possible that she stabbed him so deeply that the guy is still recovering? Is that why we haven't seen any action from him? Hell, maybe she even killed him."

"Not enough blood at the scene for that." Tucker had crossed his arms over his chest. "And I have the FBI techs doing a rush job on the blood we recovered from the knife she had. They're comparing it to the blood we took from the knife we found on Kurt's boat."

"If it's a match, we bring the guy right back in." Josh knew those tests took time, but he wanted the results yesterday. "Another reason to keep a guard on him. Until we know for sure, one way or another about the blood, he stays at the top of our suspect list." Josh considered what else they knew about the killer. "Our perp is organized. Meticulous. Such a careful planner. Maybe he is intending to go after Casey again, but he has to wait. He has to pick his moment." Even as he spoke, his gut was clenching. "We had her in the penthouse, with top-of-the-line security. It could be that he just *couldn't* get to her there."

"She's not at the penthouse any longer," Hayden pointed out. His gaze was on Josh. "She's out in the open. That producer of hers had Casey filming for most of the day. Everyone could see her."

Josh's jaw hardened.

"She had guards with her. One of them, I recognized. Drew Pitch. He's an ex-Ranger. Hard-as-nails kind of guy. He'll keep an eye on her."

It wouldn't be the same, though, with Josh not being near her. Not watching out for her himself. "I'm going to talk to her." Just to make sure that nothing had happened that day that jarred her. Nothing that set off her suspicions. Letting her just walk away after what happened—yes, the FBI brass had said they couldn't force her to stay in protective custody, but Josh couldn't shake the feeling that she was just bait out in the open.

Tom Warren loved his flashy headlines. Would he use Casey, trying to attract a killer? To get the story of a lifetime?

Not on my watch.

"Look, there's Kurt Anderson!" Katrina called. "He's walking out of the station—that means they didn't have enough to charge him, right? I've got to get the foot-age." She rushed across the street.

Other reporters and cameramen had already closed in. Casey didn't move.

"Don't you want the story?" Tom asked her as he slid closer. He'd been doing that all day—getting too close. Touching her shoulder. Her arm. Hovering. Pressing. Smothering.

"Anderson isn't going to say anything right now. The woman with him—that's Sarah Hastings. She's his law-yer." Because Casey had met the woman when she'd first talked to Kurt. Their meeting had been set up—and moderated—by Sarah. "She's protective of him." Maybe even in love with him, judging by the way Casey had seen the other woman stare at Kurt. "She won't let anyone push her client right now."

Tom moved in front of her, blocking her view of the crowd. "You're coming back home with me."

"Excuse me?" Her brows rose. Her guards were just a few feet away.

"I've rented a house on the beach—there are plenty of rooms. It has great security. The guards will be close in case you need anything. If the perp comes for you, we'll all be ready."

If the perp comes... There was just something about the way he said those words. "Do you *want* him to come?"

His lips parted. "What? No, Casey, I want you safe." His hands curled around her shoulders. "You matter to me. Don't you realize how much?" His voice softened. "Maybe I didn't even realize how much, not until I heard that you'd been taken. Priorities—they have a way of becoming crystal clear in moments of danger. You think you have all the time in the world, and then—bam. You realize you could lose the thing that matters most."

Oh, no. This wasn't happening. "Tom…you're my boss."

"I could be more."

I don't want more. "I don't cross that line. I *won't* cross it." She didn't want him—had never been attracted to him that way. He could use his easy smiles on other women. They weren't for her. He wasn't for her.

She much preferred a man who moved with lethal grace, who gazed at her as if she were the only woman in any room. As if—

"Am I interrupting something?" Josh's voice. Low, drawling.

Angry?

Tom jerked back and his hands fell away from her body as he looked back to find Josh behind him. "Agent Duvane! I just— I didn't realize you were there."

Casey hadn't realized he was there, either. The guy was far too good at sneaking up on people.

"It's getting late," Josh said, inclining his head toward the setting sun. "Don't you think Casey should be off the streets?"

"I was just about to take her home," Tom replied stiffly. "But thanks for your concern, *Agent—*"

"An arrest hasn't been made. Anderson left with his lawyer."

"Yes." Tom's jaw was clenched. "We saw that."

"The FBI still has the penthouse, Casey. Your guards—" Josh motioned to the men near her. "They can watch you during the day. But you're welcome to continue staying at the safe house during the night. You know it's a secure location."

"She's coming with—" Tom began.

"I want to go back to the crime scene," Casey blurted.

Josh blinked. "What?"

"I didn't get to go back this morning, like we planned." She stepped closer to him, brushing past Tom. "We still have a little bit of daylight left. Will you take me back there now?" She'd remembered something at the hotel. Maybe she'd remember at the beach house, too. A tiny lead could make a big difference.

"Yeah, I'll take you." Josh's hand reached out and curled around hers and his touch just felt right. Warm. Strong. Safe.

"Casey!" Tom blustered. "I don't know—"

She turned her head to look at him and his words stopped. "You want the story, right? Agent Duvane can get me access to the crime scene. You can't. I'm going back. I'm doing this *my* way." Her gaze slid to the two guards. "Drew and Shamus, thank you for your help today. I won't be needing your services for the night, though. The night is covered." She wasn't staying at Tom's place. She was staying at the penthouse.

With Josh.

Tom's eyes narrowed. "That's your choice."

"Yes, it is. And we'd better hurry before that sun is gone." She didn't want to be at the scene after dusk.

She followed Josh back to the parking lot behind the station. Katrina saw her, frowned, but didn't speak. A few moments later, Josh was handing her a helmet.

Back to the motorcycle?

She didn't protest this time. Casey put the helmet on her head. She slid onto the bike behind Josh and she held on tight.

He revved the engine, but he didn't pull away. His

body was tense, his muscles hard, and she heard him say, "I missed you today."

Casey smiled. In the midst of everything bad happening, he'd just made her feel good. "I missed you, too." She didn't know what that meant—for their future. For them. But...

It meant *something*.

The motorcycle roared away.

"So..." DREW SAID as he raised his brows. "That mean we're done for the night?"

Tom had his hands on his hips as he stared after the motorcycle. "Yes, you're done. Both of you." Because he wouldn't be needing their services.

Shamus slapped his hand on Drew's shoulders. "Let's go get a drink, buddy."

Drew hesitated a moment, his gaze on Tom's face. "You sure she's good?"

"She's with an FBI agent," Katrina announced as she strode toward them. "How much better can she get?"

Drew nodded and headed off with Shamus. Tom kept staring after the motorcycle.

"Tom?" Katrina prodded. "You okay?"

"This is my story."

"Yes, I know."

"Casey doesn't get that." He shook his head. "Why doesn't she get that?"

Katrina didn't speak.

"I'm getting a drink." Then Tom stormed off down the street. He left Katrina behind him, standing alone.

CHAZ FONTEL CHECKED the lines on his boats. It was quitting time, and he wanted to make sure he stepped in early at the local bar. He'd been interviewed by Casey Quinn—and at least four other reporters that day. He needed to tell his friends about those reporters.

He also wanted to make sure he warned people to stay away from Kurt Anderson. The guy was *trouble*.

Chaz turned around. And he had to do a quick double take when he saw someone standing less than five feet away. *"Jesus!"* He put his hand to his heart. "Didn't even see you there!" He laughed. "Look, this town is jumpy enough as it is. You can't go sneaking up on people." He approached his visitor. "You here to rent another boat? Because I was shutting down early today. I'm not going to do the night rentals for a while. I get that it's a good way to blow off steam, but in light of everything that's been happening, I just think a break is needed." He walked past the customer and moved toward his office. "Sorry, but I can't—"

The blow struck him in the back of the head. Hard and brutal, swinging down at him and sending him crashing onto the wooden dock. Then he was being kicked, again and again, and he rolled, trying to protect himself. He rolled—

And crashed right into the water. He tried to kick up, breaking through the surface, but—

As soon as his head cleared the water, he was hit. Something hard and wooden slammed into his head. An oar?

He went back down.

This time, he couldn't kick up.

JOSH BRAKED THE motorcycle just beyond the line of yellow police tape. The setting sun had turned the sky a dark red. The waves were crashing nearby.

Casey was still behind him, her hands wrapped tightly around his waist. It was so odd, but the woman just seemed to fit him. Inside and out. He kicked down the stand, and she slid back. He immediately missed her warmth.

He missed *her*.

"I thought it wouldn't seem as scary, coming here with you. But…it still does." She rubbed her upper arms, as if chilled in the summer air. "Let's go inside, okay? Waiting just makes me more nervous."

He caught her hand. Josh threaded his fingers with hers. Then he hurried forward. His shoes sank into the sand and he bent, sliding beneath the line of yellow police tape. The wind blew against them, flattening their clothes and tossing their hair. The house was built up on stilts, protecting it from the storm surge that could come if a hurricane ever turned toward Hope. They climbed those wooden steps slowly that led up to the structure. A temporary construction door was in place over the main entrance, a door that didn't have a lock. He pushed it open, and even though there was still muted light coming into the cabin, Josh pulled out his flashlight.

"Let's go up to the next level," Casey said. "Because the only thing I remember down here…is seeing you."

They started walking. Her phone rang. The cry was loud and peeling and she jumped. Casey fumbled and pulled out her phone. "Tom." His name was a sigh. "Give me just a second, okay?"

Josh waited. His light swung around the cabin. Construction had halted after the discovery that the place had been a crime scene. Would the builders eventually finish? Or would they rip the place down? Josh didn't exactly see anyone wanting to live in a serial killer's old lair.

Casey put the phone to her ear. "Hi, Tom... No, no, we're not at the penthouse yet. I told you that I wanted to stop by the crime scene... I'm *fine*... No, Tom, I don't need you. And if I remember anything else, I'm telling the FBI first, not you." Her voice was brisk. "Good night." She shoved the phone into the back pocket of her jeans.

Josh raised a brow. "Trouble?"

"He's becoming so, yes. My attack has...apparently changed things for him." She edged closer to him. Their fingers brushed. "He's feeling protective, he says. Clingy, I say."

"He cares about you." That knowledge shouldn't have made him angry, but it did.

"He likes conquests. I've seen it before. For some reason, he's decided that he needs *me* now. He was saying that he didn't even realize how he felt, not until he'd heard that I'd been taken."

Josh didn't move. "And how do you feel?"

Her head tipped back. "I feel like I'm staring at the man I want."

He wanted to kiss her. Right there, in that godforsaken place. But...

Hold the thought. Do the search. Get her to safety.

He turned away. Shined the light at the stairs and then—

He swung right back toward her. His hand slid under her chin, he tipped her head back a bit more and he kissed her. Deep, quick, hard.

Enough to savor. Enough to tease.

"Josh?"

He stared into her eyes. "Just so you know, I'm staring at the woman I want." She didn't play games. He wouldn't, either. Then, taking her hand, they went up the stairs. He made sure to go first, a habit from the FBI and his SEAL days. If there was any threat there, he'd be facing it first.

At the top of the stairs, he turned into the first room on the left—it was the most finished room. The others still sported barely framed walls.

The room on the left—that had been the room she'd been held inside. The rope was gone. Sawdust was still on the ground, mixed with discarded pieces of wood.

Plastic had been put over one of the window spaces, but it flapped in the wind.

Casey slid past him. Her hand broke from his. "I woke up right there." She pointed to the floor. "He had to be strong, huh? To carry me up the stairs while I was out cold." She shivered. "He could have done anything to me then, and I wouldn't have known. I—" She shook her head. Straightened her shoulders. "I woke up right there," she said again, her voice stronger. "And I was alone in here. I screamed for help…"

But no help had come. Only the perp had come to her.

"I can smell the ocean," she whispered. Her eyes closed. "When he came in… I—I don't think I smelled the oil any longer. That means—he cleaned up, right? He must have cleaned up somewhere and then he came to me. He had his knife. He had the phone. He called the sheriff and—" Casey shook her head. "I'm not getting anything new. It's not working this time."

He wanted to pull her into his arms. But she was

pacing, her movements tight and worried, and he held himself still.

She headed toward the window—not the one that overlooked the ocean, but the one that focused back toward the city. She stared out. "He must've had a car stashed somewhere, right? I mean, for him to get away so quickly. After I stabbed him, he hit me again." Her hand rose to feather over her cheek. "I fell back for a minute and he ran out. I was afraid to follow him at first. Afraid to move at all, and that was time that I wasted. Time that let him get away." She looked back at him. "So I know that if he does kill someone else, that's on me. I should have chased him. I should have stopped him. I—"

Josh had gone to her, helpless to stop himself. His hands closed around her shoulders. "You should have survived. That's the only thing you needed to do." He turned her to face him fully. "You fought him off. You gave Hayden your location. The perp probably did have a ride stashed somewhere nearby—and he knows the area. He was able to vanish fast because—"

But his words stopped. He'd just…seen someone below. Hadn't he? It had been a quick flash of movement. Like a shadow rushing away from—his bike?

"Josh?"

He eased her to the side even as he pulled out his weapon. His gaze had narrowed as he fought to search through the growing darkness below. Yes, *yes*, someone was there. And—

He heard another motorcycle growl.

That was how he'd gotten away so fast. Since coming to Hope, Josh had realized there were quite a few people in the town who liked to use motorcycles and scooters—the smaller vehicles enabled them to access all of the trails that were scattered around Hope.

"He came back, too," Josh muttered. Because the perp had left something behind? Or because he just couldn't stay away from the scene of his kills? Josh whirled away from the window. "He's down there." And he was getting away.

No, that couldn't happen. Josh and Casey raced down the stairs. He shoved past that wooden front door and erupted into the darkness. He kept one hand wrapped around Casey's wrist and his other had his gun.

"I thought it was you," Casey said, her words tumbling out. "I heard the motorcycle that morning—but you were rushing into the cabin when I came down the stairs. That noise—*I thought it was you.*"

The perp had been clever. He'd used the sound of Josh's bike to mask his own departure.

Josh jumped onto his motorcycle and holstered his weapon. Casey grabbed her helmet, then she was holding him tight. He kicked up the stand and had the engine roaring to life. He took off, spraying up sand in his wake. He could see the other motorcycle up ahead. The driver was wearing a dark helmet, completely shielding his head. The driver was driving fast as hell as he turned on a sharp curve that led away from the beach.

"Hold on," Josh snapped. He braked a bit, trying to slow before the curve—

Something is wrong. The bike slowed, just a bit, but the control was off. There was a long, loud grinding noise that came from the motorcycle. *What in the hell?*

"Casey—"

The other driver had stopped. In the next moment, the fellow turned his motorcycle around, revved his engine and then took off, heading straight for Josh and Casey.

"Is he playing chicken?" she yelled. *"What is he doing?"*

He was coming right at them, and Josh's bike was out of control. He couldn't brake, and he smelled the bitter odor of oil.

Casey smelled oil in her hotel room.

The guy was almost on them. "Casey, you'll need to jump."

"What?"

He tried to steer toward the side of the road, but the motorcycle just gave another horrible groan of metal. The other driver was closing in. The SOB slammed the front of his motorcycle into Josh's bike. Josh and Casey went swerving. Their motorcycle hurtled across the road as sparks flew from the tires and spokes.

They were crashing, hitting too hard. Josh spun back and grabbed Casey, trying to get her off that bike and to safety.

But then he wrecked. The motorcycle didn't hit the soft sand dune he'd been aiming for, but it slammed into the hard base of a tree. The metal didn't just groan then. It screamed as both he and Casey went flying.

Chapter Twelve

She hurt. Casey moaned as she opened her eyes. She was on the ground and her whole body ached. When she lifted her hands, she felt the blood on her palms. When they'd crashed, she'd gone flying. She'd hit the pavement, hard, and the skin had torn off her hands—and maybe her knees. Her jeans were wet near her knees and she was—

Someone was standing over her. A man in a black motorcycle helmet. She still had her helmet on, too. "Josh?" Casey whispered. Had he been wearing a dark helmet? Was he—

The man lifted his gloved hand and she saw the knife he gripped tightly.

"Get away from her!" Josh's roar seemed to echo around her. *"Now! I'm a federal agent, and I am telling you to back away!"*

Casey kicked out with her feet, aiming for the guy's shin. He staggered and yelled behind the lowered visor of his helmet. She saw nothing in that darkness—nothing that told her who he was.

"Drop the knife!" Josh yelled.

The guy in the helmet lunged toward her as he swiped down with the knife.

Josh fired. The boom of the gun seemed to erupt

around her. Her attacker staggered and the knife dropped
from his hand. Josh had hit him high in the shoulder.

Casey shoved to her feet and stumbled back a few desperate steps. She could see Josh running toward her and
the perp. Josh's gun was still out and aimed at her attacker.
The guy had grabbed his shoulder. He whirled toward her.

Again, she saw only blackness.

But…she heard the rumble of another motor. One
that was coming toward them. So fast.

She looked to the left and saw another motorcycle
hurtling down the little road.

And—

The bike braked. The rider lifted his hand and Casey
saw that he was armed, as well. Only not with a knife.
A gun.

There are two of them.

"Get down, Casey!" Josh yelled.

She was already diving for cover. In the next instant, he was above her and she heard the blast of gunfire once more. Josh rolled them, tumbling them down
the small sand dune, and she knew he was trying to
shield them both.

Gunfire thundered once more, but nothing had hit
her. Her breath sawed from her lungs. *Safe.* For the
moment and—

A motorcycle revved. Tires squealed.

"He's getting away," Josh snarled. "Stay down!" He
leapt to his feet. She peeked up just enough to see him
take aim and fire.

But it was too late.

Her attacker and the second rider—they were both
gone.

"Damn it!" She could feel his fury, but in the next

instant, Josh turned toward her and his voice shook with worry. "Casey! Are you hurt?"

"No, I'm okay." Scrapes, bruises, a little blood. Nothing fatal. She took off the helmet—she'd still been wearing the thing.

"My bike is trashed—I can't follow them." He'd yanked out his phone. "We need an APB out for them right now. *Two* of them. A team, I should have considered it... Two would make everything so much easier. Subduing the victims, transporting them. One could be lookout. One could drive the boat. The other could get rid of the body—"

She could still hear the roar of that motorcycle.

Josh had his phone to his ear. "Tucker, Tucker, listen man. I need you to start a hunt for two motorcycles. Yes, yes, listen to me. We were at the beach house and we were attacked. They just left us—get deputies and agents on the road *now*... Here's the description of the bikes..."

THEY FOUND THE MOTORCYCLES. They were located less than twenty minutes later. The bikes were dumped near the public beach. The place was deserted after sunset, and the perps had used that to their advantage.

Josh paced near the scene, fury riding him hard. "I let them get away."

Tucker sighed. "From the sound of things, you and Casey are both lucky to be alive." He shook his head. "You really think the guy tampered with your bike?"

"I know he did. The brakes were barely working, steering was a nightmare and we were freaking sitting ducks when he turned on us." The guy had set a trap and Josh had fallen right into it—and he'd nearly taken

Casey down with him. "He was going to kill her. The bike was still on top of me, and I couldn't get to her fast enough."

Casey had been thrown, and thankfully she'd had the helmet on.

"She didn't like motorcycles," Josh muttered, raking a hand through his hair. "The first time I tried to get her on one…" His gaze sought her out. She was in the back of a patrol car—the sheriff's car—sitting still in the middle of that madness. "She didn't want to go with me. I had to convince her."

That moment seemed like it had occurred so long ago.

"You shot him?" Tucker prompted.

"In the right shoulder. So if you want to know with certainty whether or not Kurt Anderson is our perp, you don't have to wait for tomorrow and the results of the blood work." His lips twisted. "Go find him right now. See if he has a gunshot wound."

Tucker nodded. "I already got agents searching for him right now."

They needed to search faster. "*Two* of them. Can't believe that—when the second rider came up, I barely had time to cover Casey."

"She's okay." Tucker gripped his shoulder. "She's safe."

"He came after her. *They* came after her. Just like we feared. She's in their sights, and they won't stop, not until they have her." He gave a grim shake of his head. "I'm not going to let that happen. Casey isn't going to wind up in the ocean. I won't go diving down there and find her that way—I can't." He forced his gaze to move away from her. His eyes met Tucker's. "She matters too much."

"Like that, is it?"

Too fast, too soon, but... Why deny it any longer? Why pretend? "Yes, it's like that."

Hayden came rushing up toward them. "The motorcycles were both reported stolen in Pensacola—that was four weeks ago."

Josh scraped his hand across the stubble on his cheek. "There's no way they transported the victims on those bikes. They used something else. Something that was at the scene of each crime. There must be a van or an SUV that they have—probably had it waiting right here at the beach so that they could make a clean getaway." But he didn't think they'd gone far. No, not far at all.

They would be hunting for Casey again soon.

The local authorities had fanned out, searching the scene. They were going up and down the beach, shining their flashlights across the sand as they searched for possible tracks or evidence.

"You should get Casey out of here," Tucker continued. "If we find something, I'll let you know. Screw what FBI brass said—she's obviously still a target, and her protection should be the FBI's priority."

Her protection was his priority. "I almost lost her." Josh shook his head. "It can't happen again." *It won't happen.* He stalked toward the sheriff's car.

"STAY STILL! THE bullet went right through you. I just need to stop the blood."

He clenched his back teeth against the pain. His body had been marked—for a second time. Not part of his plan. He liked to give the pain. Like to watch his victims moan and beg.

"I'm not supposed to be the one bleeding," he rasped.

The needle jabbed into his skin. A stitch job, to stop the blood. He'd carry that stupid mark forever now.

"Then maybe you shouldn't have gone off the script and gone after them! I *told* you to wait. I told you I had things covered."

"I got sick of waiting." He was also sick of being told what to do. It had been his plan. His moves. His victims. "It's ending." He knew just how it would end, too. He'd known from the beginning.

"Yes, well, it's not over yet. While you were out screwing things to hell and back, I was eliminating loose ends. That guy at the dock? Chaz? I couldn't risk him talking. It was only going to be a matter of time."

The needle jabbed him again. He grunted. "He never saw me."

"No, he saw *me*. And I'm not going down for this." The needle stilled. "Do you understand me? We are in this together. You aren't going to leave me taking the fall."

Of course, I am. "Of course, not. You know we have a deal. I'll get what I want...and you'll get what you want. Everything will work out."

"Provided that Josh Duvane doesn't kill you first."

He laughed, but the sound held no humor. "I won't be the one dying."

The needle jabbed him once more. "Don't be so sure of that..."

And there was just something in that low tone... His eyes narrowed.

"But the first thing we have to do...we need to make sure the Feds have the right suspect in their sights."

JOSH WAS COMING toward her. Casey hurriedly climbed out of the patrol car. "Tell me you found something," she began.

"Agents! Sheriff Black!" a voice thundered out.

She whirled around and saw that Finn was running toward them. His flashlight bobbed. "Found…something…got to see…" He gasped out each word. "Body…" He motioned behind him. "On the beach…come on…"

They all rushed to follow him. The sand flew in their wake and sure enough…

Oh, God. She saw the body, sprawled on the shore. The waves were hitting it again and again. A man's body, facedown, a heavy gash near his forehead. The flashlights lit him up and she saw his swollen, too pale skin. She also saw the tribal tattoo around his upper arm—an arm that was cast out to his side.

"I know him." She wanted to look away, but couldn't.

"Chaz Fontel." Josh's voice was grim. "Damn it."

Yes, it was Chaz. He'd been talking to her—flirting with her—just hours before.

Now he was dead?

She looked up at Josh. He was still staring at the body, a hard frown on his face.

The wind blew against them, and the waves rushed toward their feet.

"I'M SORRY."

Casey's feet were dragging as she crossed the threshold into the penthouse, but at Josh's words, she glanced back. "For what?"

He shut the door. Secured the lock. "For not taking better care of you."

"It's hardly your fault *two* psychos came after us tonight."

"I shouldn't have taken you to the beach house. The guy was obviously waiting there. I led you right into his trap."

She ignored the aches and pains in her body. "We were *both* in his trap. And I'm very glad that we're both okay right now."

He stared into her eyes. "I don't like for you to be hurt."

Casey offered him a wan smile. "Fair enough, I don't like being hurt, either." But her smile slipped away. The tension between them was so thick and dark. "Have you seen this before? Two killers, working together?"

"It's rare, but it happens. Tucker would say that one's usually the dominant and the other is following orders."

Right. "Do you think... Chaz's death has to be related, doesn't it? I mean, you saw his head—he'd been hit. More than a few times." She'd never get that image out of her mind. "He's talking to you—to me—and later the same day, he's dead. No way that's coincidence. He knew something, and someone out there didn't want him talking to us anymore."

His head inclined. "Looks that way."

Frustration beat at her. "Don't do that."

His brows lifted.

"Don't treat me like I'm just some reporter who is pressuring you for details on a case." She marched toward him and jabbed her index finger at his chest. "This is me. This is you. What's happening—it's about *us*. So don't pull rank and shut me out. You don't want me hurt? Fine, but understand this, I don't want *you* hurt, either. You matter, and because of me, you're in the crosshairs, too." Her words were fast and angry and she couldn't stop them. "You can't pull back on me now, so don't even think of doing it, got me? We're in this together. You and me, until the end." She sucked in a deep breath. "If that's a problem for you—"

He kissed her. The deep, toe-curling kind of kiss that she wanted. The kind that told her she was safe, that she was alive, and that the need between them was as strong as ever.

Fear wasn't going to stop her. Fear wasn't going to stop him.

This is you. This is me. This is us.

His hands were around her, warm and tight. Hers had locked around his shoulders. His head lifted and he stared into her eyes. "I was afraid I couldn't stop him."

"I was afraid you'd died when the motorcycle crashed." She'd flown through the air, helpless, and when she'd looked up… "How about we promise not to scare each other that way again?"

He nodded. His expression was still so tense.

He caught her hands and pulled them down. His gaze fixed on the bandages that covered her palms. "Just scratches," she said. "I must have…tried to brace myself when I hit the pavement."

"You were lucky."

They both had been. "Luck won't last forever."

"We'll catch them."

She had to believe that.

"You want to shower?" Josh asked her. "It will make you feel better. Wash away the bruises and the aches."

Sounded like a plan to her. "Come with me?"

He smiled. The smile didn't lighten his eyes. "You get the water going and I'll be right behind you."

She turned away from him and headed for the hallway, but she hesitated and had to glance back. Casey found him staring after her with a hard, hooded gaze. She faltered. "Josh?"

"I will do *anything* to keep you safe." His eyes glittered. "I hope you know that."

She did. Once, a man had tried to destroy her by taking away all that she held dear. Josh was the opposite of Benjamin. She saw that so clearly. He was a protector. Fierce and dangerous, yes, but at his heart, he was a man who would fight desperately for the victims.

He'd fight desperately for her.

Did he know…she'd fight just as desperately for him?

KURT ANDERSON STARED at the prison. His old man was in there, locked away behind the heavy walls and secured behind the bars. He wanted his father to rot. To *never* get out. To never be free.

It was exactly what the guy deserved.

Kurt lifted the beer to his mouth, but stopped, catching himself. Sarah had told him not to drink again. She said that when he drank, he didn't think clearly. He made mistakes. He wasn't supposed to make mistakes anymore.

Why am I even out here? He should be at home, but… at his house, the reporters kept showing up. He'd told them to stay off his property, but they were still there.

Only this time…they were asking him different questions. Asking him if *he* was the killer.

He wasn't. He'd *never* be like his father.

He shifted his car into Park. He needed to get out of there before some of the guards came toward him. They'd ask questions. Hell, they might even call Sheriff Black. The last thing he wanted was to deal with that guy again. Did Hayden think he didn't see the hate in his eyes? Every time that Hayden looked at him, Kurt knew it was there. Hayden blamed him for what had happened to Jillian West. Hayden had *always* been crazy for Jill, and Kurt's dad had nearly destroyed her.

He blames me. Just as much as he blames my father.

What Hayden didn't get—what no one in that town seemed to get—was that Kurt blamed himself, too. He should have stopped his father. He should have seen the truth, so long ago.

He backed out of the lot, sending gravel spitting up from his tires. He wasn't going back home. He'd find some little motel and crash for the night. Maybe tomorrow, he'd listen to Sarah and start the therapy that she kept trying to shove down his throat. It was just that he'd thought that sharing crap wasn't for him.

But I can't keep going on this way. Hayden actually thought I might be a killer.

He wouldn't be. He *couldn't* be.

His phone rang, startling him. It was his personal line. He'd only given that number out to a few people.

He braked on the side of the road and, fumbling, he pulled out his phone. He stared at the number and name on his screen, confused. *Casey Quinn.* Right. He'd given her his number after their last meeting. When he'd thought she might actually tell his side of things.

Before she'd been taken.

Why in the hell was she calling him?

Curious, he swiped his thumb over the screen. "This is Kurt."

"I need your help..."

Chapter Thirteen

She'd taken off her bandages. Stripped. Slid beneath the warm spray of the shower. Casey had left the lights on. She could have showered in the dark. Could have hidden in the dark. But she didn't want to do that.

She was tired of hiding.

For years, she felt as if she'd just been pretending to be someone else. Cassidy had become Casey and she'd bottled up all of her fears. She'd locked herself down, not letting anyone close. She'd reported on other victims in an attempt to help them.

But inside, she'd stayed the same frightened girl.

She put her head under the spray, and maybe she used it to wash away the tears that trickled down her face. There was so much pain out there—the world was full of pain. But if you really looked, it was also full of good things, too.

She heard the squeak of the door opening. Her head lifted and she saw Josh standing in the doorway. With his eyes on her, he stripped. There was no hesitation from him. No shyness. She wasn't entirely sure he understood the concept of shyness. Not Josh.

He eased open the glass door and slid into the shower with her. It was a truly massive space, easily big enough for them both. He grabbed the soap and then his big, rough hands were gently washing her skin. Massaging her as he tried to take away her aches and pains.

She closed her eyes and turned her face back toward the spray.

Then she felt his hand still on her back, right over the old scar that had marked her for so long. The scar that had changed her life—and her—forever.

There was a light, soft feathering over the scar and she glanced back—he was kissing the scar. Using such tenderness with her. Her heart ached as she turned to lock her arms around him. Their bodies were wet and steam drifted in the air around them. Their lips met. The kiss was slow at first, sensual as his tongue stroked past her lips. Her breasts pressed to his body, her nipples tight and aching. Every time they came together, the need surprised her. The way the desire built and twisted within her, a hunger that wasn't weakening. It was just growing stronger the more that she was with him.

He reached behind her and turned off the water. The last *drip, drip, drip* seemed too loud. They didn't speak as they slipped from the shower. Right then, Casey didn't think there needed to be any words. He took a towel and dried her carefully, being extra gentle near her palms and her bruised knees. Then it was her turn. She picked up a towel and slid it over his chest. Her mouth followed the towel's path. Kissing. Savoring. She pressed her lips to every inch of him.

His body shuddered beneath her touch. She was pretty sure her own desire was making her tremble. She took his hand and led him back into the bedroom. In moments, he had on protection and he was sliding into her. He filled her completely, so perfectly. Her breath came faster, her heart raced and the gentle pace gave way to fierce need. Her nails raked over his back. Her hips surged up to meet him. He slid in and out of her, and Casey had to bite her lip to muffle her cries.

"Don't." He stilled. "Give me everything. That's what I'll give you."

He withdrew, only to thrust deep. Her legs locked around his hips and Casey let go. She cried out as the pleasure hit her, and he was right with her, driving hard until he found his own release. Then he shouted her name.

No holding back, not for either of them.

Not ever again.

HER PHONE WAS ringing again. Casey opened her eyes. She was still in bed, but Josh wasn't there. Her hand slid out but the pillow next to her was cool to the touch, as if Josh had been gone awhile.

Her phone rang again.

She frowned even as she rose from the bed. It took a few stumbling moments, but Casey found the phone discarded on the floor. Her finger swiped across the screen. "Hello?"

"Kurt Anderson is missing!" Tom said, his voice sharp. "He's missing and I just saw about your attack on the *news*. On a freaking competing show! What in the actual *hell*, Casey?"

She blinked and tried to push her sleepiness away. It was still early, barely 10:00 p.m. according to the clock on the bedside table. She'd just crashed hard after making love with Josh.

Where is he? She wrapped a sheet around herself, toga-style, and crept toward the bedroom door. The door squeaked when she pulled it open. "I'm sorry— I didn't think to stop and call you while the guy was shooting at me."

"*Casey.* I care about you—this isn't about the story! This is about my *friend* getting hurt. I'm worried! We've known you for years." His voice actually shook. "I want to know you're okay. Are you still with the agent? Is he keeping you safe?"

She'd reached the den. "I'm at the safe house."

"Casey…" He sighed. "Did you hear what I said about Kurt Anderson? He's *missing*. You're attacked and the guy goes missing. He's coming for you. I know it."

"He'll have a hard time getting to me." Not with the security at that place.

Josh stepped from the kitchen. He was completely dressed—dressed in his khaki pants and button-up shirt. His "FBI clothes" as she thought of them. And he had his holster in place. He frowned when he saw her.

"I can send your bodyguards over," Tom said quickly. "Katrina said they were down at the club having a drink, and she just went to get them. They'll be back in no time. Let me send them to you. Let me help—"

"I'm all right for now. I just— Let me talk to Josh for a moment, okay? I'll call you back, I promise." Because she had to ask him about Kurt. Had to ask why it looked as if he were about to walk right out of that place without her. She ended the call and set the phone on the counter. "Josh, that was Tom. He said Kurt Anderson is missing."

A muscle jerked in Josh's jaw. "The Feds couldn't find him at his house or any of his usual hangouts. The cops tried tracking his phone, but turned up nothing. His lawyer says he's just gone to cool off but…"

"But you don't buy it."

"He could be on the water," Josh said. "At least, that's what Hayden thinks. When it was cut-and-run time for his father, Theodore Anderson tried to go out on a blaze of glory on the water. With the victims turning up in the ocean, it seems like that might be a possibility we can't ignore."

"Do they want you on the search?"

He shook his head. "I'm not leaving you." His jaw hardened. "And…there's no reason for me to dive into the water. We aren't looking for a victim—we don't have one yet—"

Her phone rang. She glanced at the screen and recognized the number there. *Katrina.*

"Go ahead," Josh said. "Let your friends know that you're all right."

She exhaled and grabbed the phone. Casey answered and quickly said, "Katrina, listen, I don't need the guards right now. Josh is with me and—"

"I've got someone new," a low voice rasped.

She almost dropped the phone.

"It's time for you to find her."

Casey lunged forward and grabbed Josh's arm. Then she frantically switched the phone to the speaker option so that he could hear—

"She's going to die in your place. Hardly fair, isn't it? I mean, she doesn't even have any secrets to tell me. She isn't like the others. There's no story with her."

"Who is this?" Casey demanded.

He laughed. "I have your friend. And she's going to start bleeding soon. Too bad you got away. I never would have gone after her. But you made me so mad tonight. I don't like getting shot, you see. Now someone else has to feel the pain."

"Don't!" Casey cried out. "You don't have to hurt her."

"Don't have to do anything," that low rasp told her. "Want to do it."

Josh had his own phone out. He was texting rapidly and she knew he was probably messaging Tucker and Hayden.

"Think you can find her?" the caller taunted her. "Sheriff Black never got to them in time. Do you really think you can?"

Her frantic gaze met Josh's. She didn't know where the perp was—she had no clue. The last time she'd seen him, he'd been rushing away on that motorcycle.

"The agent is with you, isn't he? Josh Duvane. He finds my bodies. He brings them to the surface. Duvane…do you think you can find me?" Laughter drifted to them. "But then, you've already been looking, haven't you? Looking, but not finding. I've been right there, and you couldn't catch me."

"I could shoot you, though," Josh growled. "I'm the one who did that. Not Casey. Not Katrina. So if you want to hurt someone, why don't you try me? Or do you just enjoy targeting the people who you think are weaker than you? What kind of man gets off on torturing women, anyway?"

Silence.

Casey's eyes had widened. She knew Josh was deliberately taunting the guy. Trying to pull his focus so that the perp would take out his rage on Josh.

"You think you can face me?" The caller's rasp was

even rougher. "Come on, try, FBI Agent. Come face me. You take me down and the woman can go."

Where was he?

"I'm up high," the guy continued. "I can see for miles. My light is shining. I'll see you coming. If you bring someone else with you,if you bring backup, I'll know. Just you and me, Agent Duvane. You come alone, you face me and maybe I'll let both of the women go. Or maybe…maybe you'll be the one who dies."

Casey shook her head. She mouthed *no*, but Josh said, "The lighthouse. That's where you are, right, you SOB? Up high, with your light shining…you're at the old lighthouse out near the jetties. The place was supposed to be condemned."

The caller laughed. "I think I'll get started. Katrina has some secrets to share."

A woman screamed.

The call ended.

Goose bumps had risen on Casey's arms. "No. You can't go in alone."

He was checking his weapon.

She wanted to shake him. "He'll kill you. *They'll* kill you. We know he has a partner. He could just be waiting to shoot you on sight. Then he'll kill you and Katrina." Her voice was rising. "You can't follow his orders!"

He gave her a grim smile. "You really think I'd play by his rules?"

She hoped to God not.

"Tucker and I will handle him. He'll never see Tucker coming. Hayden Black will have our backs—that guy knows how to go in undetected. I'm not fool enough to go in that place alone, not knowing there are *two* of them out there. He has a partner, so I'll have two partners." He nodded grimly. "This is ending tonight. He *wants* a final face-off. That's why he's calling. The guy is breaking apart, and I'm going to be there when he shatters into a million pieces."

That didn't sound good.

"You stay here," Josh told her gruffly. "This place is secure. You're safe. The building has a security guard stationed below *and* Hayden sent Finn over to stand watch downstairs a bit earlier. I'll get him to come up here."

"I don't need guarding. You do. Katrina does. Don't worry about me!"

But he stared into her eyes. "I'll always worry about you." His hand rose and touched her cheek. "I've still got my laptop set to receive the security feeds from the building. You can see everything that's happening outside this penthouse."

"I'll be fine."

A muscle jerked in his jaw. "I'll be back before you know it."

She locked her hand tightly around his. "Be careful. You'd better not have so much as a single new scratch on you when you get back."

His slow smile flashed. "Sweetheart, you keep talking like that, and I'll think you care."

She didn't smile back. "I do care, Josh. I care a whole lot…because I think I'm falling for you."

Shock flashed on his face.

"So come back to me. Come back safe." She kissed him. *Come back safe.*

JOSH RUSHED FROM the elevator, his phone at his ear. "Yes, yes, Tucker, we're closing in on him. I'll be there in ten minutes." He hung up and waved to the deputy who'd been stationed in the lobby. "Finn, Casey is still upstairs. Go up there and make sure she stays secure, got it? Keep watch up there and don't let anyone else in the penthouse."

Finn nodded. "Got it."

Casey's words rang through Josh's mind as he hurried out toward the SUV that waited. Good thing he had a backup rental vehicle, especially considering that his motorcycle had been totaled. *I care a whole lot... because I think I'm falling for you.*

He jumped into the vehicle, cranked the engine and shoved the gear into Reverse. He wanted this threat to Casey eliminated. He wanted to find Katrina alive. This time, things were going to be different.

This time, the victim had a chance. And he was going to fight with every bit of his power to make sure that the perps out there—the two sadistic perps who'd killed three women in that town—were stopped.

FINN ROLLED BACK his shoulders as he rode the elevator up to the penthouse. He wouldn't screw this up. Casey's safety would come first to him. He'd prove that he was good at his job. No more screwups.

The elevator opened.

A man stood near the door to the penthouse, bent over the lock. *What in the hell?*

Finn's hand immediately went to his holster, but the guy was whirling around, alerted by the ding of the elevator doors.

Light glinted off the man's glasses and his face flashed with relief when he saw Finn. "Thank goodness you're here, Deputy! I heard Casey scream."

What? Finn recognized Casey's producer, Tom.

"She called me—said Agent Duvane had to leave and for me to come over right away."

Finn had been downstairs, checking the guests who came back to the condominium with the security guard who'd been stationed there. He didn't remember seeing Tom come through the check-in. And Josh had *just* left...

"I got here—I heard her scream." Tom's eyes were bulging behind the glasses. "I think she's hurt in there— I think... I think that freak has her! He lured Josh away and now he has Casey." He pounded on the door. "We have to get to her! She's in trouble! Do you have a key?"

Finn's fingers still hovered over his gun.

"She needs help, damn it! We have to help her!"

He hesitated. Josh had *just* left. How had Tom gotten up to the penthouse so quickly?

CASEY HURRIED OUT of the bedroom. After Josh had left, she'd gone to dress as quickly as she could. There was no way she'd just hang around in a sheet while she waited to find out what was going to happen next. He'd taken her phone with him, just in case the perp called again, and she felt lost as she rushed back into the den and checked the security feed.

Finn. Tom.

Her lips parted. They were both right outside the front door. Had Finn brought Tom up? How had Tom gotten there so quickly? She turned for the door even as she heard someone pound against the wood. "I'm coming!" Casey yelled. She hurried forward. Her fingers curled around the lock. She fumbled, opening it quickly. She yanked the door open. "Tom!" Her breath heaved out as both men whirled toward her. "The killer has Katrina! But Josh is going to get her—she'll be okay." *I hope. I hope she's okay. She has to be okay.*

He nodded. "I—I know." He smiled at her. There was something about that smile...

How did he know?

Tom's hand whipped up—only it didn't come at her. He drove his hand right toward Finn's chest. His hand—and the knife that he'd gripped in his fist. The blade sank into Finn's body and a choked gasp broke from the deputy.

"Finn!" Casey slammed into Tom, knocking him back. Finn staggered, then his knees seemed to give way as he fell to the floor, the knife still in his chest. *"Finn!"*

But Tom grabbed her from behind, yanking her up against him. "Don't worry, love. I've got another knife for you." And he pulled her back into the penthouse, slamming the door shut behind them.

Locking her inside...with him.

to the darkness... and let the light up there... if she

Chapter Fourteen

Josh pulled on his bulletproof vest. He and Tucker were
in the shadows, well away from the lighthouse. The
spotlight was on at that place, blazing out, circling into
the water, but as far as he knew, the lighthouse should
have been shut down.

"Who's been paying the power bill?" he muttered.

"Hayden checked on it—nothing is shut down here
for another month." Tucker had his vest in place. His
voice was guarded, and he seemed...oddly hesitant as
he stood in the darkness. They were far enough away
from the lighthouse that any watchers up there wouldn't
see them, not yet. "It feels like another game."

"It *is* a game—one that has a woman's life as the
prize."

Hayden slipped from the darkness and closed in on
them. "I scouted the area. There's one car near the lighthouse." His voice was a gruff rumble. "I know that
car—it belongs to Kurt Anderson."

Hell.

"You go in first," Tucker said to Josh even as he
checked his own weapon. "I'll be right behind you."

"I'll have lookout," Hayden added. "I've got my

night-vision gear ready. We'll be ahead of every move these guys make."

Josh hoped so. He stuck to cover as much as he could, moving quickly toward the lighthouse. When he neared the car—Kurt's car—he paused a moment and put his hand on the hood.

Cold. The guy had been there awhile.

Josh slipped inside—the front door was partially ajar. The place smelled old, stale. His eyes quickly adjusted to the darkness, a good thing because he didn't want to risk shining a light in there and giving his location away. He looked up, noting the spiral staircase and the illuminated peak of the lighthouse. The only light in the whole building came from that spotlight, but it was shining out, not down, so he stayed in the dark. There was a room to his right—probably the old office in the place. He edged closer to it. The door was shut.

He pushed it open and went in fast, coming up in a crouch.

A new scent hit him. Coppery. Acrid.

Blood.

There was no furniture in that room, nothing at all but the body. He could see the man lying in the middle of the room. He looked more like a twisted heap than a person.

"I'm FBI Agent Josh Duvane!" He called out, just in case this was some kind of trick. "Identify yourself!"

But the heap didn't move.

Josh rushed forward. There was a gun on the floor near the downed man, inches from his hand. Josh kicked that weapon away. He kept his own gun in his right hand even as he reached for the other man's shoulder.

Blood. Soaking wet with blood...because there was a gunshot wound to the guy's shoulder.

In the exact same spot Josh had shot the perp who'd come at him and Casey. He pulled out his light and shined it at the man's face.

Kurt Anderson's skin was a stark white. Blood trickled from his pale lips, and his eyes were closed. Josh swore as he lowered the light over the rest of the man's body. There was another gunshot wound to the fellow's stomach. And so much blood.

"Josh!"

Tucker ran in after him. Josh glanced up. "It's Anderson." His hand went to the man's throat. The guy's skin was cold but...was that a pulse? Faint? Thready? He pushed harder, searching for that sign of life.

"The rest of the place is clear. Katrina isn't here." Tucker dropped to his knees beside Josh. He gave a low whistle. "This isn't right. This whole scene...*it's wrong.*"

Wrong because their victim was missing. Wrong because—

Kurt's pulse jumped beneath Josh's fingers. "He's alive."

Tucker immediately started applying pressure to the man's stomach wound.

"Not...me..." Kurt whispered, the words little more than pained gurgle. "Not..."

Josh's shoulders stiffened. *It was a game, all right. All along.* A setup. He'd been lured to the lighthouse, but the victim wasn't there...

Because Katrina was never the victim that the perp really wanted.

Casey…she was the victim he'd wanted. And she was the woman who Josh had left behind.

HE'D HANDCUFFED HER.

Casey sat at the kitchen table, her hands cuffed behind her back, and she stared up at Tom—a Tom she didn't know, not at all.

He'd pulled out another knife from his boot—and he'd put that knife to her throat as he stared into her eyes.

"Why are you doing this?"

He shrugged, rolling his shoulders, then stopped to wince.

Because he's hurt! Now she realized that his right shoulder appeared a little bigger than the left, as if… he had bandages beneath his shirt.

"Casey…" He sighed out her name. "You're my star reporter. In your last moments on earth, I really expected you to have better questions. *Why are you doing this?* I mean, that's just so typical. I wanted more from you."

"And I wanted my producer *not* to be a killer!" The words shot from her.

He smiled. "There we go. Got a little fight back, huh?"

She blinked. "You aren't going to get away with this—"

"And we're back to boring."

"Josh will figure out it's you! There's a dead body in the hallway. There is no way he will think—"

Tom leaned in close to her. "I have a secret." He smiled. "You thought you were the only one with a secret?" The knife cut into her throat. "So wrong. I have a big one. That secret will be here soon."

Her heart felt as if it were about to rip right out of her chest.

He backed away from her. "We have to work fast, though, there isn't a lot of time."

Then he started opening drawers in the kitchen, one right after the other. She jerked against the cuffs even as her eyes stayed on his gloved hands. The same gloves he'd worn before…

"Here we go." He lifted up a roll of duct tape. "Perfect." He ripped off a piece, came back to her and slapped it over her lips. "If you're not going to say anything useful, then you'd better not say anything at all."

Her nostrils flared. The cuffs bit into her wrists.

"I'm going to stab you. Actually, I'm going to stab you a lot. You'll hurt. You'll bleed, and then your FBI agent will come back to find your body." He leaned in close to her once more. His lips feathered over her ear. "But don't worry—I'll have killed the sick animal who attacked you. I'll be the hero."

The hell he would—

There was a rap at the door.

Her gaze snapped to the side, desperate, as she tried to look toward that door.

He stalked away from her, holding the knife. She saw him head toward the laptop—and the security feed. "Ah…and here she is. Just in time." He tucked the knife behind his back. He disappeared from view.

Casey twisted her wrists, struggling desperately. The jerk had learned from last time. No more rope. She couldn't cut or twist her way out of the handcuffs. They were too strong. But he'd left her legs free, his mistake. So she shoved down hard with her feet and rocked back, sending the chair crashing to the floor.

Part of the wooden back broke beneath her, and she squirmed, getting her arms from behind the remains of that chair. She rolled and pushed to her feet.

"Casey?" Katrina was suddenly in front of her, staring with wide, shocked eyes.

Tom was right behind her friend. He'd hidden the knife. He'd—

He didn't need to hide it.

Casey stilled.

Tom had said that he had a secret, a big one. And the perp hadn't been working alone—she and Josh knew that truth. A woman had screamed on the line when the killer had called her. And Casey had been so sure she was hearing Katrina's scream.

Because I was.

"Sorry, Casey," Katrina said, her lips curving down. "But it's time for someone else to be the star. I'm done working behind the camera. This is it for me. My big break."

What?

"The cops are going to find the Sandy Shore Killer. I left him dead in the lighthouse, complete with a gunshot wound to the shoulder. They're going to find him, and I'll give them a terrible, sad story about how I had to fight my way to freedom. I'll have injuries, of course. A knife wound or two to prove the terrible hell I've been through. And I'll say that the killer's accomplice ran away when I got the gun from Kurt."

From Kurt? Kurt Anderson? They're trying to pin all of this on Kurt?

"I'll be the story. You'll be another dead victim. Sorry, but in this business, sometimes, you really have to be ready to do the dirty work if you want to hit the big time."

Dirty work? They were *killing*.

"Let's get rid of her first," Katrina said, nodding, as she glanced back at Tom. "And then I'll get a slash or two—"

He was already slashing.

Casey tried to scream as she lunged forward, but Tom had driven his knife into Katrina's chest.

"I think you need more than a slash," he said. He caught Katrina's body as she slumped. "For this story to work, the partner has to be dead."

Casey kept rushing forward. She plowed her body into Katrina's slumped form—and into Tom. They all fell to the floor, landing in a heap. Casey rolled away fast, then she brought her cuffed hands up beneath her now kneeling legs. She strained and maneuvered until her hands were in front of her, and then she ripped the duct tape off her mouth, barely feeling the sting. "You bastard!" she yelled. She grabbed for Katrina.

The knife was still in Katrina's chest. Her eyes were open, wide, shocked.

Blood was pumping from her, covering her shirt. Her lips parted, as if she'd speak.

Tom laughed. "Can you believe she truly thought she'd be my next lead reporter? She never had the killer instinct."

A soft gasp slid from Katrina's lips. Her eyes closed.

Casey's hand curled around the hilt of that knife.

"Did you know…if you take the knife out, she'll just bleed out faster? I read that once—somewhere. If you leave a knife inside the person, they actually have a better chance of survival. It's when you take it out—and all of that blood starts pumping so frantically from the body—that's when the victim dies."

"I think she's already dead." Casey was pretty sure he'd stabbed Katrina straight in the heart.

"Yes, you're right." And she heard a sound behind her, a long glide, almost a *whish* of air.

Casey glanced back. He'd pulled a butcher knife from the block on the counter.

"Got a new weapon," he said, still smiling. "So why don't we get this show moving?"

Casey yanked the knife from Katrina's body. The other woman didn't move at all. *She's gone.* Casey clutched the bloody weapon with her right hand—still wearing the handcuffs. She whirled on Tom. "Stay away from me."

"Can't do that. You have to die, you see. Just as Katrina had to die. She was useful, for a time. After all, I needed someone to rent the boat for me so I could dump the bodies—couldn't very well do the renting myself. That would have created a trail and just come back to bite me in the ass."

She thought of Chaz's bloated body, washing up on the shore.

"Katrina was worried the boat manager would tell the cops about her. He would have, of course, eventually. The guy obviously loved being the center of a story. It would have worked in with my plan perfectly, but she got nervous…and Katrina took matters into her own hands."

Katrina had killed Chaz?

"Right now, your lover is finding the body of Kurt Anderson. Kurt has been quite shot up, by the way. A bullet went in and out of his right shoulder. And another—well, it was a gut shot. Highly painful. A terrible way to die, or at least, that's what I've been told."

She backed away from the kitchen—from Katrina's prone body—and tried to ease toward the front door. He followed her, stepping right over Katrina as if she didn't matter at all.

"Eventually, Agent Duvane will make his way back here. He'll find the dead deputy in the hallway. He'll find you, stabbed in this den, and then he'll find me... grief stricken as I huddle over Katrina's body. I had to kill her, you see. I came here, I realized what she'd done—I realized she'd been working with the killer all along—and I had to stop her before anyone else died." He sighed dramatically. "I just wish I'd found you sooner. Maybe I could have saved you."

"You're sick."

"No, I'm smart. I'm a man who knows how to create a killer story. When the situation presented itself, I had to act." His jaw hardened. "It's all Kylie's fault."

Kylie? Kylie Shane? The first victim?

"She recognized me. Can you believe that? It's been *years*, but she knew it was me. Saw me on the beach while you were filming a segment. I looked up—and she was staring at me as if she'd seen a ghost."

Her lips felt numb as she said, "When she was sixteen, Kylie was attacked. Stabbed twice, by an unknown assailant."

His smile came again. "Not really unknown...but I did get away. I wanted to see what it was like, you see. To drive a knife into a pretty girl."

Nausea rolled in her stomach. *He'd wanted to see years ago...and he was still stabbing women now.*

"I knew Kylie recognized me. I couldn't let her talk. She had to die." He took another step toward her.

Casey took a frantic step back. The front door was locked—could she get it unlocked before he was on her? Could she stab him before he stabbed her?

"But after Kylie was dead, well, I saw the interest buzzing in town. A new story. A better killer… So I found another victim, and I kept going. It's easy to spot the wounded, you see. You just have to know what to look for." He laughed. "Bridget still had a limp, courtesy of her hit-and-run. I met her at a club, asked her what had happened, and the woman just told me *everything*. I was a complete stranger. She should have been more careful."

It was hard to be careful with a killer.

"And Tonya? Her scars were out for the world to see. I knew she'd be perfect." His smile still curled his lips. "I knew about you, of course. I make a point of learning everyone's secrets." He glanced back at Katrina. "Like Kat over there? The woman has a bit of a drug problem. She'd do anything to get what she needed. *Anything*."

She was going to run for the door.

"You had been attacked before. I understood how fragile you were. Sometimes, I could see you almost breaking in front of the camera. I think that was what the viewers loved about you—you weren't perfect. You were weak, just like everyone is. Got to say, though, I never expected you to fight back."

Her hand was slick around the knife. "I don't believe in giving up easily."

"No?" His brows rose. "Thanks for the warning. Now, sorry, but we really need to hurry along. Can't have Agent Duvane arriving before you're dead."

He rushed toward her. She spun and grabbed for the door, fumbling with that lock. She managed to get the lock to turn, managed to rip the door open—

The blade sank into her shoulder. Casey cried out and her bound hands flew out as she whirled back to him— she stabbed at him, hitting his arm again and again with the blade. Hacking at him. He swore and jumped back.

She could feel the blood on her back. Sliding over her skin, soaking her shirt. She rushed through the doorway.

"Casey!"

Josh was there. He caught her in his arms and stared at her with wide, blazing eyes.

"He...he's in there... *Knife*..."

And she still had her knife, too. It was gripped in her hands.

Josh pushed her behind him. He had a gun in one hand, and Tucker Frost—Tucker was right there, too. His face was just as grim as Josh's.

She looked back at the doorway. She'd expected Tom to follow her out. He hadn't. What was he doing in there? The penthouse seemed dead quiet.

And then...

Laughter.

The door was still open, just a few inches.

"You're back too soon...she's not dead," Tom called out.

Josh's hold on Casey's hand tightened.

"If you don't all leave, I'll kill her right now. I'll slit her throat, from ear to ear."

What? She wasn't even in there with him any longer. She was safe. She was—

Josh pushed open the door to the penthouse.

Katrina.

Tom stood in the middle of the den, and Katrina was slumped in his arms. He had his knife at her throat. Her head was tilted down, her lashes closed.

"I think she's already dead," Casey whispered.

"Is she?" Tom shouted. "Don't be so sure. Things aren't always what they seem." He jabbed the tip of the knife into Katrina's throat.

Katrina's body jerked.

Josh swore. Then he was shoving Casey farther back. "Sweetheart, get to the elevator. Go downstairs—get *out* of here—"

"Don't go anywhere, Casey! I'm not finished with you!" Tom bellowed.

She froze.

"Casey Quinn. Casey Too-Good-For-Me Quinn. But you weren't too good for the agent, were you? The night I took you, I was watching when he brought you back to the hotel on his motorcycle. I saw the way you looked at him, the way you let him touch you. You played hands-off with me, but I saw the truth...and I knew you were going to feel my knife."

Tucker slipped into the penthouse. His gun was aimed at Tom. "It's over. Let the woman go, now."

"Nothing's over. It's just beginning. I'm beginning. And *you're* the one leaving. You and Agent Duvane are going to walk out of this building. If you don't, I'll slit Katrina's throat right here and now."

Casey knew he would.

"You'll walk away," Tom continued. "Casey will stay. And then I'll—"

"You'll kill them both," Josh said, his voice a hard

growl. "That's not happening. You aren't going to touch Casey again."

She trembled, her shoulder throbbing and the blood soaking her.

Josh edged into the open doorway. He and Tucker fanned out a bit, closing in on Tom. Casey knew she should probably run, but…her legs trembled. *How much blood am I losing?* She grabbed on to the door frame so she wouldn't fall. Her hands were bloody. She'd gotten Katrina's blood on her when she grabbed the knife.

"Casey!" Tom shouted her name.

Her head whipped up. She stared straight at him.

"This isn't the ending I wanted."

She knew that. "You…you went to the prison. You're the one who kept trying to convince… Theodore Anderson…to talk to me…"

"I also convinced him that his son was an ungrateful failure who deserved to be punished. Theodore was all too eager to point the finger at Kurt. Everything would have been perfect." He sighed and his shoulders slumped a bit. "But they came back too soon." His gaze swept to Josh. "Couldn't stay away from her, huh? Have to be close, every moment. There was another man who fell for Casey that way. Fell so deep and hard that he killed for her."

"I never wanted Benjamin to kill," she whispered.

"You'll have to kill, too, Agent Duvane," Tom continued. Katrina seemed to be a dead weight in his arms. "Because I'm not stopping. Casey will see you kill. She'll know you're just like the other one. She'll turn from you. You'll lose her as surely as if I put my knife in her heart."

"No!" Casey yelled.

He looked at her. Smiled. "I chose the ending. It was my story, never yours." His hand tightened around that knife, and she knew, she *knew* he was going to slit Katrina's throat.

Casey screamed and raced forward.

Gunshots blasted.

One shot hit Tom in the shoulder. The other…in the head.

He fell back. The knife cut across Katrina's neck, but it didn't sink deep.

Tucker and Josh both closed in. Tucker kicked the knife away from Tom, and Josh grabbed for Katrina. Casey's breath heaved from her as she hurried to Josh's side. The shot to head—it had killed Tom. She'd seen— no, she didn't want to think about what she'd seen as that bullet tore into him.

Josh was pressing his hands to Katrina's wounds. Tucker was on his phone, demanding to know where backup was, and Casey—

"It was my shot," Josh said, not looking up as he worked frantically on Katrina. "My shot killed him. I did it."

"I know." Somehow, she'd just…known.

His head turned. "I'd do it again in a heartbeat. He wasn't going to hurt you again."

Her lips were trembling.

"I'd do it again," he said quietly.

A tear slid down her cheek.

I know.

KATRINA WELCH HADN'T SURVIVED. Josh stood in the condominium's parking lot, the swirl of police lights illuminating the scene. A gurney rushed past him—Finn was strapped down and two medics were working feverishly on him. The knife was still in his chest, and he was still breathing, barely. Josh hoped the kid survived.

There had been enough death.

"No, no, I don't want to leave!"

His head whipped to the right at the sound of *her* voice. Casey was in the back of an ambulance. She should have been on the way to the hospital, but the woman was trying to push her way past the team surrounding her. She looked over at him. Their gazes locked. "Josh!"

Instantly, he ran toward her. She'd been stabbed—her blood had soaked her clothes. "She needs to get to a hospital right now," he snarled, glaring at the EMTs. "What are you waiting for—"

"You," Casey said.

He shook his head.

"I can't leave without you." She licked her lips. The EMTs pushed her back onto the gurney. "He was wrong. Tom was *crazy*. I don't see you differently. You're a good agent, Josh. A good man. I need you to know that."

His chest seemed to burn. He should stay at the scene, help Tucker tie up loose ends but…

Casey.

He climbed into the back of the ambulance. His hand caught hers. Did she get it? To him, Tom Warren had been a dead man the instant Josh saw the guy holding that bloody knife. Tom had come after Casey time and time again. Josh had never intended to let him walk.

Did she understand?

"I'm sorry—" his voice came out rough "—that you were hurt." He looked down at her wrist. The handcuffs were gone and dark bruises banded her wrists. "I should have kept you safe."

He'd nearly lost her.

"You can't save the world."

It wasn't the world that mattered to him right then. It was Casey. And when he'd raced back to the penthouse, so desperate to get to her, every instinct in his body screaming at him that something was wrong—to get *to* her…he'd felt something splinter inside of him. He'd tried calling the condominium's front desk, but the line had been disabled. Before he'd gone upstairs, Tom had been busy. He'd taken out the phone line and even turned off the alarm so that he could access the top floor via the service elevator. Since he'd gone through the service area, the guard in the lobby hadn't seen the fellow. Tom had been smart.

Sadistic.

Josh was glad he was dead.

When he couldn't reach Casey, Josh had tried calling Finn—no answer. He'd demanded backup at the condo building even before he'd rushed inside, but that backup hadn't arrived soon enough to help.

It had been him and Tucker.

"He chose death," Casey said. "That was on him. He did that. He could have dropped his knife. You were trying to save Katrina."

He stared into her eyes. Her beautiful, dark eyes. The woman had gotten to him. She'd gone far beneath his skin and straight into the soul that felt battered. "I didn't want to lose you." Even as he'd pulled the trigger, Tom's words had echoed in his head.

But he'd had a choice to make.

There had been no going back.

"You're not going to lose me." Casey smiled at him. The ache in his chest finally eased. "You're going to get the chance to start over with me. No murder. No stories. Just us."

He wanted it to be just them.

The EMT cleared her throat. "Uh, about the hospital…"

Josh pressed his lips to Casey's. "Something you should know…"

She blinked up at him.

"I'm falling for you, too, sweetheart."

Her beautiful smile stretched, lighting her eyes.

"Uh, yeah, I got things here," Tucker called out as he cleared his throat.

Josh's head turned and he found Tucker standing near the open ambulance doors. His friend gave him a little salute. "Why don't you make sure Ms. Quinn gets to the hospital all right? I'm sure she would appreciate an escort. Hayden and I will handle everything at the scene."

He didn't have to be told twice. Josh brought Casey's wrist to his mouth and pressed a kiss to the bruised skin. He felt her pulse surge beneath his lips.

Tucker slammed the ambulance's back doors closed. The siren screamed on. Moments later, they were taking off.

And Josh was holding tight to Casey. The woman he never planned to let go.

Epilogue

Josh Duvane broke from the surface of the water, pulling the regulator out of his mouth and then shoving back his mask. He grabbed for the side of the boat.

"See anything interesting down there?"

He glanced up and straight into the sparking gaze of his new bride. *She married me. She actually married me.*

Casey Quinn—now Casey Quinn-Duvane—smiled at him. He'd never get used to that smile, not in a million years. That smile lit her up from the inside out and it made him feel as if he were staring straight at a miracle.

Maybe because he was. To him, Casey was a miracle. The dream he hadn't even realized he had. The woman who loved him—bright spots and dark.

And he loved her more than anything in the world.

He carefully climbed aboard the boat, then he reached into his bag and pulled out the two perfect sand dollars that he'd just retrieved from the ocean floor. Casey laughed and crowded in closer to him. "Gorgeous!"

He was staring straight at her. "Yes."

She looked up. They were on their honeymoon—sailing in the Florida Keys. The Sandy Shore Killer wasn't in the headlines any longer. Both Finn and Kurt Anderson had survived. Casey had recently covered their stories in an exposé for her new television show.

Kurt was getting counseling. He was putting the pieces of his life back together.

And the town of Hope? It was finally healing. The monsters were gone.

Josh pulled Casey against him. "I love you." He'd never get tired of those words. When he thought of how close he'd come to losing her... Hell, no. He didn't even want to imagine that life. Because *his* life...everything he wanted...she was it.

She rose onto her toes and her lips pressed to his.

* * * * *

"All right." He came up beside her and covered one of her chilled hands with his.

"What if we enjoy what is sure to be an outstanding dinner and then head back to my place and handle whatever is coming together as husband and wife?"

She studied his profile, seeing none of the tension or stress in the hard square of his jaw, only resolute determination. "Together?" She was bewildered as much by the offer as she was by the easy way he delivered it.

"Exactly." He faced her, giving her a heated, toe-curling smile.

If only it would be that easy. "You stepping up publicly as my husband could very well put Gray Box at risk."

"I've factored that in."

His absolute fearlessness despite the unknowns made her want him more. She hadn't known it was possible to sink deeper into her infatuation with him.

"You expect me to live with you at your condo?"

MARRIAGE CONFIDENTIAL

BY
DEBRA WEBB &
REGAN BLACK

First Published in Great Britain 2017
By Mills & Boon, an imprint of HarperCollins*Publishers*
1 London Bridge Street, London, SE1 9GF

© 2017 Debra Webb

ISBN: 978-0-263-92899-0

46-0717

Our policy is to use papers that are natural, renewable and recyclable products and made from wood grown in sustainable forests. The logging and manufacturing processes conform to the legal environmental regulations of the country of origin.

Printed and bound in Spain
by CPI, Barcelona

Debra Webb, born in Alabama, wrote her first story at age nine and her first romance at thirteen. It wasn't until after she spent three years working for the military behind the Iron Curtain—and a five-year stint with NASA—that she realized her true calling. Since then the *USA TODAY* bestselling author has penned more than one hundred novels, including her internationally bestselling Colby Agency series.

Regan Black, a *USA TODAY* bestselling author, writes award-winning, action-packed novels featuring kick-butt heroines and the sexy heroes who fall in love with them. Raised in the Midwest and California, she and her family, along with their adopted greyhound, two arrogant cats and a quirky finch, reside in the South Carolina Lowcountry, where the rich blend of legend, romance and history fuels her imagination.

For my grandmother, ever the diplomat in the family,
for being a boundless source of wisdom, inspiration
and unconditional love.

—Regan

Chapter One

Shoulders back, head high, Madison Goode kept pace with the silent and stoic Special Agent Spalding from the FBI at her side. Her high heels clicked softly on the exquisite black marble tile. The sound was the only acknowledgment of their progress. Every inch of the Artistry of the Far East Museum was elegantly appointed and thoughtfully designed, not just the galleries displaying the invaluable collection. To Madison, who'd been behind the scenes of many of the most elaborate venues here and around the world, it seemed as if the museum founders had been as eager to inspire the staff as they were the visitors. She appreciated such excellent attention to detail.

As she turned her wrist to check her watch, her platinum and diamond wedding set glowed beautifully under the perfect lighting. She'd had it cleaned yesterday for this occasion, a little unnerved by how awkward and vulnerable she felt in the hours it wasn't on her finger.

She took comfort in the familiarity of the jewelry in its rightful place, a calming reminder in what hopefully wouldn't blow up into a crisis.

The countdown for the evening was running in her head. The dignitaries from China's foreign ministry would be here within forty-five minutes for a pregala toast and a private viewing of the new exhibit on loan to the United States. She knew from her years of experience as a State Department liaison that they would arrive five minutes earlier than scheduled.

Special Agent Spalding held open the door, encouraging her to enter the museum security office ahead of him. Even here, in the controlled lighting, she noted the aesthetic details that would empower the staff and boost efficiency. Her gaze slid over the monitors and the personnel watching each screen and status panel. No one was panicking and everything seemed to be in order, yet the tension simmering in the air was completely different than on her previous visits during the negotiation of the exhibit. When Spalding requested—demanded—her review of a potential security breach, he'd explained the threat was not as clear and easy to locate as a thief lurking in the building for his chance to strike.

"Technicians monitoring the computer systems found a problem," Spalding said, his voice startling her after the long minutes of silence.

She followed him over to a small work space at the far end of the room. Although Madison had met with the cyber security managers on her previous visits, she'd only been introduced to the full team once. She smiled

at the man and woman—very early twenties at best—
wearing museum security uniform shirts with skinny
jeans. Clearly uncertain how to proceed, they stood nervously beside their workstations where two FBI agents
in subdued suits had assumed their seats and were working feverishly on their computers.

Madison's stomach twisted, but years of practice and
discipline had perfected her ability to hide any outward
signs of distress or insecurity. She extended her hand
to the woman first and introduced herself. "Madison
Goode, State Department. Special Agent Spalding tells
me you've found some kind of threat?"

"Yes. I'm Carli," the woman said as she bobbed her
head. Her bright red glasses framed blue eyes high-
lighted by purple mascara. Her pursed lips and scowl
gave away her exasperation at being pushed from her
station. "We were handling it."

"Devon," the man beside her said. He unfolded his
arms long enough to shake Madison's proffered hand
and bump up his round, wire-framed glasses. Arms
crossed once more, the fingers of one hand drummed
against his opposite arm. She recognized how eager he
was to get his hands back on his keyboard. "Carli and
I saw the chatter about the attack and followed protocol," he explained.

"These two just took over," Carli said.

"We could be helping," the two finished in unison.

Special Agent Spalding cleared his throat and gave
a small tilt of his head. At the signal, Madison motioned for the technicians to step aside with her. "You
did exactly the right thing," she assured them. "Thank

you both. I'm sure the FBI will only require another few minutes to make an assessment. Can you walk me through it, please?"

"We've been gearing up for weeks," Carli began. "Staff meetings, search parameters—"

"And likely troublemakers," Devon interjected. "There hadn't been a whisper of a problem until an hour ago."

"Then we found the chat room," Carli continued. "Chatter about how America was selling the country to China one piece of art at a time. We saw blatant threats to the new exhibit. A rallying cry to take a stand."

"Ugly stuff, really," Devon added. "We notified our manager, took screenshots and started tracking usernames—"

"And IP addresses," Carli finished.

By the time Madison had heard the entire story, she was nearly convinced Carli and Devon were twins with the way they completed each other's sentences. The FBI agents at the stations continued working as Devon and Carli grew increasingly impatient. "I promise they'll be out of your space as soon as possible," Madison said.

Devon snorted and Carli elbowed him with a whispered reminder to be polite. Although Madison hadn't hit thirty yet, these two suddenly made her feel old as they fidgeted and murmured in tech-speak about the situation.

Catching Spalding's eye, she walked over. "Any progress?"

"Looks as if a group of American radicals is making a legitimate threat," Spalding replied. "What my team is unraveling implies a direct, credible threat on the delegation from China. You need to postpone the reception. Possibly delay the exhibit."

In her head, she raged and screamed, though she kept her expression neutral and her breathing under control. This unprecedented exhibit was scheduled to open to the public tomorrow. Ticket sales had exceeded their projections and officials at the Chinese consulate were openly thrilled. Delaying tonight's event would undermine significant progress in the diplomatic arena and she wasn't ready to toss that out the window, yet she couldn't put lives or the displays at risk. "Can you run the vocabulary and threats against the emails our office received earlier this month?"

"Yes." He signaled his crews to do as she asked. Spalding was grim, his voice low as he continued, "From all appearances this group is organized and ready to strike." He went on with an explanation of his on-site security team and standard precautions. FBI and local police both in uniform and undercover had the museum surrounded and the Chinese delegation's route from the consulate to the museum under surveillance, as well. "When we discussed this last week, we decided those emails came from a hacktivist group based in Asia."

"The internet brings people together," she replied. She braced a hand on the edge of the desk and leaned forward. Her sleek ponytail slid over her shoulder as she reviewed each correspondence and she pushed it back as she straightened. "The language is quite similar." Similar enough that she was almost positive they were being strung along, dancing to someone else's agenda.

Security wasn't her assigned area of expertise and yet Madison needed to weigh all threats and consequences to the exhibit and the Chinese delegation. The political fallout of canceling the event or postponing the opening could be a serious problem. Her intuition told her they had trouble, though she disagreed with Spalding that the trouble would strike in the form of an immediate personal attack. "The radicals on the other side of that computer screen are noisemakers," she said decisively. "They've never struck in person. We're prepared and we'll continue with the program as scheduled."

Spalding's eyes were hard and his voice was barely audible. "If you're wrong?"

Since accepting her role within the State Department, she'd been walking the tenuous line of relations between China, Vietnam and other interested parties in the South China Sea long enough to trust her gut instinct. "There is trouble, I'll grant you, but it is *not* a physical threat tonight. Someone is playing us, saying enough of the right things to make us doubt and potentially cause a rift. I refuse to make a decision based on fear that will undo the progress we've made in the past year."

Spalding glared down at her and only her years of ballet training kept her spine straight, her gaze direct. "Listen, Goode, if you—"

"Sir! Ma'am!"

Madison peered around Spalding to see a member of the museum security staff waving frantically from the various readouts that confirmed priceless objets d'art and artifacts were secure in their displays. "What is it?" Spalding demanded as he crossed the room, Madison on his heels.

Her famous self-control almost snapped when she saw which exhibit caused the concern. The first troubling email her office had intercepted two weeks ago specifically mentioned the cup with dragon handles carved from white jade. The cup signified more than exceptional artistry and craftsmanship. Bringing a prized item from twelfth-century China to this museum in America indicated growing trust between their countries. Priceless, it wasn't the oldest piece China had shared in this exhibit, but certainly one of the best known. Any impression that it wasn't secure could destabilize the agreement.

"We read a spike in the display temperature first," the man at the controls explained, bringing up a graph. "Now the electronic lock is flickering."

"Flickering? What does that mean?" Spalding asked.

Madison already knew. She'd been through the museum a dozen times already, reviewing every detail of the items selected as well as the security measures necessary to protect the extraordinary exhibit China planned to share as a gesture of good intentions. A flickering electronic lock meant someone either was in the security system right now or had planted a virus to weaken it.

While Spalding sent his team along with museum staff to verify the safety of the cup and secure the galleries, she pulled her phone from her clutch and prepared to make an uncomfortable call. Whether or not the cup or any of the other priceless treasures were stolen tonight, a perceived flaw in the security would raise suspicion. She debated with herself over how to keep the head of the consular staff informed without wrecking the confidence she'd worked so hard to establish.

She turned to the man still monitoring the control panels. "Is it possible to isolate what type of interference is affecting the lock?"

"I can do that." Carli stepped up when the technician hesitated.

Madison watched the younger woman conduct a swift search of the programming until she found what they were all looking for. Madison wasn't an expert in computer languages or coding, but she recognized enough groupings on the monitor. The source of the problem in the locking mechanism on the display case was a hacker who'd been pounding at the State Department computer system firewalls in a chaotic effort to make his point about the insecurities plaguing the world. The official position was the hacker was tilting at windmills for the sheer joy of annoying cyber security. Now Madison wondered what they had overlooked. Only a thorough investigation would determine if this stunt was a timely coincidence or if he was in fact part of the outrageous, threatening chatter Carli and Devon had discovered.

"This is a hacker," Madison stated. She kept her opinions and curses to herself as she opened a menu on her cell phone and located the right name in her contact list. "The reception and gala will go on. I want security increased around the cup please," she said to Spalding.

"Carli, please take a screenshot and do what you can to hold the hacker's attention," she added.

"I can help her." Devon plugged in a wireless keyboard and jumped into the technological fray. "How much do you want us to do?"

"Don't strike back directly," Madison said, keeping the phone to her ear. She listened as the line rang and rang, hoping for a miracle. From what they'd been coping with at the office in recent weeks, she suspected the hacker was better than Carli and Devon, even combined. "Make him jump through enough hoops that it keeps him entertained." Madison wrote her cell phone number on a notepad and left it between them. "Keep me in the loop."

"You got it," Carli and Devon said in unison.

As she left the security suite, Madison heard Spalding reorganizing his staff and she hit the redial icon. Again, the one man she needed didn't answer and her call went to voice mail. Irritation plucked at the tense muscles in her neck and shoulders. *She* had answered immediately when he needed her last year. Of course, he'd reached out by email that day. Rethinking her approach, she disconnected the call and opened her email application. After entering an admittedly desperate message, she hit Send. All she could do now was wait and hope Carli and Devon would be enough.

She made a last-minute adjustment to the guest list in case her secret-weapon expert did show up, alerting the team assigned to the rear entrance of the museum. Ignoring the raised eyebrows and a low whistle at the name she added, she headed for the main museum entrance. The lead dignitaries from the Chinese consulate would arrive within minutes.

"Hope you're right about this," Spalding muttered, his gaze sweeping the area.

"I am," she replied with more confidence than she felt. There would be time for recriminations and self-doubt later when she was home alone. Plenty of time if this became an assassination attempt, since she'd either be dead or unemployed by morning.

Minutes later the formal greetings were exchanged on the red carpet outside and she gave her full attention to the delegation while Spalding watched everything else. Everyone in this first, exclusive group from China appeared as relaxed as she'd ever seen them as she guided them into the museum entrance hall. The invitations had specified black-tie and she thought the group resembled a stunning kaleidoscope with the colorful silk dresses of the women spiraling about the backdrop of black tuxedos.

Madison treated herself to an inward sigh of relief when the first group was safely inside, smiling and greeting senior staff from the State Department as well as the museum director, Edward Wong. Stepping out of view, she confirmed preparations were on schedule for the champagne toast in front of the prized white jade cup.

Brief, scripted speeches were exchanged between officials along with gestures of confidence and trust. If the hacker had attempted to rattle a saber on the Chinese side, the group showed no signs of distress. For the first time in over an hour, she believed the evening would run without any visible hitch.

At either side of the doorway to the premier gallery, golden champagne sparkled and bubbled in narrow crystal flutes ready for guests. Seeing that the key players from China and America were all smiles as they gathered together around the white jade cup display, Madison wanted to give a victorious cheer. With the drama and bids for power that filled the news most days, creating these moments of peace and goodwill was the big payoff in a career she loved.

She'd met and spoken with every person scheduled to work in this room, down to the museum security guards posted discreetly at intervals throughout the gallery and museum at large. Before she could fully relax, her phone vibrated against her palm. The incoming text message had her smothering a wince, arriving too late for her to clear the room.

Suddenly the lighting flickered inside the display case of the white jade cup and the lock buzzed and clicked. With everyone so close, there was no chance for the problem to go unnoticed. The hacker had grown bored with Carli and Devon and was obviously exerting his control on the system. Across the room, Madison saw the museum director bring the guards to attention as Spalding issued orders for his team.

Xi Liu, the highest ranking official on station at the Chinese consulate, aimed straight for Madison. They had worked closely with the museum staff in preparing for this exhibit. "What is the meaning of this?" he demanded.

Mr. Wong joined her immediately. An older gentleman and first-generation American born to Chinese parents, he remained fluent in both the language and the behavioral expectations. "This is a standard test," he explained calmly to Mr. Liu. "My apologies for the incorrect timing. This is a routine we typically employ after closing. The schedule change must have reverted. I assure you all is well and your generous exhibit is secure." Mr. Wong's serene expression was tested when the lock whirred and buzzed again. "There are no weaknesses in the system that prevent us from displaying the piece publicly."

Mr. Liu didn't appear entirely convinced as he turned to Madison. "You assured me all was in place. What is happening?"

"As you are aware, sir," she began, "cutting edge technology is often finicky." Madison felt a bead of sweat slide down her back. Where was the backup she'd called in? "Despite the mistiming of the normal security routine, your exhibit is quite safe." She extended an arm to indicate the room. "The collection, in fact, the entire museum, is guarded by the finest technology systems as well as by the finest personnel. Your guests and friends remain unconcerned. In fact, they appear quite eager to continue with the festivities."

Barely appeased, Mr. Liu motioned a man forward and murmured at his ear. To Madison and the director he said, "My man will stand guard with yours."

"Absolutely," she agreed. The director nodded with her. "If you would feel more comfortable, we can adjust the access of reception attendees." It wouldn't be too difficult to keep traffic out of this room and there had been no trouble at all in any other gallery. She didn't believe for a moment that theft of the cup or any other object was on the hacker's mind. Whoever had launched this attack was interested in dealing chaos and fostering mistrust. She sensed the true goal was to create a rift that would set back relations indefinitely.

Although Mr. Liu politely declined the offer to restrict access, Madison understood the nuances in his statement that emphasized his displeasure. She escorted the dignitaries from both countries to the receiving line to greet guests and checked her phone for any new messages.

Still nothing. Carli and Devon would have to find a way to end this game. Madison struggled to stay calm on her return to the security suite. The man might be out of town. If so, she'd excuse this lack of response. However, if she found out he was simply ignoring her calls and emails, she'd find Sam Bellemere and put a hammer through his most precious hard drive.

Chapter Two

Sam Bellemere sank into the plush seat of the limousine and tugged at his bow tie, letting the ends hang loose. He popped the button at the collar of his tuxedo shirt and pushed his hands through his hair. Able to breathe at last, he felt a thousand times better than he had just ten minutes ago surrounded by a ballroom full of wealthy people eager to support the Gray Box youth programs. The June fund-raiser was the one event his business partner, Rush Grayson, refused to let him dodge. The codevelopers' proprietary encryption technology had led to their founding of the cloud storage service giant, Gray Box. For the former smart-ass teenage hackers, mentoring the next generation of responsible computer geeks was a cause near and dear to both of them.

Knowing how shy Sam was, Rush had willingly assumed the role as the front man of the company, handling most of the public events and meetings. It had become an ideal partnership over the years. Rush's extroverted nature thrived on time spent in the limelight and Sam happily kept himself behind the scenes. Without Rush and the company, Sam knew he'd be labeled an eccentric hermit—or worse—by now. The label held a certain appeal for Sam, but his friend insisted that kind of notoriety set a bad example for the kids they were trying to help.

"Back to the office, sir?" asked Jake, one of the drivers Gray Box kept on staff.

"Please," Sam replied. The privacy screen rolled up between them and he withdrew his phone from the inner pocket of his jacket and turned it on. Within a minute, the device buzzed and chimed as if he'd been offline for weeks rather than hours.

He shook his head, skimming the alerts he'd missed while rubbing elbows with San Francisco's elite. No phone was another rule for social events that Sam wasn't allowed to argue with. He and Rush both knew if he'd had his phone on, he would have hidden behind the device rather than mingle face-to-face with the guests. Per their agreement, that behavior would have meant Sam was required to attend another event later in the year to make up for the gaffe.

Once a year in the monkey suit, smiling until his face ached, was more than enough time in the spotlight for Sam. Didn't matter that by the sole measure of net worth he was technically one of the elite he struggled to connect with.

Terminally shy, he felt like a fish out of water in social situations. Anything more than dinner out with his closest friends left him wound tighter than a high wire. After several awkward failures, he'd met with counselors and psychiatrists to help him, without much success.

He tried chemistry as well, in the form of medication to erase his anxiety. The unpleasant side effects hadn't been worth it. He'd since resigned himself to limiting his social exposure and created a recovery plan that involved a double shot of whiskey and an online warfare game as a reward for making the attempt.

Several missed calls were from the same number, one he didn't recognize. Half a dozen emails with a similar time stamp caught his full attention. With luck, this would be a security crisis at Gray Box that only he could resolve. Then Rush would have to let him keep his phone on during future events.

To Sam's astonishment, all of the messages were from Madison Goode, an old friend from high school. Well, he'd known her for the two years he was allowed to attend public high school after his stint in juvenile detention. The government hadn't appreciated the skill or restraint when Sam and Rush hacked into sites just to prove it could be done.

Sam had tutored Madison through a couple of classes, helping her pump up her GPA as well as her comprehension on some required course work. To this day, she sent him an email Christmas card every year. As much as he resisted those conventional traditions, because she respected his preference for digital correspondence, he always sent one back.

He put the voice mail on speaker and listened, then quickly read and reread the emails, each more desperate than the last, which was only two sentences: "Come on, Sam. You owe me."

Sam shifted to the seat closer to the driver and lowered the privacy screen. "Change of plans. I need to get to the Artistry of the Far East Museum." He buttoned up his collar and started on his tie. "Fast as you can get there."

He hit Reply on the last email, letting Madison know he was on the way. Her first email had arrived over two and a half hours ago. Damn. He never would've left her hanging intentionally. She was right, he did owe her. Big time. Just before Christmas, she'd helped bring Rush and Lucy, Rush's new wife, home from France, sparing everyone involved delays and inquiries that were better off as unconfirmed rumors. Next, he tapped the icon and returned one of her three phone calls. She didn't pick up. He left a voice mail message that he was on the way.

While the driver made quick work of the bottlenecks of Friday night traffic, Sam checked for any breaking news at the museum. He came up empty and was ready to start a different search when the driver hit a detour about a block from the museum. "Looks like some big event," Jake said. "There's a red carpet out and everything."

A red carpet event with no news teams nearby? It didn't make sense. "No problem. I'll walk from here." His curiosity piqued, Sam reached for the door handle.

"Do you want me to wait?"

"Not necessary. I can call if I need something."

Before he'd exited the limo, the familiar tension lanced across his shoulders and turned his mouth dry. At least at this event, without Rush nearby to glare at him, he could use his phone as a shield if necessary.

Although he was dressed for it, he didn't want to brave the red carpet, so he turned away at the last second and looked for a side entrance. The museum was crawling with local uniforms as well as a team that gave Sam the impression the President of the United States might be in attendance. He hoped not. Rush's last meeting at the Pentagon had become urban legend in certain circles by now.

Sam took comfort again in the lack of news crews. For a split second, he considered the fallout if he walked away and caught a cab home. He waged an internal argument that there wasn't any kind of favor worth the agony of walking into a world of strangers.

But he couldn't do that. Madison had used her connections for him, coming through in the midst of a crisis to smooth over what might easily have been an unpleasant international incident for Rush, Lucy and the company. Not to mention she was one of two people from high school—aside from teachers—who consistently kept up with him. The other was Rush.

He was climbing the stairs to the side entrance, still waging that internal debate, when a uniformed museum guard and a man in a dark suit holding a tablet blocked the door. "Sam Bellemere," he told the man in the suit. As the man brought the guest list onto the tablet, Sam saw names and photos in two columns. "Madison Goode asked me to stop by," he added, shamelessly dropping her name to speed things up. "Is she here?"

The suit didn't reply, focused on scrolling through the long list. From Sam's view, he could see the last page was a different color and to his surprise, he recognized the head shot used on all of the Gray Box publicity.

"Mr. Bellemere." The suit said the name with reverence and a little shock. As he stuck out his hand, a smile erased the stoic gatekeeper's expression. "It is a *pleasure* to meet you." He pumped Sam's hand and then signaled for the museum guard to open the door. "I'll walk you back."

"Thank you."

"It is a pleasure," the suit repeated. "I'm Brady Cortland. Has Madison mentioned me? I've been on her planning team for this exhibition and reception from the start."

"Not that I recall," Sam said. Why did this guy think Madison shared any details about her work? When the man's face fell, he knew he had to say something. "But I'm terrible with names."

"No problem," Brady said. "Everyone who knows anything has heard how your work consumes you. Give me Mandarin any day over a computer language."

"You and Madison must have worked night and day on this event," Sam guessed.

"Yes!" Brady's smile reappeared. "It took most of the office at one point or another. This exhibit was a logistical nightmare," he said conspiratorially, "but so worth it in the long run." He paused outside a door marked Security. "I need to get back to my post. Madison will be relieved you're here. If you can sort out this mess, you'll be the most popular spouse in the State Department."

Sam was sure he'd misheard the man, but when he stepped inside the room, the question faded to the back of his mind. Here, surrounded by technology and the low murmurs of voices, he was instantly at home. Monitors showed views of the museum inside and out. Panels of status displays offered rows and blocks of colors and the soft click and clack of keyboards in action created his favorite background music. This tech-filled room was a world he understood.

Madison's gaze collided with his immediately. As she crossed the room, her face was the epitome of calm with not a single sign of the tension he'd heard on his voice mail and in the unhappy tenor of her emails. She was a vision in a black sleeveless dress that poured over her curves, slits high at each leg allowing her to move with the dancer's grace he remembered from school.

"You came," she said. Her lips, painted a deep red, curved into a warm smile. Her soft green eyes, framed with long black eyelashes, drifted over him head to toe and back up again. She'd pulled her blond hair back from her face. "Dressed for the occasion too." She leaned back and studied him and he wondered what she saw.

"I would've been here earlier if my phone hadn't been turned off." Her eyebrows arched. "Rush's orders for social events," he explained.

He soaked up every detail of her. They hadn't seen each other in person since their ten-year high-school reunion, another event Rush had forced him to attend. Madison had been the only bright light that evening. He remembered her in a softer dress, her hair in loose waves around her shoulders. Tonight, the sleek dress and hair created the illusion of a blond version of perfect Far Eastern elegance. As if being shy wasn't bad enough, her lithe dancer's body left him tongue-tied. He knew it would be polite to offer her a compliment. If only he could trust his mouth to deliver the words in the proper, flattering order. The years of exercises in composure and confidence in social settings were lost in the ether of his brain. He was terrified of saying something wrong in front of so many people. These were her coworkers and he wouldn't compound her current trouble with some embarrassing blunder.

Apparently understanding his discomfiture, she leaned close and feathered a kiss near his cheek. "Thank you for coming." When she took his hand, her tight grasp was his only clue to her distress. "Did we pull you away from something important?"

"No. I'd finished my part for the evening."

Her hand slid over his arm as she guided him to a workstation. "My apologies for being simultaneously vague and persistent," she began in that perfect, unaccented voice. "I wasn't comfortable putting the details in an email. As this evening approached, we had the typical threats against the dignitaries from China and the exhibit that opens tonight with this gala reception. I chalked it up to normal background noise until the museum system was breached a few hours ago. Whoever is behind this has disrupted display settings and the electronic locks on the centerpiece of this exhibit. The consensus is if those settings can be reset, he can do more damage at will to any part of the museum."

"Sounds about right," Sam said. "Is the primary concern preventing a theft?"

"On that we all disagree. I find the threat of a theft low." She gave a quick shake of her head. "I can't rule it out, of course. The head of the Chinese consulate has added his men to the security team. If theft is the goal, a hacker messing with the display through the computer has made their task additionally difficult. I'm more concerned with what's going on in here." She circled her finger at the nearest monitor.

Her voice rolled over him as easily as surf kissing sand before it slid back to the ocean. He could listen to her for hours, a strange revelation for a man who preferred working either in near-silence or to the pounding beat of heavy metal music. Bending forward, he reached up to bump his glasses and hit his nose, forgetting he'd worn contacts. Hoping she hadn't noticed, he examined several screenshots of coding. "You caught this?" he asked, impressed.

She laughed. "No." She rolled her hand, inviting two younger people into the conversation. "Carli and Devon noticed some increasing negative chatter directly tied to the event this evening. The primary person in the chat room had too many specifics of the agenda tonight for it to be random. The FBI has been running down the source, which left Carli and Devon to try and amuse the hacker until you could get here. Pardon me," she said. "Carli and Devon, this is Sam Bellemere."

"O-M-G." Carli clapped a hand over her mouth. Her blue eyes were huge behind her glasses. "I cannot believe you married Sam Bellemere. You're the—"

"Mastermind of Gray Box," Devon said, finishing her sentence. "We're *huge* fans," he gushed.

They both tried to shake his hand simultaneously and Sam laughed it off. Though he'd never be completely comfortable in the spotlight, their overwhelming greeting gave him a pleasant distraction from another mention of marriage. Marrying Madison—or any woman—wasn't something he considered forgettable.

Reflexively he looked at her hand and caught the wedding set on her left ring finger. It was timeless and elegant, much like the woman wearing it. The classic beauty of the wedding set contrasted with the larger ruby ring on her right hand that accented the sleek lines of her dress. So he hadn't misheard the suit with the tablet. Madison had listed him as her *husband*?

"Was Rush your best man?" Carli asked.

"If we could stay on point," Madison interjected coolly.

Happily, Sam thought. Whatever her reasons for calling him her husband, he trusted she'd tell him later. He wouldn't embarrass her with questions now, in front of people who clearly respected her. "What do you need?" He reached for the mouse and scrolled through the screenshots Carli and Devon had captured.

"I need to know the white jade cup and the museum as a whole are secure and will stay secure. This exhibit is a huge honor for the US and a big show of trust from China. Any perceived trouble could undo months of negotiations." She waved over another man. "If you'd coordinate with Special Agent Spalding, I need to circulate with the guests for a few minutes."

"Sure." He pulled out a chair and sat down. Within a few keystrokes, he was into the museum system and feeling his way around. He'd much rather be here than out there with her among a crowd of strangers.

While Spalding brought him up to speed, Sam felt Carli and Devon watching every keystroke as he looked for how the hacker had wormed this code into the display controls.

The code caught his full attention and everything around him faded into the background. He was always happier working with computer code than trying to unravel the mysteries of people. People had secrets and hidden agendas such as pretend marriage. Computer code, no matter how convoluted or infectious, always retained a sense of logic, if only to the coder. He couldn't imagine how Madison managed all the protocols and people day in and day out. He'd go crazy under that kind of pressure.

As he worked, he kept up a running litany for Spalding. "The chances of finding his location with the tools here are low." Sam wasn't ready to risk a connection and upload his personal tool kit to a compromised system. "For tonight," he continued, "I can isolate the issues and prevent him from causing more havoc."

"Can you keep him out?"

"That requires a major upgrade for the museum. They're well-protected from the things they know about. This…" His voice trailed off until he ran into another annoying speed bump. "Well, this kid is good."

"How do you know it's a kid?" Spalding asked.

"Just an educated guess based on the language, creative approach and execution. He gained access through a gap in the contact page."

Devon and Carli added their opinions and voices to the discussion, speculating on who was behind the attack and where they were hiding. Though Sam wasn't willing to give away the online security programs he used at Gray Box, he was happy to weave in a few improvements and lock out the hacker for tonight. "Display controls and locks are back in my control," a man said from across the room.

"The group from China will be delighted to hear it," Spalding said with obvious relief. "Almost as much as the museum director."

Sam imagined Madison would be pleased, as well. "The hard work isn't done," he warned. "This stopgap will buy the museum forty-eight hours at best. If he wants back in, he'll find a way."

"The exhibit runs through the end of the year," Madison said from over his shoulder.

Sam swiveled in the seat and met her serene gaze. "I didn't hear you come in." He checked his watch, surprised he'd been working on this for nearly an hour.

She gave him a small smile. "Can you create a solution that will last?"

"Yes, but not from here." He stood up from the workstation. "I'll work on it more tomorrow. For tonight, everything should run flawlessly."

"Wonderful." Her eyes were filled with gratitude. "Thank you, on behalf of all of us."

"We'll need to coordinate with your efforts moving forward," Spalding said. "My team needs to know what you're implementing."

Startled at the man's audacity, Sam laughed. "I'll

keep you in the loop, but you're not coming anywhere near my lab at Gray Box."

"This is an ongoing FBI case," Spalding countered, planting his hands on his hips.

"All right, it's yours. What a relief I'm not needed here anymore." Sam stepped away from the workstation and shoved his hands into his pockets before he gave in to the urge to pop Spalding on the chin. At one time, he'd been a scrawny nerd. After high school, when his days were his to manage, he started putting in almost as many hours at the gym as he did at the keyboard.

"Gentlemen," Madison chided. "I'm sure we can come to terms at a more appropriate time in the morning."

Sam wanted to snarl at the insinuation that he'd cave on this point. "FBI, Department of Defense, or whoever, can sign a contract if they want a consultant. I don't work for free."

He and Rush had seen a need and gone after it, cornering the market of online information security. They'd both developed and sold ideas for millions, so founding Gray Box hadn't been strictly a money-motivated endeavor. Although no one seemed to believe it, they had an altruistic side, professionally and personally.

Hackers once themselves, they'd been disowned by that community when they launched Gray Box. He couldn't recall a week since the company went public without an attempt on the servers. Every hacker in the world wanted the instant reputation and recognition that would come from breaking into Gray Box. The legitimate businesses they supported now still held a reserve of distrust, despite their zero-breach record. Sam reminded himself public image wasn't his problem. He left that to Rush and Rush left the lion's share of the day-to-day technology to him.

"If you're set," Sam said to Madison, "I'll be on my way." He shook hands with Carli and Devon and signed a business card for each of them. With a final nod to Spalding, he let Madison walk him out of the security suite.

"You haven't heard the last of Spalding," she murmured. "He takes his role in this seriously."

"As he should," Sam said, matching her low tone. "I'll cooperate with him, but I'm not handing over proprietary technology or software." Again he reached to push his glasses up so he could rub his eyes and remembered in the nick of time he was wearing his contacts. "By noon tomorrow, I'll have better location intel for the FBI to work with as well as a comprehensive protective program for the museum. At a fair price."

"Remarkable." She stopped, placing a hand on his arm again. "I have one more favor to ask."

He arched his eyebrows, waiting.

She glanced up and down the hallway before meeting his gaze. "Spend a few minutes at the reception with me. News of my, *um*, husband's arrival has made people curious."

He kept her waiting, but she didn't flinch. "Okay, on one condition."

"Only one?"

He reconsidered his position. "One condition and I

reserve the right to add conditions based on your answers."

She held her ground and his gaze. "I reserve the right to refuse on a per item basis. Name your primary condition."

He felt the smile curl his lips, saw her lovely mouth curve in reply. "Tell me where and why we married."

"Not here." Her smile faded. "You deserve a full explanation and you'll get it, I promise. As soon as I navigate the minefield this evening has become. I don't have any right to impose further, but I could use a buffer in there."

He suddenly wanted to step up and be that buffer. For her. "I'm no asset in social settings, Madison."

"No one's expecting you to be a social butterfly. You only have to be yourself and pretend to be proud of me."

He didn't care for her phrasing. Before he could debate the terms further, she leaned her body close to his and gave him a winning smile. "Later," she murmured, tapping his lips with her finger. "Let's go. There's only an hour left." She linked her hand with his and turned, giving him a start when they came face-to-face with one of the guests.

Her moves made sense now. She'd known they were being watched while he'd been mesmerized by her soft green eyes. The intimacy had only been for show. Thank goodness.

If her smile was any indication, he'd managed the first introduction flawlessly. They were soon surrounded by others eager to meet Madison's elusive husband. Beside her, working the room wasn't difficult.

She never left him to fend for himself and listening to her answer the same repeated questions, he learned she'd kept details of her married life private. It made the hour easier to bear.

The only thing that came naturally to him was demonstrating pride in his fake wife. She had a flare for diplomacy—no surprise, considering her career. He admired her ability to say the right things or politely evade questions she didn't want to answer.

When they entered the gallery where the prized white jade cup glowed under soft lights surrounded by guards, he was the only person close enough to catch her relieved sigh. She squeezed his hand. "Thank you, Sam. You saved me tonight."

He couldn't recall ever hearing similar words aimed at him. "We should dance," he replied, noticing other couples dancing on the terrace where live music was under way.

"You don't have to do that," she said, resisting.

This was a new role. Not the one she'd created for him with the marriage ruse, but being the eager and willing dance partner. He tipped his head to the open doors, urging her to come along. "It's a gorgeous night and it's our public debut as a couple."

"It's not necessary," she murmured as they lingered on the fringes of the dance floor.

"Afraid I'll step on your toes?" He managed to keep the growing list of questions to himself, though he couldn't wait to hear how she'd passed her security clearances with a fake husband. "Come on," he cajoled. "We deserve a little fun." Besides, he had more he wanted to say. Nothing as eloquent as the cheesy lines he'd just delivered—something far more relevant to his real reason for being here.

With a little spin, he turned her into his arms and they joined the flow of dancing couples.

"Impressive." She gave him an open, friendly smile that suited her better than the cool reserve she'd shown all evening.

"My mom was a stickler for all the traditional manners." If he focused on her, he didn't mind the other people milling about, watching them.

Madison peered up at him through her lashes. "Was that before or after juvie?"

"Both, actually," he admitted. Why conversation had always been easy with her was a perpetual mystery to him. She'd always been out of his league and yet she'd never been rude about what she needed when he tutored her. The sobering thought brought him back to the reason she'd called on him to help.

He bent his head close to hers and whispered in her ear. "There's more to the problem you had tonight, isn't there?"

Her hand smoothed a small circle across his shoulder. "Yes." The serene mask she kept between the world and her emotions fell back into place.

"I'd like to talk about it in more detail."

"As soon as I'm home I'll call you and fill you in."

"No." Based on who she was, the people around them and the disjointed threats from the hacker and online chat rooms, he didn't trust her phone or email right now. Knowing how she'd reached out to him, he had a few concerns about the security of his phone and email. "In person is better. Smarter," he added.

Her body tensed under his hands. "Sam, stop. You've done enough for me. I can handle it with the FBI's help from here."

"I'm serious, Madison." He guided her through a turn and brought her closer to his body. "You know the history of this situation. You know the protocols and risks in your world better than I do."

When concern flared in her eyes, he knew she was following his line of thinking. If she'd used his name from the beginning of her marriage charade, he had reason to worry that his condo might be compromised. It wasn't simply his fondness for spy novels fueling the paranoia. He and Rush had survived several corporate espionage attempts, from local to global threats. As he'd watched Madison work the room, he realized several people in the Chinese delegation recognized him and were reassessing her because of it. He sensed serious trouble brewing and he needed her insight to get ahead of it.

"How long have people believed I'm your husband?"

Chapter Three

Madison knew precisely what he was asking and she was ashamed for not thinking of it earlier. Her desperate action had put *him* at risk. She blamed her oversight on being near him, close enough to touch. Holding his hand, having that strong, warm palm pressed against hers, brought her persistent fantasy to life with vivid detail. Despite the crazy twists and turns of the evening, despite knowing there were likely more problems ahead, this past hour with him had been nothing short of a dream come true.

And now she was waking up with a jolt. "Only the security clearance team is aware the wedding set is only for show." The rings had been enough of a buffer for her, until tonight.

"That doesn't answer my question," he stated, executing another perfect turn in the dance.

Of course it didn't. Sam Bellemere, master of logistics and computer code, was searching for the bug—*the flaw*—in her story. "I have no reason to believe your home has been compromised." She pushed the words through the tight smile she kept plastered on her face.

"A good start."

"I never once used your full name in any conversation or correspondence until tonight."

She felt more than heard his disbelieving snort. Did he have to push this here and now? She was worn out, had been working toward this evening for the better part of a year. She had a bottle of her favorite wine chilled and waiting at her apartment for her private celebration. "I will tell you the whole story. In person."

"I know." His hands flexed, underscoring the inevitability of those two words.

Was that a threat or a promise? Her body had an opinion, but that was nothing new. She'd worked her tail off through high school and college until finally realizing her goal of becoming a liaison with the State Department. The joy had dulled quickly when she ran up against the preconceived notions of men and women from different countries and cultures. It wasn't a shock, she knew her research, yet facing it head-on day in and day out had challenged her resolve. The illusion of having a husband smoothed out those rough edges and gave her the respect and distance she needed to excel in her position. Even the team who handled her security clearance had been on board with the idea, since there wouldn't be any issues with questionable romantic relationships.

At the office, with the people who knew her best, she'd found having a particular man in mind made the lie easier. Even if she didn't share the details of the whirlwind wedding and happy marriage, it gave her story credibility. No need to fabricate height, hair and eye color, or how her husband smiled at her over a shared joke. All she had to do was picture the man dancing with her now.

Sam Bellemere, reclusive, wealthy and brilliant, was the embodiment of her ideal husband and she had no intention of admitting such a thing. At six feet, he was the perfect height for her. His brown hair and brown eyes might sound bland, yet thinking about the flecks of gold in his irises she'd noticed when he tutored her, recalling his exasperation and amusement with her struggle to learn what he mastered so easily, always made her smile. It was those sweet memories that convinced her coworkers she'd found her soul mate.

If only it could be true.

It was impossible to ignore how he'd bulked up as he matured, filling out through the shoulders and everywhere else since high school. He was light on his feet, his muscles firm under his tuxedo. She'd read in an interview that he kept fit by boxing at a gym across town. It was obviously working.

She reeled in her attraction before it became obvious. Her crush on him had begun that first week of his tutoring. No matter where she went, who she met or dated, or how many birthdays she celebrated, he was the standard by which she measured all men. She knew being stuck on a high-school crush was ridiculous. She worried there was something wrong with her emotionally. Every attempt to break through those persistent feelings had failed.

"Madison?"

Tonight was a dream twisted within a nightmare of

potential embarrassment. She'd never meant for them to play the happily married couple in public. Her body heated with every sway and step she took near him, believing the impossible. If she were brutally honest, she'd admit her entire system had gone on full alert when he stepped into the security office. Without an ice bath, she didn't stand a chance of cooling down any time soon.

"Madison?" He spun her out and back to him once more.

"Hmm?"

"What's on your mind?"

She jerked herself back into work mode. "The hacker." It wasn't really a lie. She'd mastered the art of compartmentalizing and showing interest in one thing while her mind raced off in another direction.

She really should credit that skill to Sam, as well. In high school, he'd never done more than shake her hand the first day the teacher introduced them. Her fantasies had been outrageously different. Looking back, she knew the only reason Sam's tutoring had been effective was that she'd been determined to prove she wasn't the typical dumb blonde. She wanted to earn his respect as a student and win his attention as a person. It hadn't worked, although she passed the classes she needed to keep her career goals on track. By the time they went their separate ways at graduation, she'd settled into the reality of being his friend, knowing she'd lost the chance to be his girlfriend.

"Madison?"

"Yes."

"The music's over."

Feeling the gaze of others on them, she stepped back and grinned up at him, playing the role of enamored spouse to perfection. Indulging herself, she brushed nonexistent lint from the lapel of his tuxedo so she could feel the solid muscle of his chest under his clothing. The images that flooded her mind nearly undermined her reserve and self-control.

"I need to stay until the guests are gone. Would you like me to call a car for you?"

His palm trailed down her arm until his hand engulfed hers. "Now that I'm here, I'm reluctant to leave without you."

She knew he didn't intend for those words to twine around her heart and yet she couldn't stop the response. "When did you start enjoying social outings?"

"It's a recent development." His voice, low and rough, sent a shiver of desire over her skin. With another man she'd chalk up the comment as innuendo, but that wasn't how Sam was wired.

Pulling herself together, she returned to her responsibilities of giving each guest a proper farewell and seeing everyone out of the museum as she gave more vague answers about their relationship.

Mr. Liu found her mingling with his wife and the other members of his party near the gallery and he signaled for a tray of champagne. "One last toast," he said, holding his glass high. "May the gods of happiness, wealth and longevity smile upon you both, this day and always."

They all drank to her marriage and Mr. Liu urged Madison and Sam toward the white jade cup on display while those who had arrived with him headed for the car waiting out front. "I had concerns, Mrs. Goode, as you know. Please also know I appreciate how efficiently you handled them." He slid a look at Sam.

"It is my honor, Mr. Liu," she replied. "We want you to be at ease, confident that we value the treasures you've shared here as much as China does."

Mr. Liu met her gaze with direct, pointed interest. "I find it intriguing, Mrs. Goode, that you've kept a treasure of your own so well hidden." He bowed slightly at Sam, maintaining eye contact. "Mr. Bellemere, it was an honor and good fortune to meet you personally this evening. Your company is of great interest to me."

It shouldn't have shocked her that Sam was known to leaders in China. He and Rush had established a global influence within the market of data security.

Assuming someone from the consulate hadn't tried to plant listening devices in her apartment previously, they would be desperate to do so now that she was known to be married to Sam. Mr. Liu wasn't even bothering with subtlety. If someone managed to bug her apartment, they'd soon learn she wasn't really married to Sam. Madison was calculating the fallout, the timing and how to handle it as the men chatted about computer advancements.

With no more than a glance, Sam understood what she needed and helped her guide Mr. Liu toward the car and those waiting for him.

"My son has a great interest in the computer sciences," Mr. Liu said, deftly shifting to an indirect tack. "He lacks follow-through and motivation, despite the best efforts of his family and educators. I've often thought it might motivate him to see what is possible."

"How old is your son?" Sam asked.

"Nearly eighteen," Mr. Liu replied. "He will begin at Stanford in the fall."

"A very good school," Sam said.

Mr. Liu ignored Madison's attempts to lead him down the front steps. Resigned, she watched for an opening to rescue Sam from the conversation, but Sam seemed content. She let her mind wander over the evening, considering it a success. Regardless of the invisible, contained antics of the hacker, no one had suffered a misstep or misspoken word. Except her, by calling in her fake husband to save the evening.

She owed him more than an explanation, she thought, as Mr. Liu finally joined those waiting for him in the long black limousine. With a wave, she stepped back inside, startled to find herself alone with the museum director. Had Sam decided he didn't need the full details of their fabricated marriage after all? For some inexplicable reason the idea made her sad as she and Mr. Wong chatted during the final walk-through of the museum.

When they reached the back hallway, she heard raised voices in the security office. Through the open door she saw Sam and Agent Spalding locked in a heated discussion.

"It's not something I handle so casually," Sam was saying. "You'll have to go through the appropriate channels."

"I am leading the only official investigation," Spald-

ing fired back. "It's better for everyone if you cooperate up front."

"We don't even have an ID," Sam retorted. "Bring
over a legit ID and a warrant and someone can probably tell you if he has a Gray Box. Until then you're
shooting in the dark."

"Is the overnight team in place?" Madison asked
Spalding, striding forward and inserting her voice into
the verbal fray.

"Yes," Spalding answered, glaring over her head at
Sam as if she weren't there. "The team will stay on full
alert outside and in."

"Wonderful," she replied. "Then it's time for the rest
of us to go home."

"You can go once I'm confident your husband will
keep me in the loop."

She silenced Sam's reply with a raised finger. "He
gave you his word earlier. You watched him lend us his
phenomenal expertise with zero advance notice this
evening. What else do you need to hear, Special Agent
Spalding?"

Spalding planted his hands on his hips. "Mr. Bellemere keeps secrets for a living."

"No," Sam interjected. "My company offers people
and businesses secure cloud storage solutions. That is
entirely different."

"This is neither the time nor the *place*," Madison emphasized, "to get into a philosophical discussion about
online privacy. I am grateful to the FBI for helping this
event run safely and smoothly tonight. Whatever the

hacker's goal, I'm sure we'll all work together to root him out before he causes serious trouble."

Obviously not even close to appeased, Spalding stood down for the moment. When she'd gathered her red silk shawl and her briefcase, the three of them along with the museum director walked together in a tense silence to the rear entrance of the museum. Satisfied with the alarms, Spalding offered Sam and Madison a ride. Sam refused for both of them.

"We're covered." He pointed to a limo waiting under a streetlamp on the far side of the parking lot. "My driver's waiting."

Spalding muttered something Madison didn't hear because she was nudging Sam toward the car. They had more important issues to discuss. At half past midnight, she hoped he'd let the discussion wait until morning.

The driver opened the rear door for them, giving her a small nod as she slid into the plush leather seat, followed closely by Sam. Maybe he left events with women all the time. Her heart sank a little at the thought.

When the driver was settled behind the wheel, she leaned forward to give him her address.

"Mr. Bellemere already provided the destination, ma'am," he replied.

"Thank you." She sat back and caught the grim expression on Sam's face. "What's wrong?"

He ignored her. "Jake, have you left the car alone at all tonight?"

"No, sir," the driver said. "I gassed up after I dropped you off. When I received your message, I stuck close.

Didn't park until about an hour ago and no one has been near the car."

"Thank you." Sam turned the full force of his attention to her, irritation snapping in his eyes. "You can start explaining right here, right now."

"What do you mean?"

Sam's dark eyebrows arched as if her confusion baffled him. "Do I have to spell it out? The car is clean. It hasn't been left alone for anyone to tamper with."

"Tamper?" He was deliberately trying to scare her and he was succeeding.

"How often do they sweep your office for listening devices?"

She folded her arms and stared out the window. "Often enough," she said, refusing to take the bait.

"Why do they sweep for those devices?"

"Okay, point made. Stop being a jerk." She was too tired for any more diplomacy tonight. "I'm glad your limo isn't bugged. I'm sure your house isn't either."

"If we're lucky we'll catch them in the act when we arrive."

"You're being unreasonable. Wait. We?"

"It'll raise too many questions if the first time I show up to one of your events we don't go home together."

"You're overreacting." Her molars might crack from the strain. Thoroughly exhausted, she refused to give his paranoia more fuel.

"Jake, are we being followed?"

"Always a tough call on a Friday night in traffic."

Sam grunted. "Do what you can to find out."

"Sam, I'm tired," Madison said. "I want the peace and quiet of my apartment."

"You promised me answers about this whole marriage business."

"Isn't the morning soon enough?"

"No. I'd like to hear the whole story tonight."

"Hang on." She scooted closer to him and lowered her voice. "You still don't sleep?"

He pushed a button on the console in the ceiling and the privacy screen rose between them and the driver.

Suddenly the space was far too intimate and way too reminiscent of her silly teenage-girl prom night fantasy. The illusion she'd harbored of Sam walking into the dance and taking notice of her as a girl rather than a friend. In her illusion, he'd crossed the room and kissed her right there in front of everyone. Even back then she'd known it was an impossible dream. Sam was too shy for such a public display, but she'd dreamed it anyway, night after night. Now she was a woman and she had a better understanding of what to wish for and with whom.

"Madison." His hand was gentle and warm against her bare shoulder. "Just tell me the story."

"We've been married almost two years. July Fourth is our anniversary."

"How patriotic of us," he quipped.

She tilted her head. "It came down to available time off for me, time between projects for you." She managed to play it cool until the driver suddenly took a hard right. The force dumped her into Sam's strong embrace.

"What the—"

She tried to be grateful as he righted her before she could snuggle deeper into his embrace. "He's checking for a tail," Sam explained.

"Does this happen often?"

"Rush only hires the best. You'd be surprised how many people try to hassle us."

So maybe his paranoia had stronger roots than the trouble she'd dumped on him tonight. Maybe, with a little time, he'd understand her rash actions.

"Which is my real question," Sam pressed. "Why did you choose me?"

She brought her mind back to the issue, tried to deliver the facts in a linear, logical order. "I'm aware other cultures view single women differently, even when they're in the US," she said. "I hadn't worried much about it, but it soon became obvious I needed a polite excuse to rebuff advances. Wearing a wedding band is a common tactic, although it doesn't always stop the most persistent people." She rubbed the platinum setting on her finger with her thumb.

"What do you mean?"

She glanced up, catching a flash of anger in his brown gaze. "Possessive of a wife you just met?"

His short bark of laughter was cool, breaking the tension. "Apparently." He motioned for her to continue. "Creating a mythical husband is understandable."

"I based the myth on you." She moved her hand up and down. "Your looks, skills, all of it. Easier than creating a husband from scratch." She hoped he believed her. "I promise I never used your full name. I can't recall using your first name very often and never with anyone outside of my office."

"Why was I the foundation for your imaginary husband?"

She swallowed, too mortified to give him the truth. The car swerved again and this time Sam fell her way. His big palm landed with a delicious pressure on her thigh and she marveled that the silk didn't just evaporate under the heat.

He drew back quickly, the question lurking in his eyes.

"Because you were a friend I trusted." Because using him gave her fake husband more than an image and career, it gave him a personality. "As for tonight, the most expedient way to get you on the guest list was to own the lie and make it real. No one would question the clearance for my husband."

"Ah. Got it."

He didn't, not completely. If she was lucky, he'd never know the whole story of her ongoing infatuation with him. "Besides, you did owe me a favor."

"I'd say we flew right by even and you owe me now."

He was right and she felt terrible for it. "We don't have to keep up the ruse." She could manage things from here. "You saved the day blocking that hacker. Now you can go do your thing and I'll do mine. We don't have to play happy couple anymore."

"You're wrong about that." He drummed his fingertips on his knee.

She frowned at him. "Pardon me?" She knew the schedule and while there were several events where a date would be nice, his presence wasn't required. "I can go back to attending functions alone. It's not a big deal." After the past few hours she knew having Sam around would be the real problem because she let his presence distract her.

"I disagree. Now that I've been identified, there will be repercussions. Liu already assumes a relationship to me through you."

"He's lamenting the idea that his son is a loser who will shame the family," she said. "The topic tends to come up at every opportunity."

Sam gave her a look she remembered, the one that was part query and part disappointment in her answer. "Is the kid a loser?"

She preferred discussing a stranger to confessing her personal sins. "He's young, arrogant and entitled. That may or may not improve while he's in college."

Sam sighed, apparently satisfied. "The museum will need to stay on alert. They should also take stronger measures to shut out more hacks." He opened his mouth to say more, but the intercom beeped.

"Trouble," Jake reported.

"You know what to do," Sam replied. "Don't worry," he said to Madison.

"What trouble?" Madison twisted in her seat. The street behind them was crowded with headlights. "What does he know to do?"

Sam shrugged and she wanted to slap that smug expression off his face. "He drives a specific route we can tap into later for potential identification."

"Can he do that and then take me home?" she

pleaded. "I have a meeting first thing in the morning." She wanted to get out of these heels and into her pajamas before she wrote up her report on the evening.

"On a Saturday?"

"Really?" She leaned back. "That's rich, the perennial workaholic criticizing *my* schedule."

"What happened to your famous, unflappable composure?" He patted her knee. "You pulled off a marriage charade along with mostly false assurances that an irreplaceable treasure from China is secure without batting an eye. Sitting back while my driver evades a tail shouldn't be a big deal."

She couldn't tell what he expected of her. At this hour she didn't care. "Take me home. I'll be safe in my building."

"Fake or not, tonight you're safer with your husband," he said, catching her as the driver's next turn pitched her into him again.

She couldn't control her runaway imagination. In a flash she could clearly see life as Sam's wife. It would be bliss to come home after a long day and talk with him over a pepperoni pizza and a couple of beers. Never once in her fantasy had she seen a face other than his when she thought of a husband.

Preposterous. Impossible. Wishful thinking at its finest. The car bounced a little as the driver entered a parking garage with too much speed.

"Now we're clear," Sam said a moment before Jake confirmed the status. The limousine came to a halt and Sam pushed open the door, extending a hand to help her.

Resigned to the strange turn of events, she placed her hand in his. "Where are we?"

"My place."

She glanced around at what appeared to be an average concrete parking garage without the typical foul odors. Only five parking spaces were occupied, all of them with luxury vehicles. She recognized a sporty Porsche crossover in smoke gray and the sexy lines of a deep blue Lamborghini. She couldn't name the other three without taking a closer look. Wherever they were, the neighbors were apparently as wealthy as Sam.

Her feet ached from the high heels as he led her toward an elevator in the corner. "Sam, I really should go." If she slept without removing the heavy makeup on her face, she'd wake up looking like something from a bad horror movie. That would be mortifying and a certain end to their friendship, just in case lying about the marriage hadn't done that already. "I need—"

The elevator doors parted automatically at their approach and she glanced around for the motion sensor, forgetting her protest.

"Intrigued?" His lips twitched in a smirk. "What do you need, Madison?" he asked, pulling out his phone.

You. Thankfully, she bit back that absurd, knee-jerk response. "My apartment," she managed. "I'm sure your place is…" The elevator opened to a penthouse and the sparkling nighttime view of San Francisco stole her breath. "Oh, Sam." She couldn't stop herself from walking in, admiring everything in sight.

"You like it?"

It wasn't anything she imagined his home might be.

Not the casual mess that always surrounded his work space at school. Of course it wouldn't be like that. He was a man now, a lauded expert at the top of his industry. The position obviously paid well. The furniture had a lived-in feel, modern, clean lines without feeling too stark or glossy or new. Nothing in her fantasies had prepared her for this, for seeing him in this kind of space. She could happily snuggle into the corner of that big couch next to Sam and forget there was a world out there that needed them.

Exasperated with herself, she wondered if anything would smother the torch she'd carried for him all this time. He'd never given her the first signal that he thought of her in a romantic way. Unlike his business partner, Rush, there was never a whisper of Sam having any romantic ties. Maybe that was why her heart was so stubbornly locked on to him.

She forced her gaze away from the stunning view and faced him. "I need to go home." Staying here would be unbearable. He'd already commented on her lack of composure. "I need my space and my things."

"Let me guess?" He started typing into his phone. "Toothbrush and toothpaste. Do you still prefer that striped brand you used when we were kids?"

"Pardon me?" How did he know what brand of toothpaste she'd used in high school?

"My bathroom is surely lacking." He held out the phone to her. "Put in whatever you need and it will be here within the hour."

"No." It was closing in on one in the morning. She jerked her hands behind her back and clutched the handle of her briefcase. "No, thank you. Take me home, please."

His gaze narrowed and his brown eyes were calculating something as he studied her from head to toe. His thumbs flew over the surface of his phone and then he pocketed the device.

Before she could react to that, he'd slipped a hand around her elbow. "Take off your shoes."

"Take me home."

His jaw clenched, but his touch remained gentle. "I didn't blow your secret out of the water tonight, did I?"

"No." She tried to smile. "I appreciate that more than I can say."

"Thank me by listening for a minute. Your feet need a break from the shoes."

"You can't know that." How did he know that?

"Take them off," he said. "And follow me."

She gave in, stifling a whimper when the cool hardwood floors soothed the soles of her feet. He guided her toward the kitchen, pausing to pull out two bottles of water. He opened both and handed her one. Without a word, he continued on toward an office.

This was where he lived, she realized immediately. He enjoyed the front room, but here she saw signs of the Sam she remembered. The big corner desk with three monitors and an ergonomic keyboard was cluttered with files and books, spiral notebooks and pencils and countless small toys mixed in with various awards. His masculine scent drifted through the air.

One wall was all windows, the spectacular view currently muted by a sheer shade. In a corner was a tall, antique secretary desk, outfitted with a slim laptop, a pen and notebook and none of the clutter. A padded executive chair held a point of honor at the corner desk and a smaller version of the same chair was positioned in front of the antique.

He sat down at the corner desk and brought his computer to life. "I assume you have your own computer, but I'd rather you used the laptop over there. You can start your report while we wait for the delivery to arrive."

She barely remembered mentioning the report. Her firm boundaries crumbled with every minute she spent with him. "Sam, it's late and you're losing me." Whatever his mind had moved on to, she needed more of an explanation.

"I doubt that," he said absently. "You want to go home. I understand." He stood up and took the briefcase from her hand. "Drink your water. In a few minutes you'll see why going home is a bad idea."

She started for the opposite chair because her feet were tired, stopping short when several images popped up on his monitors. Her grip tightened on the pebbled leather of the chair's headrest as she recognized what he'd done. "You had Jake drive by a string of traffic cams when you thought we were followed."

"That's right. Rush and I worked up the protocol when we realized we couldn't rely on blind luck all the time. We were being followed," he added.

She ignored that, more concerned about the next step. "The transportation or police departments don't mind you hacking in for a look?"

"They never caught me when I did, but now I don't have to."

She didn't ask, just in case knowing the details turned her into an accomplice. She drank her water while he used various views, zooming in on the driver and passenger in the dark sedan that had tailed the limo unerringly from the museum until Jake lost them long enough to duck into the building. "Those two are part of the security force at the Vietnamese consulate. Why would they follow us?"

That brought the full weight of Sam's attention back to her. "Vietnam? You're sure?"

She nodded. "In case you haven't kept up, things are as dicey as ever between China and Vietnam. I've been working on keeping things cordial all year long."

"You didn't introduce me to any Vietnamese diplomats tonight," Sam said.

"They weren't invited to the private viewing of the exhibit. Tonight was China and America only." Had someone spilled her marriage news to someone in the Vietnamese consulate? Even if that had happened, it didn't explain being followed. "I don't understand this."

"Why work so hard to stick with us?"

She knew his query was rhetorical. Good thing, since she didn't have an answer.

"What's your address?" He tugged his tie loose and popped open the top two buttons of his shirt while he waited for her reply.

She answered, surprised by the polite question when she knew he could look it up online in seconds. It didn't take long before he'd pulled up views of street corners.

He took his time while she watched over his shoulder as he searched for the car that had tailed them. "You think they're waiting for me to come home?"

"Time will tell."

At this hour speculation wouldn't get them anywhere. Even without the shoes, her feet were starting to cramp. Making a note in her phone so she wouldn't forget to bring up this detail at tomorrow's meeting, she decided that home or not, her mind and body needed rest. "Do you have a guest room?"

"Yes." Standing, he shrugged out of his tuxedo coat and folded it over the chair in front of the antique desk. "This way."

They walked through the central room, past the floor-to-ceiling windows and glorious view to the opposite side of the condo. There were two bedrooms connected by a luxurious bathroom. On the counter an array of skin care and bath products had been set out.

"Thanks," she said. It was a weak substitute for the miles of gratitude she wanted to show him. "I don't want to know how you managed this." She hadn't heard a delivery arrive or anyone moving through the condo. It was a little freaky.

"I've developed some connections through the years. You'll find pajamas and casual clothes on the bed. Hopefully something will fit. I had to guess your size." His gaze swept over her once more and her body responded with a flash of heat. "What time do you need to be at the office?"

"Weekend meetings start at ten." She nearly whined when she noticed it was just past two.

He nodded and his eyebrows came together in that familiar way whenever he crunched numbers. "That gives me some time to work. I'll make arrangements for breakfast and factor in a stop at your place."

"Great." She couldn't muster another protest tonight. It would only fall on deaf ears anyway. "Good night, Sam." She wiggled her fingers and he left the bathroom, shutting the door on his way out. Turning to the supplies on the counter, she removed her makeup, pampered her skin and brushed her teeth, all the while wrestling with the concept of anyone having cause to follow her.

Ready for bed, she cracked the door a bit and confirmed she was alone. On the queen-size bed she found a lavender camisole, matching shorts and an oversize sleep shirt in a deeper hue. Like the items in the bathroom, everything here was brand-new. What kind of staff or assistant did he have that he could summon up toiletries and clothing with a text message in the middle of the night? Taking the tags off the sleep shirt, she stripped off her dress and lingerie. The soft cotton fabric was bliss against her skin. Pulling back the covers, she smoothed a hand over the finest sheets, wondering if Sam had chosen them or left the decision to a decorator.

Unlike most nights when she grappled with the events of the day and the uncertainties of tomorrow, Madison fell asleep within moments of her head touching the pillow.

Chapter Four

Back on what he considered his side of the condo, Sam mentally turned and flipped the various pieces of the puzzle that made up Madison Goode. If anyone had told him a woman like her would use him as a fake husband, he'd call them crazy. He had it on good authority that no woman in her right mind wanted to waste a lifetime with a man as introverted, self-involved and work-centric as Sam. He supposed he understood her reasoning for calling him *husband* about as much as she understood his extensive resources and willingness to use them for her.

Did that give them common ground or was it an insurmountable divide? "Doesn't matter," he reminded himself aloud. He'd answered the call of a *friend* and done what he could to help her. End of story.

Aside from the challenges posed by the hacker, the small, personal moments of the evening replayed in his mind as he changed clothes in his bedroom. Her small touches, the knowing looks. It had been for show, he knew that. Still, the straight, glossy hair and the shape of her legs in that killer dress had left a lasting impression. For the rest of his days, he would remember her floral perfume weaving around them as they danced.

Exasperated with his foolishness, he dumped the tuxedo in the bag for the dry cleaner and pulled on comfortable shorts and a T-shirt sporting the logo of the gym where he boxed a few times each week. He removed his contacts and slipped his glasses into place. He wasn't an evening-wear kind of man. Although he could pull it off once a year as required, he was far more content at home like this, with the company of his computers.

He sat down at his desk and started researching the people he'd met tonight. How did Madison know he didn't sleep well or often? He couldn't recall making that confession to her when they were kids. Maybe she'd picked it up from an interview, except he wasn't prone to sharing such personal details with reporters.

Pushing that distraction to the back of his mind, along with the persistent awareness that an interesting, beautiful woman was sleeping in his guest room, he turned his mind to the issues that had dragged him into her world and opened windows for several searches.

He ran a search on the car that tailed them from the museum and confirmed the registration information linked back to the Vietnamese consulate. Identifying the men wasn't his priority. Madison's recognition was enough for his needs. He printed out the information so she could take it to her morning meeting.

Setting a timer, he limited himself to another hour of research before he called it a night. He'd planned to work out an insulating layer of protection for the museum at the Gray Box offices, but leaving her here alone didn't sound like the right decision for a husband to make.

Husband. The weight and responsibility of the word settled across his shoulders, even though she was only a casual friend in truth.

He understood her explanations, especially after seeing her in action this evening. He hadn't missed the sideways looks aimed at both of them amid all the polite smiles and kind words. He fisted his hand around the pen he held, remembering the way some of the reception attendees had ogled Madison. He tossed the pen down. Good grief, he'd been a *fake* husband for a few hours and he was already possessive. He supposed it was a design flaw in his brain, reading too much into one encounter and not picking up enough of the right cues in another.

Sam tugged off his glasses and pressed his fingers to his eyes, willing himself back on track. If he wasted any more time dwelling on Madison's cover story, he'd never get any sleep. He needed to be on his toes tomorrow at the office. Though he was tempted to share the news of his "marriage" with Rush in an email or text message, his best friend deserved better.

Replacing his glasses, he picked up the pen and resumed his research into the history—recent and old— between the United States, China and Vietnam. There had to be a better motive than mere mischief to explain the hacker's timing and his choice of targets. With every layer Sam peeled back, he marveled at Madison's patience. The politics and cultural differences overwhelmed him. It was like trying to use an ever-changing set of rules to sort and read the unspoken communication among strangers at a party. Given a choice, Sam would always prefer the cut and dried logic of computers over people.

When his timer went off, he made a few notes, backed up his work on a private server and then checked the security feeds in and around his building. The team from the Vietnamese consulate had double parked across the street from the building's main garage entrance. "Nice work, guys," he muttered to the screen. His address wasn't a secret, but he didn't advertise it either.

Just over three years ago, Rush had forced him to spend more time away from the office, supposedly for his mental health. Unwilling to deal with nosy neighbors or community associations, Sam had found a building he could remodel and design to his strict, personal privacy standards. He had room here for his growing car collection as well as an entire floor where he could play with computer builds, operating systems and virus solutions, as well as develop and test new ideas.

His decision had made the city happy, Rush happy and, most of the time, himself happy. Tonight wasn't one of those times.

For several minutes Sam watched the men in the car, debating between reporting the bad parking and sending down a couple of coffees. Yawning, he decided it wasn't time to rattle the saber. No one without a code could get into his building without tripping at least one electronic or physical alarm. Satisfied they were isolated and safe, he dimmed the lights in his office and retreated to his bedroom.

Saturday, June 11, 6:20 a.m.

SAM WOKE THREE hours later, ten minutes before his alarm sounded, with an idea for covering the gap in the museum security blasting through his brain. He went to his office, wrote it out and did a quick test. Pleased, he sent it to Rush for review.

By half past seven he'd showered and shaved and had the coffee brewing. The team in the car had gone and Sam couldn't identify any replacements. Maybe they'd given up or found answers elsewhere. So far he hadn't heard a peep from the guest room. The security system would have alerted him if she'd left. He should have confirmed the schedule for today. Then he wouldn't be standing here wondering how much time she needed to prep for her meeting.

He wished he knew how she took her coffee. When they were in school, she'd always had a Diet Coke nearby. Not an item he stocked. At their reunion, he'd seen her with a mimosa at brunch and a cosmopolitan in the evening. Maybe she didn't drink coffee at all. Rather than make another crazy list for a delivery that covered all bases, he decided to wait and ask her first.

Filling a tall mug with piping hot coffee, black as sin, he called himself out on going overboard to impress her last night. Regardless of her reasons or intentions, she'd outed them as married and he'd been compelled to put the right foundation under the illusion. Once people put his face with her ruse, they would have to follow through with the charade as a couple until they could pin down the hacker and the spotlight moved on to someone else. He'd tried to point out that fact last night and she'd avoided the topic. He couldn't give her that kind of leeway today. They had to have a plan in place before either of them left the building again.

The signal chimed that the paper had been delivered downstairs. Although he subscribed to the online edition as well, he still liked the feel of the newspaper in his hands first thing in the morning on the weekends. He checked the security camera views from the drop-down monitor in the kitchen, then took the elevator down to the lobby to pick up the paper.

When he returned, Madison was waiting for him in the kitchen, her gaze shifting from the monitor to the elevator door. "Nice setup," she said.

"Thanks. I like it." She looked refreshed and relaxed in a casual white T-shirt and jeans, yet somehow more vulnerable without any makeup and her hair down. "Good morning."

"Is it?" She rubbed her toes up and down the calf of her opposite leg. "I've been a terrible imposition." She flicked her fingers at the monitor. "Are we still friends?"

"Yes." His reply was instant and accurate, he decided. "Absolutely." He smiled at her. "Have some coffee." He'd meant it as a question and it sounded as if he were barking orders. "Do you drink coffee?"

Her smile brightened. "Yes, absolutely," she echoed.

Changing the monitor to a local news station, he muted the sound and then handed her a mug. "I figure we have a few minutes to get our story straight before you need to dress for your meeting."

He made a mental note as she poured coffee into a mug and added a heaping spoonful of sugar. She raised the cup, breathed in the aroma and took the first sip gingerly, her eyes closed.

The sight might as well have been a sneaky left jab to the jaw. His muscles went slack for a second and then everything felt too tight as he fought for balance. He pulled out the nearest counter stool and sat down, dropping the paper onto the cool surface of the marble counter.

Her eyes popped open, her gaze locking with his. "Why don't I make breakfast?"

"I'd planned to handle that." He just needed a minute, maybe an hour, to get a grip and some perspective on what was becoming an all-too-domestic morning.

"Let me," she said. "It's the least I can do."

He chose not to argue. "Make yourself at home."

She did, pulling ingredients from the refrigerator and with his cues finding the equipment she needed for whatever she had in mind. He reviewed the headlines on the front page and tried to find the best words to broach the topics of her trouble and the ideas brewing in his head for moving forward.

"I have a security upgrade almost ready for the museum. After Rush reviews it, you and I can offer it to them at least as a trial for the duration of the exhibit on loan from China."

She shot him a look over the top of his paper. "You didn't sleep," she accused.

He'd expected a warmer reply, maybe even a thank-you. "I did too." He turned the page and flattened the paper. "How do you know about my sleep habits?"

"You mean your habit of *not* sleeping?" Her golden eyebrows puckered and smoothed out again as she smiled. "You told me once during a tutoring session." She turned back to tend to whatever she had going in the skillet. "I thought you remembered everything."

"Not exactly," he admitted, trying to recall the conversation from so many years ago and coming up blank. "What was I helping you with that day?"

"It was a test prep day," she said with a sassy grin on those natural, peachy lips. "You dozed off and on while I practiced the timed sections of Mr. Denning's midterm torture session."

Based on her expression, she seemed to remember it fondly. "Denning wasn't that bad."

She snorted. "You were his *star*. I routinely brought down the class average."

Sam grunted and picked up the next section of the paper. When she announced the two-minute warning, he set the paper aside, moved around to her side of the counter and pulled out plates, utensils and napkins for them.

He was pouring juice into glasses as she carried the skillet filled with a mouthwatering mix of shredded potatoes, bacon, cheese, peppers and eggs to the plates. Her startled cry brought him around, too late to save her from the hot skillet that landed on her foot or the plate that broke into a million sharp pieces against the slate floor.

"Sam," she gasped, hopping on one foot and pointing at the monitor. "Volume."

Whatever had set her off could wait. He scooped her up and swiveled around. Setting her on the counter near the sink, he ran cold water over her burned foot.

She hissed at the shock. "Hit the volume."

"In a minute."

She swore under her breath. At him, the mess, or the pain of the burn, he wasn't sure. He chuckled. "Is that proper language for a liaison?"

"You might be surprised," she replied. She peered past him at the mess. "Crap. I'm sorry."

He didn't care. Most days, breakfast was as overrated as sleep in his schedule. "You're more important than a little mess."

She pushed her hair back over her shoulder. "We have bigger problems anyway."

"What are you talking about?"

She jerked her chin toward the monitor and tried to slide away from him. "I need my phone. My boss is probably already calling me."

With one hand at her waist and the other just above her ankle, he kept her in place. "I'll get it. Stay here until this burn cools off."

"It's fine, Sam."

He held her with a bit more force when she tried to squirm again. It was impossible not to notice the shape of her under his palms. Only an idiot wouldn't appreciate it and Sam was frequently praised for his brilliance. "I'll give you the phone if you promise to stay put."

She agreed, though the corners of her mouth turned down into a frown. "You're bossy."

"You should've remembered that too." He relaxed when she agreed with him.

He handed her the cell phone and dealt with the mess on the floor while she made her call, checked her messages and then started in on a text or an email.

"I'm sorry," she said again. "I should be doing that."

"It's no big deal." He dumped a full dustpan into the trash and then checked her burn again. Turning off the water, he patted her foot dry with a towel and wrapped some ice in another towel. "Sit still and keep that in place for a few more minutes."

"It's better, I swear."

"What set you off?" he asked, going back to cleaning the floor.

"There were news vans outside my apartment building. The ticker mentioned a disturbance reported by residents on my floor."

"Could be anything," he pointed out. "You have lots of neighbors."

She was absorbed with her phone, likely trying to find out more through social media. "Sam, look."

He dumped the last of the broken plate and ruined food into the trash. With her foot out of the sink, he ran water into the skillet to let it soak.

Drying his hands, he took her phone and flipped through the pictures. Two policemen blocked a doorway and someone had caught an angle that showed a search going on inside. "That's your place?" he asked, half-afraid he knew the answer.

When she didn't reply, he glanced up to find her face had paled. "Why would a disturbance lead them to search my apartment?" she wondered aloud.

He tilted her phone so she could see it. "That's Spalding, right?"

She nodded, her soft green eyes full of worry. "I have to get over there."

"Not yet and not alone," he said.

"Sam, I have to change clothes before my meeting. I'm sure they'll want a statement."

"Probably. What can you tell them? Better to go in armed with information," he said. "Do you have a security system?"

She tilted her head. "Kind of. It's a passive nanny-cam setup."

"It's a start."

She checked her phone again, then turned it to him to show him the status on the app she used. "The cameras have been disconnected, but I have the feed linked to a Gray Box. I just need to log in to that or sync the apps."

"There's some good news. Log in is better," he said. He could get a better timeline and idea of the problem by accessing her building security. There was a decent chance he could manage that from his home office. If not, he could definitely do it on-site. "I doubt Spalding would let you in there right now."

Her hands fisted at her sides. "It's my place."

At the moment it appeared to be the FBI's place. He wisely kept the opinion to himself. "Whatever happened overnight, you have a rock-solid alibi with me. Your husband," he added to drive the point home.

She rolled her eyes to the ceiling.

"You also have our driver as well as an entire series of traffic-cam confirmation of our whereabouts between the museum and here."

"Right." She pulled her hair up and back, resting the bundle and her hands on top of her head. "I just need to think."

"We need information," he said. He plucked her from the counter and carried her out of the kitchen, her hair cascading over his arm in a wash of lemon-scented silk.

"I'm not an invalid, you know."

He knew. "There could be bits of glass on the floor. Your feet have been through enough."

"Fine." When she was steady on her feet, he refilled their coffee mugs and added sugar to hers.

She arched an eyebrow. "Ever the quick study."

"May good habits never change." His gut told him she needed a fast problem-solver as well as the illusion of a husband to unravel this mess.

His system chirped an alert at the street level and he groaned when he recognized the car. The camera showed Rush behind the wheel and Lucy in the passenger's seat. He glanced at the clock. "Is your meeting mandatory?"

"Yes."

"Call your boss again." He jerked a thumb to the monitor. "You're going to be late."

He should have sent that heads-up text about the marriage charade after all. Sam knew the coming encoun-

ter was inevitable; he only wished they could have had
the discussion man to man first rather than as couples.
It was shaping up to be a long day.

Chapter Five

Despite her lack of professional attire, Madison wrapped herself in her calm, all-business, State Department attitude as soon as the elevator doors parted. Rush Grayson and his new wife, Lucy, stepped into the condo in a cloud of happy good-morning greetings. Their gazes skipped over Sam and unerringly locked on to her. This might have been a planned breakfast Sam forgot, though Madison didn't believe it. The overbright smiles didn't mask the underlying concern. She felt like a bug under a microscope.

A bug wearing clothing that wasn't even hers, she thought, fighting a bout of nerves. She laced her fingers at her waist, subtly covering the wedding set she forgot to take off last night.

Rush, in a red polo shirt, khaki shorts and deck shoes, carried a large picnic basket. Beside him, Lucy beamed. She wore a strappy, pale green sundress and had a straw tote looped over her shoulder. Her summery sandals coordinated with the tote and she practically glowed with contentment. Madison stifled the reactive spike of envy for the shoes and the couple.

They might be dressed as if they'd stopped in on their way to the bay for a day of sailing, or whatever billionaires did on Saturday mornings, but Madison knew they'd popped in unannounced to protect their friend. How had they heard about last night? Braced for the worst, she knew diplomacy would be the word of the hour when explaining her sudden presence in their friend's life.

When the basket and tote were set aside on the countertop, Sam startled her by drawing her to his side for introductions. He quietly emphasized Madison's role in getting Rush and Lucy out of the jam in France just before Christmas. Instantly, the tight smiles relaxed into relief and courteous handshakes turned to warm hugs. She took it all in stride, politely giving Rush and Lucy her full attention when she wanted to check her phone for missed calls, emails and news updates.

"Well, we brought champagne," Lucy declared with another warm smile. "And orange juice in case you were out, Sam."

"Champagne?" He frowned in confusion, his gaze darting from Lucy to Rush. Then he grinned, his dark eyebrows arching high. "You're pregnant?"

"No," Lucy replied, exchanging a confused glance with her husband. "We wanted to toast your marriage." She shot a look at Madison's left hand and the wedding rings still on it.

"Since we weren't invited to the ceremony," Rush added pointedly.

Madison had opened her mouth to tell them the truth when Sam spoke up. "I was planning to stop at the office later today and fill you in." He slid his arm around her waist. "We've kept it quiet for some time now."

"Really?" Rush arched an eyebrow. A wealth of doubt dripped from the single word. "Why would you do that?"

"It's complicated," Sam hedged.

Madison shifted enough to catch his attention. Why was he duping his friends? "How did you hear the news?"

Lucy, unloading the tote, held up the society page from the morning paper. "We brought you an extra copy, in case you wanted to frame it or something."

Madison wanted a hole to open up and swallow her as she stared at the pictures under the headline: Is Another San Francisco Most Eligible Bachelor Off the Market?

The collage of incriminating photos strung together with speculation and clever quips took up half the page. Her stomach churned with guilt. Sam would hate this kind of exposure. There was a shot of him under the bright lights of a hotel leaving the event alone and a picture of him walking up the block to the museum. The photographers had caught shots of them dancing at the gala and a grainy image of them in the museum hallway, her finger to his lips. How had they caught that? The article finished with a picture of the final toast Mr. Liu had offered, along with the purpose for it. Oh, she should have seen this coming. No photographer would turn down a chance to broadcast billionaire Sam Bellemere turning up married. This was her fault.

"You're very photogenic," Sam noted, giving her waist a friendly squeeze.

"Tell them," she murmured through clenched teeth. The smile he gave her, packed with shared secrets, set something aflame deep in her belly.

"Let's save the champagne for later." Sam set out fresh mugs and poured coffee for each of them. "Did you bring food?" he asked, eyeing the basket. "We had a small breakfast mishap."

"We brought half a dozen maple glazed bacon doughnuts from the kiosk near the boathouse," Lucy said. "Along with half a dozen of the chocolate rose they had today." Rush took the bags of doughnuts to the low coffee table between the sofas flanking the stunning view and Lucy brought a stack of paper plates and napkins.

With her coffee cup in hand, Madison tucked one foot under her and curled into the corner of the couch. If Sam understood her signal to distance himself from her, he was blatantly ignoring it, sinking into the cushion next to her.

Wasting no time, she launched into the explanation of why she'd listed their friend as her husband on the guest list last night. "I should have found another solution. You all have my apologies."

"I'm not surprised the staff wasn't up to a hacker, but I'd expect better from the FBI," Rush said with a frown, ignoring the husband detail entirely. "The government keeps telling us we're not needed when Gray Box bids on contracts."

Lucy patted his knee and spoke to Madison. "The wedding set is lovely. Do you always wear it?"

"She does," Sam answered. "Helps her ward off the unwanted advances. You should see the jerks that come to these things," he added for Rush.

"I can imagine," Lucy said with a sympathetic glance.

"It had never been necessary to use more than a first name with my coworkers," Madison explained. "Until last night, no one ever knew the Sam I mention was Sam Bellemere." It sounded more ridiculous with every telling. "I never expected Sam to be forced into the spotlight this way."

He rolled his shoulders and took a sip of coffee. "I owed you."

"We all owe you, Madison," Rush agreed.

"Taking care of the hacker more than covered any perceived debt." She hated the formality in her voice. "I know I overstepped and put you in a bad spot," she said to Sam.

"It might be too soon for past tense. I'm not so sure we've taken care of him." Sam leaned forward, bracing his elbows on his knees. "Did you look at what I sent over this morning?"

Rush nodded. "I figured we could discuss it here once we sorted out your marital status."

"Married." Sam's gaze caught hers and held. Then he winked at her. "We tied the knot in Las Vegas, on July Fourth almost two years ago. I forced it into the public records last night while I was doing research."

"You hacked the State of Nevada?" Rush demanded.

"Only one database," Sam confirmed. "No biggie."

Rush swore and Madison jumped to her feet and Lucy sat back, laughing merrily at all of them. "What did you expect him to do?" she asked her husband. When Rush merely swore again, she put the question to Madison.

"I, *um*. I don't know." What had she expected? "Definitely not that." She stared down at Sam. "You were supposed to be done with the illegal access stunts." At his shrug, she planted her hands on her hips.

"Rewind a minute," Rush said, settling back to the sofa. "What did you mean about too soon for past tense?"

"The more I dig, the more I think last night's hacker is up to more than he seems." Sam patted the cushion beside him. "Sit down, Maddie. We can fight over whether or not I'm reformed later. I need you back in full diplomat mode right now."

Maddie? He'd made it sound like an endearment. She shook her head as she resumed her seat, pressing herself back into the corner of the couch to do as he asked. "I'm listening."

"The hacker clogged up a chat room with threats against the exhibit and a few people at the Chinese consulate," he explained to Rush and Lucy. "Petty stuff, easy to see through unless you're looking at it with FBI-colored glasses." Sam gulped down more coffee. "And messing with the exhibit was nothing more than showing off his access to the systems."

"You think he'll strike there again?" Lucy asked.

"If the museum installs what I worked up, the people

and exhibits will be fine. The tracking program will eventually expose his location, which helps everyone in the long run."

"What aren't you saying?" Madison asked.

Again, Sam addressed Rush. "We were tailed back here by two men Madison recognized from the Vietnamese consulate. Today, her apartment is breaking news while the FBI conducts a search after a disturbance last night. The reasoning isn't clear yet." He reached over and covered her knee with his hand. "I think you're being used and your apartment is one piece in an elaborate mousetrap that was sprung last night. Exposing our secret marriage, coming here, may have saved your life. The hacker had every reason to think you'd go home to your apartment after the event."

The implication shocked her. He had to be exaggerating the threat, but she didn't want to say so in front of his friends. The one thing she understood was the need for clear facts and more of them. "No one has any reason to kill me."

"The Vietnamese security team followed *us*," Sam repeated, as if she needed the reminder. "They knew you were here with me all night, since they staked out the building until dawn."

Madison clutched her coffee cup in both hands. "I thought your driver lost them."

"It's not *impossible* to find out where I live, just challenging," he said. "I certainly wasn't the only one with a busy cell phone last night." He jerked a thumb back to the newspaper on the counter. "The proof is how fast news of our marriage hit the paper. We need to keep up the appearances of wedded bliss for your safety."

Last week, spending time with Sam would have been a dream coming true. She knew acting this out as husband and wife would strain their friendship. When she sent out his email Christmas card this year, he'd probably delete it unread. This could even be the year he didn't send her a card in return. The thoughts weighed heavily on her mind as she searched for a solution that would give him a graceful exit from this mess.

"You think the hacker is from China?" Rush asked Sam.

"That can't be," Madison interjected. "No one from China would have risked harming the white jade cup, not even to make a point."

"A rival, then," Rush suggested. "Is someone trying to make Madison a scapegoat or something?"

"In light of the search at her apartment, I think we have to consider that possibility," Sam said. "Whatever is going on," he continued, turning to her, "we need to get ahead of this before the hacker drops the anvil on your head."

"What do you mean?" She heard the tremor in her voice and ordered herself to stay calm.

"I admit it's not much more than guesswork right now," Sam began. "You're surrounded by some serious problem-solvers. Together the four of us are better than any one of us alone. Can you explain how you're familiar with the hacker who struck last night?"

"Familiar is overstating it," she said, resigned and frustrated. "There have been several small computer glitches and hack attempts at the office in the past six months." At Sam's hard look, she tallied them. "Five. There have been five small attacks. The first one came on the Vietnamese New Year when a spam virus ripped through our email system. Nothing sensitive was compromised, just pesky little annoyances. Aside from that, our cyber security team deals with the usual attempts to break down the firewall. Naturally our office is very careful about what devices we use, the classified statuses and how it's all backed up."

"Understandable," Rush said.

Sam was frowning. "Have you told anyone at your office you recognized the group hacking the chat room last night?"

She sipped her coffee, letting the liquid soothe her throat. "I had to treat the threat as credible," Madison said. "When we compared screenshots from the chat room to the previous emails and compared the vocabulary, I knew the personal threats were bogus."

"How?" Rush and Sam asked in perfect unison.

"I picked up a few things when he was my tutor." She tipped her head toward Sam. "In the screenshot, I saw one line of code that repeated and called Sam in rather than call off the gala."

"That sounds like a big risk," Rush said.

Madison set her coffee on the table and sat back again, folding her hands in her lap. "It was easier to make that call knowing the extent and professionalism of the security team on-site. I've been in constant contact with the museum staff while they prepared for the exhibit. None of the security cameras inside or out showed signs of tampering. It seemed to me that theft wasn't the goal, embarrassment was. I quickly determined we could and should proceed."

On the table, her cell phone rang. "My boss," Madison said. "He'll be furious I'm late." She excused herself to the guest room to answer the call.

Her boss, Charles Vaughn, replied to her immediate apology with a whisper. "Where are you?"

Considering Sam's speculation, she reworded her answer. "I'm at my husband's condo. Didn't you get my message?"

"No. Where is your laptop?"

"Here with me."

"That's a plus. Don't turn it on." Charles sighed heavily. "They all have GPS tags and I need you to lie low for a while. The reason Special Agent Spalding searched your apartment was that he received an anonymous tip that you've taken payoffs to influence the players in the South China Sea."

First horror and then outrage funneled through her veins. "That's absurd," she managed through gritted teeth. Even if she had that kind of influence, she wouldn't risk her career and reputation by selling out.

"I know. Spalding won't give me any details. Legal is working on it. They advise you to avoid any publicity or public outings for now."

"You're telling me to hide."

"Yes," her boss said. "Having a billionaire husband is your best defense against the presented motive right now. Do not access any office files or connect to our network."

"I'm innocent," Madison protested. She wanted to deal with the trouble head-on. "Spalding knows me. He must have doubts about this tip."

"He wouldn't move on unsubstantiated rumor," Charles said.

Her boss was right. She knew Spalding's reputation. The tip must have given the FBI something solid for them to leap into action so quickly. A chill swept over her skin. "Who does the tipster claim paid me off?"

"Spalding hasn't shared that with me. If it looks credible, he has to follow all the steps," Charles reminded her. "You know how this goes. Take some of that vacation time you've built up. Let your husband take you to Hawaii and have a real honeymoon."

She snorted. They both knew leaving town for something as simple as a day trip to Monterey would make her look guilty. "If I do that now, it's as good as a confession."

"Help me out here," he insisted. "Protect yourself. The apartment search on the news is trouble enough. Once the reasons for the move come out, if you're in the office, the consulates will be in an uproar."

Right again. Still, she fought against the unfairness of it all. "I didn't do anything wrong."

"I know. I'll have Legal contact you through your husband," he said. "It's the best way to keep you off the radar."

She cringed at that. "Yes, sir."

When the call ended, she stared at her cell phone long after the screen faded to black. So much for dodging the anvil Sam mentioned. She was off the radar all right. In Sam's private fortress, her only possessions were rumpled eveningwear, her phone and a laptop she couldn't open without the risk of serious repercussions.

Knowing how Sam valued his privacy, she hated trampling all over it. She glanced at the red mark on her foot. Under the burn a bruise was swelling, a fraction of what it might be without his first aid. She'd screwed up breakfast, the one nice thing she'd tried to do for him.

Worse, if he kept being so understanding about her intrusion, if he kept touching her and caring for her, she might explode from pent-up desire. She dropped her phone to the bed and went to the bathroom to splash her face with cool water.

He was too decent for his own good. Far too decent for her after the predicament her lies had created. Good grief, he'd nearly lied to his best friends about the fake marriage she'd concocted. If there had been a time in her life when she'd been more upset with herself, she couldn't remember it now.

At the knock on the door, she turned to see Lucy smiling at her. "The guys have switched to a geek language I don't want to understand. I told them I'd check on you. Are you okay?"

"I didn't mean for this to get out of hand." Tears of frustration clogged her throat. "It was lazy of me to call him my husband when a little extra legwork and a few calls would've gotten him into the reception."

Lucy walked over and handed her a tissue from the box on the counter. "There are times when we're forced to do things in ways that aren't comfortable." She patted Madison's shoulder. "Was your boss terribly upset?"

Madison frowned at her reflection as she blotted her eyes and nose. "Sam's right that someone is targeting me. Rather than go in to the office and discuss it, I'm to stay off the radar." She snorted a sardonic laugh. "I want to fight and my boss suggested taking a honeymoon. I promise you, Lucy, if I could get out of Sam's life this instant I would." She turned her back on her blotchy reflection. "I'll find another option and let him have his privacy back."

Lucy smiled gently. "I hope that's not true." She picked up the full-size box of makeup remover towelettes. "Do you like these?"

"They worked really well last night," Madison admitted. "Why?"

"I've never seen this bathroom stocked beyond hand soap. My guess is a woman planning to invade a billionaire would have packed travel sizes of her favorite things."

"It wasn't my idea," Madison said quickly. "Sam insisted I stay here. He wouldn't let me go home after we were followed. Somehow he managed to get all of this delivered in the middle of the night. Clothes too. Come look."

She showed Lucy the pile of clothing she'd moved from the bed to the chair so she could sleep. The memory, along with the illogical upheaval of the last eighteen hours, brought a burst of laugher out of her. "Does he keep a personal shopper on retainer?"

"Yes." Lucy chuckled at Madison's shock. "It began as a business investment. You should ask him about it sometime."

A personal shopper on retainer. The concept wasn't new; it was the twenty-four-hour access and instant delivery that boggled Madison's mind. She had no intention of prodding Sam about his investments.

"Sam enjoys spoiling his friends," Lucy said, shaking her head at the obvious overkill.

"In my experience he enjoys extending his generosity from a distance," Madison said. "I'll think of another solution," she said again. "You don't have to worry about me abusing his hospitality."

"Hmm." Lucy wandered over to the bedroom window. "Do you think that's why we came over? To protect him?"

"Didn't you?"

"We were concerned," Lucy confessed. "Sam is so shy and the paper didn't mention his reason for being at the museum reception." She sank onto the window seat and pleated the flowing fabric of her dress between her fingers. "I think you'd offend him if you bailed out now."

Madison flopped back on the bed and stared at the ceiling. Lucy was right. Sam had gone the extra mile for her, from defeating the hacker at the exhibit to making sure the record of their marriage held up. Rush and Lucy stopping by might have caught him off guard, but Sam, true to his nature, had anticipated the potential fallout of her lie.

"I don't handle 'helpless' well," Madison admitted.

"Want my advice?" Lucy asked.

"Sure." She didn't move.

"I say we hand over any electronic devices to Sam

and Rush and go have a girls' day. I think I should get to know the woman who is effectively my sister-in-law."

"Fake sister-in-law," Madison clarified, sitting up to better study Lucy.

"You're not saying the society section is wrong, are you?" Lucy's dark eyebrows arched in comic horror. "Come on, sis. Today is a day to exert some feminine power. Nothing says crisis management like a girls' day."

Madison offered logic, the only argument she had left. "Girls' day doesn't sound like an off-the-radar event."

"Have a little faith." Lucy grinned. "Are you in?"

At Madison's agreement, Lucy pulled out her phone. She sent several messages and then beamed at Madison. "Let's go run it by the tech twins."

Madison found herself up against an immovable force in Lucy. She carried her briefcase back to Sam's office and let Lucy deliver the plan to the men. She was more than a little awestruck as Lucy conquered each argument. To her surprise, Lucy already had confirmation from a massage therapist and an aesthetician that they would be at the Grayson boathouse by noon.

"Come on. You know the security setup. We'll be safe inside all day," Lucy promised for the third or fourth time. "Not anywhere in public view." She swatted away another protest from Sam as confirmation for lunch came in from a restaurant. "Shall I schedule dinner at our place?" she asked with an overdose of sweet innocence. "Or at the office?"

"Office," Sam said, seizing on the option. "We'll

head that way in my car within an hour. That way, if the FBI or anyone else is watching this building it should throw them off."

"I doubt they can get a warrant for this building, but we know there's no cause to search the offices," Rush added. "Excellent plan," he said to his wife.

"I do have them once in a while," she replied with a grin, leaning into him for a quick kiss.

The flirty, relaxed manner went against everything she'd heard about Sam's business partner. Oh, he had a reputation as a playboy—before Lucy. The obvious contentment and easy happiness between them was something the press and paparazzi never adequately captured.

"Are you sure it's safe to open my laptop at all?" Madison didn't want to risk her problems creating a blowback on Sam or Gray Box. "It has a GPS chip."

"Let them worry about that," Lucy replied before Sam could open his mouth. "We need to get moving." She tugged Madison out of Sam's office and blew Rush a kiss. "Bye, love."

He came out of his chair at lightning speed and pulled her into his arms for a proper farewell kiss that left Madison blushing. Feeling Sam's gaze on her, she studiously avoided eye contact.

"Stay out of trouble," Rush said. "Both of you."

With only her driver's license, her State Department ID and a lip gloss in the beaded clutch she'd carried last night, Madison didn't have enough technology to get into any trouble.

Sam was scowling at her anyway. "Hang on."

Her heart gave a hopeful zing that he might kiss her. Instead he walked right by her to the coat closet tucked into the corner near the elevator. "Here." He handed Madison a zippered hoodie and a Gray Box ball cap. "Put those on."

The jacket nearly swallowed her and it smelled like him—sunshine and oceanside cliffs. She had to stifle the urge to bury her nose in the fabric. "Thanks."

"Do you have sunglasses?"

"Not with me."

"She can use mine." Lucy ushered her through the motion-activated elevator doors and down to the same parking level where Jake had dropped them off last night.

"Is the building newly renovated?" Madison asked. "I'm surprised there aren't more tenants."

Lucy gave her a long, speculative look as they walked down the row to Rush's Tesla. "Sam didn't tell you he owns the building?"

Madison shook her head. "We haven't had many normal conversations." That explained the sparse garage. Sam would be extremely choosy about who he allowed into the building.

In the driver's seat, Lucy started the car and pressed the code to exit the building. "Sunglasses," she said, pointing to a pair hanging from the visor.

"Thanks."

The car glided almost silently toward the exit. "Rush told me he forced Sam to get a place away from the office when they moved into the new building. Being such an introvert, he bought a building and renovated to his specs. He's the only tenant."

Madison glanced back, though they'd turned the corner and she couldn't see the building any longer. "All those cars are his?"

Lucy nodded. "As far as I can tell, the cars are his only hobby beyond his computers."

Madison thought he'd held his own last night, as if being an extrovert and meeting new people came naturally. "No one would've guessed how shy he is at the party last night," she said, feeling miserable all over again for putting him through that ordeal. "He greeted everyone, danced and chatted as if he went out every weekend."

"You're kidding." The utter disbelief on Lucy's face exacerbated Madison's guilt.

"Rush and I didn't even see him leave the fund-raiser. The next thing we know, his face is plastered on the society pages next to yours. He did look happy in those pictures."

So he'd become a better actor since high school. Good for him. "He enjoyed shutting down the hacker," Madison said.

Lucy sputtered out a laugh. "Maybe that's how we'll get him out of the office more often."

"Why does it bother you that he's always in the office in the first place?" It dawned on Madison that his friends seemed to be pushing him out of his comfort zone consistently. She gave in to the need to defend him. "He loves his work and he's brilliant at it. He stays fit and sharp. It's not like he's wasting away or anything."

"Oh, I like you a lot." Lucy bounced a little in her seat. "We're going to have a great time today."

Hiding under Lucy's sunglasses and Sam's sweatshirt and ball cap, Madison wasn't as convinced. Although she couldn't argue that Sam's closest friends cared about him, she wondered if anyone really knew the man who'd so easily rescued the exhibit from disgrace and stepped in to give her lies substance when he could have easily walked away.

In some ways, his consistent concern for her surprised her more than the car collection, the refurbished building and the twenty-four-hour personal shopper. From her vantage point, he'd more than fulfilled the favor owed. The way he kept sticking his neck out for her amplified her crush on him. She'd had it bad before, but now, assuming she got out of this current mess, no man would ever measure up to Sam's standards.

Chapter Six

In the back of his mind, Sam kept track of the schedule
Lucy had outlined. He and Rush had been alone no more
than ten minutes before they took Madison's phone,
State Department laptop and the doughnuts downstairs
to the lab he'd built when he refurbished the building.
Knowing the women were fine, he breathed a sigh of
relief when Rush shared the text message and a picture
from Lucy when they were safely behind the armed security system of the boathouse.

Sam shook his head at the instant camaraderie. In
the picture, the women grinned as if they'd been friends
for decades rather than an hour or two.

When his stomach rumbled, he reached for another
doughnut. He thought of the hearty breakfast Madison
had prepared and he worried about her. She must be
famished after running on a smidge of sleep, a jolt of
caffeine and the sugary doughnut chaser. Last night was
proof that her career kept her hopping, but he'd held her
close enough to know she was in the kind of shape that
resulted from taking excellent care of herself.

"You sure you want to do this?" Rush watched Sam

from his place at a computer where he was putting the new software for the museum through another test.

"I understand if you want some distance," Sam replied. "Why not take the Lamborghini and head over to the office?"

Rush whistled. "With that kind of offer, I have to assume you want me gone."

"What?" Sam looked up from his study of Madison's phone and blinked a couple times to bring Rush's face into focus. "Stay or go. It's your call." He took a bite of the doughnut before he started protesting too much. "You could go work your charm on the museum, though. If we can interrupt the circling sharks, maybe we can narrow down this situation."

"Let's go through it again, then," Rush said.

Together, they reviewed the program and the embedded code that would track the hacker if he struck again. When they were satisfied it was fully functional, Rush made the call and set the installation appointment for just after the museum closed tonight. "Do you want me to handle it or send someone else?"

"I think it sends a stronger message if you and I go together," Sam replied.

"It might, except her boss told her to spend time with her husband. How will it look when you decide to work instead of cozy up with her?"

Sam cringed, for reasons other than the obvious. Rush was right and the last thing Madison needed was for her husband to appear to leave her alone. "Fine. You handle the program install." He pulled a flash drive from his pocket. "Install this too."

Rush gave the small device a wary glance. "Will I regret it?"

"No more than we regret juvie," Sam answered.

"Yeah, but we can take any of those punks now."

Sam laughed with his best friend. "We won't regret it. It's a simple filter to let me monitor specific problems from here. Only the code I need to see will show up."

"I was kidding." Rush clapped him on the shoulder. "I trust you, man."

"Thanks."

Sam was downloading all the apps and programs from Madison's phone for analysis, his mind struggling with who had taken aim at her and why. "She called me while my phone was off last night," he said, mostly to himself. "I almost didn't call her back. I was tired of being on display."

"And you're wrestling with the what-ifs," Rush said quietly. "What do you think would've happened if you hadn't gone over to help?"

Rush knew him too well. The hair at the back of Sam's neck stood on end. He didn't want to think about her being ogled by diplomats with only a wedding set as a shield. He didn't care for the idea of her being tailed home by men from another consulate. She probably wouldn't have noticed until it was too late. He'd studied her apartment building and knew she would've been vulnerable before too long.

"Do you remember her at all?" he asked.

"I remember you complaining about the tutoring to fulfill your community service." Rush boosted himself up on one of the long worktables littered with cables, fractured electronics and various tools. "What a whiner. I had hours of janitorial work."

"Same thing," Sam joked. "No one cared about how I could help, except Madison. She needed better grades in the upper-level math and comp-sci classes to stay competitive and Denning had no use for her. She worked her ass off with me."

"Sounds like she liked you," Rush said in a goofy singsong voice.

Sam leaned back in his chair. "We got along okay."

"You're oblivious," Rush muttered. "Come clean with me. Why in the hell are you really going all out with the husband routine?" He stopped and his eyes narrowed. "Unless you want to. That's it, isn't it?"

"Shut up," Sam barked. "It's not like that. She cleared the fib with her security clearance team and would never have given my full name until last night forced her hand."

"Uh-huh." Rush folded his arms and waited.

"On second thought, I'll work better alone today." Sam turned his back on his friend.

"Give me a break." Rush walked over, lending moral support as Sam opened Madison's laptop. "You're going above and beyond and you know it."

When the system asked for it, Sam inserted Madison's department identification card into the reader. "I'm not so sure. Her world isn't at all what I expected."

"What does that mean?"

Aware of the GPS and her boss's orders not to turn on the laptop, Sam took precautions to hide his investigation from the State Department and FBI. Once he was convinced they were in the clear, he immediately started duplicating the hard drive. "It was a private reception and viewing at the gallery. Only the Chinese and the American diplomats were invited. A few people from China recognized my name and made a couple of awkward insinuations."

Rush swore. "We do have a global clientele. What kind of insinuations?"

"That's just it." Sam sat back while the systems worked. "The comments could have been small talk. Possibly, one diplomat from China extended an invitation to a conversation I don't want to get tangled up with. There was even a veiled query about mentoring one of his kids," he said with a shrug. "You know me. I might have read too much into it. Regardless, I played off the comments as generous compliments and kept moving through the room."

"You working the room," Rush said. "What a concept."

Sam ignored that and started picking apart the hard drive, searching for anomalies in Madison's typical computer behavior. Rush pulled up a stool and sat down beside him, helping him make notes to explore and expand on when they returned to the Gray Box offices. They wouldn't connect Madison's computer to the servers there unless it was clean and only once they were sure the connection wouldn't drag them into this mess.

"Did you recognize the hacker's signature?" Rush asked after an hour.

"No one using that signature has made an attempt on our encryption," Sam replied. "One of the first things

I checked." He pointed Rush to a secondary file he'd created last night to further protect their business interests. "I figured if the Chinese diplomats knew me, it wouldn't be long before the hacker learned who'd ended his party early."

"Always anticipating," Rush said.

"That's why we split the big bucks," Sam murmured, lost in his evaluation of Madison's email correspondence. When they finally had a log of the data patterns he wanted, he shut down her computer.

"Ready for me to call a driver and take this to the office?"

Sam pushed his glasses up his forehead and pressed his fingers to his eyes. Glasses back in place, he checked the cameras overlooking the street outside the building. "We've got company again," he said, pointing to the sedan at the corner. He ran the plates to be sure. "Not the same crew as last night. Why don't we use public transit? I doubt anyone watching us is prepared for that move."

Rush agreed and they made a plan to divide and conquer the team on the street. Although his appointment wasn't until this evening, Rush wanted to visit the museum earlier and see the galleries and flow. There were both straight and convoluted routes by cable car or bus from Sam's building to both the museum and the Gray Box offices in the heart of the financial district.

"As long as we grab lunch first," Rush said as his stomach rumbled.

They walked a block from Sam's building to his favorite deli around the corner. Rush sent a text message, checking on Lucy and Madison, while they waited for their order. With a remote connection to his building system, Sam kept an eye on the men tailing them. Seeing the picture of Rush's boathouse turned into a shopping boutique eased another layer of Sam's tension. At least Madison would be effectively distracted.

"You're not as pissed as I thought you'd be," Rush observed after they were settled at a high-top table with thick-stacked roast beef sandwiches and a couple of beers.

"You mean about the hacker?" Sam snagged a homemade potato chip from the basket between them and dipped it in mayonnaise.

"No." Rush glared at him. "About the *woman*."

Why wouldn't Rush drop this? "She's a good friend."

"As far as the world is concerned, she's now your *wife*," Rush said. "Have you even called your mom?"

Sam had to work to swallow the food that had turned to sawdust in his mouth. "Forgot that," he admitted. "I'll call her as soon as we get to the office."

"Bet she's furious," his best friend said with a smirk.

Sam's mood brightened suddenly with another memory. "Bet she isn't." His mother had been a major proponent of the tutoring program and had even met Madison once. It had been a rainy afternoon and Madison's ride was late, so she waited in the car with Sam and his mom. "Mom might've suggested I ask Madison out."

Rush snorted. "And she won't be at all surprised it took you more than a decade to do it. Still, I've got fifty bucks that she'll read you the riot act before she pops any champagne."

"You're on." Sam knew better than to believe he had much grace time before his mother caught wind of his marriage. If his face wasn't all over the society page, he might've had a chance. The fact that he hadn't sent so much as a text proved how much Madison's trouble preoccupied him. He never had been able to let go of a good puzzle once he had his teeth in it. Madison's work and her current predicament were definitely a puzzle he wanted to solve and fast.

Rush's eyebrows arched in shock. "I want proof."

"Fine." Sam grabbed another chip. "I'll put the call on speaker for you."

"Nice." A gleam of triumph flashed in Rush's eyes. "Will you tell her the whole story?"

"No way," Sam admitted.

"So you'll let her believe you got married in secret?"

Sam bit off a big chunk of his sandwich as a stall tactic. He'd been working on it since last night and still couldn't find a good answer for why he'd gone along with Madison's story so easily. If the friend line wasn't enough for Rush, it would fall well short of the explanation his mom deserved.

"The best way through is through, right?" he said at last. It had been their mantra in juvie when surviving came down to the two of them against other kids far bigger and meaner. "We'll figure it out."

Rush's mouth fell open. "You're seriously playing it out."

"May as well." Sam shrugged and took a deep drink of his beer. He didn't know how things would end up, only that he wouldn't leave Madison to cope with this alone. "She needs a friend." Too bad he wasn't thinking entirely platonic and friendly thoughts about Madison. When he wasn't researching the players or evaluating the code options, his mind drifted to decidedly more intimate areas. He knew how enticing it felt to dance with her. What would it be like to kiss her, to sift his hands through that golden hair, or to have her body under his?

Rush waved a hand in front of his face. "Sam? Pretending doesn't make it real."

"Just drop it," Sam said, a low growl in his voice.

"Crap." Rush snatched the basket of chips out of reach. "You want to keep her. You deserve a better relationship than a convenient accident," he insisted. "When will you stop being such a coward?"

"Shut up." He would *not* take this from Rush, of all people. "You've got no room to talk. Lucy *ran away* from you."

Rush's eyes narrowed. "She came back."

Sam snorted. They both knew Lucy came back into Rush's life because she'd been blackmailed. Somehow the two of them had made it work, but Sam didn't need this level of hypocrisy out of his best friend.

"At least I didn't just roll over for the first woman who wanted to use my last name," Rush said.

Sam's temper sparked like dry kindling. He carefully crumpled his sandwich wrapper into a tight ball of wax paper and foil. If he gave voice to all the things on his mind, their friendship would be nothing more than a bloody lump on the deli floor and Rush would be nursing a broken nose. "You've got your methods. I've got mine," Sam said with deceptive calm.

He pushed back his chair and gathered up his trash. "Thanks for taking care of the client," he said for the benefit of the man who'd walked in.

"Sam, I'm—"

"Honest," Sam cut him off. Hearing an apology right now would make the turmoil churning through him worse. He walked out of the deli without a word. Yes, he was furious with Rush, but also with himself.

He walked by the bus stop and caught the cable car on the next block, just to clear his head and think. Hopeful he'd lost the men from the sedan, he let the cool breeze off the bay blow through some of the delusions Rush had so helpfully pointed out.

No, he didn't really expect Madison to stick around and play the happy housewife once they sorted out her current problem. Despite the records he'd wedged into the Nevada system, she wasn't really his wife and his attraction to her notwithstanding, he couldn't just keep her in that role because it was the easy answer to his awkward social life. That would be the worst abuse of a friendship.

Worse than breaking your friend's nose because he pushed the truth in your face.

His only consolation was that she didn't seem to have a steady romance in her life beyond him as her false husband. Again, he wondered why she'd choose the solitude that a fake marriage would impose over an active dating life. She was smart and beautiful and accomplished. Her choices were another layer in the puzzle he was naturally inclined to solve.

Maybe Rush was wrong and he *could* keep Madison

in his life. Not because he was a coward, but because the solution could work for both of them. There were worse reasons to create a partnership and call it a marriage. They'd need to discuss it. He would show her the pros and cons and listen to her hopes and concerns. Then they could draw up a contract and—

The bump and pinch at his side yanked him out of his pleasant thoughts. "Phone and wallet," a man said in heavily accented English. "Give over now."

"No," Sam answered. He glanced down under his arm and saw the flash of a knife. The lousy timing was unbelievable. Did the mugger behind him not understand they were on a moving cable car? "Find another mark."

The knife sliced his shirt, nicked his skin. "I find you. Phone and wallet."

"All right. Take it easy." Sam knew the route, calculated the time to the stop and how the cable car would slow and brake. "Take that out of my side so I can move."

He couldn't get a good look at the man's face from this angle, though the mugger was close enough Sam could judge his general size. The mugger was shorter than Sam by an inch or two and that most likely gave Sam a reach advantage. Slowly reaching for his wallet, he let his elbow graze the man's torso. The guy felt lean, another advantage for Sam.

"This is my stop," Sam said as the cable car braked. "Let's finish this outside."

"Here and now," the mugger countered.

The people packed into the car shifted and swayed

with the stop. Prepared to move, Sam sucked in a breath as the knife slid through his shirt and caught skin. Twisting, he drove his elbow into the mugger's midsection and followed through with a forearm to his throat. He gripped the mugger's collar and jumped off the cable car, bringing him along.

No one on the cable car or sidewalk appeared overly concerned about Sam or the mugger. Sam pushed the smaller man off the sidewalk and into an alley and slammed his knife hand against the hard stone of the building. The knife clattered to the ground and Sam kicked it away.

"Who are you working for?" he demanded.

The mugger tried to shake his head. "Me. Alone."

Sam made his opinion on that lie clear, with a quick punch. "Who?" he asked as the man wheezed. Sam gave him a shake, unconvinced this was a random robbery. The world didn't function under that much coincidence.

He catalogued the man's distinct Asian features, general height and build and guessed at the age. A full description was possible if he chose to report this. Going through proper channels would take time. "What do you want with me?"

"Wallet and phone." The man squeezed the words through Sam's tough grip. "Work alone."

Sam kept the man pinned to the wall with a forearm while he pulled out his phone and took a picture of him. "Last chance," he said. "Why me?"

The man shook his head. "Mistake."

"Fine." Sam kicked him just above his knee. The man slumped to the ground and Sam followed him down, keeping his voice low and controlled. "Tell whoever sent you they are swimming in the deep end now. Got it?"

The man nodded.

Sam snatched the man's knife and left the sorry excuse for a mugger groaning in the alley. By the time he'd doubled back and reached the Gray Box offices, the wound in his side burned as if he'd been stuck with a hot poker. He didn't think the mugger had gotten that much of him. His skin and shirt were sticky under his palm and the familiar copper-tinged scent of fresh blood stung his nostrils. Once he was safely inside the building, he moved straight to the men's room off the lobby to catch his breath and assess the damage.

He swore when he saw the shirt was beyond salvation. It had been a favorite. He stripped it away and dumped it in the sink for now. Swearing again at the gash in his side, he debated his options. The first aid kit wouldn't be enough. He needed stitches. And a clean shirt. If he went to the hospital, they'd insist on filing a report.

While the legalities didn't bother him, he had other things to get done first. He sent a text message and a picture of the wound to the gym where he boxed and added a request for a clean shirt. The trainers there had plenty of experience stitching up split eyebrows, ears and cheeks. A slice over his ribs wouldn't be any challenge for them.

He flushed the wound with warm water and soap while he waited for the reply. When it came, along with criticism about leaving his weak side open, Sam laughed at his reflection. In the context of the last twenty-four hours, he had to admit life had become infinitely more exciting.

Chapter Seven

5:45 p.m.

The girls' day Lucy had arranged had turned into one of the best days in Madison's recent memory. The massage therapist, a man with a body and face worthy of a Nordic god, had worked out the kinks and knots in her shoulders and neck. Thoroughly loosened up, she'd enjoyed at least a gallon of lime-ginger water provided by the caterer. Lunch had been the ultimate girl feast of salads, white wine, more water and delightful, purely feminine conversation.

Facials had followed lunch and Madison and Lucy indulged in mani-pedis while a private shopper turned the living room into an exclusive boutique. With little encouragement from Lucy, Madison splurged on a week's worth of clothing covering everything from lingerie to a strappy, sexy little black dress. At least she had the shoes at Sam's condo to go with that one. The shopper had her sizes and notes about her style preferences and left Madison with a business card and instructions to call if she needed anything.

If this was life as Sam's wife, she could get used to it all too easily. While that love-struck teenager she'd been did a victory cheer at the idea, older and wiser Madison recognized the gross mistake of enjoying this level of service and indulgence. Though she'd paid for everything, guilt niggled at the back of her mind with each step she took deeper into this farce.

It was one thing to wear a ring and pretend to be married to a busy entrepreneur who never needed to be present in her career, much less her life. Now everyone knew her husband's name and *face* and she'd dumped him smack in the middle of her problems.

As she and Lucy lounged outside on the balcony overlooking the city marina and the Golden Gate Bridge, Madison asked again how Lucy had pulled this off.

"Connections," Lucy said. "The people you met today I met through my MBA grad work. Having a secret password known as Rush Grayson doesn't hurt."

Madison sipped her wine and circled a foot, admiring the bright berry polish on her toes and the perfect daisy decorating her big toe.

"I heartily approve of your whimsical side," Lucy observed with a smile. "Sam needs that in his life."

Madison was too relaxed to start protesting again. Besides, it was probably true about Sam. Lucy would know. "I could use it too," she replied.

"You finally look as relaxed as you should." Lucy tapped her wineglass gently to Madison's. "Cheers, my friend."

Madison wanted Lucy to be a friend. She, like Sam,

often pushed everything other than work to the edges of her life. "I am relaxed, although I spent too much of the day imagining Special Agent Spalding storming the gates."

"All the more reason to enjoy a girls-only safe space," Lucy said.

Madison swirled the wine in her glass. "Have you heard from Rush?"

"Not since he messaged me about installing the new cyber security update at the museum." Lucy sighed. "We'll have to tell them the dinner plan soon or they'll insist on having pizza at the office."

"Is that typical?"

"Less often since Christmastime," Lucy said with a wink. "I call myself the good influence. Melva, the woman who has kept that pair straight since the start, helps me get both Rush and Sam out of the building as often as possible."

"I bet Sam is tough to budge."

"You do know him well," Lucy observed, her gaze on the sun-warmed water.

Well seemed like an overstatement. Madison simply made educated guesses based on how he'd behaved in the past and what she read in the tech and business journals. "I'd be happy to cook for the four of us," Madison offered, shifting the topic to safer ground.

"With that manicure? Absolutely not. I made reservations already."

"Out?" A double date sounded like the perfect cap for her day. Except, marriage rumors aside, she wasn't actually dating Sam and doing something so public went against the orders from the legal department. All Sam needed was for his name and face to get dragged through the gossip columns again as his wife got yanked away from dinner by the FBI.

"I can hear the wheels turning in your head, Madison." Lucy tipped down her sunglasses. "If the FBI or any other agency had issued a warrant, we'd know about it. If your boss tried to reach you on your cell or email, Sam would've told you. We'll take your new dress on a test drive with a lovely dinner at a private dining room. Then you can test out that new lingerie for dessert," she finished with a grin.

"The shoes that go with that dress are at Sam's," Madison said.

"He can bring them along when they pick us up."

Madison gave in with a weary chuckle. "You really are a force of nature."

"I confess I've always been headstrong." Lucy gave her long, dark hair a sassy flip over her shoulder. "What's the point of knowing what you want if you don't go after it?" She sighed, thoroughly content. "There was a point when I thought I'd settle," she mused. "I'm glad I didn't and more important, I'm glad I took the second chance when it rolled around."

Madison thought about that as it related to her desire for Sam and nearly choked on her wine. Going "after" Sam was likely to get her tossed out on her ear—a consequence she wasn't prepared to face.

Lucy's phone rang with an incoming call rather than the text message chime. She frowned at the screen and excused herself to answer.

Madison wasn't entirely comfortable out here alone with her thoughts. Every stately black sedan or beefed-up SUV left her feeling vulnerable and exposed. The daisy on her toe lost its whimsy as she beat herself up for slacking off instead of working to sort this out. Her boss said lie low. Extreme pampering and private power shopping didn't seem to fit with that order. Something was very wrong and she'd been out of touch for an entire day. No news cycle, no staff meeting, no assessment and discussion of last night. Without Lucy out here distracting her, Madison's contentment fizzled.

What had Spalding been looking for in her apartment? She didn't have anything to hide, but she knew things could get twisted around and misinterpreted during an investigation. What did he think he'd found?

As the tension gripped her shoulders, threatening to undo the benefits of the massage, she set her wine aside and tried to meditate. She hadn't made it halfway through the first round of breathing before Lucy returned.

"We're still on for dinner," Lucy declared brightly. "Rush is sending a driver to pick us up. He and Sam will meet us at the restaurant. I told Sam to bring the shoes," she finished with a brilliant smile.

Too brilliant, Madison realized. "What's wrong?" She got to her feet.

A quick debate played out over Lucy's expressive face. "Rush said they wanted to wait until after dinner to discuss it," she said.

"Discuss what?"

"Everyone is okay, I promise. The guys don't want to ruin dinner."

Madison folded her arms over her chest and waited. Lucy wasn't the only woman who could be a force of nature when necessary.

Lucy huffed out a breath. "Fine. In your shoes I'd insist on knowing too." She drew Madison back down to sit on the chaise beside her. "Someone tried to mug Sam this afternoon. Don't worry, he's completely fine! I made Rush put him on so I could talk to him myself."

Madison sucked in a breath. "What happened? I thought they'd be together."

"The important thing to remember is the mugger wasn't successful." She rubbed Madison's clenched fists. "Relax. Rush tells me Sam handled himself."

"Did Sam get a description?"

"Better," Lucy said. "He took the mugger's picture. Rush has one of his investigators working on the identification as well as pulling any prints or DNA from the knife."

The wince on Lucy's face when she realized what she'd said would've been comical under better circumstances. "I want to talk to Sam," Madison said.

"He's fine, I promise. He asked me to assure you he'll tell you everything tonight."

Madison looked around for her cell phone out of habit and swore when she remembered why it had been such a quiet, peaceful day. "I can't stand being out of the loop this way. I don't think I'm wired for hours and hours of bliss."

"Of course you are," Lucy soothed. "It just takes

some practice." She checked the time on her phone. "Let's go ahead and dress for dinner. You'll feel better when you see Sam hale and whole."

Madison tried to get into the spirit of it as she and Lucy dressed and fussed with makeup and hair until the last possible second. They chatted over the silly look of Madison in the black dress and flip-flops on the short drive to a restaurant a block past Ghirardelli Square.

Lucy was right. As the driver parked at the side entrance and Sam stepped up to the car looking perfectly healthy and stunning in a dove gray suit, his pale blue dress shirt open at the collar, a wave of relief crashed over Madison. He opened the door and Lucy slid out. Before Madison could follow, Sam motioned her back and joined her in the backseat.

"Have a great time," Lucy said to him, closing the door.

The car pulled away from the curb and Madison stared at Sam, hoping he'd explain. Although her evening shoes dangled from his fingers, he seemed to have forgotten them as he stared back at her. "You look great," he said.

The fascinated intensity in his deep brown eyes turned her muscles to jelly as effectively as the massage therapist. "Thanks," she replied. "I know you can't possibly want to be out on the town two nights in a row."

"I'm okay if it's just the two of us." He handed her the shoes. "I know how to talk with you."

The two of us had such a lovely ring to it and the sincerity in the statement melted something inside her as she slipped her feet into the heels, careful of the small burn on the top of her foot.

Sam finally broke eye contact and sank into the cushions. "I'm sorry for the cloak and dagger routine. It's been a long day. Did you have a good time with Lucy?"

"Yes," she replied. "Don't take this the wrong way, but you look a little less fine than Lucy implied."

Sam dropped his head back on the seat and pushed his glasses to his forehead. With one hand pinching the bridge of his nose, his other hand found hers. "I'm not un-fine," he said after a long moment.

"Is that a word?" It was the only question she could think of with his hand wrapped around hers as if they sat this way every day. It felt more intimate than dancing last night. Despite the obvious toll of his day, this particular moment gave her an unexpected sense of contentment.

He turned his head and offered her a faint smile. "I sure as hell hope so."

She smiled back. "What can I do for *you*, Sam?"

His brown eyes glinted and his mouth opened before he abruptly changed his mind and snapped it shut again. "Just enjoy yourself tonight," he said after a long moment.

She wondered what he left unsaid. With all her practice reading people, interpreting the signs behind the words, Sam remained a mystery. "I will. I already am enjoying myself," she replied. It was a simple truth and if she wanted him to open up, she figured she should set the example.

"Lucy knows how to pack the most fun into an impromptu girls' day," she began. "I almost forgot why we were doing it in the first place."

"Lucy probably had that plan in motion before they reached the condo," Sam said. "It just made selling it to you easier when your boss asked you to stay out of the office."

"I understand the necessity for that." Madison let her gaze roam over the passing city. "It shouldn't have been a surprise that I'm uncomfortable being out of touch. Have you heard anything more about the FBI search of my apartment?"

"Heard or gone snooping?" he asked.

She faced him, hoping he had news. "Either."

"I'm good enough to do the snooping," Sam said, a wicked grin flashing across his face, "but I promised not to hack the FBI again for a year."

She gawked at the comment, realized he was serious and burst into laughter. "Does Special Agent Spalding know about your promise?" she asked when she caught her breath.

"Probably." He sat up straight in the seat and righted his glasses. "Never met him before last night," he added.

It was clear his mind was moving through scenarios and options invisible to her. He had a remarkable ability to pay attention to his surroundings without appearing to care or listen. It was an ability that made the experience all the more intense when he focused completely on her.

She wasn't entirely surprised or pleased to learn neither age nor determination dimmed her feminine reaction to him. Not even the circumstance—her *lie*—that had shoved them together. She was starting to think being older only made her reactions worse.

She swallowed. "What are you thinking?" she asked, certain the answer wouldn't be what she wanted to hear.

"I'm thinking about you," he said.

Madison drew in a small breath, caught in a web she'd created where delight and caution tugged her in opposite directions. Sam wasn't a flirt and he'd never looked at her as more than a friend. "What are you thinking about me?" She tried to regret the breathy way the words emerged, but when his gaze landed on her lips, she couldn't manage it.

Did he—could he—feel this electric chemistry in the air? She desperately hoped it wasn't all one-sided.

"Well, you and your apartment," he amended.

She knew better than to let her hopes about Sam take flight. She had to find a way to control this unquenchable crush. "I see."

He reached up and wrapped his finger around one of the curls framing her face. "Your hair is softer tonight."

"Thank you?" Startled he'd noticed, she wasn't sure how to take that compliment. Considering the source, she forced herself to accept that the words might be a polite, straightforward observation.

"Last night, pulled back, it was sleek and cool. Unapproachable." He frowned, his thoughts carrying him away momentarily. "Tonight you look warmer. More like yourself."

She was starting to feel downright hot, her body overheating from the supreme effort of staying still when she wanted to launch herself at him. She smiled in reply, not trusting her voice.

The car glided to a stop and Sam covered her hand with his. "You're not afraid of boats, are you? I should've asked earlier."

"No." She didn't remind him they lived in a city surrounded by water.

His face lit up in a big smile. "Good."

He offered his hand as she climbed out of the car and she stared at the luxury sailboats, cabin cruisers and yachts docked around the marina. She caught Sam's low voice, but not the words, as he gave instructions to the driver. "Let's go," he said, taking her hand in his again.

They didn't chat along the way. The evening was calm and yet curiosity and anticipation danced over her skin. What did he have in mind? She worked to remind herself they were friends only. He was here to help her through a temporary crisis.

"Here we are," he said, stopping at a narrow gangway at the end of the dock.

"You said boat." She'd expected a cruiser and Sam had brought her to a yacht. It was a large, well-appointed vessel with a crew of five standing by ready to welcome them aboard. "Is this yours?" she whispered as they followed the steward into a plush salon with a dinner table set for two.

"Rush owns it," Sam replied. "He uses it primarily to wow potential clients and shares it with the executive staff."

"*Wow* is right."

Another uniformed man asked for their drink preferences. Sam ordered a beer and she requested water, knowing another drink on an empty stomach would only make it harder to keep her hands to herself. The vessel glided away from the dock and they settled into soft chairs on the stern deck. The water churning in their wake as the vessel quietly moved into the bay mesmerized her. "Why didn't he and Lucy come along tonight?"

Sam studied the bottle of beer in his hand for a long moment. "A few reasons."

She waited, sensing his shift to practical issues. Whatever intimacy she'd imagined was blowing away in the sea air.

"After everything that happened today," he continued, "we adjusted the arrangements tonight so you and I could speak privately with no worry about interruptions."

"Does 'everything' include you being mugged?"

"Everything includes an *attempted* mugging," he clarified with a smile.

She noticed the smile didn't put a spark in his brown eyes. "You're not okay."

"I am." He shifted in the chair. "I got the man's picture and his knife." He sipped the beer. "The guy got nothing from me."

Madison wasn't so sure about that. Something serious weighed on his mind, had him more distracted than usual. "Will you tell me the whole story?"

"Maybe later." He sat back in the chair and propped an ankle on his opposite knee. "First of all, the museum and the white jade cup are now secure from online threats through the run of the exhibit. Rush just finished installing the new program as a courtesy trial. If they want to keep it when the exhibit returns to China, they can buy it."

"That was more than generous," she said. He had her almost convinced he was simply a carefree, wealthy entrepreneur out for a private dinner cruise. She spotted the tension in his clean-shaven jaw and the uncharacteristic stillness of his hands.

"You didn't want us to give them the upgrade for free?" He shot her a quizzical look.

"Why would I want that?"

"I just thought as a friend or whatever we are here, you might expect us to throw in a freebie."

"Sam, that's ridiculous." Too edgy and overwhelmed from the events of the previous twenty-four hours, she couldn't hide her offense. "Stopping the hacker pro bono was all the favor I needed. You're brilliant and should be paid well for your expertise." On a roll now, she ignored the curious lift of his dark eyebrows. "I'm well aware how much you and Rush give back to the community. You have every right to call me on the marriage lie and yet here we are, acting it out."

"Right down to our first fight, apparently," he said.

The charming grin made her knees weak. "You know what I mean."

He nodded, his gaze full of an earnest sincerity. "I'm happy to help you, Madison. We've been friends a long time."

She didn't trust herself to reply.

"I've been through your computer." He stayed her

protest with a raised palm. "Off network. No one will ever know it was even turned on. I needed to study and evaluate your typical habits on that computer."

Work computer, she reminded herself. Her personal documents and such were in a password-locked file on her tablet at home. Great. Spalding probably had that now. Not that there was anything more incriminating than her banking and charity interests. Unless she counted every saved email she'd ever received from Sam Bellemere along with an electronic scrapbook of headlines he'd made through the years. If anyone found that, her fake husband might have cause for a restraining order against her.

"Madison, you're not listening. I know the details can be tedious—"

"It's not the details," she said quickly. "You've always made the details interesting for me." Through necessity, she'd developed the ability to listen to and assess multiple topics simultaneously. "The computer behavior assessment algorithms to prevent hacking and breaches are cutting edge."

"Yes, they are."

She sat forward, eager to hear more about what he was developing and what he'd do with it. "Will Gray Box market the new software publicly?"

He frowned at her. "You were listening."

She smiled and sipped her water.

"We're a long way from having a reliable program ready to market." He tipped his head back as they passed under the Golden Gate Bridge. "What's more important and relevant is the string of recent email messages I found buried in your official inbox."

She shivered and it had nothing to do with the chilly breeze on the bay. Sam set aside his beer and removed his suit jacket, sliding it over her shoulders. Being surrounded by the fabric warm from his body and the scent of his cologne was almost better than dancing with him at the gala. He lingered there in front of her fussing with the jacket panels as if he didn't want to go back to his own seat.

If she leaned forward just a few inches, she could kiss those firm lips and learn the taste of him at last. He was right there, within easy reach and she lost her nerve, too afraid of scaring him off. Far more frightened that kissing him would snap that last thread of hope that she might be content with another man.

"I clean out my inbox every day," she said, though the words came out as if she'd been chewing sandpaper. "I have folders and a system and—"

"I know." He pushed back from her. Standing, he tucked his hands into his pockets. "Behavior, remember?"

"Then where and how did I miss these emails you found?"

"It's not easy to explain. The dates and times show up over the past three or four months, but they didn't actually hit your inbox until after the gala. More specifically, just after the first disturbance call from your neighbors."

The inexplicable and sudden rash of trouble bumped

around in her head until it fell into place. "You believe I'm being set up."

"Yes," he replied, his gaze searching the night beyond their boat. "I just can't pin down why."

Her mind raced back through recent months and the attempts on the State Department firewall. "What did the emails suggest?"

He sighed. "The implication is an ongoing conversation that you're interested in sharing confidential information about Vietnam's interests with China for the right price."

"I would never." She swore. "That's outrageous."

"I know."

"No wonder Spalding is after me. My boss said the FBI got a tip that I've already taken payoffs. It must be this hacker, or a group, trying to embarrass the State Department."

"I agree. Having more than one person or group come after you right now is too much of a coincidence. Unfortunately, it will take me some time to identify him." He removed his glasses and hooked them at the open collar of his shirt. "I've worked on this all day, Madison. Depending on how things come to light, the problems at the reception could be read as retaliation for your potential betrayal. That's a spitball theory, of course," he said quickly. "There are too many unknowns right now. Even looking at the pieces separately, it's clear to me the hacker has latched on to you. He or she took offense at your suddenly publicized marriage and me as your high-profile husband."

She understood why she might be a target as a liaison, but why did the appearance of a husband make any difference? She'd been behaving as married for a long time. "Should we publicize a separation or divorce instead?"

"Hell, no."

His swift reply had her looking up at him in shock. "What are you suggesting?"

"I can take care of myself." He picked up his beer and drained it. "You—we—have options. FBI involvement or not, Rush and I can get you out of the country. Tonight, if you like."

She glanced around the harbor as understanding of their location struck home. "You're suggesting we sail to Canada?"

"It's closer than Mexico," he quipped. "I'm just laying out your options," he added.

"Lay out another one. I'm not running from some punk hiding behind a wall of technology."

"Have you forgotten I used to be that punk?" he asked with a rough bark of laughter.

"Oh, you were not." She stood up, swaying a little with the movement of the boat as she walked over to the rail. She gripped it hard, willing herself to find a graceful way out of this twisted mess. "Lay out another option," she repeated over her shoulder.

"All right." He came up beside her and covered one of her chilled hands with his. "What if we enjoy what is sure to be an outstanding dinner and then head back to my place and handle whatever is coming together as husband and wife?"

She studied his profile, seeing none of the tension

or stress in the hard square of his jaw, only resolute determination. "Together?" She was bewildered as much by the offer as she was by the easy way he delivered it.

"Exactly." He faced her, giving her a heated, toe-curling smile.

If only it would be that easy. "You stepping up publicly as my husband could very well put Gray Box at risk."

"I've factored that in."

His absolute fearlessness despite the unknowns made her want him more as a friend and an ally as well as on a personal level. She hadn't known it was possible to sink deeper into her infatuation with him.

"What did Rush say?"

His gaze slid over her shoulder, as if he could see the office from here. "We discussed every angle of the situation and while there's no foolproof plan right now, we know our options and basic tactics."

"You expect me to live with you at your condo?"

"Yes. The building is covered by the best security team in the business," he said, his eyes on her again. "It's all legal too, should the FBI believe a hacker's antics and claims over the proof we'll eventually provide to clear you."

"What about your real life, Sam?"

"You're as real as my life has ever been outside of the office," he replied. "Seriously, it's the best solution for you."

He started to say something else but the steward stepped out, announcing dinner. Sam laced his fingers with hers as they walked into the salon. "I did speak with my mom, since she's a society page junkie."

"Oh, no." Madison groaned. "She must think I'm the worst for dragging you into my fib," she said as Sam pulled out her chair at the table.

"Not at all." He took his seat across from her and waited while wine was poured. "I told her the 'true story.'" He added air quotes to the phrase. "The way you gave it to me."

Appalled, Madison struggled to catch a full breath. "You didn't." His mother must be furious and hurt. "Sam."

"I admit she wasn't happy we eloped. She was thrilled to hear I have a wife who adores me."

Sheer embarrassment heated her cheeks. He'd figured out her infatuation. The stereotype that tech experts had no personal observation skills was thoroughly debunked. Sam, both a famous tech innovator and notoriously shy, a soft-spoken rejecter of typical social conventions, had recognized her desperate crush on him.

She knew it was all her fault. Yes, she could see his point about the need to play the parts she'd cast for them and the definite short-term benefits. What worried her more was the long-term fallout for her, him and the people who cared about them.

To her immense relief, any need for a response was delayed by the arrival of salads and a basket of aromatic herb bread, brushed with a gloss of melted butter. It gave her time to get a grip on her runaway thoughts so she could match his logical approach to this monstrously uncomfortable box she'd built.

Chapter Eight

"I explained our reasons," Sam continued, wondering about Madison's prolonged silence. Her cheeks were turning red, her lips caught tight between her teeth and she stared deliberately at her salad plate.

"You don't have to really adore me," he said quickly. "Obviously we won't be out and about much. I was selling it for Mom, that's all," he blathered on, fighting the rising panic. This wasn't how he'd envisioned the conversation. "I told her we kept the wedding quiet because it was better for your career not to go public until we had to."

"Had to," she echoed.

"Yes." He offered her a slice of bread and took one for himself. "To best protect you now, I think we'll need to let the public in a little more."

"My boss said lie low," she said. "Stay off the radar."

"I know." He leaned forward, willing her to look at him and see what he was offering. She didn't. "I promise you, Madison, we can manage this. We'll be careful and deliberate about the what, where and when of every piece."

"You'll hate that kind of invasion of your privacy."

He shook his head. As her husband, he wouldn't be coping with the scrutiny alone. It had been the personal teamwork he'd longed for. "We'll be invaded together." His joke fell flat. There had to be a way to convince her.

He'd spent all day thinking about it and decided this marriage offered them the best of both worlds. No longer an eligible bachelor, he could go out with his wife and enjoy the city without unflattering speculation or bizarre attempts to get his attention. Granted, when people approached him it was more often about technology than a personal interest in his life, but still. "Whatever attention we get, you can be a social asset for me. The company and I will be a legal buffer for you."

She met his gaze and her moss-green eyes were as cool and hard as the jade artwork in the exhibit. "You see that as an equal trade?"

He wished she'd spit out whatever was bothering her. Either his suggestion made her angry or there was more going on that she didn't want to share with him. "You're not enthused about this at all."

"My apologies." She raised her glass of wine. "A toast to wedded bliss." Her smile was brittle, far more fragile than the warm expressions they'd shared out on the deck.

He gently tapped his glass to hers and held her gaze as they sipped. "I've irritated you? Overstepped?"

"No." She closed her eyes a moment. "No," she repeated. "That's on me. I did the wrong thing with the guest list by dragging you into this on a personal level." She placed her hands in her lap, her body so still, her eyes solemn. "I appreciate the remarkable patience you've extended to me."

"There's more," he prompted when she picked up her fork and stabbed at the mixed greens on her salad plate. "I'd rather we were honest with each other." To that end, he should probably come clean with her about what he really wanted.

She choked, sputtered and then waved off assistance as both Sam and the steward moved to help her. "I'm okay. Maybe you should send me out of the country," she said morosely when the coughing spell was over.

Sam knew he didn't understand women, but this moodiness didn't fit with the Madison who'd shown exceptional grace under fire six months ago, last night and again this morning. When the salad plates were removed he walked over and pulled up a chair to her side of the table.

"Madison, I don't believe you're guilty of any wrong-doing."

"That's not it." She fanned her face with her hand and blinked rapidly.

He thought he caught the glimmer of tears welling in her eyes. He was bad enough at the personal stuff and lousy at soothing crying women. "If there's some-one else in your life, I'll talk with him. I'll take care of the fake divorce as soon as this mess is resolved." Rush would have a field day that he couldn't keep a fake wife.

"No. There's no one else." She sniffled through a wry chuckle. "Only you."

"Same goes," he said, clutching her admission like a lifeline. Lasting marriages had started on weaker foundations. If he handled this crisis well, he might convince her to stay with him. Just because the situation was unconventional didn't mean it couldn't work. The more time he spent with her, the more he believed *they* could work.

"Pardon me?" Her eyes went wide, the soft green shimmering with emotions he couldn't label.

He understood that. He'd struggled all day with the potential pitfalls and, frustrated, he shifted his focus to the more enticing potential rewards. "Why don't we move forward with this?" He picked up her hand and kissed her knuckles, hoping she found the gesture romantic.

"This?" Her gaze locked on the point where his lips met her skin.

Probably laying it on too thick, he decided. Releasing her hand, he moved back to his side of the table as the main course arrived. "This," he said when they were alone. He pointed a finger between them. "Us. Being husband and wife. We'll play it out publicly, cautiously as your situation requires and in private we can see how we get along. I've drawn up a contract for your review with a plan to reassess and make adjustments in thirty days."

"What?" Her voice traveled up a full octave in the single syllable.

From the corner of his eye, he saw the steward hesitate before stepping out of view. Good. He didn't need witnesses to his humiliation. Sam sliced into the beef medallions and took a bite, savoring the flavor. He'd rather hear the litany of his inadequacies on a full stomach. Across the table Madison stared at him, still clearly mortified by his suggestion.

"I need you to clarify what you mean," she said with more edge than his steak knife. "Precisely."

"I am—" He caught himself before he used the word *propose* and started over. "In the simplest terms I am suggesting you move in with me for a month, with an option to extend our arrangement after that time."

"You think it will take that long to track down the hacker who is targeting me?"

"I can't be sure," he admitted. "For your career, I hope it won't take that long." He'd done his best to bait the jerk tampering with her email and State Department systems. "I can't make any promises on the timeline. The contract specifies that we live together for a month, regardless of any outside circumstances and see how being married works for us."

"You're serious." Her eyes went wide.

He gave her a smile, though it didn't ease the misery straining her lovely features. "It was your idea," he said kindly. "I'm taking it a step further, that's all."

Her knuckles turned white as she clutched her knife. "It was my cover. It wasn't meant to be real, Sam." She lowered her gaze. "I don't think I can pretend for thirty days," she finished on a whisper.

"Right." Of course she couldn't. She hadn't meant to pretend at all. She hadn't shared his name until she needed his skills, not him personally. Rush was right, he was a coward. A coward and an idiot for thinking he might win her over if only they spent more time to-gether. A normal man wouldn't latch on to a convenient, familiar woman and try to shape a friendship into something more.

Seizing an unexpected opportunity was smart business. That didn't make it an equation for a workable personal interest. He was second-rate when it came to the small, attentive gestures women enjoyed, tonight being plenty of evidence of that. According to the advice from relationship experts he'd studied this afternoon while a few test programs cycled, women wanted men who could offer romance, consideration and responsiveness.

All things Sam didn't know how to give. He could save her career—probably—and keep her out of harm's way—again, probably—but it wouldn't be enough to give her a happy, fulfilled life. He didn't seem built for that. Even the women he'd dated, the ones after his money or financial backing on a business deal, didn't put up with him for long.

"You're right. I'm out of line. Forget I mentioned it. It wasn't meant to be this awkward. You take the condo and I'll stay at the Gray Box office until we figure out who's gunning for you. I respect our friendship, all evidence to the contrary. Use the condo," he repeated. "Use the marriage cover as long as you need it. You'll have all the legal resources Rush and I can muster until we clear your name. Whatever you need, personally or publicly, let me know and I'll be there."

Embarrassed and discouraged, he couldn't sit here and act as if nothing had happened. Knowing it was rude, he excused himself.

"Sam, wait."

"I'll be right back," he promised without turning

around. Hell, he couldn't figure out why he was upset. It had been a long shot, trying to squeeze something more permanent out of a friendship. With luck, she'd forgive him by Christmas and he'd get another email card from her to add to the collection he'd saved through the years.

What the hell had he been thinking to take advantage of her on the basis of proximity when things were going to hell in her world? He might have talked with Rush about it. Better if he'd gone over his idea with Lucy for some female perspective.

"Sam!"

He kept walking, taking the stairs two at a time up to the upper level and out onto the open deck at the bow. He dragged in a deep breath and pushed his hands through his hair. The move made the fresh stitches in his side sting. Whose bright idea had it been to have this conversation on a damn boat where he couldn't get away from her? Rush's idea, he remembered. Though he hadn't confided his thirty-day plan to Rush, his best friend knew he liked to hole up with his computers when things got sticky. *Sticky* was definitely a nice word for the hole he'd dug for himself tonight.

"Sam, I'm sorry." Her hand landed on his shoulder, soft and gentle.

He held still, reveling in her touch despite his foolish behavior. "Don't apologize. This is on me. I made an outrageous suggestion," he said, unable to look at her.

Her hand smoothed down his arm, stopping just below his elbow. His entire body seemed to start at that particular point, all of his attention zeroed in on the feel of her.

"I'm grateful for all your help," she said.

"But?" He met her gaze, her eyes unfathomable in the starlight.

"No *but*s," she replied quietly.

She seemed to lean into him and he knew it had to be his imagination. Or the motion of the ship. Not of her free will. He didn't draw women in; he was the guy who ignored them until they drifted away.

"Do you remember the first day we met?" she asked.

She'd been wearing faded jeans with a tear at one knee and a pink football jersey with the quarterback's number from the prior school year's powder-puff game. She'd moved with a ballerina's grace, making him feel more awkward than usual that day. "Vaguely."

"I asked if you could help me and you said you had to try."

"That sounds like me." Blunt and braced for rejection. "You were a good student."

"Thanks to you, my grades eventually reflected that." She shifted again, rubbing her hands over her arms. She was chilled again, having left his jacket in the salon. Even he knew giving her his shirt would be going too far.

"You should get out of the wind," he said.

"In a minute. I need to say this."

He waited, captivated now as she nibbled on her lip, her gaze sliding to his mouth, his chest, then away to the water. Whatever it was, she clearly wanted to keep it to herself. The polite thing was to let her off the hook. He was the poster child for privacy and yet he wanted to coax out all the mysteries lingering in her soft green eyes.

"I knew who you were when we were introduced," she said. "I knew why you'd been out of school the previous year."

He glanced away. "It wasn't a state secret."

"No. The secret was how much I admired you for taking the chance."

"It was a cocky stunt," he countered.

One narrow shoulder rose and fell. "You did something no one else had done. Plus…" She stopped, took a deep breath. "Plus I had the biggest crush on you."

He stared at her, waiting for the straight face to crack into laughter as she delivered the punch line. She didn't laugh, didn't add to the statement. "I don't get the joke." He shoved his hands into his pockets and leaned back against the rail.

"I'm not joking." She shivered a little and hugged herself tighter. "I had the biggest crush on you in high school and you were oblivious."

In his head he heard Rush teasing that Madison had liked him. "You dated…" His voice trailed off. He couldn't remember whom she'd dated, only that it hadn't been him. Of course, he'd never asked her out. She'd probably gone out with guys who had the confidence or bravado to speak to girls without stumbling over every other word. To call him a late bloomer was an enormous understatement for Sam's dating life.

"I didn't date," Madison said. "I went out with friends on the weekends."

"Strict parents?"

"Well, yes," she answered. "And the boy I really liked—you—was oblivious."

He could see her honesty in her eyes as easily as he could see the moon in the sky. "Madison, if you sent me signals back then, I'm sorry I missed them. Even if I'd noticed a signal, I was terminally shy and petrified of casual conversation." He reached out and rubbed her arms, chasing away the goose bumps. "My mom thought the tutoring would help me with the shyness and she convinced the judge to count it as my community service."

"Did it help?"

"Not really." He looked down into her gorgeous face with the sharp cheekbones, wide eyes and inviting lips. Out here in shadow and starlight, cruising across the inky velvet of the water, she looked delectable, a woman well out of his league. Still, he ached for her. She was smart to avoid one extra day of a fake marriage with him. His needs would overwhelm her and wreck their friendship within a week. By the end of thirty days she'd be begging for the State Department to move her to New York or anywhere he wasn't.

"We should go inside," he repeated, forcing his hands away from the supple strength in her arms. "You're chilled."

She stepped closer, her legs bracketed by his, yet he was the one who felt trapped. He was caught in a sensual cage between her lithe body and the hard deck rail at his back. The ache ratcheted into a serious need. "Madison."

She lifted herself onto her toes, her body a soft glide

against him and pressed her lips to his. An instant of featherlight contact and then gone.

The touch sent a frantic pulse skittering through him. Reaching out, he cupped her jaw in his hand, brushed her lower lip with his thumb. Her eyelids were heavy as he pushed his hand into her hair and brought her mouth back to his for another taste, a full taste. He kissed her, slowly at first, giving her room to push back or to tell him off. Instead, she sighed and the soft, wistful sound thundered in his ears. When her lips parted, he took the kiss deeper. Exploring the angles and touches that made her gasp and lean into him.

Desire and pleasure built touch by touch as the kiss deepened. Her palms were warm at his hips, her fingers digging in a bit for balance as the boat rocked. And then her hands slid up his rib cage, stirring bliss on one side and sparking fire on the other. He flinched at the pain.

She froze, eyes wide staring up at him. "What's wrong?"

"Nothing." He caught her before she could scramble away. "It's nothing." He was not losing this chance, not with that kiss rocking through him.

She ducked her head, evading his attempt to reclaim that stunning sensation. "Sam, look." She curled her fingers into her palms, then spread them wide and tugged at his shirt. "Wait, you're bleeding." With an accusing glare, she added, "You *are* hurt."

"I'm fine," he said while she pulled him toward the better light at the stairwell. "I'm sorry for bleeding on you."

"Oh, hush." She called for the steward and demanded

hot water and towels. She supervised Sam's return to the salon and pushed him into a chair and started unbuttoning his shirt.

"This is escalating quickly," he observed. "I like it."

She rolled her eyes. "So says the man who offered me a thirty-day contract to cohabitate with an option to stay married."

"We all have our strengths." He wouldn't apologize. Not after that hot, searing kiss full of dark, tempting promises. He wanted more of her, all of her and preferably right now. Hackers, the FBI and diplomacy could wait in line for her attention. He wanted her, wanted to indulge his urge to spoil her with the best life could offer.

She tugged his shirt from his waistband and batted his hands out of the way when he tried to stop her. "I knew you looked pasty when you got into the car."

"Computer nerds always look pasty. It's the persistent lack of sunlight." His breath caught as she pressed a hot, damp towel to the stitches in his side.

"You have never been pasty," she countered. "Hold still."

He didn't have much time to appreciate what might have been a compliment. "I'm not sure that's supposed to get wet."

"It's not supposed to be bleeding either. Did the doctor give you any antiseptic ointment or instructions?"

"Are you a qualified nurse?" he asked, growing impatient. If she was going to put her hands on him, he had better suggestions for where to start.

"We have a doctor on board," the steward replied.

"Get him," Madison answered before Sam could reply. "This looks infected."

"It can't be. We cleaned it, stitched it up."

She pressed a dry towel to his side and covered it with his hand. "Easy pressure," she instructed. She used the warm soapy water and a second towel to wash her hands. "When you say 'we,' who do you mean?"

He stalled, hoping the doctor would distract her. She wasn't fooled.

"Sam." She took his chin and steered his face so he had to look at her.

Not that the view was any hardship. "You're prettier than ever," he said, hoping to distract her. She'd had a crush on him once and he didn't think she could kiss him that way if she didn't still like him a little. That hadn't been a kiss between friends.

"And you're going to answer me. Who put in these stitches?"

"One of the trainers from the gym." At her obvious disgust, he quickly defended his choice. "I couldn't run out to a hospital without raising questions and causing more trouble."

"You might have been killed."

"This was more accident than intention," he said. She glared again. "I handled it." His pride bruised, he said, "I'm not the scrawny nerd I used to be."

Her eyes swept over his chest, exposed by the open shirt. "I noticed."

Was that a little flutter he heard in her voice, or was she simply exasperated and done with him? "Does that mean you approve of how I turned out?"

"I'd be either a fool or blind not to," she muttered, turning away. "Where is the doctor?"

He dropped the towel and caught up with her. "Maybe he fell overboard," he said, pressing his lips to the top of her shoulder. "This isn't serious."

"You were stabbed because of me."

"I was scratched, deeply," he agreed, turning her to face him. He couldn't figure out how to hug her without bleeding on her again. "The investigator is still working out if the incident had anything to do with the trouble surrounding your work."

"However you came by the injury, you've popped stitches and need them repaired." She stepped out of his reach as the doctor entered the salon.

Sam obediently stretched out on his back on a sofa and let the doctor come to his own conclusions.

"Not bad work," he said, prodding at the repair. "Just in a bad place. You need to take it easy for several days."

"Good thing nerd work isn't taxing," Sam replied, his eyes on Madison.

She snorted. He caught her staring at his chest again and wondered if they were finally thinking similar thoughts.

By the time the doctor finished, leaving him with another admonishment to rest, the steward had found a clean shirt for Sam. When he offered to serve fresh meals, Madison declined and Sam followed suit.

"Back to the city is best," Sam said.

Madison picked up her wine and stood at the window overlooking the stern deck. Sam joined her, keeping his silence. He didn't want to say the wrong thing and ruin any chance of kissing her again.

"I'm not signing any contract," she said at last. "We don't need that kind of formality to do what's necessary."

"Okay." A string of what-ifs trailed through his mind, but he recognized that was his business sense clamoring for certainties that a personal relationship never demanded or guaranteed. "I'll follow your lead." That would be the best solution for both of them, publicly and privately. "Whatever you need, Madison, just ask."

Once they were back on land, he'd be preoccupied again with tracing the hacker and the tech issues. He wouldn't have the time or inclination to research how to romance and woo her the way she deserved. He would leave the next step, together or apart, up to her.

She lifted her face, those green eyes studying him. "What do *you* need, Sam?"

More time with you in my arms. He bit back the revealing response, annoyed with his infatuation and searched for a more palatable reply. "I need time to root out the hacker," he managed. "I believe I can do that and still play the role of your husband effectively." Good grief, could he make it sound more sterile or calculated?

"All right." She closed her eyes on him, on the view and rubbed her temples. "While you work on the technical side, I'll keep prodding at the diplomatic side."

"Your boss told you to back off."

She snapped her eyes open once more. "He told me to take a honeymoon too. You'll need my expertise to find the hacker," she insisted. "The cause and motives he presented in the chat room before the museum stunt are bogus. If he's the same person or group accusing me of taking bribes, it's even more essential to know the nuances and intentions of all the parties involved."

Sam mulled that over as he considered the circumstances that had drawn him into her life again. "Reviewing what we have so far, I think he's after more than making his reputation with a notorious hack or new virus."

"I agree," she said.

"So we'll stick with the marriage cover story and stay off the radar together?" he asked, wanting to be clear about where they stood.

"At least until the FBI dumps me in a holding cell."

"That will never happen," he vowed.

She shook her head and more of her silky hair spilled out of the clip holding it, loosened by his hands and the breeze. "You say that now, but mine wouldn't be the first diplomatic career ruined by false allegations."

"You have me on your side," he said, wishing she'd accept everything he could offer. "And I have resources most people can't imagine." He wouldn't hesitate to employ any of them if it meant keeping a friend safe, keeping *her* safe.

As another tiny frown tugged at her lush mouth, he wondered why every reassurance he offered seemed to make her more uncomfortable. He told himself it wasn't relevant to the problem. Better to believe that than admit he still didn't have the guts to ask her out on a proper date.

Chapter Nine

They didn't speak at all on the drive from the marina to his building. Madison was grateful for the quiet. She needed time to think and to come to terms with the realization that he'd given his mother Madison's version of the truth. What did that mean? She had no idea. Just when she was sure she thought she understood this thing between them, he said something that made her doubt her conclusion.

At least by her refusing to sign the strange marriage test-drive contract, they seemed to be back on the stable footing of a friendship. After the doctor's visit, Sam had swiftly shifted back to business mode while she struggled to quell the pent-up desire thrumming through her veins. How was she supposed to feel about that?

He didn't touch her, aside from offering his hand to help her in and out of the car. She couldn't make up her mind if that fell into the pro or con category of the evening. Doctor's orders or not, having kissed him once, she wanted more. More kisses, more of that sensual way his hand in her hair made her body pliant. What would it be like to uncover his body inch by inch and explore the strength and shape of him? To learn what made him weak with desire? If they kissed again—preferably *when*—she would refuse to stop until she knew all of him and he'd learned all of her.

I'll follow your lead, he'd said. If he knew the images those four words evoked, he'd run away or drag her to the nearest bedroom and lock the door.

Although his "unimaginable resources" had been unquestionably helpful in her current crisis, she wanted to know Sam as a person, not as a wallet. The way he poked and prodded at any sort of problem or puzzle until he untangled the solution had always intrigued her. She might have had a crush on him, but that teenage fascination was shifting into something else with every passing hour. It sounded crazy in her head, standing next to one of the wealthiest, sexiest men in the world, to say she loved his mind first.

Loved?

She sighed, abruptly recognizing how much danger her heart was in. For a teenager, the concept of love came with loopy hearts and flower doodles. The real thing had been too big to even entertain. Growing up, being out in the world, she found it impossible to label her persistent hang-up on the cute, nerdy guy from high school as *love*.

In the elevator, she peeked at him from under her lashes. She wasn't feeling anything that qualified as cute or nerdy when she looked at him tonight. When they entered his condo, Sam said her name and her body pulsed with anticipation.

"I'm going to change clothes and get to work," he said.

The memory of his sculpted chest flashed through her mind. She bit her lip so she didn't beg him to let her watch.

Sam gave her an odd look. "If you're tired, you don't have to join me. We can pick up this discussion again in the morning."

"It's not that," she said breezily. Stepping out of her heels, she hooked the straps over her finger. "I'm thinking about the clothes." It was mostly true. "Lucy's private boutique today does me no good if my purchases are all at her place."

"It should all be here by now." He raised his chin toward her side of the condo. "I asked her to have everything delivered to your room." He turned in the opposite direction, heading for his office.

Excited to verify the claim, she hurried to the guest room. Her room, to use Sam's phrase, for the foreseeable future. While it was far better than a holding cell, living with Sam would give her plenty of other pitfalls to avoid. She couldn't believe she'd told him about crushing on him in high school or that she'd kissed him. She touched her fingers to her lips, recalling the feel of that amazing kiss. Oh, the risk had been worth it when he took control.

Desire warmed her skin and that quiver in her belly was back with a vengeance. She sank down on the bed, wondering if he'd meant it. Would he really follow her lead if she asked him to make love to her?

No, that was insanity waiting to happen. She didn't know how long they'd be stuck in this limbo. Immersion in Sam's daily life, without the distraction of her career, wouldn't be a dream come true. It would be a nightmare when the idyllic time ended. She had no illusions about his dedication to his work or his view of her as a friend. Just because a man knew how to leave her breathless with a kiss didn't mean he could love her. She'd been on the opposite side of the equation with a man who'd loved her in ways she couldn't return.

Because her heart was devoted to Sam.

She was an idiot, convincing herself her career would be enough satisfaction. That eventually the right man would walk into her life, a man she could trust with her marriage secret, a man who'd be patient while she undid that secret to make room for him. A man with qualities that would shatter everything she'd idealized about Sam.

Now that she'd kissed Sam, the man she'd fantasized about for nearly half her life, she knew her "someday" man didn't exist. It wasn't a pretty thought, being so enamored and infatuated and—yes, damn it—in *love* with a man who wasn't looking for the same thing from her.

A thirty-day test-drive marriage contract wasn't a marriage. Not the way she wanted to be married and share her life with someone. She didn't want to be his social butterfly. She wanted him to be more than a legal buffer for her. She wanted them. Together, as a team. Despite the sizzling potential packed into that kiss, she wanted a lifetime partnership with more lasting affection than sexual chemistry keeping them in the same room. She wanted them to be more to each other than various convenient reasons.

When she'd sought a psychologist to help her get over

Sam as Mr. Perfect, she assumed they'd find an answer for her lingering crush. She'd anticipated that a professional could identify why she idealized him, that maybe he exemplified a particular quality or trait she admired.

No. The best suggestion to come out of a year working on the issue from every angle was that she should reach out to Sam and tell him her feelings. Accepted or rejected, that sort of action would allow her to move on. He'd been spotted around town that holiday season with a regular date, an actress he'd met while consulting on a movie project in Los Angeles. She'd sent the usual Christmas card and put a lid on her feelings.

Unfulfilled sexually and emotionally, she carried the lavender sleep set with her into the bathroom. Pulling the pins from her hair, she brushed it out, then piled it high on her head, securing it with a band to keep it out of the way while she washed her face. She reached back to unzip her dress and felt the zipper catch in the fabric. Twisting around, fumbling with it, she couldn't quite wriggle out of the dress. On a heavy sigh, she accepted she had unpleasant choices. Ask Sam for help, cut the dress off or sleep in it and hope for a better result in the morning.

Embarrassed and frustrated, she stalked across the condo to his office and knocked on the open door.

"Come in." He sounded annoyed and for a second Madison reconsidered not disturbing him.

"I'm stuck," she said, stepping forward into his domain.

"Me too," he muttered without turning. He'd changed clothes. A black T-shirt stretched across his back and he'd pulled on gym shorts. His feet and legs were bare. The man did not get that body from his "nerd work" career in cyber security and development.

She dragged her gaze away from the delicious view of him to the monitors that held his attention. It wasn't code or museum protocols. Those were articles and reports about the situation and key players in the South China Sea. She came closer until she was able to read over his shoulder.

"Resources," she murmured. "You weren't kidding." He'd tapped into reports that were stored behind layers of security and permissions.

"I've gone back and forth through the instances where the museum hacker took credit. He shows up with an affiliation with a group of American radicals who claim we've sold out to China, but in the hacks, the code and language are just different enough to make me think that's bogus."

She was skimming articles on the other monitors. "This guy doesn't care about the fishing rights or shipping lanes in the South China Sea. It's only an excuse, something that matters to the countries I work with as a liaison."

Sam leaned back in his chair. "You do realize China and Vietnam will never be good friends."

"We just need them to be civil," she replied in her cool, State Department voice.

"I keep asking myself what anyone gains by embarrassing you or sending the FBI into your apartment."

"Distraction? Collateral damage?"

"No."

His stern reply pulled her attention and she glanced down to find him staring up at her as if she was one more piece of research he needed to solve the puzzle. Before her eyes could lock with his mouth, she forced her gaze back to the monitors. "These articles aren't related," she said, trying to stay on point.

"Why haven't you changed clothes?" he asked.

"The zipper is stuck," she said. "Hang on. You shouldn't have access to this report." She pointed to a draft of a report she'd written last year. The final version had supposedly been sent up the line and stored on secure State Department servers.

He followed her finger. "Technically, I don't have access."

"Sam." Fresh panic made her palms sweat. "My boss told me not to log on." They'd need to come up with an excuse and fast. She thought of calling the office, but it was late and Sam had her phone too.

The chair creaked. Sam stood up and walked around behind her. "Relax."

At his touch she jumped, having blanked on the real reason for entering his office.

"Madison, it's okay. You're not logged in. Neither one of us has disobeyed your boss." He pointed out a flat black rectangle. "That report was copied from your hard drive and the copy was made in my secure lab when I picked apart your laptop."

"Oh." She clamped her mouth shut when one of his hands slid between the fabric of her dress and her skin as he started working the zipper at her back. Finally it gave, lowering with a slow, subtle rasp to the base of her spine. The office air was cool as the panels parted, exposing her bare skin to his view and the warmer touch of his fingers.

"Thank you." Too late, she remembered the new black lace lingerie with the sexy red bow at the back that he could probably see perfectly. If she asked, would he put those lips to her skin?

"Do you still dance?" His rough voice set her pulse skipping.

"No." Her last performance had been for a stage production during the spring semester of her sophomore year of college. "I take ballet classes when I can, just to unwind. There's a studio near the office."

"You move so gracefully," he murmured. One blunt fingertip trailed down her spine to her bra strap and back to the nape of her neck.

How could there be so much pleasure, so much significance, in that small caress? She turned to face him, feeling exposed by far more than the open panels of her dress. She ached to wrap herself around him and caught herself as the doctor's orders clanged through her mind. Sam needed rest. The best way to be sure he obeyed that order was to stay up with him. "I'll be right back," she said.

Behind his glasses, he blinked a couple of times. "You don't have to stay up with me."

"I'm your best resource. That's fact, not ego," she assured him, pushing her lips into a smile. If she could focus on the puzzle the way he did, she'd get through this in one piece. "Give me just a minute."

She dashed back to her room and shimmied out of

the dress. She pulled on her new denim shorts and a boxy loose-weave sweater, pushing up the sleeves to her elbows. When she returned to his office, he was back in his chair studying the multifaceted issues between the countries she served as liaison. He'd pulled up the second chair beside his.

"Why did China choose to feature the white jade cup?" he asked when she sat down.

"We've been working on this exhibit for more than a year. They want to show Americans a trusting, touchy-feely side to encourage understanding and foster co-operation."

"Did we send something to a museum over there?"

She chuckled. "People. In general our best-received asset overseas is our innovation." She explained a bit more about what the cooperative effort entailed.

"Tell me about Liu." Sam's hands were bringing up the general information from typical online searches of the name. "How long have you known him?"

She watched him work while she explained the developing professional relationship. Sitting here, talking over the issues with him, was so satisfying and compelling. "Why don't you like him?"

Sam shrugged those broad shoulders and then stretched his arms high overhead. "I don't dislike him. You know I'm better with computers than people."

She disagreed, though she kept the thought to herself.

"Some of the questions he asked at the reception made me uneasy."

That put Madison on alert. "What questions?"

Sam waved off her concern. "Rush and I can get paranoid when people ask about our software."

"He wanted to talk about Gray Box during the reception?"

"We have a global reach," Sam said. "He's probably a customer."

She stifled a yawn and checked the clock. They were creeping up on midnight and he seemed fresh as ever. She pulled her feet up to the chair and wrapped her hands around her knees. "That's not what you mean."

"No. I ran it by Rush. It might've been a polite way to show interest, the way you described him. Something about it felt like fishing, but what do I know?"

Quite a bit. She kept that thought quiet, as well. "He can't want to poach you," she said. "His personal business interests don't run to software."

Sam didn't reply. He was rolling the mouse around another article until his gaze had landed on her toe. "How did I miss this?" He leaned over for a closer look at the daisy.

Her heart hammered. Being the object of his single-mindedness made her knees weak and her skin prickle with awareness. "Spur of the moment, girl day decision," she said in a voice barely more than a whisper. She wiggled her toe, silently inviting him to touch.

He did. That one teasing stroke along the tip of her toe had her biting back a moan. "It suits you." When he met her gaze the yearning in his brown eyes scorched her.

"I want to kiss you," she admitted.

"I'm right here," he replied. He swiveled a bit, tugged

her chair closer to his between his knees. He ran his hands over her feet, up to her knees and back down.

"Sam, the doctor said—"

His lips twitched up at one corner. "He isn't here." He ran his hands up to her knees and down over her thighs this time, his fingertips sliding just under the hem of her shorts before retreating. Started over.

Feeling boneless, she was primed and ready for him already.

"Your legs are gorgeous," he said. "I could do this all night."

She'd never survive it if he didn't do more.

"Your lead," he reminded her.

Her pulse stuttered, but her hands were steady as she laid them over his on top of her knees while she caught her breath. She dropped her feet to the floor and leaned into him. Stroking the length of his arms, she relished the thick, carved shape of his biceps, the solid curves of his shoulders. She dragged her hands down the hard angles of his chest and teased the skin of his stomach just under the hem of his shirt.

She wet her lips, watched his eyes, dark with need, follow the motion.

Her lead. She eased her chair back, hiding a smirk when his eyebrows dipped into a frown. He would let her go, she knew it. She wanted to stay right here in this moment. With him. Standing, she peeled her sweater off over her head, let it fall to the floor. His frown was gone, his eyes on the black lace bra as he ripped off his T-shirt.

She laughed when he hooked a finger into the waistband of her shorts and tugged her closer. Leaning down, she kissed him, with all the tenderness and urgency a lifetime of fantasies had built up. She poured all she had into those kisses, everything she wanted to share with him and didn't dare speak the words. His wide palms slid up her back and she pushed her fingers through his hair as he nuzzled her breasts through the lace. Then he flicked open the bra clasp and tossed the lingerie aside, his mouth closing over the tight peak of one nipple. She arched into the marvelous heat of his mouth. He nipped and suckled and tormented each breast in turn until he was her only balance.

"This is better than any fantasy," she whispered.

He chuckled, the light stubble on his chin rasping her sensitive flesh as his mouth blazed a trail down to her navel. "Just wait."

He dropped to his knees and popped open the button of her shorts, lowered the zipper. His tongue dipped and swirled over her skin, inch by inch as he dragged the denim shorts down her legs. He lifted her foot and planted a kiss on the toe sporting the daisy.

"Gorgeous legs," he said again. The words hummed against her skin as he kissed a meandering path from her foot to her inner thigh.

She looked down into his hot brown eyes and surrendered the lead to him. He slipped a finger beneath the thin triangle of black lace and she gasped and bucked at the intimate touch. She was slick and ready, rolling her hips to meet each passionate caress. His devotion was clear in every velvety touch of his tongue, hot press of his lips and bold, claiming touch of his hands.

His name burst from her lips when she climaxed and he caught her, cradling her close when her knees threatened to buckle. "Hang on to me." He surged to his feet, carrying her into his bedroom.

"Your stitches."

"I can only feel you," he said.

Stretched out on his massive bed, she was mesmerized by his body as he stripped off his shorts. "You're a sculptor's dream." She sat up on her knees and he let her hands trace the fascinating ridges and hollows of his torso. She peeked at the injury—which looked fine now—and reached lower, her fingers circling his arousal. He closed his eyes and dropped his head back as she explored and experimented with what pleased him.

Groaning, he rolled her back and kissed her until they were both breathless. "What about your dream?" He trailed kisses over her ear, along her jaw, down the column of her throat. The dusting of hair on his chest teased her aching nipples.

His erection pulsed against her entrance in the sweetest torture. She opened her legs, wrapping them around his. Brushing his hair back from his face, she gave him the truth. "You've always been my dream, Sam."

Holding her gaze, he filled her with one full, deep thrust and her body gripped him in response. He pulled back, just a little and thrust again. She matched his driving rhythm, craving more and more. She clutched his arms as the pleasure built and the second climax ripped through her moments before he found his release.

Sated, she kissed him lazily as he relaxed and

stretched out beside her. When he tucked her into the warm shelter of his body, it was such a remarkable sensation she stayed awake as long as possible to savor the experience.

Chapter Ten

Sam blinked awake, startled by the soft glow of sunlight creeping around the edges of his bedroom windows. He never slept past dawn. More startling, Madison's supple legs were twined with his. Careful not to disturb her, he reached for his watch. Just past seven. He couldn't recall the last time he'd slept for six hours straight.

"You're a wonder," he whispered, kissing her forehead. She challenged him, tempted him and seemed to genuinely care for *him*.

Regardless of the many ways she wowed him, he hadn't intended to leave his search for the hacker undone overnight. Slipping out of bed, he went to the bathroom to clean up and get back to work. The sooner they put her life back together, the sooner he could start working on his next challenge: convincing her to remain his wife.

While she slept, Sam picked up their scattered clothing and dumped it in his hamper before settling at his desk. He poked at the original code some more, testing theories and runs, making little progress. Nothing had popped on the traps he'd set to locate the hacker either.

He was halfway through a second cup of coffee and still didn't have a rock-solid plan to keep Madison safe and restore her career. He wasn't convinced that preventing another attack on the exhibit would annoy the hacker enough to force a mistake. There was an element he was missing. He could sense it; he just couldn't pin it down.

Restless, Sam messaged the investigator Rush had assigned to the mugging incident. With a little luck, that would create a lead they could follow. Sam agreed with Madison that this hacker had an agenda beyond the crap he—or she—was spouting.

Her boss wanted her away from the office. The FBI had yet to demand an interview with her. Still, the pieces swirled around in his mind and he sensed a storm waiting for the perfect conditions to become a hurricane.

Sam fought the temptation to jet away and put her well and truly out of danger. He had the resources, rabbit holes both online and real-world, where they'd never be found. What the public *thought* they knew about him hardly qualified as the tip of the iceberg. Billionaire was a number—an amazing number that garnered immediate influence—but it didn't define him. Brilliant innovator meant more and fit him better, although people generally didn't want to understand how he worked his way from broad concept to finished product.

Madison deserved to hear equivalent praise from her peers. She'd worked hard to make her dreams a reality. Having seen her in action, he knew removing her from that would be akin to taking away his computers and access. Those months in juvenile detention had been the worst of his life. He couldn't do that to her, wouldn't cut something so vital from her life.

I admired you, she'd said. The recollection was nearly as shocking as hearing her say those words last night. No one said things like that to him and never for getting caught in a criminal act.

He had definitely been oblivious of any admiration she'd expressed when they were kids. Of course he'd been wearing the angst and piss-poor attitude as a badge of honor with the singular tenacity unique to teenagers. By some miracle and no small credit to his mom, he'd churned that angst into drive and focus and here he was, on top of the world and so lonely that he'd offered his friend a contract to stick around.

She should've pushed him overboard rather than kiss him. His mind wandered over that delicious terrain without a single regret. With an effort he yanked his mind back on track and returned to his computer. Her current professional crisis needed his full attention.

On his desk, his phone chirped with another automatic update from the museum. Rush had set the program to send immediate alerts and all clears every six hours. The system was clear, no physical or technical glitches found. Their computer systems from administration to the electronic security measures remained virus-free.

"Behaviors," he muttered to himself. He downed another gulp of hot coffee. Without more data he couldn't get a full read on the hacker who had snooped State Department email and attempted to embarrass the US at the museum. Where else could he look?

He opened another search window on the computer and started over. They needed hard facts to go along with his gut instinct and Madison's professional insight. "Behaviors," he muttered. "Behaviors and anomalies."

"Is this a private conversation?"

Madison's voice at his back felt as warm as a ray of sunshine. Swiveling in the chair, he started to answer and went speechless at the sight. Her blond hair rumpled from sleep, she'd pulled on one of his faded black T-shirts, the hem riding high on her sexy thighs. She couldn't have anything on underneath it. His mouth watered and his body went hard.

"I didn't see a robe," she said, watching him closely.

"A perfect substitute," he managed. He wanted to turn her around and take her right back to the bedroom and never let her leave. She'd never want for anything. Neither would he.

"I'll, *um*, go change clothes and then you can catch me up."

The insecure side step toward the door brought him to his feet. He wrapped her in his arms and indulged the need, kissing her until she melted into him once more. "Nothing much to add yet," he admitted, drawing her hips snug against his.

She hummed and her eyes were soft and liquid when she looked up at him. "You might be my cure for coffee." She trailed a finger down the center of his chest. "Can I check the stitches?"

He let her lift his shirt and endured the gentle touches as she gave the healing wound a wide berth. "Well?"

"Looks good," she said.

"Told you." He tipped her chin up for another kiss, smoothed his hand down the soft column of her throat. Somehow he let her go without following her or telling her to hurry.

With the programs running, he killed the waiting time in the kitchen, searching for a breakfast solution. His usual day for grocery delivery was Monday and his supplies were low. She deserved better than the two best options of frozen pizza or cereal with a dash of milk.

She walked back into the kitchen, wearing a halter-top sundress in a blue as soft as the summer sky over the bay. Her hair was down and the golden waves framed her lovely face. His gaze skimmed down to find her feet were bare, that daisy taunting him again. He forced himself to assess the burn on her foot, pleased to see it was healing well.

Please, God, let her need help with this zipper tonight.

"You look like you're ready for a brunch date in the islands." Though he'd meant it as a compliment, she frowned at him, her eyebrows shading those glorious green eyes.

Was she having second thoughts about him? Last night? The next step? He forced his mind away from that gerbil wheel and focused on her. "Why don't we go for brunch?" he said, stopping awkwardly in front of her. "Let me change."

"We should stay in," she reminded him.

Right. "Then why are you dressed up?" She put his graphic tee and worn jeans to shame.

"Because I didn't really buy anything casual. It's

either this or your tees." A blush stained her cheeks. "I need coffee," she said, scooting by him to reach the coffeepot.

He didn't see a zipper on this dress, probably because his mind was too busy conjuring the image of her wearing his T-shirt.

"Have your coffee," he said, surprised his voice didn't crack. He pulled his cell phone from his pocket and set it on the countertop. "Check the directory and make your choice for delivery."

She stared at the phone as if it might explode. "I can't get delivery in the middle of Sunday brunch rush. I'm not you."

"And the world rejoices." He grinned, came back and kissed her cheek. "Per the society page, you're my wife, remember? Whoever you call will deliver."

And if they didn't, he'd make sure they understood the gravity of the slight. He hustled to the bedroom before she could argue.

He chose khaki slacks and a white, short-sleeved polo shirt. He found his deck shoes in the closet and slid his watch over his wrist, his wallet into his pocket. They had a great deal of waiting ahead of them and the day was gorgeous. He decided they would take the Lamborghini for a drive along the coast after breakfast. Thankfully, Madison wasn't the type shallow enough to sell out as his wife for the wealth, but showing off a little and giving her a taste of how smooth life could be couldn't hurt his long game.

"That was fast," she said, her gaze cruising over him from head to toe when he returned to the kitchen.

"Fast isn't all bad," he said. "In the right context."

Her tongue darted over her lips and her cheeks colored again. He gave himself a point on the imaginary scoreboard in his head and picked up his phone. "How long do we have?"

Her gaze dropped to her coffee. "Maybe ten more minutes?"

"If I had my choice, we'd be going out." He leaned across the counter and smoothed a lock of her hair behind her ear. "We still can," he said.

She didn't lift her gaze. "I don't want you embarrassed if the FBI shows up. Or worse."

"You're innocent." He had to work to hide his frustration. "We'll prove it." He had to prove it sooner rather than later.

"I know." She backed away from his touch and hugged herself, effectively shutting him out.

Something snapped inside him and he reordered his day. He was letting his personal desire and pervasive loneliness shift the top priority. He couldn't waste time selfishly thinking of romantic drives when she so clearly needed a resolution.

"You stay here and eat." He opened the panel near the door and chose the keys to the Porsche. "I'll go in to the office and prove it."

She rounded the counter and hurried forward, catching his arm in her slender hands. "I'm not trying to insult you or ignore your generosity, Sam."

Generosity? That wasn't the word he'd use for last night. He swallowed the knee-jerk sarcastic response. "I know that." He toyed with the keys in his hand. Man up, he told himself. "You called me in to help you with the hacker." He'd blurred the lines, hoping to win her affection with a little time and superb sex. "Stay here. You'll be safe." Somehow he managed not to grab her close and kiss her goodbye.

"What happened to working together?" she asked.

"I'll focus better working alone." He used his phone to reset the security system for her.

Her curls swayed over her bare shoulders as she shook her head. "You need my input."

He shrugged. "I'll call when I hit that point."

He was walking out when the bell rang at the delivery door downstairs. He angled the camera and confirmed the restaurant logo on the ball cap and bag. He glanced down and saw Madison's feet were still bare. "I'll get it. Wait here."

Naturally, she didn't listen, slipping into the elevator with him. "I paid already and added a tip."

"You didn't put it on my account?"

"No." She shook her head. "Why would I do that?"

Because I'm your husband, he thought, unable to come up with a sane answer. For some reason, that made him angrier than her common sense about staying in for brunch. Irrational, but true. Silently, he cursed Spalding for being dumb enough to follow a hacker's trail and make Madison paranoid.

He heard her exclamation when the elevator doors parted on a standard building lobby. All glass and marble, staged with a desk, plants and a waiting area.

"Why go to the trouble when you live here alone?" she asked.

"In case I want to develop or sell," he answered. "Wait here." He tapped a code into the panel and opened the door to accept the delivery.

The deliveryman—woman, he noticed—smiled at him. "Good morning," she said politely.

"Hi," he replied. "They gave Nate a morning off?"

"Yes." The name tag on her shirt looked brand new, with Kellie printed in bright red on the white background. "Your wife's credit card did not go through."

"That's impossible."

In the reflection off the glass, Sam saw Madison rounding the corner. He waved her back. "Just put it on my account," he said.

"Yes, sir." The deliverywoman held out a small clipboard. "Sign here please."

"Sam!"

His hands occupied with clipboard and pen, Madison's warning saved him. He dodged when the deliverywoman swung the bag at his head and blocked with an elbow, trying to push her onto the street. He had to jump back when sunlight bounced off the blade of a knife in her hand. He was damn tired of knives.

"Hit the alarm," he shouted to Madison.

Kellie used the advantage, lunging into the lobby. He countered, using the clipboard to jab her and push her back to the door. He didn't want her to get away, yet he couldn't let her too close to Madison.

Kellie clearly had superb martial arts training, but Sam learned to fight dirty in juvie. As they circled, he judged the reach, the options. Get under the knife and he could do some damage. She was quicker than the mugger and had a clear, deadly intent about her.

She came at him in a flurry of limbs, slithering around him like mercury. The clipboard cracked in two when he used it to block a kick. Better than his jaw, he decided, tossing the pieces aside. Sam changed tactics, not playing to win, just buying time. All he had to do was keep Kellie busy and not die before help arrived. As she spun by him again, he landed a hard jab to her kidneys.

It only pissed her off. With a terror-inducing scream, she leaped at him, knife leading the way. He struck the elbow of her knife hand. Her grip held. Driving a fist into her gut, he heard her breath explode from her chest and still she snarled as she rolled to her feet.

He'd miscalculated his position and now she was between him and Madison. Why hadn't he shown Madison the safe room? He jerked, ready to chase down Kellie, but she didn't bolt for Madison. She remained fixed on him. He waited, determined to draw her to him like a bullfighter in the ring. He watched her coil and spring into another attack and fell back as the knife whizzed past his throat. He caught her ankle and yanked, dumping her on her face. She twisted and kicked out. He reached for that foot and missed. Her shoe scraped the side of his face and plowed into his shoulder.

He rolled with her, his only hope against the next arc of the knife, when he heard a muffled clang and her body went limp.

Sam looked up into Madison's furious face, letting his gaze trace down to the fire extinguisher she held in both hands. She was braced to deal another blow. "Is she out?"

"Kick that knife away." When Madison had the knife out of reach, Sam shook Kellie's limp leg, then extricated himself and stood up.

"Nice job," he said. "Thanks."

She blew a strand of hair from her face, unwilling to release her hold on her makeshift weapon. "You had her."

He wasn't so sure. "I let her too close to you." He pulled Madison into his arms. "I'm sorry. I should have shown you the safe room."

"I wouldn't have left you." She silenced his apologies and erased his regrets with a swift, hard kiss. "I'm fine, Sam. She was after *you*."

Chapter Eleven

While he processed her statement with a confused stare, Madison leaped into action, running her hands over his face, down his arms and chest. She knew what she'd seen and that woman had been after Sam. She was about to reiterate that when a swarm of men poured through the lobby doors. Uniformed police, along with two men dressed in street clothes and, to her dismay, Special Agent Spalding and three men in FBI Windbreakers.

Two of the four from the San Francisco Police Department cuffed the woman. They bagged the knife as evidence and hauled her away to an address specified by Spalding.

"Is there somewhere we can talk?" Spalding asked.

Madison ignored him, looking to Sam. "He should see a doctor before we do anything else."

Sam waved off her concern. "I'm good enough," he said. "Let's go upstairs."

She didn't want to spoil the serenity of Sam's condo by inviting Spalding and his team into the space. "Why don't we go to the office? After a trip to the doctor," she offered.

Spalding eyed them both, as if he wasn't sure where things stood. She wasn't about to put a definition on it for him.

"You can start here and now," Sam said. He slid his arm around her waist. "I'm not leaving until I know the lobby is secured."

Disgusted, Spalding shook his head, then turned and barked orders to the personnel working the scene. When Sam was satisfied, he led them around the corner to the elevators. Madison expected him to call the elevator they'd used to return to the condo, curious when he pressed the button for a different elevator. As they traveled up two floors according to the display above the door, Madison wondered how many secrets Sam had built into this building.

They exited the elevator into what appeared to be a standard office suite. She raised an eyebrow at the man playing her husband and almost missed the answering, fleeting smirk.

"How many cameras are on me right now?" Spalding asked, looking around.

Sam tipped his head as if counting. "You might be more concerned with the signal jammers."

"Seriously?" The FBI agent planted his hands on his hips.

"Take a seat," Madison said, leading by example. She settled into one of the four upholstered chairs surrounding a low table in a waiting area in front of the windows overlooking the front street. "How can I help you?" she said, determined to prove she had nothing to hide.

"You're married?" Spalding asked.

"You knew I was," she replied.

"Actually, nothing in our standard observation we ran before the reception confirmed it," he shot back.

Sam stood at her back. "Not even the marriage license on file in Nevada?"

"That has held up," Spalding allowed.

Madison felt like an insect about to get flattened as the FBI agent watched her. "What happened at my apartment?"

"Why do you maintain a separate residence from your husband?"

"Privacy," Sam answered before she could open her mouth. "In light of current events, you can see why we'd find it prudent."

Spalding cocked his head. "According to the neighbors, on the night of the reception a man was buzzed into the building. He pounded on your door, demanding you let him in."

"No one was buzzed in by Madison," Sam said. "We weren't there. Have you identified the man?"

Spalding shifted. "Yes. He was a low-level assistant at the Chinese consulate. His body was found this morning behind a garbage bin in an alley two blocks away."

"No." Madison's self-control fractured. Without Sam's palms on her shoulders she wouldn't know up from down. "Have you made some connection between that man and me?" She hated how her voice quavered.

"Not beyond his appearance at your door. What concerns me is the timing, Mrs. Goode."

"Bellemere," Sam corrected.

"We received a tip shortly after the reception ended

that you've been taking bribes, Mrs. Bellemere," Spalding emphasized the last name with a glare for Sam. "Then this man comes to your door, apparently desperate and now he's dead."

"You know this wasn't her," Sam muttered.

The doubt was clear in Spalding's eyes. Madison swallowed around the panic in her throat. "You couldn't call and ask me about this directly?"

"You weren't there to ask," Spalding replied. "I'm asking now." He withdrew an envelope from his inner pocket. "Do you recognize any of these men?"

She studied each face, all of them with Asian features, none of them familiar. "No." She knew Spalding didn't believe her. "I'm excellent with faces," she said. "If these men were essential to the staff within the consulates I work with, I would know them. How can I help you close this investigation?"

"Our investigation is only getting started," Spalding evaded.

"You'll never be able to close the investigation if you keep chasing bogus tips," Sam snarled. "I'm calling our lawyer."

She appreciated his protective nature and the way he played his part as her husband with such dedication. "Did you receive the tip by email?"

Spalding tucked the pictures back into the envelope and the envelope back into his jacket. "Yes. We received another communication this morning that you were helping extricate a spy from the Chinese delegation."

"You believe the spy is the dead man?" She laughed. She clapped a hand over her mouth, but the hysterical giggles kept bubbling up. "Excuse me," she said, catching her breath. "First of all, you've interviewed my boss and coworkers by now. You must know an accusation like that is pure fiction. If it *were* true, it would be well above my pay grade."

"Your boss said the same thing."

She took comfort in his sincerity and pushed aside her fears to get a better read on him. "Can I be candid?" On her shoulders, Sam's hands tensed. Spalding seemed relieved by the offer, rolling a hand for her to continue. "My guess is you're investigating this absurd accusation for appearances only. You already know I'm innocent."

"We aren't finding anything to contradict that conclusion," Spalding allowed.

"If you drop it, the tipster will know we're onto him," she said.

"Yes." Spalding leaned back, holding up his hands in surrender. "Candidly, the cyber team is having no luck with the hacker who targeted the exhibit. You didn't help us when you blocked him out with the added security," he said to Sam.

"My wife expressed a desire for the exhibit to be safe. I will always do what I can to support her."

Wife was an amazing word when Sam used it. It would take a valiant effort to remember their marriage was fake when they were alone again.

"Since the reception you've been attacked twice, am I right, Mr. Bellemere?"

Madison's intuition spiked with the new line of inquiry. Spalding knew more than he was willing to share.

"My bad luck for being in the news lately," Sam replied, blowing off two attempts on his life.

Spalding sat forward. "With your permission," he glanced up at Sam, "and with your assistance, I'd like to pull Mrs. Bellemere's banking records."

She caught herself before she looked around for a Mrs. Bellemere. "You want to bait a trap for the tipster or hacker or whatever group is behind this?"

"He agrees with me, sweetheart," Sam said, squeezing her shoulder. "The hacker—by any definition—is targeting you." Sam came around and sat down, obviously intrigued now. "There has to be a reason. We'll help."

Spalding's gaze narrowed. "Are you volunteering Gray Box resources or solely your individual efforts?"

Sam grinned. "You can't go wrong by either answer. Consider me a consultant to your cybercrime team. We can work out a payment schedule if you can't afford my standard fee up front."

"Sam," she murmured, shaking her head. "Don't do this. Not on the record. You've been attacked twice already since our marriage went public."

"Because I'm in the way and my well-known skills are a threat to the hacker's big plan." He reached out and took her hand. "Putting your bank records in jeopardy is far better than putting you personally in the line of fire."

She couldn't argue with his logic and yet it made her nervous. "What measures will you take to protect him?" she asked Special Agent Spalding.

"Us," Sam amended.

"I've had you both under surveillance since the initial tip came in," Spalding admitted.

"Pardon me?" She came to her feet and crowded Spalding. "Your team allowed Sam to be mugged and stabbed? That hardly encourages our trust. And today, you didn't even try to help. You didn't walk in until we knocked her out."

Spalding laced his fingers, tapped his thumbs together. "I know how it looks—"

She cut him off, gaining steam without raising her voice. "What about the real delivery person? Have you sent anyone to find out how that woman got a uniform and name tag? I want some ground rules. We'll need some assurances in writing or we'll handle this on our own."

Spalding jumped in when she paused for breath. "We're on the same team. I promise you we'll share everything we have," he said, aiming a look at Sam. "Unless you already know what we know?"

"He hasn't broken any of his promises," she snapped before Sam could say something to make Spalding wary. "I have one more question before we move forward."

"Yes?"

"Do you have a theory about why *I* have been the target of this scheme?"

"I believe the person, or persons, behind this feels as if they can abuse some perceived connection to you. It's something I'd like to review with you if you'll come to the office."

Her knees trembled a bit at the idea of voluntarily visiting the FBI office. She sat down, perched at the edge of her chair. "Do you believe Sam's intervention at the museum caused this person to escalate?" She was already creating a short list of people with the skill and reach necessary to pull off such a stunt. Unfortunately the list grew when she added in people with the resources to hire the talent.

"Someone is working very hard to make us believe you're abusing your position for personal gain."

It made no sense. The idea of someone maligning her was bad enough. Having confirmation that Sam's troubles were a direct result of her inviting him into the mess made her sick to her stomach. "Can we leave him out of it?" she asked.

"Not a chance." Sam caught her hand, held tight. "I have some ideas to corral this troublemaker," he said, his fingers twitching as if the code was coming together in his mind already.

"Great. For convenience, we'll work at my office," Spalding said. "My team has traced the informant to IP addresses all over the world."

"You're not buying that, are you?" Sam asked. He flicked a hand. "I can sit right here and make people in England think I'm tucked up at the bar in their local pub. I'll go along and bring your team up to speed, but I'll work better in my own space."

"That's true," Madison said absently. She trusted Sam's safety to Gray Box security over the FBI at this rate. They'd come a long way from email viruses, haphazard attempts on firewalls to conflicting manifestos, fraud and murder in a short time frame.

"I'll keep you dialed in to my progress," he promised.

Before they could argue, Madison stepped in. "What can I do?" She wouldn't sit back and twiddle her thumbs while they did all the heavy lifting necessary to find the root of the problem.

Spalding sighed. "According to your boss, you're one of the best at analysis and you have that personal X factor that makes you some paragon of diplomatic interaction. I believe the hacker knows you, is possibly afraid of you since your marriage went public. I need your expertise. While the tech geniuses can pin down the hacker's location, you and I can work the case from the personnel perspective."

Although she worried she was leading Sam into a legal trap, she knew they had to cooperate in any way possible.

"Mrs. Bellemere, I've been through your apartment, your office and your background." He paused, holding her gaze. "We need to show this hacker that I believe what he's spoon-feeding me so he makes a mistake."

She looked at Sam, hoping for confirmation or a dissenting opinion. He was scowling at his phone display.

"There is an event at the Vietnamese consulate tonight. I'd like you and your husband to join your boss and his wife for cocktails. I've cleared it with your boss."

She cringed, knowing Sam would hate that. "I can manage it alone," she said to Sam.

He turned the phone upside down on his thigh. "Not after this morning." He shook his head. "I don't care if Rush's top investigator and all his dark ops buddies are tailing you, we're not splitting up now."

She couldn't argue with him. Not while her heart did silly pirouettes in her chest over his declaration.

"With your permission, Mr. and Mrs. Bellemere, I'd like to bring you both in," Spalding said. "Since the society page hit on Saturday morning, there have been paparazzi and teams from the consulates hovering around your building. Our exit won't resemble an arrest," he added quickly. "Let's capitalize on the opportunity. Officially, we'll have a candid conversation. Unofficially, Sam will meet with the cyber team while you and I sort out who's who in this drama."

"I need my purse and shoes," she said. "We'll meet you at the front doors in ten minutes."

"And you're stopping to pick up breakfast for us on the way," Sam added.

The FBI headquarters in San Francisco were modern and clean and although Special Agent Spalding had been grim in public, his friendlier side returned as she and Sam wolfed down their breakfast at a table in the small conference room near his office. Although Sam gave her a quick kiss before moving off to confer with the cyber team, Madison felt the skepticism rolling off the FBI agent in charge as he watched them.

When she was alone with Spalding in his office, he rolled up a map of the city covering one wall to reveal a board with her official head shot surrounded by co-workers and associates from the foreign ministry divisions she served.

Panic flared and for a moment she was sure he'd fooled them. Sam had called Rush and had the legal team standing by, but it was little comfort right now.

She braced for someone to cuff her and read her her rights. "That's intimidating."

"It's meant to be," Spalding admitted.

Madison was reluctantly impressed with what Spalding had accomplished in less than forty-eight hours. He had outlined all the key players at the consulates and their latest interactions with her. He also had left up the initial information from the anonymous tip.

"What are you thinking?"

She hesitated, even though she'd promised to cooperate. "These men followed us from the exhibit gala," she said, pointing to the Vietnamese team. "Does their consulate find me suspect, as well?"

"If you go by the round the clock surveillance, they are curious." Spalding removed his suit coat and draped it over his desk chair. He studied her, hands in his pockets. "They haven't admitted anything to me, of course. It would be helpful to know if they're having similar attacks on their systems."

She made a mental note to reach out directly when she got home.

"Not one person I've spoken with has anything untoward to say about you or your work," Spalding said. "Usually, I wouldn't consider that a good thing, but I've seen you in action. Your instincts at the museum were spot on. Either you were expecting the problem because you were in on it, or you've gained some expertise from your husband through the years."

"My knowledge is summed up by the fact that I know when to call in an expert." Turning back to the board, she thought of the stories—the good and the awkward—

to go with nearly every face. "I've been liaison to these two consulates for nearly five years," she mused.

"From the interviews I'd say you've made real friendships."

"No." She shook her head. "Not friends, strong acquaintances. There tends to be frequent turnover with consular staff." She wished she was wearing one of her suits rather than this sundress for this meeting. "What's your end game?" she queried. At the startled lift of his eyebrows, she tapped the big board. "Everyone you've put on this board has diplomatic immunity, except me."

"The US has successfully prosecuted diplomats in the past."

She folded her arms over her chest. "We both know that is a rare occurrence. Someone out there is using me and making a mockery of foreign relationships. You started this board looking for a scapegoat."

His hesitation was all the confirmation she needed. "I started this board, Madison, because a solid tip told me you were a problem child. How long have you known Bellemere?"

"He tutored me in high school," she replied.

"In what subjects?"

That wary feeling returned tenfold. She faced him with the calm and composure her boss lauded. Her gut churned with nerves, but she'd be damned if Spalding knew it. "Math and computer science. Both subjects have changed quite a bit since I was a junior in high school."

"I'm aware." Spalding dragged out his chair and

dropped into it. He pointed at the board. "You aren't going to throw anyone under the bus, are you?"

"No." She came over and took one of the chairs across from his desk. "I'm a professional, Special Agent Spalding. There are enough challenges with this situation already if you hope to make any charges stick. What do you have in mind?"

His candor startled her as he listed out the possibilities, all of them connected with fraud and criminal computer behavior. Making her banking vulnerable opened up a few international options, as well. "You're assuming this hacker is in the States," she said as the key to his case dawned on her.

"It's a long shot," Spalding admitted. "Although my team is on board with that theory." He leaned forward. "When do I get to hear your analysis?"

"My analysis hasn't changed much from the ornery stunt at the museum." She studied the board again. "The person orchestrating this is someone who knows the right buttons to push with the big-issue chatter but is interested in a more personal outcome. The people with the real access are either hiring a young person or unaware that someone young and cocky is using them."

She walked him through the personal relationships and business interests of the people he'd tacked on to that board. No one had any obvious reason to take such a convoluted route through her to stir up discord. "Even when the insults are subtle, the rhetoric is clear," she mused. "All of the countries with an interest in the rights and resources of the South China Sea know what's at stake. National pride and revenue top the list.

Framing me doesn't fit with the usual up-front bluster or behind the scenes negotiating."

When Spalding's phone rang he ignored it and they continued to discuss the latest sound bites and agendas of the foreign delegates she knew. A few minutes later, Sam burst into the office and she had to assume the people trailing behind him belonged to Spalding's cyber team. "Answer your phone," he snapped at Spalding. "He's in the States," he added. "I'll show you."

Sam took her hand and pulled her from the chair. "You're gonna love this." Clearly expecting the others to follow, he hurried out of the office. He was practically vibrating with excitement as he led her down the hall and into a stairwell. "You okay?" he asked in a whisper.

She nodded.

Sam pushed through a swinging door into a hallway with zero aesthetics beyond the glossy cream paint on the concrete block walls. He stopped short at the secure door at the end of the hall, waiting impatiently for Spalding to put a card to the panel and unlock the door.

The big square room had several stations similar to Sam's office at home and along one wall, monitors were set up for video conferencing. She had the feeling Sam's equipment and skill would still outdistance Spalding's team.

Sam reminded her of a kid bursting with pride over a perfect report card as he gave her a crash course on the program they were using to find the hacker. "He wants us to believe he's in the Philippines."

"My team found his code signature in use in Amsterdam."

"Both sites are bogus." Sam signaled another member of the cyber team. "Bring it up."

As the graphics filled the largest screen, Sam explained the origination of several attempts on the State Department software. "I don't believe any of these locations are legit. It gives us a starting point. I can work with this and pick up his trail."

"You did this in less than an hour?" Spalding squinted at the colors crisscrossing the world map.

"You have a great team," Sam said. "They pick up quick."

Madison clamped her lips together, smothering a giggle at his casual, unintentional arrogance.

"I don't see anything stateside."

Sam nodded to the man at the keyboard. "The sites used overseas are known cells for kids like this one. We can build on it," he repeated.

Madison caught Sam's eye. "Are we done?"

"No." Spalding answered, although she'd spoken to Sam. "Not until I have a suspect identified and under control. I'll be requesting your pay history this afternoon."

"I already did that," Sam said, oblivious of Spalding's glare. "If he's in the State Department system, the hacker won't be able to resist pushing his luck for a look at your accounts. He'll want to tinker in there if only to give his tips more weight. We can use that for insight into tactics and motive." He checked his cell phone again and scowled. "I can use this. I need to get to my place. I've called my driver."

"Go work your magic," Spalding said. "Just be on time for cocktails tonight."

"We'll be there," Madison said.

Sam nearly hauled her out of the lab, then the building, his eyes on his phone the entire way. Hopefully she hadn't promised something she couldn't deliver. If she couldn't drag him away from his computers, she'd sneak out and handle the cocktail party on her own.

His attention didn't waver when the black sedan pulled up at the curb. As soon as they were in the car, she said to Jake, "To the condo, please."

"You got it, Mrs. B."

She wanted to laugh at the nickname the driver had given her, but instead she gave Sam's tough shoulder a shake. "What are you doing?"

"We have the programs running," he said. "Museum and now the bank." He pushed his glasses to his forehead and rubbed his eyes. "It's not fast enough." He swore.

"Sam, what haven't you told me?"

He turned the phone and shuffled the information displayed, enlarging it until a spreadsheet filled the screen. He leaned close so she could see it too. "I can show you more when we get home, but I think this line is a countdown operation."

"To what?" she asked.

"Nothing good," he replied. "If I'm reading this right, the first deadline coincided with the reception and the second with the disturbance at your apartment."

An icy chill dripped down her spine and she shivered. "There's no reason to target me."

"That's what's happened." He looked up from the phone and met her gaze. "You're being set up. You, the office or the country. I can't be sure which, can't make a plan without more information."

"I'm scared," she admitted. For herself, her office and her country and for him.

He tossed the phone to the opposite seat and took her hand in his. "Me too."

"You are?" The raw honesty in his voice shocked her. "Scared of what?"

"Letting you down." He glanced at the boarded-up lobby door as they passed the front of his building. "I won't lie, this kid is good."

"You're better," she said with a quiet conviction. This wasn't the confidence of an infatuated girl coursing through her. It was the utter certainty of a woman who knew how amazing and lucky she was to have him on her side. She did all she could to let him see that radiating from her, to feel how much she believed in him.

"Maddie…" His brown eyes flashed with unspoken emotion.

The car bumped as Jake pulled into the garage and then they were around the corner, up the ramp and stopped at the elevator.

"All clear?" Sam asked.

"Yes, sir."

"That's your cue, genius." Madison kissed him lightly on the lips. "Let's get to work."

Whatever he'd been about to say, the moment had passed. She told herself she was relieved. She didn't want to know what he'd been about to say, wasn't sure she could cope with any more revelations or limitations just now.

For now, it was enough to love *him*. She knew she couldn't survive in a one-sided relationship long-term, but for now, she could manage. He liked her, that was obvious and they were great in bed, she thought with an inward smile. Loving him would make the show more convincing for anyone watching tonight, tomorrow or however long it took them to find the hacker.

Chapter Twelve

In his private computer lab, Sam worked through the afternoon. He'd called in reinforcements in the form of Rush and an extra-large sausage and black olive pizza. Together they'd isolated the countdown, though they weren't much closer to making an identification or finding the accurate location of the hacker.

After she'd gotten past the shock and awe of his lab, Madison had set herself up at another computer, creating a digital reconstruction of the investigation board in Spalding's office. Occasionally Sam heard her muttering or making notes; for the most part he blocked her out. Realizing that he could ignore her bothered him. On the one hand he was grateful that she wasn't distracting him and on the other hand he wondered what was wrong with him.

"Your building is all perfect and pretty again," Rush teased, pointing out an email with a picture of the completed repairs downstairs.

"Thanks for handling that," he said. "This guy isn't over twenty," he added, pushing his glasses up and rubbing at his tired eyes. "Well, I think the hacker is male. Either way, not over twenty. Can't be."

"I'll keep at it," Rush said. "You need to go upstairs and get dressed. Madison left half an hour ago."

"She did?" Sam swiveled around on the stool, more than a little unnerved he hadn't heard her leave.

"Go on and have fun."

"Fun." Cocktails with strangers while someone was playing a dangerous game didn't sound like fun. "Fun," he repeated as it dawned on him. He sat back down at the keyboard and typed in new parameters. "Behaviors. Fun. Follow these stops." He pulled up the map from the FBI. "He's been to these places."

"You got it."

"I have to tell her." Sam jumped back from the work counter and bolted for the stairs, ignoring Rush's laughter. "Madison will know what that means."

He stormed through the stair access door of the condo, calling her name. "Madison!" He turned for his office and bedroom to find her. "Madison?"

"Right here," she replied in that serene voice that smoothed over all his rough edges.

She was behind him, emerging from the guest room side of the condo. He did a double take, realizing he'd expected her to be in his room. Later, he told himself. They had a hacker to find. Then he saw the dress, the same dress as last night and his mind fixated on the idea of the lingerie she wore underneath. He cleared his throat. "Need any help with that zipper?"

She blushed. "Not yet." She tipped her head to put on her earring. The long spill of cool, sparkling silver caught his eye. "Lucy." She answered the question he hadn't yet asked. "The car will be here in fifteen minutes."

"I know. He's young," he blurted.

"You've thought so from the start."

Sam checked the wall clock and moved toward his bedroom. "Come on. I'll explain while I change clothes."

He stripped off his shirt on the way and had his jeans halfway down his hips when he caught her leaning in the doorway, her green eyes hot, her teeth buried in her lip. "Like the view?"

"Absolutely," she admitted in her unflappable way.

"You're in diplomat mode," he stated, stripping off his boxers and reaching to turn on the shower. In the mirror, he caught the sheer longing on her face when she thought he wasn't looking.

"I am." Her voice halted. "You were saying the hacker is young?"

He knew it wouldn't take much to get her out of the dress and into the shower with him, but that would wreck the schedule. He and Rush had discovered a countdown in place for this evening.

He turned the water to cold and cleaned up in record time. Toweling off, he walked her through the bouncing IP address locations and the creative code language and behaviors Sam had found unique to one person shadowing the hacker group. "I think he's been to the places he's using to bounce the signal."

"A globetrotting teenager."

"Isn't that common in your circles?" He pulled out a

dark suit and dressed quickly, the task more challenging as his body responded so readily to the passion simmering in her gaze as she watched.

"Yes." Her eyebrows dipped and her lips pursed in thought. "Doesn't that give us a bigger pool of suspects?"

"Only if you know them all," he teased. "Rush and I used to be thrill-seeking teenagers, without the global access." He buttoned the dress shirt, tucked it into his slacks. "We put out a few things we hope will catch his attention." He found his cuff links. "Do I have to wear a tie?"

"Yes." She walked into his closet and pulled one from the organizer. Looping it over his head, she proceeded to tie it for him.

His mind spun out visions of making love to her right here, in the closet. Man, he had it bad. "That's a lot more enjoyable when you do it."

A sexy grin played at the corner of her lips. "Just wait until I take it off later."

He kissed her, long and deep, reveling in the way she kissed him back with those lush lips and her whole body pressed close. If he was lucky, all the words that kept jamming up in his head and throat would be clear to her in his actions. "Later it is," he agreed, resting his forehead against hers.

Consulate General of Vietnam, 8:40 p.m.

NORMALLY TWO MINUTES of cocktails and polite chatter would have Sam running for his noise-canceling headphones and a computer. Circulating and socializing with Madison on his arm was a completely different experience. Her warm and gracious manners put him at ease rather than on edge. The pride in her voice when she introduced him made him believe they'd married for love.

"You make this easy," he said quietly as she made another graceful exit from a conversation.

"Years of practice," she reminded him. "Do you need a break to check the phone?"

"No," he replied. It was true. "Rush knows what to do." He waited out another brief conversation. "You're pondering the hacker's ID, aren't you?"

"Among other things." She took a sip of her wine. "Spalding insisted we attend and I can't figure out why. No one seems troubled to see me. There hasn't been so much as an awkward pause in conversation. Even Mr. and Mrs. Liu are having a good time." She nodded to them across the room.

"Is anyone you expected to see missing?"

"No," she replied, smiling.

"Any party crashers?" he queried.

"Not one."

He could tell she was frustrated, though it didn't show at all on her face. "Well, maybe he wanted me to fully appreciate your skill with small talk." He marveled at her ability to make him feel included. He'd always been an outsider at these things. She introduced him to another couple, chatted and moved on again. "If Rush gets wind of this, you're likely to get a job offer," he said.

"Oh?" She paused in her scan of the room to peer up at him.

He winked. "Definitely. He'd give you a high-powered title along the lines of 'Certified Sam Handler.'" When she giggled he felt as if he'd slayed a dragon. "I wish there was dancing tonight."

Her lips parted. "You're kidding."

He angled his body closer, just enough to block her view of the room. "I'm not." Holding her hand, he ran his thumb over the wedding set. "I want to hold you, Madison. Forever."

"Sam, I can't. Not here."

I can't. The blatant plea in her eyes startled him. Silenced him. "Let's get some air," he suggested, unable to keep the stiffness out of his voice.

"Please."

On the terrace, with the breeze ruffling her golden hair, he resisted the temptation to try and voice his thoughts more eloquently. "When will we have done enough mingling to satisfy Spalding?" he asked with forced brightness.

"Fifteen minutes, maybe?"

She wouldn't meet his gaze and he knew it was because he'd pushed her. *Wrong place, wrong time*, he scolded himself. His phone hummed in his pocket and since they were alone on this corner of the terrace, he checked the display. "Rush is making progress." He showed her the current screenshot.

She snatched the phone from his hand, scrolling up and down the limited information on the display. "I know who it is."

"You do? Who?"

Inside the ballroom, the fire alarm sounded and the sprinklers came on. Guests in dripping finery ran for the terrace and exits as security teams scrambled. "The countdown," he muttered, shaking his head. "Brat."

"Now I'm positive." She tucked his phone back into his pocket and patted his chest. "Let's get you home so you can catch him."

Home. He'd wanted it to be her home too. *I can't.* The words cut deep. "Just a minute." He pulled out his phone and within seconds, the sprinklers were off, the alarm silenced. "There."

"Do I want to know how you did that?"

He shook his head.

"Oh, Sam." She reached up and touched his cheek, her eyes swimming with tears. "I love you," she whispered. She tugged on his tie, smiling as she brought his lips close enough to kiss.

Dumbfounded, he couldn't summon a response.

Her diplomatic mask fell back into place. With her hand at his elbow, she turned him to the growing crowd on the terrace. With her signature composure and his assistance, they calmed the guests and guided everyone inside to safety.

Whatever theory Spalding was testing by insisting she be here, Sam was sure she'd passed it with flying colors.

Chapter Thirteen

Monday, 3:15 p.m.

Madison hated the waiting. She trusted Sam with every detail of the plan, but sitting here in the depths of the Gray Box corporate headquarters with nothing to do was making her more nervous than necessary.

The hacker had taken the irresistible bait Sam and the FBI cyber team had trickled out. Everyone affected by the antics from the State Department to the consulates had quietly been brought up to speed in a face-to-face meeting with Spalding. Spokesmen from each consulate delivered precisely scripted responses that the media were circulating per the usual. Unless the hacker had a wire on Spalding, he had no idea they were onto him.

Still, the waiting for the location and enough proof to make an arrest was driving her batty. They'd been so busy since last night, carefully verifying the prime suspect's travels and correspondence without tipping him off, that they hadn't spoken at all about what she'd told Sam on the terrace. She'd said she *loved* him and he had stared at her, the proverbial deer caught in headlights.

Should she say it again? Try to explain how she could love him and yet not be able to stay with him?

"Take a seat," Sam said, startling her out of the internal debate.

He'd been demonstrating remarkable awareness of her since she wiggled that toe two nights ago and invited him to make love to her. Invited? Ha. Begged was more accurate, particularly last night. A nervous giggle bubbled out of her at the memories.

His desk chair squeaked a little as he swiveled around, stood up. "Come here."

She did, hoping he had worked kissing her senseless into the afternoon schedule. She needed the distraction. His hands light on her shoulders, he did kiss her. Quick and brisk, it wasn't nearly enough. "Sam."

He put a sleek tablet with Gray Box branding in her hands. "Start searching."

"For what?"

"An island getaway," he suggested with a shrug. "A place in the mountains would do."

Astonished, she stared at the phone. "Are you saying we need an escape hatch?"

He laughed, resuming his latest cat and mouse game with the hacker. "Only if you're wrong."

She groaned. What if she was wrong?

"You're not wrong," he reassured her as if he'd read her mind. "We've talked about it, verified his skill set, access and behavior. We can track all of the trouble right back to the day he visited your office with his father last year. You were convenient. Your system was a conduit he used and exploited. Every layer we peel back confirms your analysis, Madison. Jonathon Liu is the root of this mess."

"His father will be devastated," she murmured.

"Rightly so," Sam said. "There are consequences for interfering and tampering where you shouldn't be." He shot her a glance over his shoulder. "I know from experience, remember? I can promise you this kid is not a normal hacker. He incited people to violence and to do the legwork he couldn't. He needs to be stopped and then he needs help."

She knew he was right. "I won't snap," she said, coaching herself more than anything else.

"You exemplify fortitude," he said.

Her jaw dropped at the compliment. She didn't mind at all that he'd delivered it in that distracted manner he used when he was concentrating on something else. In fact, it somehow gave the compliment more credibility, as if it was as basic a truth as two plus two equaling four.

"Islands," he murmured. This time he wasn't talking about a getaway. "Damn. His creativity is off the charts." Sam's fingers flew over the keyboard.

She didn't hover, forcing herself to sit down with the tablet and do as he asked. Hawaii was lovely. At the moment, it wasn't far enough away.

When Spalding had Jonathon in custody, she wanted to go somewhere she'd never been. Somewhere isolated. She glanced at Sam, hoping he'd be willing to go with her. She studied each location, making sure the amenities he appreciated would be available. There were the Calendar Islands in Maine and summer was the best time to head out there. The Caribbean was never wrong and if he wanted seaside cliffs, there was always Ireland.

While he murmured at the screen, her attention was divided between the island debate and how to break the news to Mr. Liu that his son had turned into a criminal.

She heard the chime as the elevator arrived. Glancing up, she saw Rush striding over. "How is he doing?" he asked.

"He's in his element," she said. Holding up the tablet, she added, "He gave me a toy because I was hovering."

"She was pacing," Sam interjected without skipping a beat. "Hovering would've gotten her kicked out."

Rush grinned at her and then turned to Sam. "Have you found him yet?"

"Getting closer," Sam answered. "I know he's in town. I just have to prove it."

Rush caught her eye. "And if he's in the consulate?"

It was the biggest point of concern with their plan. If Mr. Liu's son was causing this trouble from somewhere inside the consulate, it would require a delicate negotiation to stop him. The consulate was technically outside US legal jurisdiction. "My boss has been assured China will respond swiftly even if we prove the culprit is in the consulate."

Rush moved closer to Sam's desk for a moment, then returned to her. "Officially, do you trust that assurance?"

"I have to." It wasn't ideal. She'd had a nightmare, dreading Mr. Liu's probable reaction to the news. "No system is perfect," she added softly.

Rush winked. "We've made sure Gray Box comes pretty damn close."

"If you were looking for an island, where would you go?" she asked, needing a lighter subject.

"Don't answer her," Sam said. "It's her choice."

"To buy or to visit?" Rush asked, ignoring him.

Madison looked up, saw he was serious and laughed. Rush and Sam were both so easygoing and down to earth that she occasionally forgot they were both billionaires. On the rare occasions when the super-wealthy mind-set appeared, it caught her off guard.

"To visit," she answered politely.

His gaze narrowed and he lowered his voice. "Are you looking to move out of the area?"

"No," she replied. There was a subtext here she was missing. "Sam mentioned a weekend getaway."

Sam snorted. "I've promised her a two-week excursion anywhere in the world."

"A weekend is definite. The rest depends on my boss approving the time off."

Rush's eyebrows lifted. "After your service record, you think there's any doubt?"

"Only in how and when things settle out with all of this." She swiped the tablet screen and tilted it to show him a picture, desperate to change the subject. "Trinidad and Tobago?"

"Never been there," Rush said. "I'll have to put it on my list."

"Got him!" Sam shouted.

Madison and Rush surged forward to flank him. "Seriously?"

"He's in Chinatown." Sam pulled over a laptop, ignoring them, while he continued working. "We just have to keep him there."

Rush held up a hand for a high five and Madison obliged, bouncing a little on her toes. It was almost over. Officially, she was thrilled. Personally, not so much. When Jonathon was in custody and things were sorted out, she'd indulge in that weekend with Sam and then the interlude was over. She'd return to her apartment and career and Sam would do the same.

"Anything I can do?" Rush asked.

"Extra eyes would be welcome at this point," Sam said. "I have it recorded for analysis later, but bring on the real-time assessment."

Madison distracted herself, watching them work. They were an excellent team, assessing and adjusting on the fly. Rush might be considered the face of the company and Sam the brain, but these recent days had proven to her they were equally committed and could manage either role well if necessary.

"Look," Rush said to Madison, pointing at a monitor coming to life with a grainy view outside an internet café. "Street cam. Live feed. You can watch the takedown."

"No view inside?" she asked, suddenly concerned.

"No."

Sam swore. "Hold. Hold. Hold." He keyed the same message into the FBI communication program.

"What's wrong?"

"He's one step better than I thought," Sam groused. "Spring it," he said to Rush. He pulled off his headset and jumped out of the chair. "Come on, Mrs. Belle-mere," he said, taking her hand. "We've got one more performance to give."

"What are you talking about?" she demanded when they were in the elevator.

He kissed her, hard and her body responded. Shame-lessly, she leaned into him, her hands on his muscled shoulders. He wrapped his arms around her waist, keep-ing her close. "I didn't trust Liu. Jonathon," Sam clari-fied.

"Who would?"

"Right." The elevator chimed their arrival. "Follow my lead this time?"

"Of course." She nodded, utterly confused.

They stepped out onto the street-level lobby and Sam answered his phone with a rapid fire string of com-mands. Was he speaking with Rush or Spalding?

"We're almost out," he said furtively, heading for the front door. He was into the part, his grip on her hand so hard her bones ached in protest. They were in the airlock when Sam swore. "He's here."

He tugged her behind him. When he reached for the door to get back inside, she heard the electronic locks slam into place.

"We're trapped?"

"No," Sam said.

Madison knew he was lying. Whatever he'd had in mind, this wasn't it.

An image of the South China Sea rippled into focus on the monitor installed to greet Gray Box visitors. "Yes, you are trapped, Mr. Bellemere." Although the voice was being distorted, she knew it was Jonathon. "And you thought you had all the answers. How fitting to beat you at your own game, right here in the house that hacking built."

"Drop it," Sam shouted, yanking on the doors. "You've lost. The FBI knows what you've done."

"Knowing it and proving it are not the same. I am untouchable. Your laws don't apply to me."

Sam's face had gone pale under the dark whiskers shading his jaw. "I'm sorry," he whispered at her ear. "Let her go," he shouted up at the camera positioned in the corner of the airlock.

Glass shattered with a shriek and she screamed. Sam swore, covering her with his bigger body. At the sting of splinters lancing her feet, she didn't want to think about what was happening to Sam. A loud boom brought down another panel in a sickening shower of glass.

Over Sam's shoulder, Madison saw Jonathon crossing the street, a device in one hand and a gun held at arm's length. Where was the backup, the FBI?

"I am untouchable." The monitors repeated the phrase over and over until she wanted to cover her ears.

She knew he intended to kill them. She knew he'd get away with it despite any number of witnesses or security cameras catching him in the act. With diplomatic immunity, he could do anything at all unless China disavowed him and handed him over to the US court system. For Mr. Liu's youngest son, she couldn't see that happening.

"Sam." He wouldn't even be here if she hadn't dragged him into the mess. Tears blurred her vision.

"I'm sorry." She heard the gunshot at nearly the same time the lobby window behind her disintegrated.

The air exploded from her chest as Sam drove them through the broken window and into the scarce shelter of the wide open lobby. He kept his body between her and the danger behind them. She'd never forgive herself if Sam died protecting her.

She heard shouted commands and pounding boots and the distorted voice on the monitor ceased at last.

"The cavalry arrives," Sam said, turning her face side to side. "Are you hurt?" he asked.

"No, not really." She shook her head. Her hands raced over him, came back bloody once more. "You are."

"Scratches," he promised. "I'm fine." He brushed her hair back from her face and kissed her tenderly. "You were so brave."

"This was staged?"

"Not this, exactly. Rush and I agreed to give him an irresistible target," Sam said. "I'm sorry, sweetheart. If we'd had any idea he'd turn violent, I would've left you downstairs."

Leaving him to clean up her mess alone. "I thought this was a together thing?"

He helped her to her feet and kissed her forehead. "It is."

"What will happen to Gray Box if it gets out the building itself was hacked?"

Sam grinned. "Rush and Lucy were handling those details."

His confidence soothed her. "His father will be heartbroken," she murmured, watching Spalding put hand-cuffs on Jonathon.

"We'll give him the proof and hope for the best," Sam said. "Let's get some of these scrapes and splinters treated before we give our statements."

Knowing he was right, knowing her time with him was nearly at an end, Madison wished Sam would say the words her heart craved. She knew it wasn't fair to expect so much so soon. Maybe if they took a weekend trip, they could talk about building a true relationship.

Or maybe she needed to accept the inevitable and allow Sam to return to the quiet, private life he preferred. Hopefully some time and space would make her path clear.

Chapter Fourteen

US Diplomatic Field Office, Wednesday, 7:30 p.m.

The butterflies in Madison's stomach were pushing the envelope of aerial maneuvers as she and Sam waited in a formal receiving room. Charles, her boss, had cornered her this morning, asking her and Sam to be available this evening. She didn't tell him she'd moved back to her apartment after a double-date dinner with Rush and Lucy Monday night. She failed to mention that she'd only exchanged text messages with Sam since Jonathon's arrest.

They had both needed the distance.

When Jake picked her up half an hour ago, Sam had been in the backseat, looking dashing as ever in a soft gray suit. He'd even chosen the tie he'd worn for cocktails. He'd held her hand, casually noted she still wore the wedding set and then reminded her she hadn't given him a weekend destination yet.

"Do you know what to expect?" he asked her now.

She shook her head. "Only that Mr. Liu wants a private word before returning to China." Without his son.

His decision to allow the United States to prosecute still surprised her.

She couldn't imagine the disgrace Mr. Liu had to be feeling. Knowing him to be a proud man, she'd found his aloof nature a mask he'd used only on formal occasions. He'd always been kind and warm in their more casual interactions. It saddened her to know his son's misguided stunt would bring his career to an end. China had yet to name Mr. Liu's replacement and careful, thoughtful communication would be required to repair the relationship between the countries Jonathon had exploited.

She hoped the exhibit at the museum would not be withdrawn on principle.

"Relax."

Sam's whisper at her ear launched a fresh flight of butterflies. She told them to wait their turn. This meeting would test her composure enough as it was.

The double doors opened and Mr. Liu entered, flanked by two men from his security detail. Her boss followed, flashing them an encouraging smile.

She wasn't surprised by the formal greeting and deep bow Mr. Liu offered, only that he honored her before Sam.

"I am thankful to both of you for my son's life," Mr. Liu began. "There is no excuse to be made on his behalf. Were he trustworthy, he would be here himself to apologize. In his absence, I extend my apologies to you, Mrs. Bellemere, Mr. Bellemere, for his unfortunate actions against you and your country."

Tears gleamed in the older man's eyes. Madison had

to fight the urge to soothe him as a friend. Beside her, she sensed Sam was waging the same war.

"Mistakes of youth, with time and care, become the wisdom of men grown," Madison replied.

Mr. Liu's son had made a dreadful, misguided attempt to embarrass his father and stir up national ire against countries he perceived as enemies of a supreme nation. As Sam had said, such choices had consequences. All she could do now was trust those higher up and say a prayer that the Liu family recovered from their youngest son's blunder.

Mr. Liu turned to the man on his left, who placed a slim box in his hand. "In honor of your superb service and dedication as a liaison to our country, I offer this gift."

She opened the box and stared down at a white jade pendant carved with the Chinese character for *peace* nestled into the center of black silk. Surrounding the pendant was a bracelet of jade beads, alternating white and green and amber, smooth and luminous as pearls, with a centered space for the pendant. She held a treasure and they both knew it.

"I am deeply humbled and honored," she said to Mr. Liu. She wanted to toss formality out the window and give him a hug. Only training and his obvious grief stayed her. "You have given me a treasure beyond value, a lasting reminder of what trust and friendship are meant to be."

From his station near the door, her boss nodded his approval.

Without a word, Mr. Liu handed Sam a smaller box.

With another deep bow, he left the room with his men. When the doors closed, Madison relaxed and leaned into the immediate support Sam offered.

"You did great," he said.

The praise eased the sadness of her farewell to Mr. Liu. "What is it?"

Sam opened the box to find a jade tie pin. "Wow. What does this symbol mean?"

She smiled at him. "Prosperity."

"Safe bet. Hope no one's offended if I have it scanned for any electronic signatures before I wear it to the office."

She laughed and elbowed him. "Behave."

"Open yours again," he said. "That is stunning. Should it be in a museum?"

"Probably, but I'm not giving it up." She touched the edge of the silk lining the box. "This is my name followed by the characters for deep and abiding friendship."

"That covers it," he said, his palm warm at her back.

"You think so?"

"Definitely. It's how I've always seen you," he said.

She should be grateful to have that friendship from him. She was grateful. Having had more, she knew it wouldn't be enough. "I'll never see him again," she said, desperate to avoid her personal minefield.

She closed the box with a snap as her boss peeked into the room again. "You ready for round two?" he asked. "The group from Vietnam is in the elevator."

Sam set their gift boxes on the table under the window, near the floral arrangement. "We're set."

The meeting with the Vietnam diplomatic team was far more effusive and genial. They'd brought champagne and made a toast to long life and happiness for Sam and Madison and continued positive relations between their countries. Along with their thanks came more gifts.

Madison gasped at the long strand of pearls with a spacer for the jade pendant she'd received from Mr. Liu and a large, perfect pearl on a charm clasp that would complete the jade bracelet.

When they were done, Madison wanted to leap for joy. She kept her face in neutral when her boss walked back in. His relief clear, he extended his hand to each of them in turn. "My thanks to both of you," he said. "Sorry I don't have gifts. You two kept the peace in a volatile area. The world owes you, Madison. You too, Sam."

For the first time in her career, Madison didn't care about the good opinion of her boss, her country or the world at large. She was pleased and proud of Sam. He'd skillfully corralled a troubled young man on a violent bender. Weary of diplomacy, she was ready for a more personal and no less delicate, negotiation.

She'd put him on the spot naming him as her husband. His willingness to play along and stand by her until they figured it out had surprised her.

Even now, with his hand at the small of her back, she wondered how things would go once they left the office. The time away from him had been agony for her. She couldn't tell if he felt the same. Once they were alone, would he suggest they announce a quiet, quick divorce?

"Take a vacation, Madison," Charles said, snapping her attention back to the present. "I'm serious. You've earned it a dozen times over by now." He turned to Sam. "I don't want her back in the office before August."

"Why not?" Madison asked, aghast.

"It's paid leave," Charles said as if that explained it. "You'll need some time to rest up and rejuvenate before taking on your new responsibilities."

The news blindsided her. "I'm getting a promotion?"

"You don't want it?"

Happy excitement bubbled through her. "Yes! I didn't expect it."

"You earned it," he repeated.

This entire mess had been one risky stunt after another with more than their fair share of close calls thrown in. She hadn't been sure, until right now, that she'd have a job once the legalities were settled. Recovering swiftly, she smiled and said, "I'll want to see the terms."

Charles smiled broadly. "Of course. But if you pop in here before August, I'll have security haul you out with plenty of publicity on hand for the gossip rags."

"Got it. Forewarned and forearmed and all that." Sam took her hand. "I'll come up with something to keep her mind off work."

"You've both been invaluable," Charles said. "Take care of her for us, Sam."

SAM BREATHED A sigh of relief when they were done. He had to find a way to make his case that they should get married for real. He'd rehearsed the words with Rush and Lucy and still he couldn't seem to get them rolling.

His house didn't feel the same without her in it. He hadn't slept more than a few hours since she moved back to her apartment and his sleeplessness was affecting his work. But those weren't the right reasons. He wanted her to want him for *him*. He wanted that sweet "I love you" she'd given him to be real.

He understood how much she valued her career and he wanted her to have that. He understood why Madison had been honored so generously. He knew what others saw in her, though his reasons were rooted in his heart rather than public diplomatic interests. She was amazing as a liaison. If this situation had taught him anything, it was that they were an excellent team. That was something he'd never known could fit into his life.

She cared passionately about her role with the State Department. For her, the career was more than civic pride and the essential mission of keeping communication open as a path to peace. She never forgot the people involved in the complex equations and that set her apart.

"The gifts alone are a remarkable gesture of cooperation," Sam said quietly. "You've made a significant, positive impact on each delegation."

"It's a chapter closed," she replied, turning to smile at him. "We wouldn't be here, with a happy ending all around, without your help."

The finality in her tone gave him pause. He wasn't ready to walk away or return to their previous status of exchanging annual Christmas e-cards. There had to be a way of encouraging her to come back to the condo.

He suspected it would never feel like home again without her.

He hadn't handled the personal nuances well since she called him to the museum last week. He had to improve and quickly. Here, he had one more chance and he couldn't squander it. He'd promised to follow her lead and he'd done his best to honor that.

"Well," he said, gesturing to the car. "How should we celebrate?"

Chapter Fifteen

As Jake held open the car door, Madison slid across the seat to make room for Sam. "I'm overwhelmed," she admitted, pressing a hand to her belly. She wanted to celebrate with Sam, privately, for a long time.

"I need to be honest," Sam said. "Charles gave me a heads-up about the promotion and vacation. Rush has the plane and crew standing by and Lucy said she packed a suitcase for you to cover any locale or occasion." He reached to the opposite seat and handed her a leather portfolio. "Your passport, airport information, everything you need to go anywhere you like."

"And you?" she asked.

"I'll follow your lead."

The words sent a delicious tremor dancing over her skin. This was her moment, the private solitude she'd been hoping for to make her case for staying together.

"I even built you a clean laptop," he said, breaking the silence.

"You did?"

He dragged a finger over the back of her hand. "Absolutely. You need a fresh start."

Tears clogged her throat. She couldn't see any happiness in a fresh start without Sam, yet she couldn't seem to get the conversation started.

"Thanks for everything." She turned up her palm and wrapped her fingers around his hand. The scrapes from his fight with the deliverywoman were scabbed over, but she suspected his hands still ached. "You were amazing every step of the way. I don't even want to think about how awful things would be now without your help."

"I was just your technical backup. You and the FBI did the hard stuff."

"Now you're modest?"

He grinned, unrepentant. "We were a good team."

She shifted closer to him, leaning in to kiss his cheek. He brought her closer and caught her lips. She gave herself up to the heat and passion of him. If this was the last chance she had, she would take every inch he gave.

"What will you do with nearly three months off?" he asked, his fingers toying with the ends of her hair.

"That depends." Get married. Have a honeymoon. The thought burst into her mind along with an image of standing at the front of a church, exchanging rings with Sam. It was less elaborate and more real than her first visions of their wedding when she'd been seventeen. She had to be brave if she wanted her happy ending.

"Sam, when I figure out a destination, will you…will you come meet me?" Not quite how she'd practiced it in the mirror. The ring she'd worn for more than two years as a fake wife felt as heavy and awkward as a boulder on her finger. How was a real proposal supposed to go after pretending for so long?

He didn't reply, though she waited, her worry mounting.

Jake took the exit for the airport. She knew Sam would drop her off, let her go anywhere in the world. Giving him more time was the right solution, although the idea of another night without him made her stomach cramp.

Still, giving him space was the smarter play, she told herself as her heart pounded a denial in her chest. Being clingy wasn't a good answer. Just because she was ready to commit didn't mean he was. Being excellent lovers and sharing an affectionate bond might not be enough for him to build on.

Sam was different, private and she led a public life. Her work would always pull her from their time together. Worse, her work would pull him into the limelight—the one place he resisted above all. Loving him might not be enough to make up for that and she didn't want to lose him over careers. Decision made, she smothered her proposal. She'd put her shy, fake husband on the spot enough for one lifetime.

"We're here," he said as the car turned toward the hangars for private planes.

Too soon, she thought as he tipped up her chin and kissed her softly. The tenderness brought tears to her eyes as she felt the inevitable farewell in his touch.

The car rolled to a gentle stop and the kiss ended as Jake opened the door for them.

Sam didn't want to let her go, but they were here.

Jake was loading her luggage into the plane. She'd invited him to join her. *Later.* He wasn't sure he could wait that long and yet he knew he'd wait forever. For her.

"Sam? Will you join me?"

He heard the reservation in her voice. She wasn't sure he'd like what she was about to say. Clenching his teeth against the inevitable, he forced himself to meet her gaze. "For a weekend?"

"Longer. If you like. I know you have projects to get back to."

Always diplomatic and thoughtful. "Sure. Just let me know where you end up."

Her hands clasped in front of her, the smile on her lips trembled. He would not beg her to stay with him; he loved her too much for that. All he had to do was man up, smile and give her whatever she asked for. He'd already removed their marriage record from the Nevada database.

"Thank you again, Sam, for everything."

The words landed like a punch to his sternum. "You're welcome."

"Sam—"

He held up a hand and stepped back. If she dragged this out, he'd lose his mind. Rush needed him to get the new software up and running so they could start planning the launch and marketing. He seized on the thought, trusting the technology to save him again. "Have a wonderful trip," he grumbled, stuffing his hands into his pockets.

"Sam." Her voice turned sharp. "Do you understand that I love you?"

Did he? She'd said the words, but he hadn't been sure if she meant she loved him as a friend and for what he'd done or if she *loved* him. Gazing into those lovely green eyes, he understood that friendship was a type of love. But was it a strong enough foundation to build on? Was friendship a powerful enough magnet to keep people together for a lifetime?

"I love you too," he said, blurting it out. *As my friend, as a lover, even as the fake wife who somehow made my real life brighter. I love you, Madison.* That was what he wanted her to know. He fisted his hands in his pockets. If he touched her, she'd know beyond all doubt how terrified he was of her rejection. "Where do you think you'll go?"

"That depends," she said again. Her teeth nipped at her lower lip, the way she used to do when she struggled over a new concept. She balanced on one foot. "Just one last question, Sam."

Man up, he told himself when he wanted to bolt. They were both alive and neither of them was headed to prison or exile. It was situation normal. They'd succeeded, she was a hero and he had a new product halfway developed.

She twisted the wedding set off her finger, tucking it into her jacket pocket. His heart shriveled in his chest. Apparently that phase of her life—*their lives*—was over.

"Sam Bellemere." Her voice cracked on his name. "Would you be my husband?" She swallowed. "Through politics or technology, as my friend and lover, in sunshine or computer labs, please share my life. I can't imagine any aspect of my world without you to come home to."

He stared into her serious green eyes, then down at her bare finger. Should he return the ring to her finger, the one she'd bought for herself? Did it matter? He'd buy her a wedding set for every day of the week if that was what she wanted.

"Say something," she prompted, her voice thick with tears.

"How about 'I do'?" He stepped up and fished the wedding set from her pocket. He slid the engagement solitaire back into place on her finger and pocketed the matching wedding band. "I researched engagement rings and wedding sets," he admitted. "Turns out I couldn't picture anything suiting you better than the one you've been wearing."

"You researched rings? For me?"

"Yes. It kept me entertained through the last couple of sleepless nights." He stroked his thumb over the back of her left hand. "It only confirmed what I knew. You have superb taste."

She kissed him, wrapping her arms around his neck. "Yes, I do." She brushed her nose to his. "Should I infer that your research meant you were going to propose?"

"It was on my mind," he admitted. "But I promised to follow your lead."

"True." She laid her hand gently over the healing wound on his side. "Although you bolted out in front more than once."

"That was teamwork," he said. He didn't want to argue or dwell on his faults, afraid she'd come to her senses about him. "I said yes," he reminded her, pulling her into another kiss before approaching the plane. "Now you're stuck with me, right here beside you." He stopped at the steps. "Where to?"

"Las Vegas," she said. "I don't want to waste time and we should make things right with the records there."

"Already took care of that," he said, urging her up the stairs ahead of him. "I didn't want anything hanging over your head when we were finished. Although I doubt anyone would've been looking at that anymore."

"Our heads," she corrected. "We're a team. You've always been the only man for me."

He'd never heard sweeter words. With his hands on her slim hips, he guided her into the plush passenger area while the crew prepared for takeoff.

But they weren't alone. Rush and Lucy were waiting at the back of the cabin and Lucy was bouncing on her toes a bit. "She said yes?" she asked Sam.

Sam looked at Madison. "She asked me!"

Rush shook his hand, pulled him into a brotherly hug. "Have you called your mom?"

"Thought I'd send her a first class ticket by messenger in the morning."

"Great plan," Madison said. "Will the ticket and news arrive with flowers?"

"And her favorite chocolate truffles," Sam confirmed. "I promise she'll be half in love with you before she arrives." He moved to the sofa and drew Madison to sit beside him.

She laced her fingers through his. "I won't change my mind, love."

"I know." He brought her hand to his lips. "That doesn't make me less eager to make it officially official." She laughed, the sound music to his ears.

Rush popped open a bottle of champagne, Lucy passed out the filled flutes and the four of them shared a toast to love and happiness as the plane lifted into the evening sky.

* * * * *

Love Debra Webb & Regan Black?
Check out the bestselling COLBY AGENCY *series:*

BRIDAL ARMOR
READY, AIM... I DO!
WOULD-BE CHRISTMAS WEDDING
GUNNING FOR THE GROOM
HEAVY ARTILLERY HUSBAND

Available now from Mills & Boon Intrigue!

MILLS & BOON®

Why shop at millsandboon.co.uk?

Each year, thousands of romance readers
find their perfect read at millsandboon.co.uk.
That's because we're passionate about
bringing you the very best romantic fiction.
Here are some of the advantages of
shopping at www.millsandboon.co.uk:

* **Get new books first**—you'll be able to buy
  your favourite books one month before they
  hit the shops

* **Get exclusive discounts**—you'll also be
  able to buy our specially created monthly
  collections, with up to 50% off the RRP

* **Find your favourite authors**—latest news,
  interviews and new releases for all your
  favourite authors and series on our website,
  plus ideas for what to try next

* **Join in**—once you've bought your favourite
  books, don't forget to register with us to rate,
  review and join in the discussions

Visit **www.millsandboon.co.uk**
for all this and more today!